# The Girlfriend Book

# The Girlfriend Book

Gwen K. Harvey

Jan 2024

Clare,
This is a light
read, but with
"heart". I've so enjoyed
our bringing chats. Looking
forward to having longer ones!
Warm wishes
Gwen

Published by Tablo

# CONTENTS

# DEDICATION

This book is dedicated to those who trust and share, listen kindly and take the time to care.

# PREFACE

From early days as a child, the weight of life was eased when I could share a problem and talk it through. Initially the listener was my mother and I am grateful for her non-judgmental ear. As teenage years arrived, so too did "the Girlfriend". And so began the sharing of a parallel life with women.

It has been fascinating to witness the power of conversation as a tool to create clarity. When thoughts are pulled out and turned into spoken words, one is on their way to finding solutions that fit. When this happens in a safe space with active listening and helpful words from friends, the load is lighter, the decisions are better and the mind finds peace.

1995

# NICOLE

That was too long. It's easy to lose track.

Driving towards home, I can see the children running along the sidewalk, heading home from school. My two will be walking through the back door at any moment, calling out my name.

I remember doing the same. Coming home with my two brothers, walking, running or scootering along the sidewalk, throwing down knapsacks inside the back door and barreling into the kitchen for cheese and crackers or cookies and milk. The stories tumbling out onto the kitchen counter where my mother was beginning to prepare dinner.

Always there was that time of contact with guiding words from Mom. A test was a stepping stone, not the ultimate. Friends were significant but family was the most important thing. Then Mom would package the boys off to their desks to make sure their homework was done with one hundred percent effort. As the girl, I was detained to help set the table and chop vegetables. Mom would frequently remind me that home economics was important for a young woman. Eventually I would arrive at my little homework desk, crammed into the corner of my mother's sewing room, where I would puzzle over my work.

In time, the boys headed off to the university in Toronto, leaving this small town and our family. New friendships were formed in an exciting city with novel sounds, smells, and lights. They experienced fashionable shops, cutting-edge restaurants and fascinating people from all over the world. They thrived in their studies and grew up with peers who challenged their minds. When my brothers came home for visits, they seemed taller as they strode into our home. Such confidence. I was in awe of the young men they had become.

Meanwhile, complying with my parents' wishes that I stay local, and be there to help them when needed, I applied to Port Colebrook's local community college in administrative studies. I followed my parents' sensible advice. They told me that secretarial work was a safe, dependable job and it would allow me to easily pick-up part-time work between children or full time work after my children were all grown up. Within two years of leaving high school, I was earning a pay cheque and wondering what to do with it. Most of my girlfriends had left for university and those that had stayed were already spending more time with boyfriends than girlfriends.

I had decided to take a sabbatical from boys. I did not want to repeat that slow burning feeling and flue-like ache that I experienced when Alex returned after his first term in university. He avoided me for the first few days and then arrived at my front door and unceremoniously broke up with me. Why did I imagine that just because we both loved sailing, cycling, cuddling up together and magically finishing each other's sentences, that someone else wouldn't come along that could do all of that too? And if that person could also join him in an exciting city life while he was at school, why would he miss out on that? I had always dreamed that he might come home after finishing university, see me sitting across the room at the Whistle House Café and I would then have a chance to tilt my head, smile and say something engaging. But no such luck. He continued to move on in life, and he settled far away in a city out west.

It was around that time that I took up long early morning runs. It was a way to take control of one part of my life. As others slept or read their morning paper, I haunted the forest and waterside trails. In time I grew to love my long slim runner's body and became a keen reader about nutrition and health. This was something I could create on my own, and those early mornings, running and thinking, were all mine.

I had been taught that life works out as it is meant to be. I had no reason to doubt that. My mother and father had always said that their family was lucky to have a great town to grow up in, with solid, kind people living all around them. My Dad, having watched his father lose everything when the family business had gone under during a recession, found security in the trades. As an electrician, there was always work and the pay was steady. While he did encourage the boys to break out and find a well-paying future, he strongly suggested that I marry a professional. He greatly admired doctors, accountants and lawyers. He said that a man who was a professional would be sure to bring financial security to both me and the family I would have one day.

In time, I met a young dentist, who was new to Port Colebrook and had come from a nearby farming community. I made a point of courting him until he noticed me, and then he spent a good six months running after me. Marriage followed and now two little kids are turning into two bigger kids and they will be racing in through the kitchen door at any moment.

I pull into the driveway and walk calmly into the house. Stopping at the front hall mirror, I stare at the tall woman who is looking back at me. I hardly recognize her these days. At thirty-five, gone is my long auburn hair from my twenties, traded in for a blunt shoulder length cut. Hazel eyes blink at me and I reach out and touch the glass. "You are late today," I whisper. "Why are you getting sloppy?" I head to the kitchen and open up the fridge. I reach in, pull out a beer and then pop the cap off with the bottle opener that is nailed to the side of the kitchen cupboard. Pressing the sharp points of the cap into the palm of one of my hands, I raise the beer to my lips with the other. I take one civilized gulp, pause and then pour the rest of the beer down the kitchen sink. I place the bottle beside the fridge, throw the cap into the garbage and sit down at the kitchen table that overlooks the garden.

A minute later Jimmy and Tessa hurtle through the back door, dropping their knapsacks and running up and into the kitchen. I wave Jimmy to the cookie cupboard and he plunges into the large tin, filled with homemade oatmeal cookies. "Leave some for your sister," I call out laughing, always amazed at my son's healthy metabolism and his total fixation on filling up his stomach as he flies in after school. I get up and pour them both a tall glass of milk, feeling like I am walking in my mother's footsteps.

After the usual banter, I make sure that both of my children are settled at their desks and doing their homework. Then I return to the kitchen alone to prepare for dinner. Unlike my mother's roadmap for her children, I will make sure both of my children have an equal shot at university and a life beyond here.

The phone rings and I answer.

"You made it home in time?" he asks.

"Yes," I reply. "But barely. I can't stay that long next time."

"Understood. See you next week?"

I pause, "Okay, see you then." I lower the phone and place it softly on the receiver.

Having the freedom to leave my job in the early afternoon each day, had been a life saver. Originally it was to give me time between running the behind-the-scenes administration of Michael's busy dental practice, and picking up all the pieces at home. Once the children descended from school, there was always homework, dinner, laundry, preparing lunches for the next day and being perky and upbeat when Michael arrived home and needed to unload. But during the mid-afternoon, that was my time. It was peaceful being alone and it had become a family joke that I had an interesting alternative to a cup of tea. I would open one beer during that time. That beer's cool passage down my throat calmed me and I would silently float away, leaving this small town on Georgian Bay. Family and friends all knew that when it was *beer time*, I wouldn't be answering the phone. Everyone had been trained to leave me alone and not interrupt my afternoon.

But for the last couple of months, the beer had been swirling down the sink on Tuesdays. Decompressing had found a new form of self-expression.

# DIANNE

Filing through the wide school hallways, plastered with art projects depicting a frantic clash between nature and civilization, I lead a long trail of hyper nine year old's. I am aware that I am short and only hover over my class by about a foot. Thankfully those twelve inches mean they physically do tip their heads back and look up to me. But I do know that stature is more than just height. Having always been the *short, little blonde,* I have worked hard to speak out, create a presence and to be very good at what I do. However, I continue to be amazed at the credit given to a tall male when they enter a room, even before they have spoken. I would have to do handstands to get that type of attention.

My grade three class is bursting with enthusiasm, delighted to be heading away from paper, pens and desks and towards the school auditorium. As we enter the gym, they scamper into the neatly lined rows of unstacked chairs, and continue to bounce even while seated. Shortly the stage will be full of song and dance, as the eighth graders share their *Welcome Back from Summer* show. For the past couple of years this spirited extravaganza has turned into a sentimental time of reflection, as I watch the fourteen year old's, who were once my nine year old's, move about the stage. Some predictably take on leadership roles, and others uncharacteristically move into the spotlight. Watching them interact with each other, and knowing their individual backstories, makes the clapping and standing ovations a chance for me and others to celebrate their success both on and beyond the stage.

My love of school started day one, when I bolted into my kindergarten class and left my bewildered Mother at the door, where other children were dewy-eyed and clinging to their mothers. Books were a passion from an early age. Colliding with C.S. Lewis's *The Lion, the Witch and the Wardrobe* when our teacher read the book out loud to us in grade three, pulled me into Narnia, never to return to regular life again. If the magic of Narnia existed, then other books too must hold adventures, experiences and secrets to explore. And there were so many books out there. I dove into them one after another.

And then one year when I was thirteen, Uncle Darren visited our lively family home. Unlike the rest of my mother's family, this brother had moved away from Port Colebrook, lived in multiple big cities and traveled extensively. With a generous, broad smile, he always seemed to glow as he described his adventures. He was so articulate and had vocabulary that cast a spell on me. I hung on every word and animated analogy. After sharing stories of a recent trip, he leaned in to me and confided, "Dianne, the world awaits you. And the secret about who you will become lies in the books you will read and the people you will meet."

"Well," I remember thinking, "I am nailing the part about reading books, but I guess maybe I need to spend more time talking with people". And as if fairy dust had been sprinkled on me overnight, I woke up the next day and became one of the most inquisitive and extraverted girls in my class, always seeking out others to talk to and learn from. This trait continued to expand as I grew up.

And then I met Tom in grade eleven. He was the captain of the football team. His athletic build, summery smile and good nature made him a hit with everyone. However, what I loved most about Tom was that he was an enlightened male. While he loved his sports (all of them, and there were many), he also enjoyed school and did well. He would wrap me up in his arms on the living room sofa, as we either read books aloud together, or quietly read on our own and then stopped to share an observation that had suddenly bounced off the page.

However, while I had caught Tom's attention, he spent the next couple of years of high school trying to keep mine. It wasn't that I was interested in dating anyone else, but I just found people so interesting.

I continued to engage in long and varied conversations with teachers, store keepers, gas station attendants, and fellow students. It often meant I lost track of time and was late for a date, or sometimes completely forgot there was one. My fascination with other people and exploring thoughts about the world unfolding around me was often manic, and it kept displacing time for Tom and me, as a couple.

When we split up after high school finished, it was meant to be mutual, but it wasn't. He initiated it. I realized too late that my continuously growing assortment of friends, was to the detriment of those I cared for most. And this was playing out with girlfriends too. I began to witness that among my many girlfriends, some were becoming closer to each other, and I wasn't a part of their inner circle. I finally understood that time *in* the friendship mattered, and that applied to boyfriends too.

While dating other men in university, I was always bewildered when they seemed insecure, defensive or worst of all, narrow focused. I wondered why there weren't more men out there like Tom, and how sad it would be if there really weren't more like him.

In university, I continued to grow my love of learning through both studies and the people I met, but I made a point of figuring out who I really wanted to be closest to and spent more time and effort with them.

Kate was one such person. While Kate took Commerce and was heading towards business, and I was now eyeing a Masters of Education after my undergraduate degree, we met when we lived side by side in a rather boisterous first-year dormitory. We shared our anxieties over our studies and our elation over our well-earned grades. In second-year we moved into a small, low rent, dilapidated house with four other girlfriends and Kate and I became the best of friends, cheering each other on through graduate school and into the work force.

With my teaching degree in hand, I focused on finding a way to return back home, where one of my sisters, Gemma, was a nurse at the local hospital, and the other one, Caroline, had twins on the way.

I had definitely come full circle and knew who I cherished most in life. With my parents ageing and my sisters settling into comfortable lives in our hometown, I yearned to be near them and teaching in the familiar rooms within my old school.

When I opened the letter that offered me the grade three teaching position at Port Colebrook Elementary School, I smiled and curled up in my armchair. I could feel my body being transported through the air, to my childhood classroom and into the snowy woods of Narnia. While I was returning to a place I knew well, I felt adventure and excitement ahead. Being able to share and then follow young minds into imaginary places was something I found thrilling. It all felt right to be heading back to where it all began.

On my first day home I was settling into a tiny, freshly painted apartment on the second floor of a house, just a few blocks from the school. A loud knock rattled my open front door. Tom peered in through the door frame. He had a bottle of bubbly in his hand, and he had come to congratulate me on coming home to what he knew was my dream job. His smile at the door melted away any hard feelings, and we became inseparable. I was never late for him again.

Now seven years and two children later, we are a happy family. We are not as busy and loud a family as the one I came from, but we are close. And most importantly, I have learned to protect time so that I spend more time with those I love most – and right now that is Tom, and our sweet little Sara and Sam.

# KATE

Frank? He seemed so much like Frank, but apparently his name was Trevor. He was perfect. Charm sparkled through him. He moved with ease and his smile warmed up his whole face and unbeknownst to him, all of me.

I rushed along the hallway to my office. Holding my laptop tight to my chest, my eyes narrowed and I saw only the runway in front of me. Noise filled my head. His laugh. His clever and well-chosen words as he confidently shared his presentation about how children's toothpaste sales could be improved with cartoon characters and a targeted reward program.

Where did he come from? Did they say he had been transferred from another division or did he come from outside of the company? I had not paid attention to Terry as he had introduced our new team member. It was only when Trevor began to talk that I was captivated, instantly.

I turned into my office, closed the door and leaned against it. A flood of mistrust surged within me. A smile and words from long ago floated onto my mind's movie screen. "Beautiful girls, can we join you?" Dressed in freshly pressed khakis, a pink golf shirt and Adidas running shoes, an eighteen-year-old Frank straddled the picnic bench beside me and stared directly into my trusting, teenage face. In those days that face of mine was completely blemish free and as pure as porcelain, due to a day and night regime inherited from my mother. "Well, yes!" chorused Debbie and Suzie as I sat stunned by this sudden attention. And so, Frank and his friends began a six-week summer interest in me and my two girlfriends.

That summer, I was a naïve, over-protected sixteen-year-old, working part-time, with a lot of free time on my hands. It was a formative period of my life and an indelible mark was left by Frank that summer. Day after day we met up, butterflies constantly in my tummy. Amazing soft kisses led to folding into each other's arms. Frank's adventurous nature created excitement and wonder as we tripped through forests, looked for out of the way garden sheds or unoccupied summer cottages, and in hindsight, searched out places where we could escape and explore each other. He was so handsome, like a movie star. And he had chosen me and spoken out in public about how beautiful I was, and how lucky he was. He made me feel incredibly special, and simply on top of the world.

It all ended with something we both wanted. I thought that having sex and giving ourselves to each other made us a real couple. But then just three days later Frank ran into a pretty red-head with a shapely figure in the grocery store and he was off in pursuit. I was totally crushed. Being with Frank had been all consuming. He was the first male in my life who doted on me. For a month I had seen myself through his eyes and saw a beautiful face and a desirable body.

Afterwards, I could just imagine what my mother would say if she knew about it. "Some men just follow beautiful women and it will never stop, they move from one to the next". I had never known my father, but understood from my mother that he loved beautiful women, but loved too many of them at one time. That wasn't a way to live so Mom had left and my father had never been curious enough to follow. When I was twenty-five I tracked him down, but after doing so and keeping him under surveillance for a few days, I decided that I too didn't like who he was - married but charming every female he met. And so I left my sleuthing behind me, without ever approaching him.

But being dumped so suddenly at age sixteen was a problem. The brightness of Frank never had the opportunity to dim. I never had a chance to find his imperfection (beyond him liking someone else). Without having something about him to hate, I continued to like him, or what I imagined he was. Since then, I have pretty much been looking for another Frank. But because who I am looking for likely doesn't exist in real life, I have had difficulty finding him. Sticking to the narration I have concocted about Frank has helped to keep dating a short, sporadic and unsuccessful series of events, that has kept me, my story book heroine, all on her own.

But now, after two decades, Frank is back. But his name is Trevor. I moved over to my desk, sat down and pulled out my makeup mirror and weighed in. What was Trevor seeing? A brunette with long, dark hair, carefully curled at the ends with a curling iron and then sprayed lightly so as to keep all in place through a long day. A face with smooth skin and a light layer of foundation that helped to cover small marks of time that were beginning to show up. But the beauty coaching from Mom had been extreme and, in hindsight, most helpful and well informed. Cleansers, toners, moisturizers and avoiding sun as if it were poison had all done an excellent job. All those hours perched beside my mother's beauty stool at a large mirror with lightbulbs glowing around the edges had paid off. Fabulous skin and a keen awareness of how to apply eyeshadow, blush, and lipstick, and how to properly draw that perfect eyebrow arch. The result was being the subject of on-going compliments from friends and occasional dates. *Stunning* and *gorgeous* were the recurring words that came my way and I always smiled and thought of Mom, and thanked her often. I trained with the best!

Shoving the mirror back into my right-hand drawer, I flipped open my laptop and searched for Trevor's name in the company directory. A smile bounced off the screen at me and I sat back. A handsome face attached to broad shoulders that filled out an attractive dark suit stared up at me. I peered forward and squinted as I read about his short corporate background, education and university graduation date. I paused. Then I grimaced. The math was simple. He was exactly ten years younger than me. This was awkward.

There was a knock on the door and I looked up. The same face on my computer screen was staring at me through my doorway.

"Hello, Kate. I wanted to more formally introduce myself," said

Trevor. "I know you must be very busy, and the way you left the meeting, well we never had the chance to really say hello."

"Right, welcome," I said in my steady managerial voice. I closed out the computer window, stood and crossed the office to shake his hand. "Impressive presentation. I like your proposed strategy."

I could feel myself moving into professional mode. My mother had not only taught me about beauty. She was a staunch supporter of the theory that women *should* have it all, and in business that happened by tuning into the male world with full force. "Strength is admired," she taught, and "Be prepared to be on your own often, as some men and women don't always know how to deal personally with an efficient and capable woman. But Kate, my dear, they do respect a powerful woman, which is what you will become as you advance ahead of them."

"Thank you," Trevor said as he smiled and nodded. "I am hoping to learn from you. I've seen your work and it is extensive."

I shuddered at his choice of words. *Extensive work* felt like he had just circled my age in red pen. This would be one of many conversations that started warm and friendly and then had me climbing the wall, in search of a way out. I hate feeling *older*. I had had the good fortune of spending most of life looking younger than my friends. I loved it when those I met thought of me as wise beyond my years, when in fact I wasn't as young as they thought, and my insight was totally appropriate for my age and experience.

Over the next few months, Trevor and I had the good luck of working together through a number of key assignments. However, we both seemed to take great care to keep our interactions extremely professional. I had been told that Trevor was dating his university sweetheart and later I learned that Trevor had been told that I was very private and didn't mix work with my personal life. So, I took Trevor's charm and deep gazes as just part of his warm character and Trevor steered clear from ever including me in after work drinks, which of course only reconfirmed to me that he wasn't interested.

Until one day. During a long week of building a presentation for the board, we found ourselves late at night, alone and huddled over a shared computer screen. It only took the simultaneous raising of our heads and a long five second gaze, to trigger the slow moving of our heads together and the softest of kisses.

# SEPTEMBER GIRLS' BIKE RIDE
## AT 35

Dianne, barely bigger than the heavy wooden chairs encircling the dining room table, slides into one of the upholstered soft green velvet seats. Her tiny stature, pixie haircut and button nose could have a faraway observer believe a child had mistakenly joined the adult table. Nicole affectionately squeezes Dianne's shoulder as she passes behind her. Sitting down, her long, slender arms help to pull her and her comfortable chair in and up to the table. Kate strides into the room, lighting it up with her glowing complexion. "It is wonderful to be back here again," she says smiling and taking her seat.

They are seated together at the sole table set up in the library of Abigail's Bed & Breakfast. Located in the small town of Ellington, Abigail's is where they have been gathering for their annual get together for the past three years. The tradition began when Dianne instigated the idea of pressing the pause button on their busy lives. Knowing Kate from her city and university days and Nicole from her quieter small-town life in Port Colebrook, Dianne pulled the three of them together for a bike ride, dinner and overnight stay at Abigail's. While Dianne visits with both of them during the year, Kate and Nicole don't see each other through the winter and summer and are noticeably still more acquaintances at this stage, sometimes becoming cautious when engaging on new subjects. But Dianne has enjoyed watching them learn to enjoy each other and embrace their differences. She knows Kate can be brash and opinionated and Nicole is more reserved and careful. But Dianne believes all three of them share a strength and vulnerability that is similar and she suspects in time they will all become closer.

"What a day! That felt amazing to really ride a bike again," pipes up Dianne. "It's been too long since I rode for hours and hours. When Tom and I are out with the kids, we are lucky if we can get them to bike to and from the park."

Kate pulls back her long-tussled hair into an elastic band and then strips off her cashmere cardigan and ties the arms loosely around her shoulders. "Well, their little legs can only go so far right now. But in time they will be challenging you to keep up with them. Just you wait. Now, that ride has made me hungry. And thirsty too. What are you ladies going to have to drink?"

"Hmm, on weekdays I am partial to having a beer each afternoon," replies Nicole thoughtfully. "But this is the weekend, so I think I would prefer a glass of wine."

Kate frowns, "You have a beer every day?"

"Just during the week," says Nicole with a smile, as she picks up the water pitcher and pours ice water into each of their glasses. "Some people meditate or do yoga. I enjoy pouring a cold beer."

"She has been like that since I met her," Dianne chimes in with a grin. "If I ever went part-time at work and could be home for my afternoons, I think I might adapt your practice Nicole. You are one of the most together and balanced people I know. Sorry Kate, but it's true. Nicole, I don't think I have ever watched you blow your top with the kids. There may be something in a well-timed, daily dose of alcohol."

"Interesting theory. I will keep said strategy in mind if I ever have children or have the chance to go part-time. So, do we know what Abigail has cooked up for dinner tonight?" asks Kate. "Every year we have been lucky that we happen to have liked what she is serving. I find it fascinating that she survives the magazine review ratings. Her draconian behaviour around dinner time is completely against all principles of the customer comes first. Is everyone prepared to eat every single item that lands on your plate?"

Smiling, Nicole winks and reaches for the small dinner menu, sitting on the corner of the table, and reads out the details of the four-course meal. They all nod their heads in approval, and Kate waves down Abigail as she passes by their door en route to the main dining room. In time a bottle of Prosecco appears, is popped and consumed and a basket of homemade bread arrives and is quickly devoured. Having pumped pedals for five hours and having caught up with the usual light chatter while on the road, they are ready for a hearty dinner with an even heartier conversation.

"So ladies, it's been a full year since the three of us sat around this table," says Dianne. "This is where the biggest catch up happens each year. I am the lucky one who gets to see each of you more often, so sometimes subtle changes are easy for me to see. And I do have an observation to share. Kate, something is up. You have been particularly bouncy today. I don't think you have snapped at me once, and I know you take fantastic care of your skin, but frankly, you are glowing. Or maybe, that is simply how you look when you are not frowning and you are smiling full out?"

"Well," Kate pauses, purses her lips and tilts her head, "There is a reason your little grade threes don't get away with anything under your watch. You are very perceptive. I have actually been working particularly hard to contain myself all through our ride and keep my rather perplexing news under wraps until we could talk it all out."

"My," smiles Nicole, raising her eyebrows and moving in closer, "This sounds interesting."

Abigail sails into the room with pickled beets and soft goat cheese on a bed of arugula, drizzled with oil and balsamic vinegar. She lays each plate down with great ceremony, stands back to view her work and then strides out.

"So," begins Kate, ignoring the food, "I've met a Frank." Looking to Dianne and then to Nicole, she is surprised at their complete stillness. "Well of course he is not Frank, he is a Trevor, or rather *is* Trevor."

Nicole nods her head slowly and gracefully picks up her fork, prepared to hear yet another of Kate's escapades, that in time tend to become doomed encounters.

Dianne perks up and smiles, preparing herself to be open minded. She wants to encourage Kate and so she says, "This is good, keep going."

"We work together, which is a bit of a problem, but he is charming, smart, and so handsome. When he smiles or is explaining something, he just lights up the room. I love how he moves and pauses. At first, I thought the way he was paying attention to me was just part of his natural intensity because I had heard he was dating someone. And it was true, he was very much dating someone. But then we worked late one night and it was unbelievable how everything happened. It was just like in a movie. We both looked up at the same time and we were face to face. I could hardly breathe. And then we kissed, just once. We both pulled back surprised and I cried inside thinking that was so wonderful and it's so sad that it won't happen again. And then I blinked and we were kissing again and my head said, *Well, why can't it happen again? Of course, it can happen again!* And then he started saying all these beautiful things to me. How he had been star struck by me the moment he saw me in our first marketing meeting. How he could hardly keep his thoughts on the presentation he was giving. How he watched me leave so quickly after he presented and was worried somehow that I thought poorly of him. How he timidly knocked on my door and was so relieved when I came towards him to shake his hand and welcome him, because then he knew everything was okay. He was so open, so intense and it was the most romantic moment in my life, which may be a sad comment to make. But really, I hadn't felt that inner gasp and *heart standing still* feeling since I was sixteen. I really thought I might never feel that again".

"Wow," grins Nicole, "That is a lot of heat to have circling about in the office!"

"And?" asks Dianne, munching on her salad and moving in closer, "Then?"

"Well," laughs Kate popping in her first bite of salad, "We have sort of been hinged at the hip every non-working hour since then!"

"Okay, now I am really hot and bothered" laughs Nicole, pretending to cool herself down by elegantly fanning herself with her napkin.

Abigail comes barreling around the corner and into the small dining room to check on their progress. She gives Kate the evil eye when she spies her untouched plate and leaves briskly. They all break out in laughter and Kate shakes her head and dives into her salad muttering, "Unbelievable!"

After some further quizzing on the progression of Kate's new relationship, plates are removed and grilled lamb, encrusted with mustard and rosemary, new potatoes and carrots arrive. Abigail surfaces with a bottle of Pinot Noir, which is taste tested by Kate and then poured for all. There are plenty of appreciative words shared with Abigail who leaves with a big smile.

"So," Dianne queries, "You said that you had *perplexing* news. But this all sounds like wonderful news. What are we missing here?"

Kate pauses. Suddenly her animated face has gone flat. "About ten years."

Dianne scrunches her face, confused. Nicole purses her lips, pauses and then nods slowly. "Which way?" she asks.

Kate stares into Nicole's knowing face "He's missing them".

Nicole grins, and then smiles, her hazel eyes shining with amusement, "Well my dear, you are going to have some fun!"

Kate does not smile and is suddenly still. Nicole and Dianne dart their eyes back and forth. Nicole, feeling very much on the periphery of Kate and Dianne's friendship, feels she has just rammed a boat into the rocks with her light hearted comment.

Dianne jumps in so as to defuse Nicole's remark. "So, he is ten years younger than you, however you both feel similarly about each other, so this can work. It happens. The upside here is that he isn't ten years older and in time you become his nurse. Younger is a good thing. Don't you think?"

Kate looks back and forth between Dianne, her longtime friend who has always had her back and who she knows would always be there for her, and Nicole, a newer friend, met through Dianne. While she doesn't know Nicole very well, she has gauged over time that she is someone who has the uncanny ability to see straight, even around corners. The fact that Nicole thought the age gap was something to joke about, increases the vulnerability Kate was already feeling about the age discrepancy.

"Yes, Nicole, I am having *fun*. But I am thirty-five, single, and have no children. So *fun* is not what I am looking for."

Silence. The words are hard to find. Both Dianne and Nicole puzzle through potential ways to address this and opt to be silent and not chance sending Kate any further over the edge.

Kate saves them by explaining. "I want a soul mate. I want what you both have. I want someone to come home to and who I can share my life with. And the confusing part of all of this is trying to figure out how long is he in this for? Is he here for now, or forever? When you are twenty-five and you are a guy, you generally aren't looking beyond the next weekend!"

"Sorry," murmurs Nicole, "I missed the big picture here. My total mistake."

This is an unusual moment for Nicole. She rarely has the occasion to make apologies as her words are generally so carefully selected. She pulls up her long lean frame on her chair, takes a deep breath and says again, "I really am sorry."

"Kate, look at me" says Dianne soothingly. "He clearly cares for you. That's how something really good starts. Don't be scared by it. You are beautiful, inside and out. He is lucky to be with you."

"Thanks Di." Kate's eyes are wet and she fidgets with the soft arms of her sweater that are loosely tied around her shoulders. Then seeking to dispel the moment she unwraps the sweater, raises it up into the air and pulls it over her head and down and around her shapely form. Nicole and Dianne watch her, so aware that this beautiful woman is one of the most exquisite looking women they know. As she combs her hands through her messed up hair and readjusts her ponytail, they watch as casual meets elegant. Nicole and Dianne each quietly retreat back inside their own average sense of self.

Abigail appears and pours more wine into all of their glasses.

Kate smiles and nods her head. "Perfect Abigail, thank you. I definitely needed that!"

Leaving the room their hostess looks back and makes a mental note that the mood has changed remarkably since she was last in it.

"So, Kate. How long have you been seeing Trevor?" asks Dianne.

"A month. But I have known him for three months. In those first couple of months I did have a chance to watch him a lot. I really liked how he interacted with people. I was attracted to his sense of humour, his kindness and how smart he was. But we have been seeing each other for just a month. It was a bit rocky at first because he had to break up with his girlfriend, who he had been with for four years. They had never lived together, but that is a lot of shared time. I wasn't sure if he would break up with her, as he said he would. But he did. She called him a few times after they broke up and she cried a lot. I have never felt like the other woman before. It didn't feel good. But I think that has all settled down now, although I cant imagine how long it will take for her to adjust to life without him."

"Likely it will take a good while. But for you, give it time, don't worry about what it can and can't be," encourages Dianne.

"Yes," says Nicole. "Relationships need oxygen. Time will bring that. Let it develop. Don't be scared."

Kate nods and then a smile begins to bloom, "Okay. Oxygen, good image." She turns to Nicole with an olive branch. "And yes, I will have *fun* too!"

Dinner carries on with more captivating details of intimacy from Kate, with their conversation being stifled when the plates are cleared and then again when the cheese course arrives. In time the topic changes to their past summer vacations, the antics of Dianne's three-year-old Sam and six-year-old Sara, and the early academic achievements of Nicole's eight-year-old Tessa and ten-year-old Jimmy.

As chocolate mousse is served, the suggestion is made to move to decaffeinated coffee instead of opening up a third bottle of wine.

Dianne shifts in her seat, signaling she has something to say. "Dare I launch another observation?" she asks.

"Of course," says Kate. "Please do. The last one was such a hit!"

Nicole smiles demurely. "Is this one targeting me?"

"No targeting here. Just me being curious and wanting to be sure I am being the friend I think I should be." Dianne folds her napkin, and pauses. And then staring down at her place setting she asks, "How is everything with Michael?"

Nicole pauses, looks away and says, "Everything is fine Dianne." The tone is pleasant but curt. Then she turns and stares head on at Dianne. "Is there something I should know about Michael?"

"No, no," Dianne pushes back defensively. "It's not him, it's you. When I see you two together, you are there, but you are not really there. You used to laugh with him at his cautiously delivered jokes and smile at him when he would speak to the room. But the last few times we have gotten together, your face doesn't move. You don't move. And he doesn't seem to realize you aren't a part of the conversation. You would think he would miss his number one supporter. I haven't known how to ask you. I just wanted you to know I am here. Well we are *both* here, if you want to talk."

"Well, I feel a little put on the spot actually. I hadn't noticed that we were acting differently in public."

Nicole sits back, stretches her hands out in front of her and stares at her long fingers and lightly polished nails. She smiles and her right hand reaches over and touches her wedding and engagement ring on her left hand. "These have been on for a long time now. I noticed that the gold band on my diamond ring has warped in shape. Here have a look."

She pulls the ring with its small solitaire off her finger and slowly moves it from Dianne to Kate. Instead of a round circle, the metal ring clearly follows a lopsided path. "I feel a bit like that," she says quietly as she slides the ring back on her finger.

All of them are quiet. There is a puzzlement that hangs in the air. There is no clear demarcation for this conversation. Kate, as the newer friend, who has just barked earlier at Nicole for insensitive comments, has a heightened awareness that she could easily crush the flower bed if she attempts to take an experimental step. Dianne, who isn't sure what she had expected Nicole to say, isn't clear what to add next. This would have been a very good time for Abigail to burst into the room with those coffees, but no such luck.

"Relax," says Nicole. "It's okay. I am okay. Marriage is a long road. Don't judge it in one moment."

Understanding that the subject is now closed, they all nod their heads.

"Decaf coffees all round," Abigail calls out merrily as she enters the room. "And there is a small plate of chocolates coming too, because what is a *Girls Night Out* without lots of chocolate?" She gently places a coffee down in front of each of them, and then returns with milk, sugar and a small plate of chocolate rum truffles. "Can't say that I made these, but I never miss a chance to share them. Enjoy them, ladies. Thank you for coming back again this year." And then with a wink she adds, "Good to see you have worked everything out."

After a chorus of thanks for yet another spectacular meal, and after asking about Abigail's family, Dianne, Nicole and Kate are alone again.

Nicole turns to Dianne. "Thanks for caring. I do appreciate that you notice."

Kate looks to do her part, by trying to move the conversation along. "So, Nicole, what can we observe about Dianne? Or maybe we can just do this the old-fashioned way and simply ask Dianne, *How are you?* and she could tell us so we don't have to guess?"

"I'm good!" laughs Dianne. "Kids are good. Tom is good. My class is great this year. The principal leaves me alone. I have been able to write a little on weekends. That is my escape. But pretty much all is *boringly good,* although I would strike that phrase out if a child wrote that. *Boringly good* - horrendous English!"

"And I would observe," says Nicole reaching over and taking her friend's hand, "That you continue to thrive in your work with all those children. It is remarkable how you can cater to so many in one room."

Dianne smiles, "Thanks. Okay girls. Group hug first and then time for pyjamas, bedtime stories and bed!"

They push back their heavy chairs, and reach out and hug each other, letting words said and unsaid slip away for now. Climbing the stairs to their shared room, they complain about quads and glutes that aren't used to the abuse of riding for so many hours in one day. As flannel nighties and pyjamas appear, so do the jokes. Both Dianne and Nicole kid Kate that she is in need of an upgrade from puppies and bows to an alluring negligee. Kate delights them by replying, "And why buy that if it isn't staying on?" And then the words and stories continue, even when lights are turned off. How to cram in a year in one day and one night? You can't. But you try.

2000

# NICOLE

The summer is over. Back to the battle. For young teenagers, homework doesn't co-exist peacefully beside the television, or a gaming screen of any kind, and the parent ends up losing even when the parent thinks they have won. The glare, cold shoulder or muttered choice words push you even further away from your child, who unbelievably once hung on your every word and begged for bedtime stories. I am happy for the independence I have as the children grow up. But I do miss their younger years when home harmony was broken by them fighting with each other, and not battling with me.

I am told that Jimmy is applying himself in class, but sometimes misses marks when he doesn't hand in homework. Since I am the one at home supervising Jimmy after school, I receive an exasperated expression from Michael. The teacher explains about the marks Jimmy could have gotten, if he were more consistent with his work. I am ready to plough my fist through the classroom drywall, but sit with a pasted straight line across my face and raise my eyebrows.

Tessa receives rave reviews at school. It seems that every teacher thinks that their class is Tessa's favourite subject. She has a knack for endearing herself to teachers and her success becomes their success and subsequently her marks are remarkable. Michael and I smile delightedly at each other as we are told she has an outstanding academic future ahead. Michael sees himself in her work ethic and results, and I see myself in her ability to manipulate people.

But the summer, while free of worry about my children's academics, creates constraints for me. Whether we are in town, for a few days, or up at our rented cottage on the lake, their sprawling arms and legs and raised voices are all around me. I am not free to come and go. I long for the quiet when they are out of the house and at school. I miss leaving work early and having my afternoons on my own.

Our schedule is frequently changing, and moves about based on sporadic tennis games, visits to the pool, and invitations to be guests on a sailboat or at the local country club. Two things are baked in the calendar. My early morning runs, and Michael joining us Thursday nights at the cottage for a long weekend every weekend. And I have to say, those weekends do feel long.

My highlight this summer was shopping. Usually, Tessa was in tow. As a thirteen year old with a keen sense of fashion, she was excellent company as we trolled the clothing stores, picking out summer dresses for Bar-B-Q parties, and Capri pants and cotton sweaters for chillier evening cocktails and mocktails. We both enjoyed walking into a group and watching their eyes dart all over us as they examined our chosen cut of cloth, the accessories we had selected and how all the fashionable parts fit together. This year we both had our toe nails polished bright pink one afternoon, so that our braided, pink and white Jack Roger open-toed sandals, became widely coveted. I am told that the local store experienced a rush on their inventory the next day.

But my comings and goings were based on the family's schedule and I missed my independent afternoons that are available during the academic year. And so as much as I hate the boxing match over homework and the worry time I put in as I become anxious that Jimmy may miss opportunities that I had always wished for, I am happy it is September. I am back to helping out at Michael's office in the morning and then stealing the afternoons for me.

I am beginning to seek out ways to build a bigger life. I am helping some of the mothers who are running the *Annual Harvest Dinner*, the *Ho, Ho, Ho Christmas Bazar* and the fundraiser for the soccer team's visit to Chile. It's great to be a part of figuring out ways to make events more compelling and then be congratulated for making something better. One doesn't get that sort of affirmation from helping in administration at a dental office, keeping a home clean or bringing up children. I know helping out in school events must seem mundane to many, but it is helping me to keep sane. It works better than popping the little white pills that are quite easy to have filled when prescription pads sit on Michael's unattended desk. A scratchy signature and a thirty-minute drive to another community down the road is all that is needed.

Within five years, if Jimmy gets his act together and Tessa carries on with her enthusiastic academic parade, the children will be away in one city or another, experiencing what I have always wished I could have had. I watched from afar as my brothers and high school friends thrived in university, ventured into lectures in large auditoriums, and mingled with new friends in a labyrinth of libraries, campus pubs and lively house parties. I want this for Jimmy and Tessa. Not so I can live through them. I am done with that. I want this for them because I love them and I want them to thrive and love their life.

I don't want my children to feel trapped. I don't want them to see each day as a small, unimportant contribution to the world around them. I don't want them to be seen as having made good choices, when they are doubting many of those decisions. I don't want others to tell them that they married well, appear to be content, happy and in control, and know that all of it is not true.

I have built this charade and I take full responsibility. However, I am always puzzled that as the author of my own story, I can't seem to redirect it to a more pleasing conclusion. I smile when girlfriends admire my smooth existence. I seem to have the gift for pleasing conversation, getting things done on task and on time, and calling out the truth. But living the truth is something with which I have an increasing challenge.

I have someone in my life, or rather, outside of it. He makes me feel that I exist and that I have a pulse. I wonder sometimes if I might have found a different type of distraction if he hadn't offered to drive me home that night when Michael was away and the kids were young and early to bed. Having a third party in a marriage is a silent, destructive force. It has swallowed my voice.

Dianne is my antithesis. She speaks openly and honestly, without a filter. She reminds me of my children when they were little and had not learned that there were consequences if others knew everything you thought. I so enjoy her company. She makes me laugh as she retells the antics in her classroom. She makes me tearful when she shares intimate moments surrounding her dying sister's journey.

This weekend Dianne, Kate and I will be heading away for our annual bike ride and overnight stay at Abigail's B&B. Dianne will need lots of soulful time and cheering up this year. She is close to her sister Caroline, and she is already empathizing with the horrid crush the twins will feel when they lose their mother. They are just a year younger than my Jimmy. One girl and one boy, fourteen years old I believe, and they have lived the last two years with undulating hope and pain.

It will be good to see Kate too. She is more of Dianne's friend than mine and I haven't seen her all year. But what a life she leads. So worldly and full of adventure. I love how her mind thinks. Each year after seeing her at our annual get together, I come back with new ideas popping more freely into my head about how to *market* a fundraiser, or how to create ways for parents and community members to join in and contribute more to events. She has a way for encouraging my mind to move into unexplored corners and find something new. She is remarkable and has a lot on her plate now, with a child, a fast-moving career and a non-traditional relationship, that can be puzzling to the outsider.

I love the fall. The red maple tree is my favourite. Brilliant. Some are massive. Some years they are more impressive than others, or is it just that some years we live in a more colourful existence than the one before? I don't know for sure. But this year they do seem particularly vibrant. So, I guess that may mean for now, all is in a good way.

# DIANNE

These have got to be the best chocolate chip cookies. How can I eat just two? And how then, does that turn into having eight? Sitting down at my desk overlooking the back garden, my tea and plate of cookies appear to have become just tea. Cookies are my comfort food. I feel comfort in the anticipation while mixing up the batter and stirring in the chocolate chips. Comfort in the inevitable sampling as I spoon lumps out onto the tray. And comfort in biting into the cookies, while piping hot, right out of the oven. And then they are gone. I stare at my empty plate, at my oversized sweatshirt discretely hiding my frequent indulgences, and promise again to restrain from returning to the kitchen where the rest of the batch of cookies are attempting to turn into *cool* cookies.

A stack of papers sits beside me - reflections from each of my grade three students on our reading together of *The Lion, the Witch and the Wardrobe*. The girls imagine being Lucy, although two appear to think they would like to be the White Witch. I will have to look into how everything is going for them in the school yard. The boys seem to gravitate towards being Edmund, Peter, the kind faun Mr. Tumnus or the powerful and totally awesome Aslan. Definitely, there are a greater variety of male characters to choose from and once again, a woman is the villain.

As I read, I am constantly alternating from smiling, bursting out with a loud laugh, or sighing over the sweet thoughts expressed, the curious spelling and the strange use of punctuation. It may not be *Saturday Night Live*, but I find an hour of reading through the work of nine-year-old children is pure entertainment.

But then Dylan's paper appears. As he reflects on Aslan's ability to come back from the dead, he wishes that his dad could have had that power. And in a snap the happy time is gone and this child's raw moment becomes mine. I feel his pain and think back to last winter when his father's body was found after an ice fishing incident. The weather had become warmer, more quickly than the year before, and his father's usual spot on the frozen lake had thinned. It took them two weeks to find him after the ice cracked and took him away. Two weeks when Dylan's eyes dimmed slowly, holding onto his father, wanting so desperately to see his dad swagger into the room, ruffle his hair and hug him.

Gazing up and across the lawn to the blue expanse of Georgian Bay, I feel grief rising. While triggered by Dylan's, this one is mine. I hear Caroline's shrieking laughter as she, our sister Gemma and I run hand in hand into the waves as young children. I smell Caroline's favourite perfume as she hugs me, winks and heads out on her first date. I feel her warmth as she listens to my animated stories from my first day of teaching. I see her thinning body cautiously navigating the sandy path at our parent's cottage this summer. I watch her as her two children bravely converse with her by the side of the bed, and then feel her grief as she knows that they are hugging and crying outside her room.

Massive feet tread across my chest. Pressure builds in my head. As I breathe, I feel as if I am breathing for us both. Somewhere she is breathing in and out, however for her, the number of breaths left are running low.

Sam bounces into the room, chasing his soccer ball. A smear of chocolate across his cheek lets me know that more cookies have not made it to the cooling point.

"Mom, have you seen my cleats?" he asks. "Practice is starting soon."

I get up, pull him over to me and practically crush him with a hug. He tolerates the attention, loving it enough not to pull away. He grins at me, letting me know that he knows that I love him. They all know I have been a bit of an emotional mess around the family for months.

Sam, his sister Sara and my dear Tom – all letting me let it out, and hugging me back when I need it.

"Behind the door, in the cubby holes is where I thought I saw them. Have you tried there?" I ask.

"Yup" he says as he leans back and looks up at me. "Logical spot, but not there this time".

We head off to look for them and find them mixed in with his sister's ballet slippers. Totally unrelated, but the image of cleats with ballet slippers warms me up. My children's passions lying side by side. Could be a perfect picture. I smile. Balance returns.

"Ted's mom is driving me. Will you or Dad pick us up?" he asks as he edges towards the door.

"Probably Dad on his way home from work," I mumble, realizing I haven't organized my thoughts around dinner yet. "I will work on dinner so it is ready for all of us. Pizza, I think. Have fun!"

His eyes light up, he waves and bounds out the door. It never fails to amaze me how children sparkle when you mention pizza, even if they have had it twice that week already. More time intensive magazine recipes never seem to garner the same excitement. As a result, my cooking has become rather limited, with Tom leading the charge on the weekend with more adventurous foods.

How different it is at Nicole's. She has turned into such an accomplished chef over the years. When I visited her last Thursday for a glass of wine on her back deck before dinner, she had three well-worn cookbooks laid out on her kitchen counter and she was mixing and matching her evening's meal. When I asked what was the special occasion, she looked at me with a blank face. It took me a moment to realize that this likely happened every night and maybe it happened in a lot more homes than I realized.

The phone rings and I suddenly become aware that I have been standing beside the cooling cookies and one of them has ended up in my hand and is headed for my mouth. I place it back down on the cooling rack and pick up the phone.

"Hey girlfriend," says a warm voice. "How was your day at school today?"

Kate has told me that she has learned never to ask someone coping with grief, the dreaded question, "How are you doing?" It was just too big a question to answer. She explained that it is best to focus on questions that deal with small periods of time. "How was your morning? How was your day? How is your evening going?" And so, this question about my school day was one of those carefully worded questions.

"Good" I answer, which was basically the same non-descript answer she got every time.

I could feel her smiling over the phone. "Just here to bug you, my dear. So, are you still up for biking and escaping for a night this weekend?"

"Absolutely" I answer. "And I saw Nicole last week and she is totally raring to go too."

"How has she been?" asks Kate. "We spoke just a couple of times this year on the phone when we were worried about you, but you were the focus. I didn't ask about her and she pretty much didn't ask about me. All good there?"

"I think so," I answer, thinking back to sitting out on Nicole's back deck. With wine glass in hand, staring out into the quiet early evening, we told stories about the gardener, the principal and any unsuspecting soul who we both happened to know and who had the mishap of slipping up around us. And then there was her time up at the lake. What a lovely spot that seems to be.

"She was animated as she talked about her summer," Dianne continued. "Quite the social scene up there. And now with the kids back at school, it seems that they are doing really well in class, although I guess she talked more about Tessa than Jimmy. I have to say I felt like such a slob in my big cotton shirt and jeans. She had on a spectacular summer dress that looked like a classic 1950's number. If she smoked, a cigarette would have been the perfect accessory."

"She can carry that look off for sure," muses Kate. "Effortless beauty it seems with her. I love her blunt haircut and bangs. Her big eyes just pop out at you. I still can't figure out how she looks like she does with a skincare and makeup bag the size of my wallet!"

"I know what you mean," I continue. "And you know, she seems to float from task to task and nothing phases her. When I grow up, I want to be like Nicole. Know how to cook on demand. Create and manage a party or event with ease. Have children who listen the first time I ask them to do something. And when I open my mouth, always have the right words coming out of it."

"Well," Kate pauses, "Until then, I am going to enjoy who you are now, because that is who I love and wanted to call."

I feel a warmth inside, my face flushes and tears spring from a deep well that never seems to go dry. Warm, salty drops roll down my cheeks, bump into my lips and then hover around my chin.

Knowing that tears are the release that I need, I let them fall and don't even try to rub them away. Each tear says that Caroline matters, that friends matter, and I will not wipe one of those away.

# KATE

The morning mirror is a truthsayer. Before I can begin to apply my magic, it beckons me closer, revealing subtle changes. Skin that has been so well cared for, but has now had forty years to be battered by toxins on the outside - pollution, sun, wind - and toxins consumed within - generous servings of wine and potato chips come to mind. After a quick shower, I begin. Cool water compresses padded on cheeks, forehead, nose, chin, neck, as I remove the remnants from an overnight moisture mask. Careful circular motions with my cleanser to clean and stimulate the skin. Toner applied to cotton balls that are dabbed on my face and neck. And now my moisturizer, my most favourite part. Breathing in the familiar citrus scent, I smooth the cream from my nose, to my cheeks, to my chin and then a second dab for my forehead and a third dab for my neck.

With my skin happy, I force myself to drink two full glasses of water. This always seems to take forever. I can tell with each sip that my body is craving it, but my head is distracted and crying out for coffee. Leaving the warmth of the heated marble floors, I move onto the soft carpet of my dressing room, tap the start button on the espresso machine and switch on the ten globe lights that surround the mirror at my makeup table. As the aroma of Columbian coffee fills the room, I sit down, pull open my makeup drawer and over the next twenty minutes follow my daily regime to transform this face into Kate.

This is also the time I meet with myself each morning. Smoothing on foundation and touching up with concealer, I think through the day ahead. I tap my phone message function and speak slowly, "Add a back up notation about promotions to the Hiller deck." And then a moment later, "Make sure that Talia picks up my dry cleaning". A highlighter and bronzer are each carefully applied. Dabbing my brush into light and then dark powder, I focus in on my eyes. Then an eye liner for eye lids and a special pencil and brush to craft the perfect eyebrow arch. I raise one brow, smile and then get to work on my lashes. A sudden new thought stops me still and I push the button, "Ask Maureen to book theatre tickets in New York based on feedback from Gregory about what show the client would like to see. And ditto for dinner reservations. Ask Gregory and then book." I add blush (understated is best), setting powder (holds all in place), and then moisturizer on my lips. Scanning through my lipsticks I find and apply "Wild Aster", a perfect tone to compliment my new navy suit.

I can hear some activity down the hallway. Trevor is up and cooing with Sylvie. Suddenly there are screams and a trill of laughter and I suspect there are some overhead airplane antics in play. Not how I would start the day with her, but then that only happens on weekends, and I have learned to stay out of it, if I want the help. Talia will be here soon and Trevor will then hand over a turbo charged one year old and head into his day.

It's not as complicated as I thought it would be at the beginning. It is amazing how it is possible to rationalize and fit everything into a manageable box. However so much depends on who is involved and their wishes and intentions. In the end, things seem to be working out. Although I guess its not really the end. It is still very much the beginning.

Trevor peaks his head into my room. "Good morning, gorgeous," he says, his smile as magnetic as ever. "All set for your big trip?" He waits to ensure I am open to interruption and when I smile, he pulls in close behind me, bends down, kisses me gently and then engulfs me with a big man hug. "All packed?"

"Yes, pretty much," I answer, "I just need to throw my makeup bag in".

"Well, that will likely tip your carryon over the weight limit," he teases as he releases me and grins.

"Miss you already," I say sarcastically. "But seriously, it is getting harder to jump into the taxi, drag my bag through the airport and fly off without you."

But I am loving the work, and the rewards have been beyond what I had ever imagined. It's strange to think that if Trevor hadn't walked out and if we hadn't split up a couple of years ago, I would never have taken that head hunter's call. Switching out of marketing packaged goods to strategic marketing within a software startup firm was a bit of a leap. But it was exactly what I needed at the time, so I could flee from the company where Trevor and I both worked and try to escape from the hurt of losing him. Agreeing to take some equity instead of a traditional compensation package turned out to be a good move. Then when the company ran into a liquidity jam, I doubled down further by forgoing income and bonus and took more equity instead. That turned a good situation into a great one. At the time it didn't feel like a risk. I believed in the application we were marketing and could see the future for the other products that were still in development. And now my role in marketing and communications, developing the buzz that is needed to attract investors and end users, continues to be highly valued. Today I find it mind boggling how much my shares are worth should the right buyer come along, and how much salary they continue to pay me on top of that.

"I do enjoy the challenge. I do choose to do this," I declare. "But working full days and then entertaining clients at night is getting somewhat exhausting."

"It's the entertaining part that will always keep me on edge," says Trevor staring at me intently. "I know you don't give yourself full credit, but not all of your clients are thinking pure business thoughts when you are in the room."

"There is a compliment in there" I muse and swivel back to my mirror, "So I will take it and run!"

Trevor strokes my bare arms gently and retreats. I turn and look over my shoulder as he disappears through the door. I hate seeing his back moving away from me. That image still pulls strings inside that hurt. I continue to sense that our ten-year age difference is a sleeping threat. His strength, youth and beauty are forever evident to me and a constant contrast to the woman I meet with in the mirror every morning. The comments from younger women are tough to ignore. The overheard words about me have labels that make me feel as if I am a predator. And the casual comments that come to him, are openly filled with sexual innuendos. I know I need to seriously keep my doubts in check as it has been the source of way too many altercations between Trevor and me. It was the flame that turned into a full out blaze and sent him packing and moving out, after our three years of trying to make it work. And it contributed to me not only bolting from where I worked, but also diving into the next pair of arms that reached out.

"Mr. Phillip is on the phone for you, Miss Kate," calls out Talia from the hallway.

That man has impeccable timing. Telepathic almost. "Thanks Talia! Picking up now! Good Morning, Phillip," I chirp, "I was just thinking about you. How is Florida?"

"Sunny and warm, with a golf game beginning shortly," replies a friendly voice. "How is our Princess this morning?"

"A bundle of energy, from the racket I can hear right now. Talia is in there trying to change her."

"I understand you are off to New York for a few days, correct?" asks Phillip.

"Yes, the Hiller file, it should all work well. I don't see any red flags."

"Great, they will be good to have involved. And now tell me, when will you be joining us in the sun, my dear? It has been a month since I've seen Sylvie. That's one twelfth of her life!"

I smile and appreciate his affection for Sylvie. I wouldn't want it any other way. He is a kind man. A good man. He caught me when I was falling and loved me back to life. Awkwardly though, I got pregnant right away and we both blinked in disbelief at the news, completely lost for words. He knew he was my fling, and I knew I was his momentary lapse of judgement. He was twenty years my senior, a successful private equity investor, recently divorced and heading towards retirement. And he had no children, yet. We changed that. I didn't want to terminate the life of a child that might be my only child, and he was a saint, fully supportive, as long as I led the way.

So, I led the way, with him as a supportive friend, as my body swelled and I figured out how to work full out in my new position, set up a home and prepare for the little girl that was coming.

And then I ran into Trevor. Of course, he had heard I was pregnant, but what he had not known was that I was still very much single. Learning this, he started showing up, again and again. Asking me to go for a coffee, a movie, a walk. Telling me that when he had left, he knew quickly that it was a mistake. He thought some cooling off time would be wise, but he didn't think within a month I would be reattached and gone for good. We laughed about our poor timing and misguided actions – maybe more mine than his. It took some time for me to trust him again, and to trust what I felt for him. But by the time Sylvie arrived, Trevor was a fixture once more in my life. He jumped in, frequently more intuitive to the parent role. And then he moved in, totally confusing the neighbours.

"Trevor has holidays coming up, so we were thinking about coming down in two weeks time. Will that work for you?" I ask.

"Perfect. Tell him I am sharpening up my tennis game and will be ready for him."

"I will do that. I best finish up here Phillip. The taxi will be here within the next ten to fifteen minutes. Big hug to you."

"And a big hug back to you, my sweet Kate."

I dash to dress, zip up my bag and then pop into Sylvie's room. As Talia holds this super active, squirming bundle of joy, I kiss the top of her head, her cheek and her button nose, keeping her little hands away from my silk blouse. It is usually easier to scoot out than to see her for a short moment. But it is getting tougher not to make contact as she becomes more and more her own little person.

"Daddy says hello, Sylvie," I whisper into her tiny ear, encircled by tumbling blonde curls. "And now I had better go find your other Daddy, to give him his kiss good bye, too. And Sylvie, you and I are going to have to work out exactly what you are going to be calling these two men in your life. It's becoming a little confusing!"

# SEPTEMBER GIRLS' BIKE RIDE
## AT 40

Grey can be good, even if it sinks the soul when you wake up hoping for sunshine. A cool, grey day has its own charm. The eye picks up details that can be bleached out by a brilliant sun. The line of a roof becomes more defined. Texture and contrast become sharper. The contents are magically revealed behind a glass window, that has stopped reflecting the outside world. In the dull, grey day, the mind's eye sees an alternate version of its well-known world.

Kate arrives first.

Having a longer journey than the others, she made sure she was packed the night before and was up early to spend an hour with Sylvie before heading out by 8am. Saturdays were meant to be *Sylvie days*, and she did feel a bit guilty as she pulled out of the driveway, but once underway that disappeared. Motherhood, career, and relationships all benefited from girlfriend time. Having twenty-four hours to talk out life and articulate what sometimes never had a chance to surface, was beyond important, it was pretty much essential. It had taken a few years to realize the impact of their annual bike ride, dinner and sleepover. When she began to examine the critical decisions she had made and implemented after each get together, she realized that being with Dianne and Nicole was not only fun, but a much more effective and less expensive form of therapy than the counsellors she had visited over the years.

After pulling up at Abigail's B&B, she enters the dark foyer of the old Victorian home. A small brass bell at the desk is labelled *ring me*, which Kate does. Abigail, dressed in a flowing blouse and carpenter work pants, appears and true to form, takes one second to welcome her and then ten minutes to explain all the rules of the house. Kate smiles throughout. It is refreshing to transfer full control to another human being one day each year.

Having been shown to the requested large, shared bedroom, Kate notices that it has made contact with a fresh coat of paint since last year and has new pink and purple floral bedspreads. While the busy pattern, and choice of colours are not a design scheme she would select to live with, she absolutely loves that this place continues to be consistently different from her world in the city. It has old-world charm and an uncanny sense of feeling *like home*, although it isn't like any home she has ever lived in.

Kate heads back out to the car. She begins unthreading and unbuckling her bike and then lifts it off the rack. Since the bike rack for her new sports Mercedes is attached to the trunk and is imprisoning her luggage, the next part is always a bit tricky. She pops the trunk button on the driver's door and races to catch the bike rack as it flies into the air with the trunk's hood. "There has got to be a better design solution," she thinks. She then stores the rack in the back seat, wheels her bike over to the bike rack, locks it up, and pulls out her two large overnight bags.

The sound of a car on gravel behind her spins Kate around. Two smiling faces are connected to two sets of hands that are waving frenetically through the front window of a large, white SUV. Dianne is driving, which makes Kate suspect that Nicole will be jumping out of her seat as soon as the engine pauses. While their drive would only have been a half hour, Dianne was known to be a distracted driver when she was talking. Her hands would constantly leave the steering wheel so as to better express her words or describe a story more visually.

"We're twins!" yells Dianne, sticking her head out the window, and then hitting the breaks suddenly when she realizes how close she is to another guest's car.

Kate scrunches her face quizzically. "Not sure what you mean?"

"We both have new white cars!" cries out Dianne as she backs up and then pulls in beside Kate.

Nicole escapes from Dianne's car, reaches out and gives Kate a tentative, light embrace and walks around the Mercedes. "I love the lines of your new car, Kate. You must be loving it!"

"Yes," answers Kate, "It is definitely my most favourite purchase of all time. I love every moment I'm in it."

"It must be a bit of a challenge with a car seat," Dianne ponders aloud as she hugs Kate and then peers in through the car window.

"You're right," Kate admits, "It is a bit of pain getting the child seat attached and then getting Sylvie in and out. When we can, we actually use Trevor's car. We suspect Sylvie can see more out of his back window than out of mine. So, once she has the language to fully express herself, this car may have a little less action on weekends."

Dianne pulls out her knapsack from the trunk and Nicole grabs her small overnight bag. Since their bikes are locked on the roof rack, they leave them in place and follow Kate into the house. Checking in with Abigail, they too smile through the welcome, extended rule list and the showing of the room they have shared one night a year for eight years.

As they flip a coin to see who *wins* the single bed and who shares the double, they get lost in remembering who slept where and when. Dianne claims that *for sure* she had the single bed the first year. She remembers it being her first time away from the kids, who at that time were four and one years old. She recalled Kate and Nicole offering her the luxury of having a bed on her own, with no threat of a little one that might be joining her in the middle of the night. It was bliss, just anticipating the sleep ahead.

## Biking

Changing into their biking gear and adding rain and wind paraphernalia, they check out the grey skies, cross their fingers and head out. They comment that bike helmets are the perfect nerd look, and kill their sexy, skin-tight, biking outfits. Taking turns riding in twos along the old, railway trail, they enjoy the smoothness of the well-kept, sandy and partially paved biking and walking paths. While cool when they began their ride, they soon become warm from the exercise and stop to hydrate and strip off an outer layer.

Always this leisurely, three-hour morning bike ride has been for light conversation. The answer to "How are the kids?" is full of anecdotal stories, that have been saved up to share. The stories are cute, funny and heartwarming. The answer to "How is work?" and how is a husband or partner, are kept to short, positive statements, with the fuller picture likely to be shared later over dinner.

This year they add in their stories leading up to Y2K and where they were at 11.59pm on December 31, 1999. It was just last year. They recall watching with anticipation to see how their world would be functioning at 12.01am on January 1, 2000. Kate, with her tech background, leans in to say that it was all an example of narrow thinking back in the early days of technology. Why would a date locator within coding not contemplate all possible future dates? But she admits it was a lesson for the world and has stretched everyone to be more diligent. It is a good thing to always be asking, *What could go wrong here? What have we not thought about?* And since that is not the way those who think they know it all are inclined to think, it has been a good shift for the industry.

Lunch, while seated at the pub table, is generally the time that serious subjects begin to seep in. When eye to eye, it is tougher to set aside what is on one's mind. One's reality and truth begin to seek an audience and answers.

"I am trying to understand how Caroline will soon just not be here," begins Dianne, as their soda waters arrive, are set down and begin to perspire on the small cork coasters promoting a local beer. "This will be my first close death. I have parents alive, all siblings, friends and colleagues. I have felt sadness for others who have lost someone close, but that was different. I feel maybe, there is a *before*

*life* and an *after life* for those of us left behind. And right now, I am
in the before, and when Caroline dies, I will pass over and forever
be in the after. I'm thinking in the *after*, everything is different. How
you feel day to day. How you look at everything. Have either of you
experienced that?"

Kate and Nicole both shake their heads. Kate because she still has
her Mom, her few close friends and she doesn't have siblings. Nicole
because she has lost an uncle, a close cousin, and a dear book club
member, but never felt what Dianne is describing and so chooses not
to contest Dianne's theory.

"I am also starting to feel a weight I didn't feel before. I knew
logically in my head that *if* Caroline goes, my role with her children
would grow. But now I can really see that role ahead and it is big. It
is a role of a pseudo-mother, and the time it will take is not finite. It
will simply go on and on and it will never end. I hadn't realized that.
For the past two years as I assured Caroline that I would be there for
her and for her kids, it hadn't dawned on me what *being there* for her
children really meant. Andrew is great, but he is a pretty blunt father
and frequently unperceptive. Those kids will need someone listening
to them, and story telling along the way to help guide them."

"Dianne, you are the perfect person for that, and for them,"
assures Kate, reaching out her hand and resting it protectively on
Dianne's forearm. Dianne hypnotically turns her glass in circles on its
coaster.

"Caroline knows her children are safe with you," Kate continues.
"She knows you love them and that you are fabulous with kids. But
I can see your point. The role is big. But gradually as they get older
and launch, the role will reduce. None of us at forty are dependent
on our mothers. While we push back in our teens, return cautiously
for support in our twenties, we are pretty much fully launched in
our thirties. Although, it is true that when kids come along there are
still so many useful tips that are helpful. And I guess if there is ever
heartache, a mother's love is pretty special to have there to nurse you

back. So yes, I see what you are saying, I guess it is a long road and potentially it will feel endless."

"I agree with Kate about how valuable you will be to the twins," says Nicole slowly as she stares down at her two hands, clasped as if in prayer in front of her. "You are the perfect person for them. I have seen you with your kids, my kids, and kids at school. You have a gift. You talk *with* them, not *at* them. I want to say you have the patience so many of us lack, but that is not quite it, because it never looks like that. You seem to have a genuine curiosity that gives you the time to find the words they need to hear."

As Nicole finishes, she looks up and into Dianne's face. While Dianne's tears were anticipated, Kate and Dianne are surprised to see Nicole's eyes brimming. Kate can't recall ever having seen Nicole cry before.

"Thank you," Dianne responds, and reaches out to Nicole. "Thank you Nicole. That means a lot. And Kate, thank you too. I need to hear this. I need to get it all straight in my head."

The heaviness of the conversation lightens as homemade soup and fresh buttermilk rolls arrive and are consumed. They gaze down at the coasters and agree that the beer looks tasty, and they joke that it is very unkind of them not to be supporting the local brewery through lunch. But they all agree that they would be quite useless on the bike ride home if beers appeared. With the mood at the moment, it might be tough to have just one.

Typically, each year after lunch, with the prospect of showers and cocktails before dinner at the other end of their afternoon ride, the goal has become to put their heads down and push for a meaningful workout as they pedal *home*. Over the last couple of years, they have begun to clock their afternoon return time. The goal has become *beat your previous best*. They recognize that keeping this as a recurring goal into the future is a bit at odds with their imminent ageing. But they push off the future for now, snap on their helmets and press the time clock.

## Cocktails

"I love the water pressure in this house!" shouts Kate from the shower. After a number of years now, they have an established routine. Kate is first into the shower because her *post-shower* routine is twice as long as Dianne's and Nicole's. The bathroom door always remains ajar so once the water is turned off, no-one is missing any of the conversation. Cocktail hour begins during shower time, since Kate always brings a small cooler with a bottle of chilled, white wine. Music is essential and each year Dianne curates a new list from her CD collection, which generally combines their past favourites with a few new additions. And snacks are limited to one bowl of pretzels, so as to absorb the alcohol (a bit) and not kill their appetite for dinner.

The last twenty minutes of their ride turned brutally cold as the wind whipped up, and the threat of rain approached. However, drops only began as they exited the bike path and were five blocks away from Abigail's. Locking their bikes, they and their dirty shoes rushed into the B&B, and up the front hall stairs, unfortunately breaking one of the rules that had something to do with *don't bring the outside inside.*

Now in their warm corner room, with large, high windows stretching up the walls, they can see the trees bending, and streaks of rain clawing on the window pane. They would also have been able to hear the full power of the rain storm if Aretha Franklin wasn't so loud in her singing out to them for *a little respect!*

Bopping along to the music, while pulling off layers of damp clothing, they all join in. Dianne nailing every word. Nicole lip synching the verses. And Kate bellowing the chorus from the shower.

Once Kate is out of the shower, wrapped in her robe and sporting a turban towel around her wet hair, she pulls out a bottle of Californian Chardonnay, pops the cork and pours three generous glasses.

"And now for our favourite part of the day," says Nicole, winking and raising her wine glass in a salute.

"I swear there is a smile button that wine presses the second it lands in your mouth," joins in Dianne. "Cheers!"

Clinking their glasses, they begin to recount their ride home and then move to recalling past rides that were generally warmer. Then Nicole and Dianne flip a coin, with the loser heading into the shower and the winner topping up everyone's drink.

With Nicole in the shower, and the music rather loud, Kate knows that she and Dianne are pretty much out of earshot.

"Dianne, is Nicole okay?" asks Kate

"I think so," answers Dianne. "She can be quiet sometimes. I don't think it means anything is wrong. She is thinking. Is that what you are getting at?"

"Maybe that's it," ponders Kate as she sits down at the small vanity table and begins to pull out multiple sized bottles, makeup brushes and a couple of compacts. "I just don't see her enough to really judge what's up. Once a year I get a glimpse of her. But its as if each year she has faded, just a bit. When I think back to our first couple of rides some seven to eight years ago, she was larger than life. Not loud, but happier, and she initiated more topics and views. She seemed more generous with her energy in our conversations."

"Hmm," muses Dianne. "Maybe something is up with her. Her tears were a surprise at lunch. She knows Caroline, but not well. I don't think those tears were for her."

"I agree, there is something more to that," carries on Kate. "I somehow think she just seems more reserved and sedate than when I first met her. Maybe it is age. Maybe I am becoming that way too?"

"No," Dianne barges in, "You are definitely not that way. I don't see age making you sedate at all! You are firing on all cylinders these days. You have to be to keep up with what work and Sylvie demand."

As the shower turns off, so does their conversation. Dianne takes a big sip of wine, places her glass down on the bedside table and advances into the bathroom, noting aloud to Kate that she is abiding by the *no glass in the bathroom rule.*

Passing Nicole, Dianne smiles at her long-time friend and thinks back to when they first reconnected after Dianne had returned to Port Colebrook. As she tests the water temperature, and then climbs into the old clawfoot tub, fitted with a powerful shower head, she drifts back to her third day home, when she was checking out kitchen supplies in the hardware store. She ran into Nicole, who was negotiating a baby carriage carefully through the aisles, trying not to wake up Jimmy. He was a beautiful little tow-head one year old back then. It was curious to think that Sylvie is now the same age that Jimmy was then, and that Sylvie has a forty-year-old mother, whereas Nicole was only twenty-six at the time.

Dianne remembers that Nicole was animated and engaging, and after a short catch up, Dianne had been invited to a weekend Bar-B-Q. When she arrived, it turned out that the Bar-B-Q had been reoriented into a Welcome Back party for Dianne, and many of her old high school friends were there. It was a beautiful summer evening and Nicole's back yard was decked out with tiny glittering white lights, a bar tended by Nicole's husband Michael, and fabulous food, all prepared and passed by Nicole. Dianne had always been grateful to Nicole for helping her resettle into the community so quickly and continued to be amazed at Nicole's ability over the years to make things happen and entertain with such poise.

In time, they set a pattern of having afternoon tea every second Saturday when Jimmy was sleeping. They carried that on as Nicole's Tessa, Dianne's Sam and then Sara were born. Initially, it was easy to do when babies could sleep in a baby carriage, but it all became challenging when the children needed their own beds. So, they transitioned their get togethers to every second Thursday night, after dinner when their husbands were home. One of them would walk the short three blocks between their houses, and they would escape to an outside porch when it was warm, or to the basement when the snow blustered and winds blew.

But, in time, that too became difficult. There was homework to patrol and parent or work duties that were beckoning. And so, while the early years were full of vibrant conversations and sharing intimate confidences, in time that all slowed down. And it was true, what Kate was observing, Nicole was more sedate, less lively and maybe more careful with her words. She had always been thoughtful when she shared her views, but now it seemed that she was spending more time in thought than expressing them.

Turning off the shower, reaching for her towel and stepping out onto the small terry towel mat, Dianne felt that maybe she hadn't been the friend she should have been. She should have noticed. But maybe Dianne was too close, and it took Kate, and these once-a-year get-togethers, to be able to see changes more clearly.

"Dianne, if you want any pretzels," cries out Kate, "You had better get out here. Nicole is on a tear."

"Coming," Dianne calls back, and then joins Nicole, who is perched on the bed and talking to Kate's reflection that appears in the three-way vanity mirrors. Kate's beautiful face has now been transformed into an illuminated masterpiece, and Dianne and Nicole both wonder what possible face product in their little bags could help them out.

Holding up one of the pretzels Nicole announces, "Toasted flour and water seems to be the perfect stomach liner for alcohol. And a pretzel is not highly caloric, and there are no saturated fats."

"Good to know," Kate nods with a smile and reaches for more.

Munching on pretzels and sipping the oaky Chardonnay, they dry their wet hair, chatter to each other and change into their *dressed up* casual wear. For Dianne, that involves a good pair of black jeans, an oversized white, cotton shirt and large, silver loop earrings dramatically peaking out from her short, pixie haircut. For Nicole, her choice includes a tailored, plaid, wool pant, a tucked in cotton shirt and a vintage Hermes belt. And for Kate, her pick of a stretch black pant, a dark pink, cashmere turtleneck and lipstick to match seems to say no effort, which is miles from the truth, considering Kate's extensive preparation time.

Popping open a second bottle of wine seems like a good idea. After all the first one is finished, and tonight they only have to navigate getting to and from the dining room downstairs. But as they kick back, gossiping about friends in common and then moving to a topic about emotions, that *one more glass* turns into two, and that is two on top of the first two.

"I am not good with emotion at work," declares Kate.

"Why is that?" asks Nicole.

"I think it is because when I take on a leadership role in the office, I believe it is best to hide emotion from men. In the past, some men seem to have pegged me as weak when they saw me emote. So, it is easier to just pack it away completely and never bring it out. By keeping it under constant check, I lower the risk of it spontaneously showing up!"

"Wow, I don't know how you can do that," remarks Dianne, shaking her head. "I find it hard to curb my emotion even when I am in public and around people I don't know."

"I've seen that play out!" jumps in Nicole. "Remember when we took Sam, Sara and Tessa to the park last summer? Do you remember your altercation with that man with his little boy?"

"Yes," Dianne says solemnly, "I do. That was terrible. Not my behaviour. His!"

"The little boy's?" asks Kate.

"No, the father's," answers Dianne. "There was this precious, little three or four-year-old playing in the sand box, while our kids were on the swings. He was so adorable and he was playing sweetly with the other children. Then all of a sudden this big man, his father, appears and yanks this little boy up by his arm. I thought for sure the arm and shoulder joint would dislodge with the force he used. I instantly jumped up and raced over."

"It was something, Kate," Nicole adds in. "She flew at him, not physically, but there were a lot of words coming out of her mouth."

"That's my girl," smiles Kate. "Not much of an edit button."

"Well, how could you not do something?" Dianne says with a frown. "Anyways, the father seemed to know that he had best back off. There were twenty sets of parent eyes watching. So, he said it was a momentary lapse and that he was truly sorry. And the little boy seemed to be okay. I did check his arm and shoulder and he didn't wince. But then, as they were walking away and had reached the other side of the park, I saw the father swat the little boy on the head. I kept replaying that and trying to figure out if that swat was a whack on the head or just a brush through his hair. I think it was the former but I couldn't be sure. It was very disturbing."

"Do you know who that man is?" asks Kate. "Does he live in Port Colebrook?"

"We asked a couple of the moms in the park about him," Nicole explains. "But no-one knew him. They said that the little boy had been there once before with his mother. But she had kept to herself. The moms seemed to think that the family might live outside of town."

"Each child's world is so different," Dianne says, a melancholy tone creeping into her voice. "And they have no say in which one they end up in."

Kate sits up all of a sudden and checks her watch. "Shoot! Its almost seven o'clock. We had better get down there or Abigail will —"

The music stops. The room is in total darkness. Their ears and eyes search for sound and light.

"Yikes," Dianne pipes up in the dark. "Now, if I hadn't given up smoking, I would have a match nearby to strike."

"If you hadn't given up smoking, we would not have roomed together in university," mutters Kate in the dark.

"Abigail has got to have candles or a flashlight in the room somewhere," says Nicole, running her hands around the vacant interiors of the vanity drawers and then exploring the bedside tables. "Success," she calls out, as she flicks on a small flashlight.

"And then there was light!" cries out Dianne.

"This shouldn't last long," says Nicole. "Usually, the power is back on in a few minutes."

"I guess she doesn't have a generator," said Kate. "I was in Montreal a couple of years ago during their ice storm, and after that experience I promised myself that I would never be without a generator. I am no good with the sudden disappearance of creature comforts."

"Abigail must be having a fit downstairs," said Dianne. "Hmm, not sure if I'm looking forward to our dinner being the second half of our bag of pretzels!"

For the next five minutes they carry on talking in the dark, as Kate recounts her experience in Montreal when huge parts of the city lost power, and the armed forces were brought in to help out. The light from the flashlight provides a warm glow to their little circle. They each have power loss stories to share, and begin to realize that all the incidents were random, unpredictable and lasted for multiple hours or days.

"Let me go see what's up," says Nicole. "Back in a minute."

With the flashlight helping her navigate the hall, and mindful that her wine consumption was making the winding staircase more challenging than it should be, Nicole heads off in search of Abigail. Chaos can be heard from the kitchen, where a few elderly guests are looking on anxiously. Abigail is heard directing her staff, and trying to figure out how dinner could be prepared by flashlight and cooked only on the gas stove top. Finally, she comes out of the kitchen and explains to everyone that a main line is down for the area and it might be a few hours until everything is up and working. She can likely serve a few tables tonight, but not the full house. She glances over at Nicole and asks if she can have a word with her.

As Nicole is climbing back up the stairs, she meets Kate and Dianne, edging carefully downwards in the dark, where they are finding their alcohol induced lack of judgement around their foot placement particularly funny.

"What's up?" asks Kate. "We thought Abigail might have commandeered you into service!"

"Its going to be a few hours until the power is back up. A line seems to have come down for the whole area. Abigail can serve a few guests from her stove top but is asking if, since we are younger, *there is a compliment in there girls,* maybe we could head over to Ricky's Road

House. She says it's a lively spot, has good food, and a generator. But she suggested we get there quickly, as it will get packed once all the visitors in town figure out that Ricky's is one of the only places with lights still on."

They all nod and quickly retrace their steps to their room, fumble around to find their shoes, and grab their coats, gloves and purses.

"I hate lugging this big purse around," says Kate. "It's meant for when I am travelling and I have my lap top. I would have brought a small evening bag if I knew we were going out!"

"Don't take it Kate" says Nicole, "We can pick this meal up."

"No, no," insists Kate. "Here, let me get my credit card and some cash. Can you slip it into your purse?"

"Sure," replies Nicole. "Easy to do."

"Thanks!" says Kate with a big smile as she hands over her card and cash. "I will be keeping you in sight all night!"

"I'm good with mine," says Dianne. "And I am now picking up the key to the room, so we are compliant with rule number whatever - *Leave the room key at the front desk.* So ladies, let's go!"


## Dinner

Ricky's Road House is illuminated up ahead. It beams like a lighthouse, but instead of warning people to stay away, it is beckoning them to come towards it. All around is dark, with a few subdued emergency lights along the road, and the occasional small venue carrying on brightly, thanks to a private generator. The wind is cold and still blowing, but thankfully the rain has stopped. They take turns between running and walking along the sidewalk, acknowledging that the alcohol and their coats are equal contributors to keeping them warm.

Approaching Ricky's, they can see that a small line has appeared, but thankfully it is moving when they join it. Within five minutes they leave the chilly, dark night and feel the heat hit their faces as they step inside. Bright lights and loud sound greet them. They turn to each other smiling, raising eyebrows and begin to bounce to the beat of the Rolling Stones' *Start me up!*

"Our night is looking up ladies," Kate shouts over the music, and Dianne and Nicole smile back, both energized by the buzz in the room.

They follow their hostess over to a small table for two, and add a chair from a larger, boisterous table beside them. Predictably, once Kate takes off her coat the neighbouring table of young men, who are likely on a boys' weekend, take note of the bright, pink, cashmere sweater, or rather what they imagine lies beneath it. In no time, the young men are engaging all three of them in conversation. Drinks are flowing and "What do you want for dinner?" is raised, but the dance floor gets in the way.

Dianne looks over at Nicole and is delighted to see the return of the animated friend that she remembers. As Ted, Jason and Stewart pursue Kate's attention, Mark and Jordan are curiously captivated by Nicole. She has a wry sense of humour, and her sarcasm and engaging smile, has always been a winning formula with both men and women. Looking at her sparring with these men, who are a good eight years younger, she can see her appeal to them. She is attractive, fit and tonight, particularly vibrant. And when she is pulled out onto the dance floor, her rhythm takes over and eyes move to her.

Thinking ahead, to the sore heads they will be nursing tomorrow if they don't eat and if they don't hydrate with water instead of wine, Dianne takes the liberty of ordering a large plate of nachos, three healthy looking salads and another pitcher of water. An intoxicated Terrance, who has cozied up beside her agrees with her choices and then pulls her out to the dance floor as the pounding first beats of the B-52's *Love Shack* peals out across the room.

Kate finds this evening's male attention refreshingly different from her frequent unsolicited encounters on business trips. This is pure fun, with neither side believing it is going anywhere. While she doesn't wear a wedding or engagement ring, she has been clear in her opening conversation to mention that she has a one-year-old child and is happily living with a long-term partner. What she finds secretly amusing is that none of them would guess that her partner happens to be around their age, and so yes, in fact, it is possible that this older woman would find them of interest.

Curiously the conversation with these young men has moved from flirtation to business. They are intrigued by the software that Kate's firm is developing and it turns out that Ted and Stewart both have ambitions in this field. She watches knowingly as the predictable transformation occurs where men start speaking to her as if she is a person instead of an object.

In the midst of this, Kate hears a familiar melody and looks up. The tune's subtle prelude is clearly not drawing the recognition that it soon will receive. Kate scans the room for Dianne and Nicole, and seeing them both on the dance floor with a handful of others, excuses herself and races to the dance floor to join them.

Dianne, who has a photographic memory for lyrics, has already begun lip-synching the opening "Ooh boy, oh yeah, yeah," and is edging into the first verse. Aretha Franklin has entered the room and Kate and Nicole faithfully take up their positions on either side of her, swaying their shoulders and hips. While they have never formally practiced dance moves, or vocal parts, there is an intuitive feel that ripples between them. Locked in memories of bouncing about bedrooms over the years with radios, cassette decks and then CD players, their performances have always been for each other. The fact that there is a happy crowd dancing around them, looking on and joining in doesn't phase them one bit.

*Who's Zoomin Who?* fills the room, and Dianne, a five-foot two-inch bundle of energy, is remarkably entertaining. Her eyes light up as she sings. Her body dances with her voice as she reaches out her hands towards Nicole and Kate and then to the dancers all around her who encourage her on. She beckons answers to Aretha's questions and smiles as she invites all to join in

In no time, the young men from their neighbouring table have joined them on the dance floor. The sea of moving arms and legs begin to wedge together as the floor fills. However respectfully, everyone is leaving breathing room for Aretha and her two back up singers. As the lyrics continue, Kate smiles at the female empowerment present in the words. She doubts the young men present are fully hearing the words that chide men for thinking they are always smooth and in control of picking and choosing. Sometimes it is the woman who is orchestrating the final outcome. Dianne, Nicole and Kate smile and point coyly at the boys, as they bounce to the beat and sing out the final phrases together.

As the DJ blends in another tune, and Aretha fades away, the three girlfriends fold into each others' arms. Exhaustion wells up and they are in need of water.

The room seems to have changed since they left their little table. Suddenly their area has become overpopulated with someone who thinks they know Kate (an unoriginal pick-up line), or went to university with Dianne (possibly) or has seen Nicole here before (not the case). When their food arrives, they attempt to return to an intimate conversation, but abandon that as the music keeps their feet tapping, and eventually they are out on the dance floor again.

As midnight approaches, and Nicole and Dianne are singing and dancing to Deep Blue Something's *Breakfast at Tiffany's* on the dance floor, Kate makes the decision to close out the bill. She would like to suggest they head home at the next water break. She reaches under the table for Nicole's purse that is wrapped inside Nicole's coat, which was forfeited to the floor so as to keep the purse hidden. Looking into the purse, she searches the main compartment and then tries the inside pocket. She feels edges that feel like her credit card and pulls out a square packet. In shock, she pauses and then quickly shoves her hand back into the purse. She looks around for a moment and then seeing that no-one is watching her, she peers into the purse and opens up her hand.

"What the f***?" she mouths out to herself. An unopened condom package lies in her hand. She looks out onto the dance floor at Nicole, laughing with Dianne and moving suggestively with the music. In confusion, she tries to recall details of the rather serious topic of conversation a number of years back, when Dianne and Nicole had discussed why they were in favour of turning off the baby machine for good. It was a rather bizarre conversation for Kate, who at the time was still hoping to turn it on. Kate was pretty sure that both Dianne's Tom, and Nicole's Michael had had vasectomies. So, why was Nicole carrying a condom in her purse? Kate felt her brain twisting, just thinking about it.

Carefully, she puts the condom back in the purse's inner pocket. She then locates her cash and card in the opposite pocket, waves down their waitress, and pays and tips her well. She is ready to go when Nicole and Dianne come waltzing back to the table.

"Come on girls," Kate calls out, "My beauty sleep is beckoning. Time to go!"

Thankfully neither Nicole or Dianne dissent, however the boys beside them try unsuccessfully to get them to stay for "just one more." As they pull on coats, Nicole and Dianne admonish Kate for paying without them. Moving towards the door a number of patrons smile and wave a friendly goodbye to them.

"Hey, the Supremes are leaving!" shouts one of the bartenders as they reach the door. They had done a rendition of *Baby Love*, with Dianne enacting the super cool Diana Ross. Dianne responds to the shout out by blowing him a dramatic kiss with both hands.

Laughing, they burst out into the night, hardly feeling the cold. Thankfully the combination of dancing, which took time away from drinking, and lots of ice water throughout the night, ensures that they are totally capable of finding their way home in a straight line.

Half way home, Dianne notices that Kate is not joining in with the same enthusiasm as earlier, and chalks it up to Kate returning to her responsible self a little ahead of Dianne and Nicole. Later she would understand, but for now she is energized, happy, and without a worry to slow her down.

Happily, they return to a warm, fully-lit house. A note with their key says, "Thank you for your understanding. See you at breakfast, Abigail."

Respecting other guests, who are likely fast asleep, they quietly climb the stairs, keep the radio off and change into their pyjamas. With no music to perk them up, exhaustion settles in quickly and their warm beds engulf them. As the conversation trails off and sleep overtakes them, they make their goodnight rounds.

"Good night, Kate."

"Good night, Nicole."

"Good night, Dianne."

And then Dianne calls out the famous close-off line from the Walton's TV series, which had become their traditional nighttime close-off line each year. "Good night, John Boy!"

But it is not a good night after all. Either age has made Nicole and Kate lighter sleepers, or age has changed Dianne's nasal passages. Shortly after they have all slipped into sleep, loud snoring begins to fill the room. First Nicole sits up, and then Kate. They walk over to the single bed where Dianne is sleeping and try to wake her up to make her stop. But Dianne simply fades back into sleep and the snoring begins again. Nicole and Kate spend the rest of the night taking turns to walk over and roll Dianne onto her side. While sleep seems to be peacefully constant for Dianne it is frustratingly intermittent for Nicole and Kate.

## Breakfast

Kate is up early and heads downstairs to search out an early morning coffee and review her emails. In time, a well-rested Dianne arrives and Kate lights into her about her snoring.

"Dianne, we are for sure going to get you your own room next year. You were so loud!"

After Dianne's profuse apologies, they seek out a breakfast table and have some time to catch up on mutual friends from university.

Kate then shares last night's discovery of what she found in Nicole's purse.

"I don't know why she would have that in her purse," Dianne says, shaking her head from side to side. "You have to ask her outright. I can see you going through a paradigm shift about her and that's not fair for her or for you. There could be a perfectly good explanation."

"For what?" asks Nicole, suddenly planting herself down beside them, having blissfully caught an extra hour of uninterrupted sleep.

Kate looks at Dianne, pauses for a rather long minute and then faces Nicole straight on. "When I went into your purse last night to get my credit card, I found a condom. I am just trying to get my head around why it's in there. You don't have to tell me, or us, anything if you don't want to. I guess I just don't understand, and I want to believe I really know you and what is going on in your life."

Nicole seems to freeze for a moment, and looks back and forth between Kate and Nicole. Then her shoulders relax, a large smile creeps across her face and she reaches for the pot of coffee on the table. She pours herself a cup.

"You two are too funny. Have you been messing about trying to figure this out since you got up?" asks Nicole.

The table is silent.

"Relax," says Nicole. "Its actually a funny story." She reaches over and picks up the small creamer, eyes the contents, and then asks, "Is this cream or milk?"

"Cream," says Kate in a flat voice, staring hawkishly at Nicole, slightly suspicious of her nonchalant manner.

"Let me get some milk. Back in a second." Nicole leaves the dining room.

Kate looks at Dianne sideways and twists her mouth into a small knot.

"So," says Nicole returning with a small milk jug and adding some milk to her coffee, "Have you read the new novel Ziggy and Rain?"

Kate and Dianne shake their heads.

"Well, our book club read it last month. Its about a rock band

and a couple of volatile, hippy-like rock stars, who are constantly falling in and out of bed through out the story. Ziggy, the heroine is always unwrapping and making sure the condom is on Rain. We thought it was a hoot and couldn't decide whether it was put in for entertainment value or whether the author had a teenager and was possessed with teaching them about safe sex. Not a great book, but our book club meeting was pretty animated. Anyways, Cynthia, who hosted the night, passed out a condom to each of us as a party favour. It was hilarious. I guess I put it in my purse and it has been there ever since. I am thinking, that with your reaction, I had best get it out of there. While I could explain it to Michael, I am not sure I would want to have to explain the situation or the plot of the book to my kids."

Throughout Nicole's explanation, first Dianne, and then Kate, begin to smile and gradually the tension disappears.

"I'm sorry," says Kate. "You understand why I thought it was odd though, right?"

"Totally," says Nicole with a laugh. "If I had found that in Dianne's bag, I would be scratching my head too. Now if I found it in your bag Kate, I would be imagining you and Trevor just being prepared for some fabulous, spontaneous sex!"

Kate laughs. "Not much risk of that these days!"

"Truth is, Nicole," says Dianne slowly, "Kate and I were wondering yesterday if you were okay. I don't get to see you as much these days, and Kate only sees you once a year. Kate noticed that you have become more reserved, and you jump in less when we are carrying on, and I agree that sometimes you seem far away. Although, last night when we were all out, I could totally *see you* again. You were all there. One hundred percent. Please don't hate me for caring to ask. You were amazing to me when I moved back after school. You constantly checked in to make sure I was coming along. It is important to me that I be the friend you have always been to me, and that I look out for you too."

"Well," says Nicole, sitting back and crossing her arms. Then, realizing how defensive that looks, she uncrosses them and places her hands flat out on the table. "I am feeling a bit ganged up on this morning, but I am clear-minded enough to understand you are just being good friends. I do have a lot on my mind. There are things I am working through, and it does interfere with being spontaneous. Thank you for noticing and for voicing. I will try to do a better job at being more in the moment, because I really do enjoy being with you both, and I don't want to hurt that."

Kate notes that while Nicole has been open in this moment and has admitted that there is something on her mind, she is not offering up the actual source of the problem. How does that happen when you are with your girlfriends for twenty-four hours? Kate finds this irritating. For Kate, this time together has always been where she could pull out her worries, have a chance to articulate them in a safe space and seek thoughtful answers.

Dianne clenches her jaw, so as to force herself not to open up her mouth and ask, "What is going on, Nicole? What is on your mind?" She has been told she sometimes needs to stop and not force what she is thinking on others. But incredibly, it seems that Nicole has managed to confirm the allegation, admit a lot is on her mind, and is now going to walk away from the weekend and keep it all to herself. Dianne looks over at Kate and notices that she too is mad at Nicole.

Abigail is standing over them, looking at each of them expectantly. "So ladies, what can I offer you? Vegetable and cheese omelets, porridge, pancakes?"

Abigail, having interrupted the tension, has created a neutral space for them to re-group. They order their breakfast, have a moment of silence and then seek out a new subject.

"So, I do have something I have been meaning to ask your advice on," says Kate. "It has to do with Sylvie's parent population."

"That is an interesting way to describe it," chimes in Dianne.

"Sylvie is starting to form words. At six months she was saying *ma* and *da*, but more as sounds than expressing who they belonged to. But now at a year, I am for sure *ma ma*, and both Trevor and Phillip get *da da*, (and recently Talia got *da da* too), so the meaning of *da da* is not definitive yet. But you may be able to see where I am going with this. I feel I need to nail down who is Daddy and what the other one is going to be called?"

"That is a tough one," sympathizes Nicole. "Has Phillip or Trevor weighed in on what they want to be called?"

"No. They are both playing the *what ever you think is best* card. But I feel that is a trap. Eventually one of them, or both of them, will have a strong opinion. I think they are just not expressing what they want."

"So," quizzed Nicole, "How do you introduce Trevor and Phillip today to people when you are out and about with Sylvie? What words have you been using?"

"Good point," says Kate as she nods her head slowly. "It doesn't happen often, but when they are both there, I will say *this is Sylvie's father* referencing Phillip, and then I will say *and this is my partner* referencing Trevor. If Phillip isn't there, I still stick with introducing Trevor as my partner. I haven't introduced him as Sylvie's Dad, but I know some of the neighbours think he is her father, and I don't correct them when they say *your daughter* to both of us. That would be petty."

"How about when you and Trevor are alone with Sylvie," asks Dianne, and he is saying *Sylvie look at Mommy*. What are you saying to Sylvie when referencing Trevor?"

"Well, that is where I am inconsistent. I sometimes say Daddy, and Trevor will look at me in such an intimate way, that I know, deep down, that is what he wants to be called. If I had never said it, and I have done it a few times, I might not have the dilemma. Its my own fault for playing around with the word without thinking it all through."

"Omelets all round," Abigail pipes up as she arrives at our table carrying three hot plates, each with a steaming vegetable omelet, surrounded by back bacon and thickly-cut, white toast. "Careful, the plates are hot!" Checking the coffee pot she adds, "There is more where that came from, let me fill that up." Abigail returns with a fresh pot, stands back, surveys the table, nods and heads back to the kitchen.

"You mentioned you were flying to Florida with Sylvie and Trevor to visit with Phillip, right?" asks Nicole. "What feels right and what feels wrong when you think ahead to all four of you being together?"

"Well, I guess for sure Phillip is the father and should be Daddy, and Trevor is Trevor, and maybe she should just call him by his name?"

"What about *Papa?*" asks Dianne, "or *Pops*, or something fun? Wouldn't it be nice for Trevor to have a special name that Sylvie could grow up calling him? It would be their own special thing to have forever."

Kate becomes very still, and stares down at the centre of the table. Deep down she suddenly understands the bigger problem and why she hasn't been able to land on this on her own. Something deep inside continues to flinch at the thought of giving Trevor a title role in Sylvie's life.

"Kate," says Nicole, "There is something more to this. You know the answer, but something is bothering you about all of this. What are you really thinking?"

Kate looks up at Nicole, wanting to say *you tell me what is really up with you, and I will tell you what is really up with me!* But she holds back. That is just anger speaking, because she doesn't like what she is beginning to figure out.

Kate shakes her head slowly, stops and purses her lips together and then continues. "I think the problem is that I want Trevor, Sylvie and me to be the little family that Trevor and I had hoped for when we first got together. And I want to think that Trevor will be a part of our lives forever and be this *Super-dad* who will always be there for her. But I still don't know for sure that Trevor will stay. He keeps saying that our ten-year age difference is in my head, not his. But I do think both Sylvie and me are in a vulnerable position. He could leave me for a younger woman, someone who can also give him a house full of kids. Phillip, on the other hand, will be with us for all of his life. He will be there for Sylvie for sure. He won't leave Sylvie, and he won't hurt her by hurting or leaving me."

Dianne and Nicole nod their heads. The picture has been fully outlined and coloured in. They see what Kate sees. Neither attempts to console by offering another point of view. Kate hears their silence and is grateful for the honesty of friends.

They eat silently for a moment, one of their very few breaks in conversation this weekend.

Nicole puts down her knife and fork, folds her hands into her lap and slowly looks at Dianne and then at Kate. "I don't love Michael anymore."

Dianne's mouth drops. She stares at Nicole, blinks once, then twice, and then shakes her head as if to wake up. She leans over towards her friend and searches out her hand and holds it.

"I just don't feel anything anymore. I haven't for a long time. I used to say to myself that I wasn't *in love* with him, but I did at least *love* him. But now I don't love him either."

Kate furrows her brow and reaches out to find Dianne's other hand. "This is big Nicole. What happened?"

"I can't really pinpoint what happened. It happened over such a long period of time. We had constantly different ideas around parenting, so we would fight about that. Nothing really would get resolved, so that pushed us apart for sure. If we were friends way back, we don't seem to be friends any more. We don't really have shared views. We read different newspapers, magazines and books. We watch different shows and movies. He seems to like what I cook. But if I cooked a gourmet meal or a simple meat and potatoes meal, he reacts the same. I used to think he was indifferent to me when I cooked but I think it is actually that he is indifferent to food. And I love cooking. At least the kids appreciate it when I do something really adventurous or complex. Jimmy has become quite the foodie," she smiles. "And I love it when he joins me in the kitchen."

Kate wants to say, "This is so sad." But these words don't seem like the right ones. She wants to find words that are hopeful and helpful, not ones that sit uselessly in space.

"And I don't find him interesting," Nicole continues with a disheartened exasperation. "And I don't think he finds me interesting either. We seem to have settled into indifference and silence. And we just carry on. He with his work, reading and TV, and me with reading, cooking and as many out of the house volunteer activities I can find."

"Have you gone to see a counsellor or couple's therapist?" asks Kate.

"We did once, but he didn't like it. He said he was not comfortable sharing his married life with someone else. I wanted to say *that's exactly the problem. You aren't even sharing that life with me!* But I know it goes both ways. I am the co-curator of the charade of a life we are in."

"What are you going to do Nicole?" asks Dianne.

"I really don't know what I'm going to do. It is not the kids' fault that we have botched this up. I don't want them to get hurt. I don't want them to be dividing their time between two homes, and frankly, I need to know they are under my roof every night. I want to know that I can go in and kiss them while they are sleeping if I want to. I need to know that no-one can take them away. I can share anything, but not my children. So, I am not going to do anything. Not right now anyways."

"Is there anything I can do to help?" asks Dianne.

"Your brutal honesty Dianne," continued Nicole, with a vacant stare. "That was help right there. Calling me out on my demeanor. That is actually helpful. I've had my blinders on. I haven't seen what this is all doing to me. I have to work on building myself back up so I don't get washed out through this. I hadn't seen that. I see it now. Thank you."

"I can feel you more right now than I have for years, Nicole," says Kate, leaning in towards Nicole, and squeezing Nicole's hand. "We are both here for you. And we don't have to wait a year to get together. And there is the phone, too!"

"Look, Nicole," says Dianne, "Let's get back into doing something together, maybe every one to two weeks? We can do the cocktail thing, but I'm thinking that maybe a walk, snowshoe or something that gets us outside and moving might be better. Exercise is one thing I need more of and I had wanted to suggest it to you this weekend anyways. You'd be doing me a huge favour to help get me moving! What do you say?"

Kate looks over at Dianne and marvels at the beautiful person she is. Dianne is clearly reaching out to help Nicole, but she has managed to turn it around so that she is making Nicole feel that she is the one doing the helping. Kate's surge of affection is followed by a tinge of jealousy. The two-hour travel distance between her and them has created inevitable moments of exclusion in the past. However right now, new images of future missed walks, deep talks, and impromptu cocktails and dinners flood into her mind. They all seem to float in front of her, just slightly out of reach.

Later, once they have packed up and checked out, they fold into a frozen tableau of arms wrapped around each other. After this overly long hug, Nicole and Dianne climb into Dianne's SUV. With a soft, gentle wave to Kate, they back out and drive off.

Kate double checks that her reattached bike rack is centred and secure and then reverses her car out of the parking lot and begins her trek home. Annie Lennox's *No More I Love You's* begins to play on the radio as she picks up speed and moves onto the highway. Kate turns up the volume. As the chorus kicks in and the singer's sad voice laments about the loss of *I love you's* and *language leaving one in silence*, she starts to tear up. She cries for Nicole and the feeling of love lost. And she cries for her own future self, fearful of the love that she may lose one day too. She senses a distant derailment approaching in her life. While it may be far off, eerily, she feels powerless to stop it.

2005

# NICOLE

Endings bring beginnings. My ending and new beginning came into place one after another. Both were unplanned by me.

Sitting comfortably in my soft, leather seat inside my black Lexus sedan, I breathe in that fabulous new car smell that signals that this car has recently come off the production line and I am the happy first owner. Up the driveway ahead of me is a large Georgian Bay property. The post and beam architecture includes huge floor to ceiling windows that pull in the outside majesty of grasses, trees, water and sky. While the home sits out on a private point with driving winds, its solid construction creates a bunker like effect, sheltering occupants from the unpredictable weather. Huge slabs of meta-sedimentary and igneous rock circle the shoreline and masses of soaring pine trees provide the privacy so many find desirable.

I check my watch. I am early. But that is always the plan - to be early and never late. Clients remember if you inconvenience them, even if it is just once. That is understandable. Most of my clients these days are driving up from the city to view properties, so they need someone reliable and totally focused on them. Someone who will make the time enjoyable, productive and worthwhile.

Through Kate I learned about differentiating myself, and I have made a point of creating an experience for my clients that make their visit with me a highlight in their week. This generally includes having their favourite beverage and snack ready, ensuring I have done my homework well and that I am always early. I want them to remember the image of me waiting for them, ready to serve them. It seems to be working, so I am keeping this formula. And as Dianne has said to me, "It's working, so just *rinse and repeat!*"

When I look back now to a few years ago, I feel as though I was rinsing and repeating a completely different life. I was operating as if in a thick, heavy fog, and just moving through the motions of mother, housewife, administrative assistant to Michael, and community helper. I didn't seem to see anything else in the world around me. While a movie uses fog for suspense and to hide a villain, my fog was a self-inflicted malaise. And as for a villain, I was completely unaware that one had slipped into my life.

But sometimes things have to get really bad, before they can get better. When life is about to totally tip over, people get worried and thankfully get bossy and insistent. Well, at least good girlfriends do.

Dianne and I had settled back into the rhythm of seeing each other every couple of weeks for long walks. Kate, had reached out with occasional calls and made a point of coming up north for a weekend during the early summer and inviting us to her home in the city during the winter. I see now that while I was still running on auto pilot during that time, all of that one-on-one time with them allowed the trust between us to grow stronger. And so, when I tipped over, I didn't go under. They leapt in and pulled me out.

Unfortunately, the drama of that tipping point played out around Kate's wedding in Bermuda, which likely took something away from her day. She continues to insist that she wouldn't have had it any other way. And I guess when you look at my trajectory afterwards, she can at least take credit for being a big part of that. But I still want to bury my head and hide when I think about that day.

A dark blue Audi appears in my rear-view mirror, and pulls up behind me. Allison and Mark, a young couple in their late thirties step out, and I join them on the sandy driveway. It is a brisk April morning, and the couple wear matching blue jeans, with crisp cotton polo shirts and soft tailored sweaters. Brand new boat shoes on both of them tell me they are serious about looking at properties. They are seeking to find a distraction from their city life and a place where they, and their shoes, can fit into a casual weekend up north.

After handshakes and a short introduction, I suggest they pop into my car with me, where it is a bit warmer and I can go through the property tour outline. They do, and are delighted with the Chai tea latte, black coffee and homemade chocolate chip cookies. I give full credit to Mark's assistant, who was most helpful in not only helping me with these preferences, but who also in confidence, gave me a great run down on how to manage them.

Over the course of the day, we visit four properties, two that I knew they would like and two that I suspected would be quickly set aside, but that would allow them to see just how special the other two were. Overall, it is a successful day. They are not only truly interested in visiting again, but they have also indicated that they have a city friend who might also like to speak with me. I still don't know what excites me more, the actual sale of a property or the promise of a new introduction. As time goes on, I am suspecting it is the latter, which actually is a good thing, as it perpetuates the former.

Arriving home around 4pm, I have time to kick off my shoes, turn on the radio, grab my one beer, flip up my laptop on the kitchen table and make a few notes on the day. Shortly, I will pull out and prepare a light dinner for Michael and me, but for now the day is still mine. With a new housekeeper that we hired a year ago, my only house duties are managing what needs to be done and cooking dinner. Both are jobs I enjoy, so these days I am feeling pretty good about life. I miss the kids though. Tessa joined Jimmy at university this year, so it is a lot quieter here. Lots of time to think, to read, to work and to be thankful for how all is beginning to turn out.

*Smooth* by Santana comes on the radio, and as the strumming and drumming fills the kitchen, I am transported back to the heat of Bermuda. "Who has a July wedding in Bermuda anyways?" I remember hearing one of Kate's friend's mutter. They did have a point. It turns out that July is an incredibly humid month and if we weren't near a fan or in an air conditioned room we were all dripping within ten minutes.

But Trevor had surprised Kate with a proposal in May, and Kate pounced on the preparations right away. She decided on a destination wedding so as to keep it small. She had heard about the Coral Beach Club in Bermuda from a colleague and while the club was booked up for the fall and winter, they had lots of openings in July. Likely most wedding couples and guests preferred not to sweat profusely in their wedding attire.

I can still feel the emotion, both hers and then mine, when Kate called to let me know she was engaged. I could tell that she was en route between meetings that morning. Her voice was fast and she was frequently out of breath as she described her birthday the day before. She had arrived home to a house with candles lit in every room and she had to look for Trevor, because he didn't answer when she called. She eventually found him out on the back porch and there was a huge wrapped box beside him. It ended up being many boxes inside each other, seven in total - one for each year that they had known each other. The seventh one was a small Tiffany ring box. Her joy bounced through the phone, and then it was followed by her asking me if I would be in her wedding party. She wanted to have Dianne and me, and that was pretty much it. I lost it. I was crying with her on the phone. To be loved and wanted at that moment meant the world to me.

And so, Dianne, Kate and I, along with Kate's mother, travelled down to Bermuda for a few days before the wedding – a pseudo *Stagette* that would last three days. Trevor, Sylvie (with Talia helping out), our husbands and thirty or so other guests trailed the day before the wedding. With most of the preparations complete and Kate's mother preferring the coolness of the air conditioned interiors of the club, shops and restaurants, Kate, Dianne and I hopped on mopeds, explored the island top to bottom and checked out the sandy pink beaches and aqua blue water. Kate kept an eye out for small private beaches and interesting restaurants to take Trevor back to, as they would be staying on afterwards for a honeymoon week once we all headed home.

There were two defining moments for me on that trip. The first one created the momentum that led me to helping city folk find that perfect spot up north. But I realize now, that it was the second moment, that while disruptive, ensured I could carry through with this new direction.

We were having lunch at the Southampton Princess's Beach Bar, overlooking the ocean waves crashing into the rocks below us. Large blue and white striped umbrellas sheltered us from the strong sun, and a warm salty breeze kissed our skin. We had popped a bottle of champagne, knowing that we had the afternoon to stretch out on the soft, pink, coral sand. We would have time to sober up before we jumped onto our mopeds and concentrated on navigating our way home along the unfamiliar left-hand side of the road.

As we sat back in our chairs, Kate looked out at the ocean, and let out a sigh with a soft, sleepy smile. If bliss needed a poster girl to illustrate its precious pleasure, Kate was it. Dianne and I smiled at each other. It was good to see Kate taking in the moment and not in the throws of planning, creating or correcting something. She took on the world constantly but today she was taking it in peacefully. Or so I thought.

Kate shifted her gaze to the two of us and said slowly, "Do you realize that all of this is possible, because we live in a time where women can be educated and become economically independent? If I hadn't gone through university, gone out into the work force and made my own way, I wouldn't be here, having chosen this spectacular spot, and getting married to Trevor. I wouldn't have been able to choose to have a child on my own. But I have the financial capacity to take the personal risks and to stretch for what I want. I would have been trapped into making other decisions, and having another life, if I didn't have the capital and income I have."

For someone who was generally so sensitive to us, I felt that Kate had forgotten her audience. I assumed that Dianne, like me, must feel like she was on the other side of the fence peering over at this beautifully landscaped life Kate had just described.

But then Dianne joined in. "I agree, money in the bank and the means to keep the money coming in, does make a difference, when you are wondering about choices you have made or are contemplating for the future."

As the lobster salads were carefully placed down in front of each of us and our champagne was topped up, I suddenly felt like a complete outsider in this conversation. Blinking at my blurry plate in front of me, and feeling the tears on the edge of surfacing, I wondered why the two of them could be so oblivious to how I did not have their education and was totally dependent on Michael. But when I looked up, they were both staring intently at me, and the zig we were on zagged.

"We've been thinking," said Kate. "We think you would be an amazing realtor."

I stared at them, processing the words.

"You have such a great way with people," Dianne joined in. "You're smart, the right thing comes out of your mouth when you open it and people just like you."

"And you have a natural curiosity and a great eye," said Kate. "Did you notice how when we drove in from the airport, you were the one pointing out that the roofs on the houses were stepped so as to collect heavy rainfall for drinking water? And then you went on in great detail about the roofs being white because that reflects ultra-violet light that helps to purify the water. How did you know that? Why did you know that? And then when you got hold of the realtor sheet in the club's lobby, you were pointing out some of the most exquisite properties? I bet your brain loves form and structure."

"And you have a great network in town because of all the school and community work you have done," added Dianne.

"Plus," carried on Kate, "I have a network in the city that is beginning to seriously look at cottage properties. You remember when my friend Christopher moved up into your area just last year, and bought that fabulous property opposite Christian Island? Well, his one complaint during the whole process was that he didn't like his agent. She was self absorbed and not well informed about the wider real estate market."

I am still not sure if it was the alcohol, the setting or the thought of being successful at something, but in that moment, I felt a high, that kept building. It was something that I had never felt before. Through their eyes I could see an exciting future, and the word exciting had not been in my mind's vocabulary for a very long time.

By the end of our lunch, my co-conspirators had fully mapped out a path that involved a course, licensing exam, mentoring under a local agent and the beginnings of a marketing plan. Clearly the two of them had been at this for some time.

I guess when people know you well, they can sew up a coat for you, tailor it perfectly and then it becomes so easy to slide on. As I listened to them, I fully agreed with everything they laid out. It was as if I had been a part of every planned step, which I guess in hindsight I was. I may have been missing at the table but I was inside their heads and hearts, so I had been very well represented all the way along.

That afternoon and evening I felt a lightness of being that I don't ever remember experiencing before. Maybe it was because this new path had no ceiling, so mentally I could lift up and imagine a journey that was unlimited in nature.

But secrets have a weight and they separate you from those you love. If secrets are kept over a long period of time, they can define you internally as that *undeserving person*, so that you believe you alone know the truth about who you are and others are misled. The good person they see and love, is not real. When I woke up the next morning my optimism and excitement had faded. They didn't really know all of me, so I was doubting that their plan would really work. I slipped out early for a run and skipped breakfast.

When I returned, the club was in the throws of welcoming wedding guests, and I spotted Michael with his luggage standing at the concierge's desk. I came over beside him, plastered a smile on my face, and kissed his cheek. He turned, taken off guard and stared at me. Affection was not something that filled our lives at that time.

Over the next twenty-four hours, there were tennis games, a beach volley ball tournament, and a large cocktail reception. Later, the smaller, intimate rehearsal dinner was absolutely beautiful. It was held on the circular stone patio that overlooked the long beach and wide, open ocean, some one hundred feet below. The next morning, we woke to clear, blue skies and a refreshing breeze. We all agreed that the weather fairies had sent Kate and Trevor the perfect wedding day.

The late afternoon wedding and party that followed had many poignant moments. Kate arriving in a sleek, white, satin dress at the small, country church. The full wedding party gliding down the stone tiled main aisle past the highly polished, cedar pews filled with smiling faces. Trevor looking at Kate with complete adoration throughout the ceremony. The band striking up Queen's *Crazy Little Thing called Love* as the newlywed couple entered the reception back at the club. And then there was Trevor's speech that included the reciting of Josh Groban's lyrics and sharing how Kate made him feel strong and able to stand on mountains. He then pulled Kate out onto the dance floor as Groban's song *You Raise Me Up* brought tears to the eyes of all the romantics in attendance.

Comic relief also made an appearance in the form of three-year-old Sylvie. Kate had given Sylvie her long white veil. Sylvie raced wildly through the reception, eying the long white gauze trailing behind her and subsequently bumping into most guests. She was over the moon with this new, fanciful toy. And when she was summoned to say good-night, she shrieked and clapped with delight when she learned she could take the veil with her to bed!

The wedding was practically perfect in everyway, as Mary Poppins would say. Well, that is until I imploded.

Looking back, it is with the help of Dianne and Kate that I can even put together what happened. My recall was being outside on the stone patio and having had a lot to drink. It was dark and I could hear the thudding of the ocean against the sand on the beach far below. I had moved away from Kate and Dianne on my right and had stepped up to the cedar trimmed bar on my left. Suddenly I felt a body behind me that pushed up against me. I felt hands encircle my hips and an unknown voice said, "There should be a law against wearing a dress like that." I apparently lost it. I don't even remember that part.

Dianne and Kate have still not told me exactly what I screamed out, but when I fled from the patio and headed for the two hundred steps down to the beach, they followed. I can only imagine the scene. Two women in pursuit of another, one of them wearing a long, white, satin wedding dress shimmering in the moonlight.

Unfortunately for them, I am a runner, and so I managed to get a fair way down the beach until I became disoriented and stopped. When they caught up, they found me crying wildly, and they had to pull me down into the sand and hold me, so I would stop hitting them. Then with lots of soothing they calmed me down. And that is where I was finally able to speak out about what I had not shared, and in return they uncovered a buried truth that I had failed to process. The combination of Kate's commanding manner and Dianne's intuitive nature, allowed them to ask the questions that opened up what years had covered up.

Sitting on that beach, the details about a night long ago tumbled out. One of the fathers at Jimmy and Tessa's school had offered to drive me home. Michael was away and the kids were young and had been tucked into bed by their babysitter. I had asked him in for tea as a thank you, paid and let the babysitter go, and then had moved over to plug in the kettle. He had come up behind me, pressed in close, placed his hands first on my breasts and then drew them down along my body to my hips. I froze as he pressed in against me further and my body went limp. I simply stared at the kettle as it warmed up. He raised up my skirt and we went far away.

"My God, you were raped, Nicole," Kate said just an inch from my face.

"No," I said. "I was a part of it. I didn't push him away."

"But was it really consensual?" quizzed Dianne. "Were you fully a willing party at the time?"

"I don't know. I think I might have been in a bit of shock. But then I couldn't get him out of my mind. And not in a bad way. I knew it was wrong. But I felt awake. I felt I had been in a long sleep and he woke me up."

Kate and Dianne sat on either side of me; the three of us with our legs stretched out in the damp sand, facing the ocean and the huge moon hovering above us.

"When Nelson suggested I visit him on Tuesday afternoons at his office each week, I went."

"Is this Nelson Muir?" asked Dianne slowly. "The chiropractor?"

"Yes," I answered. "He didn't have patients on Tuesday afternoons, so it was easy to fit me in, as if I was his last appointment, even though his staff had left an hour earlier."

But as Kate and Dianne continued to ask me questions, there were a few things that did seem odd to them, and then to me. First, I had never noticed Nelson before that first night. I definitely did not have any feelings for him or a passing curiosity. Second, when I attempted to stop the weekly visits after a few months by fabricating another commitment he got angry with me in public when he found out I had lied to him. I was anxious to keep the peace and contain the situation, so I went back to him. And then finally, when I eventually did break away from the weekly visits, we still would see each other every few months. But each time, I now realized, was after he had shown up, sought me out and had a detailed plan on how we could see each other, *just once*.

I kept pushing back as Kate and Dianne tried to make Nelson the villain, because that was not the story I had developed in my head. But as we sat there and the cold, damp sand began to make us shiver, I eventually had to acknowledge that my reaction tonight, to the inappropriate grasp and words by one of Trevor's drunk friends, was not normal. It had definitely triggered a deep anger, an unfamiliar feeling of hate and an overwhelming fear. All seemed to line up with their theory that there had been a power imbalance to which I had been oblivious.

We heard distant voices and looked back towards the club. Quite a way down from us and perched up above the beach, we could see the club outlined in little, twinkling, white lights. Then we saw two small lights on the sand moving up and down, and coming towards us. Eventually the moonlight revealed Michael and Tom attached to two bright flashlights. Apparently, Trevor had escorted his friend out of the party so he wouldn't offend any other guests and Michael and Tom had been charged with finding us.

I can hear Michael's car. He has just pulled into the drive way. I jump up, tie on my apron, pull the prepared pork chops out of the fridge, and turn on the oven. Looping back to the fridge I pull out yesterdays scalloped potatoes and the fixings for a salad. It will be a simple dinner, but he seems to be fine with whatever lands on his placemat.

Michael comes through the back door, pecks me on the cheek and calls out as he leaves the kitchen, "How did your day go with that new couple?"

"Great," I answer, happy that he cared to ask and that he remembered. Happy that he still lives in a protected bubble.

# DIANNE

My favourite day of the week was about to be rattled. Saturday was usually when Tom and I would rise early, take our coffees out onto the back verandah and lounge in the large white, wicker chairs. We would spend hours sharing the newspaper, swapping must-read articles back and forth. Even today, a chillier September morning, we sat outside with a wool blanket pulled around each of us, and enjoyed the long fingers of the morning rays stretching out across our laps, warming us up.

I was reading the *Arts & Culture* pages, which I always went to first, so I could catch up on trends in literature and find intriguing book titles to add to my ever expanding reading wish list. This morning the review was a memoir of a young man, recounting his growing up in a small town where physical abuse within the walls of his home was impeccably well hidden from all of those around him. It mentioned in particular how he knew that one of his teachers suspected something, but chose to do nothing about it. He had felt invisible, inconsequential and completely alone.

A wave of nausea rose up inside of me. My face felt cold, my hands clammy. My head seemed to be pulsing and then I realized it was my heart. I could feel my chest. Pounding.

I lowered my head and continued to read the article. The critic was clearly impressed with the young man's resilience and his ability to seek healing through telling his story. He thoughtfully questioned if this could still happen today with the public's sensitivity to the issue, and all the measures in place with school boards, the public health system and social agencies. He concluded that he believed in time, we would continue to hear such stories, and that family violence is an unfortunate reoccurring drama within humanity.

"Tom," I said in distress, "You have to read this. There is no way I can just do nothing."

Tom reluctantly set aside the sports pages and reached over and took the newspaper section from me. I watched him intently as he read, noting his furrowed brow and the way one hand came up and rubbed his chin, again and again. He placed the paper down on his lap, looked out over the back yard and down towards the water and said simply, "So, what are you going to do?"

I felt my breath come back. I smiled, got up and wrapped my arms around him, whispering, "Thank you. I don't know yet, but thank you for not telling me to stay out of it."

He looked up at me and smiled, "The woman I love never sits still when there is a child involved."

With that confirming encouragement, I went upstairs, showered and changed into my jeans but added a fresh oversized white cotton shirt and my better pair of suede loafers. While my visit wouldn't be an official one, I wanted to be sure I looked semi-professional as I took on a task that the Principal, Henry Wooley, had expressly forbidden. But then Wooley was the older brother of Margaret Preston, so I was choosing to take his order not to interfere as a personal and not a professional request. Somehow that logic worked for me at that moment, although I wasn't quite sure how a disciplinary board would view it.

As I was heading down the stairs, Sara bounced out of her room in her baby doll pyjamas, reminding me that I needed to have a conversation with her about throwing on a cover up in the morning. At sixteen, she is becoming a well-endowed young woman.

"Mom, where are you going?" she asked, somewhat confused. "It's the weekend, isn't it?"

"Yes, it is honey," I answered as I reached out for a morning hug.

"So why are you leaving. You don't do that on Saturdays. You stay with us." Sara has developed a set mentality around time and activities. She is not very good when we colour outside the lines of her regular string of events. This behaviour was amusing at first, but has developed into something we understand will become an ongoing challenge for her, and for us.

"I just have a morning errand to do, but I will be back by lunch and then we can all go for our Saturday bike ride this afternoon. Sound good to you?" Sara nodded with a big smile, understanding that the day would shortly be back on track. "And you my dear, are in charge of getting your brother up by lunchtime," I added, as I got up and headed out the door. With Sara's extreme sense of efficiency, poor little Sam was likely to be raised out of bed at any moment, so that there was no chance he would be late.

As I headed out, crusading came to mind, influenced by the medieval history we had been covering in class that week. Strapping on armour, carrying a shield and wielding a sword were images of strength, but fear and vulnerability exist too. The future, the confrontation, it is all unwritten and has the possibility of getting very messy and difficult. My imagination was in overdrive and my brain hurt as it tried to form some semblance of a plan.

In the end, it wasn't really much of a plan at all. I resorted to what I do best. Although in truth, some would say that my open style of saying what is on my mind and bringing the problem right out in the open can be my downfall.

Freddy Preston, who was in my grade three class, lived with his parents and younger sister Lulu on the outskirts of town. Their home was set back from the road, next to a dense forest and a wide boat channel that came in from Georgian Bay. Freddy was short and slight for his age, and so in the first week of school I assumed his shy nature, his distancing from others and his inability to really look me in the eye, was a part of him being smaller, maybe less confident and just learning to find his way with his peer group. A summer is also a long stretch to be away from the clamor of a classroom with twenty-five other children. It was not unusual for some children to cautiously nudge into the rhythm of school, while others barreled in at full speed.

However, by the second week of school I noticed that on top of his reserved manner, what set him apart from the others was what he was wearing. He wore long sleeved shirts and pants, while the rest of the children were still happily sporting summer shorts and t-shirts, with a sweater for the cooler mornings. Unconsciously, I think a small alarm bell, well maybe more like a tiny doorbell, went off in my head.

But that doorbell turned into a clamoring racket when Freddy limped into class on Monday last week. When I asked him what happened, he said he had fallen down the basement stairs. I asked if he had seen the doctor and he said he had and he was going to be fine. All of this was said while looking at the floor. And with his head bent over I noticed a bruise on the back of his neck. When I asked if I could take him to see the school nurse, he said that he didn't want to and his father had told him not to.

For the next few days, I argued with the Principal, who unfortunately happened to be Freddy's uncle. He said he knew his sisters' family well, that he would vouch for them and reminded me of my overzealous pursuit of a parent last year. In truth, while I seemed to have been wrong on that one, there definitely were inconsistencies that were in my favour.

And then yesterday I had gone for my walk with Nicole. While we began our conversation focused mainly on her excitement over her new found independence and the interesting buyers and sellers that she was meeting, she quickly noticed my mind was wandering and asked what was wrong. As a result, we spent most of the walk talking about kids, dysfunctional families, and the subtleties of abuse, which Nicole was well versed in, having sought considerable counselling after the Bermuda episode. At the end of our walk Nicole stopped me, held me by the shoulders and looked at me with fire in her eyes.

"Don't let them bully you, Dianne. If you think you are right, or even have a strong chance of being right, follow that through." It hadn't even occurred to me that I was the one being bullied. But thinking about Principal Wooley's firm, dismissive and slightly condescending manner, I realized she was right.

Driving up the Preston's long driveway, I noted that the lawns were well kept. After ringing the front door bell, I admired the well-attended flower beds on either side of the door. All of it reminded me that Tom and I had a bit of work to do on our yard this weekend.

A small, smiling woman answered the door and I introduced myself to Margaret Preston, and lied. I said I was dropping in at the homes of students whose parents I had never met. Margaret paused at first, but then opened the door to me and in no time, we were having coffee and muffins in her kitchen and speaking about her children, my class of children, my own children and motherhood.

Her husband was away, visiting his family out east in Halifax she explained, so I would have to meet him at another time. As she referenced her husband, she pointed over towards a family picture on a bookshelf in the kitchen. I smiled, got up and wandered over to look at the family of four, who were standing side by side on a dock, in front of a large boat. As I peered closer to look at Freddy my eye was pulled towards his father. I knew that man - his large build, his close cropped hair and his intense expression. Where did I know him from?

Sitting back down at the table and warming my hands on my coffee cup, I asked where Freddy and Lulu were. Margaret hesitated, then looked directly at me and said they were with her eldest brother Henry, who I would know as Principal Wooley.

At the mention of the Principal's name, perhaps I should have let it go. But the opposite happened. I charged on. I laid out my concerns. I described her son's manner at school and my puzzlement with his wearing of clothing that covered every patch of skin when it was still so warm. I explained that I was worried about his fall down the stairs, his limp that lasted all week and the bruise I had seen on the back of his neck. As Margaret sat staring at her lap, I continued. I told her that I had been teaching for nineteen years and I believed Freddy needed help. I added that from speaking with Lulu's grade one teacher, she too believed Lulu might be exhibiting behaviour consistent with a child who needs help. I expressly kept from verbalizing what I thought was happening, and kept it all open to offering help.

In hindsight, I suppose I was naïve. I felt my offer to help was being made to someone who might want to seize it. Margaret was so tiny, and it was easy to assume the violent parent would be her husband. Bill Preston did appear to be a big man. His picture confirmed that. And eerily, he reminded me of an angry person, who I couldn't quite place. Margaret looked up at me and thanked me for coming by. She said the children were safe and I need not worry about them. She then stood. As she was clearly dismissing me I reluctantly got up and headed towards the door. A final thought surfaced. Passing from the kitchen, along the hallway and past the stairs leading to the second floor, I looked up at the wooden railing and said wistfully, "If only our kids would hold onto the railing when they come running down the stairs. Is this where Freddy fell?"

Margaret stopped, nodded and pointed to the lower few steps. "It was just at the end here. It wasn't that bad." She saw my frown. Freddy had credited the basement stairs as the culprit. She folded her arms and stared at me with a steely strength.

"Thank you for caring about my children. I do understand your concern. Please trust me when I say that I promise you they are going to be fine now."

I felt the oddest sensation. While I believe she had lied to me about the stairs, everything in me believed her closing words. She smiled, a tight closed lip smile, opened the door and waited until I was in the car and driving away, before raising one hand in a conciliatory wave and then closing her door. As I drove down the driveway I couldn't decide if I felt better or worse than when I drove in. For sure I didn't feel the same.

Now, as I putter around the house turning off all the lights before heading up to bed, I realize that I am feeling unbalanced. Uneven. Everything inside me told me I needed to confront Freddy's parents so that the truth could come out. I did confront and some truth was shared. But I feel as if my head knows more than me. I saw something and my mind is still trying to figure it out. And I was told something that I don't understand. I sit down in the dark. Why is it that I feel that if I stay very still and listen to the silence, I will better hear what Margaret really said?

# KATE

I think it was his eyes that I remember the most. They seemed to grow wider in front of me. His eyebrows raised in wonderment. And then a warmth moved across Trevor's face like when the sun opens up the day. I felt incredible to be able to make him so happy. And on that day when I told him the news, for the first time I felt I could see the two of us wrinkled and crumpled with age and still together.

It was just two months after our wedding, and we were happily shocked that at age forty-three, my body cooperated so quickly and easily. We had always wanted a child together, but each of us understood the odds were depleting. We recognized too that during our years of trying to figure *us* out, we had lost valuable time on my biological clock. Something we would never get back. While we spoke optimistically about giving Sylvie a little brother or sister, there was a silent centre in each of us that doubted we could. And now that centre was rejoicing and dancing on the table.

We waited a couple of months before quietly telling family and a few friends. Mom was so excited for us. She had felt my angst over Trevor's need to be a part of creating a family and we had pondered over the dilemma of how I would age significantly faster than my attractive, younger partner. If ever Trevor became disconnected in our marriage, she bluntly pointed out that a younger woman could ease her way into his life. We knew our view was jaded, but we continued to find examples around us that only served to confirm it. We always concluded with the hopeful sentiment that maybe Trevor's eyesight and sexual appetite would decline faster than the demise of my exterior!

Predictably Dianne and Nicole were over the moon about the

baby. Without saying so, they too felt a new conviction that the vows they had witnessed in July would be stronger and kept. I had decided to tell them in early December when they came to stay with me in Toronto for the night. I had the dinner table all laid out with fresh linen mats, shiny silverware and sparkling crystal wine glasses. All the tableware items were compliments of our registry choices, kind gifts from wedding guests. It had been a heated conversation when I had suggested a *no gift* policy for the wedding. I can still remember Dianne arriving with multiple brochures and pressing me to choose special items, so that she and other guests could celebrate my marriage as family and friends had celebrated hers, Nicole's and others. "Just because this is happening a little later on," she argued, "Don't sideline it! Celebrate with the traditions that were a part of what you dreamed of when you were a little girl growing up." My very expensive, and absolutely *I'm in love with it* white, satin wedding dress, was also a result of shopping with Dianne. She would not let me off the hook when I began to contemplate a cream-coloured suit.

"Well," I had said, as we sat down in front of the fireplace, for cocktails before dinner. "I am having a cranberry and soda water tonight ladies, because Sylvie is going to have a little brother or sister!"

They both peeled out of their chairs at once and stormed me in mine. I can still feel their arms and legs all over me as we hugged and re-hugged on that rather oversized leather chair. Just a few weeks later I would be curled up in that same chair with a big wool blanket enveloping me and a hot water bottle pressed to my stomach, nursing cramps that I was told were normal, and all part of the process when you lose a baby.

The one blessing was that we had not told Sylvie about my pregnancy. We had decided to wait until the three month mark. I wondered about the research and studies around ninety days. Was it really the safe benchmark? If I had lasted past that, would I have been safe? I found out the answer to that question nine months later, when I miscarried again, at four months.

This time Trevor had been away and wasn't able to calm me down when the red spotting appeared. He wasn't there to hold me, tell me he loved me and that we had Sylvie and each other. Mom arrived in record time, drove me to the hospital and later helped me home and stood close by as I called and spoke with Trevor. There seemed to be multiple deaths that my brain was contending with at that moment. Our first child, this second child and also the death of the family we had envisioned and hoped to share. I was forty-four. I would be forty-five in five months. My body was telling me that it would prefer if I didn't carry on with this irrational dream.

Dianne arrived on my door step that night with an overnight bag. My Mom had called her. She sprang at me and she held me for a very long time. Then she came in and took over. As Mom and then Talia quietly took their leave, Dianne went into the kitchen and prepared dinner for Sylvie and me. And afterwards, as I curled up in my bed, I could hear her rattling on with Sylvie as she bathed her and helped her into her pyjamas. At five years old, Sylvie knew how to dress, but she was an extraverted little thing and needed help to keep on track. And then all went quiet, but I could tell that Dianne hadn't left Sylvie's room.

I got up, pulled on my warm flannel dressing coat, slipped into my soft, squishy slippers and padded down the hallway to Sylvie's open door. As I approached, I could hear Dianne reading a bedtime story in a soft soothing voice.

"The Mommy fox explained to her baby fox:

*Our job is to keep the bunnies away from little Emily's garden. This allows Emily to grow carrots, peas, tomatoes and lettuce and all kinds of herbs. Then Emily can use the vegetables to make healthy dinners for her family and the herbs will make them extra tasty"*

And then the baby fox looked out across the snow that covered the fields and the garden, and said to her Mommy:

*But what is our job then in the winter time when there is no garden?*

The Mommy fox looked at the baby fox and said:

*The winter is when we look for food to keep us healthy and strong. Our job is to look after each other and help us grow over the winter. When we look after ourselves, we can better help others. When we are bigger and stronger, we will be even better at keeping those bunnies away once the spring comes and the little green stalks start to shoot up in the garden.*

And the baby fox smiled at the Mommy fox and said:

*Okay Mom, let's go eat and work on growing up!*

And the baby fox and the Mommy fox hugged each other and scurried off into the woods."

Sylvie laughed and Dianne reached over and kissed her goodnight. As Dianne turned around on the bed towards the side table to turn out the light, Kate realized that there was no book in Dianne's hands. That explained why the story wasn't one that Kate had seen among Sylvie's vast collection of books that lined one full wall of her bedroom.

Dianne smiled at Kate as she crept out to the hall and closed Sylvie's door half-way.

"Where did that story come from?" Kate asked.

"I made it up tonight," said Dianne, grinning.

"Wow, I only caught the ending, but it was so sweet."

"Thanks. But I have to say I was racing in my head for a credible answer, in case Sylvie asked about how the foxes keep the bunnies away. It would have sort of wrecked the story if I had to explain that they chase them and then eat them. So, let's just say, that story needs a little more work."

"Are you writing stories again?" Kate asked.

"I am always writing them in my head, and yes, some get written down too. I still fantasize about writing a story that could have the same magic and wonder as *The Lion, the Witch and the Wardrobe*. I know it is an ambitious wish to touch the mind's eye of a youngster, in a positive and lasting way."

"That is such a worthy and honest goal. It sure beats goals of meeting sales targets and consumer acceptance ratings!"

"Your goal right now is to heal. Embrace all the good around you. When you are ready, you will need to modify that movie in your head that you have told me about - the one that has you and Trevor in a park chasing Sylvie and the other children you had hoped to have."

Over time, my heart moved through the sad sweetness of breaking and mending. I learned to focus on the good around me and to keep a special place in my heart for those two little ones I had never met.

As for the movie that Dianne alluded to, I now have a new one that plays in my head. Instead of Trevor, Sylvie and I running around in a park with other children, the scene is more tranquil. The three of us sit together on the forest floor, having a picnic. All around us huge trees reach up towards the sky and bright wildflowers wave in the warm breeze. As we pass out the sandwiches, Sylvie suddenly makes us stop and presses her little finger up to her lips, signaling silence. Two little baby foxes nose their way out of the bushes and begin to tumble and play with each other in the sunshine. They make Sylvie laugh. And as Sylvie turns towards me and smiles, I feel joy. The light in her fills me up and I become whole again.

# SEPTEMBER GIRLS' BIKE RIDE
## AT 45

The warm sun blankets the manicured lawns, the wide sidewalks, and the tall maple trees that border the neighbourhood streets in Ellington. The leaves are yellow, orange and a fire engine red. The large, red brick Victorian homes, majestic in their size and stature, sit back from the street, observing the changing world around them. Once these houses were all owned by individual families, with multiple staff dusting and cleaning the many rooms and cooking and serving one family. Now they are divided into coveted apartments. The paint trim seems to tell the story of those that have enjoyed renovations and those in transition. Like gingerbread houses, some have white icing that is beautifully fluted along the roof edges, window sills and shutters, while others have chunks missing, as wear and tear, the rain and winds, have munched them away.

Abigail's B&B reflects the owner. Both are very much in their prime. It is not uncommon for guests to find Abigail, dressed in overalls and joining the painter, plumber, carpenter and gardener with their tasks. Her view has been that keeping this home healthy has always been a personal quest and a joint task with the trades. As a result, each year as Kate, Dianne and Nicole arrive, the beautiful old house seems to have had a touch up here and an upgrade there, so that over time it is gracefully ageing. They joke that Abigail is the Queen of *nip and tuck* for homes.

Today has been an absolutely spectacular one for biking and their faces sport a sunny glow when they return from their ride. With the heat of the day more similar to mid August than late September, they veer off their regular routine. With two bedrooms established since Dianne's loud night of snoring five years ago, they have two showers to jump into. They shower and change quickly and head down for cocktails out on the large wrap around verandah on the main floor. They all recall that some thirteen years ago, on their very first visit, it had been warm enough to sit outside, and there is an air of excitement as they race to recreate that moment. Back then Dianne was tight with both Kate and Nicole, and she had been optimistic but a bit anxious, as to how Kate and Nicole would get along. While the bike ride and lunch had been social and the three of them managed just fine, it was when they sat back in the large floral cushioned whicker chairs on the verandah that sparks were ignited, stories and secrets were shared and bonds were formed. The fact was not lost on them that the variety of cocktails sampled at the time had helped to lower inhibitions. However, the chemistry between the three of them surfaced on that verandah, and since that day has continued to grow.

## Cocktails

"Let's have a look at that cocktail menu," says Kate, stretching across the low glass coffee table in the centre of their three comfortable chairs, and picking up a small menu under a heavy, brass paperweight. They have moved the fourth chair away, so that they can all sit in a semicircle and look out past the wooden slats of the verandah and down into the fading colours of the autumn garden.

"Cosmopolitan sounds tasty" muses Kate, "Although they do have beers and ciders here too."

They all elect the celebratory Cosmopolitan, citing it as a drink one would not generally make at home on your own. Abigail slips out from the kitchen to take their order and catch up on their ride. They remark on the weather, with the predictable comment about the warmth in the fall being an upside of global warming. It is always strange, they confide after Abigail has left, how there is a sense of guilt when that point comes up. You know you are not supposed to be happy about global warming, but the gift of unexpected warmth from time to time is hard not to enjoy.

Speaking about changes in weather patterns, easily brings Hurricane Katrina to mind. It was just three weeks ago, and they talk about how everyone thought at first that New Orleans had been spared from the storm's gale force winds. But then levees and flood walls failed and within two days eighty percent of the city was flooded, with some parts under fifteen feet of water. They found it unbelievable when they had learned that about half of the city was built below sea level and was completely dependent on the levees. They try to imagine living in an area knowing that if water broke through it would threaten life, and then destroy your home and your neighbourhood.

"The power of water," says Nicole. "This year it was Katrina, but remember last year it was the Tsunami in Indonesia. Tough to imagine the eeriness of the water silently retreating way out into the ocean during the undersea earthquake and then the horror of that wall of water suddenly approaching, getting larger and larger and then pounding into the land and tearing up everything in its path."

"When I was on the beach in Florida this year," injects Kate, "I would look out at the horizon and try to visualize a huge crest moving towards me. I almost felt physically sick with fear just imagining it. But for those who were there and survived through the initial hit, the additional surges and the aftermath of seeking out family and friends in a torn-up infrastructure, it must have been a nightmare. I found I just couldn't go there very long, and I had to pack it up and put the thought away."

They all become silent as they seek to make sense of it all, and can't. Staring out at the garden, they nestle back into their comfortable chairs and listen to the sounds of evening. Muted clinks and bangs drift out from the food and table preparations inside. Murmuring words and gentle laughter hum towards them from the people walking home together along the streets.

"So," says Dianne seeking to launch into another topic and change the mood, "Nicole, how are you managing with both Jimmy and Tessa away at university? Are you aching to see them? I just can't grasp what that is going to feel like with kids no longer at home."

Nicole smiles and tilts her head, contemplating the question. "It is actually okay. I think my head was prepared, and that helped the heart. It certainly wasn't the case when Jimmy left for university two years ago. That was when I had a hard time, as you two will recall. I think I had a good cry over dinner with you."

"Yes," chimes in Kate, "I remember that well."

"It was tougher when Jimmy left because he was the first one to go and suddenly it was real. It seemed like all at once I gained complete clarity that these children are going to leave. They are going to go off to university and while they may come home for vacations, once they start summer jobs and then full-time jobs, well, they may not be sleeping in their rooms and living in our home anymore. When Jimmy left, the continuity of their presence from birth until that moment suddenly snapped. So, the shock happened when Jimmy left. Then I had two years to nurse that along, and so surprisingly I am okay right now with Tessa just having left. I thought I might have had another foot stomped on my head, but it didn't happen. Of course, Tessa doesn't know this. She saw how messed up I was when Jimmy left, and she is so cautious and sweet with me on the phone when she calls home. I think she would be devastated if she learned I was actually doing fine."

"So true," says Kate. "The kids are always watching our reactions and tend to measure themselves by what they see."

"Very much a human trait to mirror" agrees Dianne. "They look for clues about themselves by looking at how others perceive them. How much are they loved by a parent is very much on display when they move away. Disinterest would be devastating. Tears are a good thing. Having said that, I am confident that I will have no problem in helping my kids feel hugely loved with the torrent of tears I will be pouring out when Sara heads away in two years. But it is good to know that maybe it will be easier when its Sam's turn to go."

Abigail arrives balancing a tray with three large martini glasses. A bright pink concoction sways back and forth in each glass, as she fusses with small white napkins to act as coasters, and carefully places each drink down on the table. She suggests that *nuts and bolts* might be a helpful snack as dinner is still an hour and a half away, and returns with a generous bowl full of crunchie spiced Shreddies, pretzels and nuts. The contents disappear at an accelerating rate as first a few pieces are gracefully picked out and then returning fingers begin to scoop up the rest.

"It's strange actually," Dianne begins as she carefully lifts and sips her drink. "I sort of had the reverse scenario going on with the twins. Having looked out for them after Caroline died, I was at peace when they headed off to university a year ago. Tom and I went with them and their father to Kingston to get them settled in. They were so excited, and it was a happy time. So even now a year later, when I think of them away, I think of them as happy and I feel happy for them. And I guess what I am also feeling, is relieved. I am no longer constantly thinking, *Should I drop over to see how they are doing tonight?* That was okay when they were here, but I know for sure that would not be a good thing if I showed up out of the blue at university! They know I am on call. I have told them that. But the great thing with twins who are close to each other, is that you know and they know, that they have a built-in safety valve with each other."

"Wow," Kate says softly. "They were just fourteen when they lost their mother. And now they are at university and launching into adulthood. Time goes so fast. Caroline would be so pleased to know they are coming along so well."

"You know, it was curious what Christine said to me as I was helping her unpack last year," continues Dianne. "She said that it was kind of nice to be somewhere where everyone doesn't know what happened to her Mom. She said that she and Ethan sort of got labeled as those poor little kids who lost their Mom, and it just continued to come up all the time. Either in words like, *So how are you doing now?* or a sad look in a neighbour's eyes as they treat you like you are made of glass. She said she was really looking forward to the anonymity of a new place."

"Amazing," says Nicole, shaking her head, "We think that a small town has the benefit over a big city, when it comes to helping to look after people when we lose someone. I think we might even have pride in that. But I had never thought about how someone then has to contend with the label of being a child without a mother, or being a widow or a widower. I can see in a city how that anonymity could be therapeutic."

"Well, it will be a good while until Sylvie is joining in with higher education," Kate pipes up. "Grade one is her current academic challenge, which includes learning how to sit still in her seat. Honestly, while she can be a real old soul with Phillip and sit and talk quietly for extended periods of time with him, when there are kids around a switch flips and it's show time. She becomes a real spark plug!"

"Children are highly situational in nature," leans in Dianne. "If Phillip has been that chilled parent that always sat quietly with her and nurtured that adult conversation with her, she will reserve that for him. If Trevor is the one bouncing her around since she was little, she will be wired up as soon as she sees him. Similarly, when pre-school kids are steeped in a past where play is synonymous with being around a lot of children at one time, like going to the park or a birthday party, it is no wonder that they arrive into class and are confused by desks and chairs. Even though kindergarten prepares them, grade one is a bit of a shock. This is when the teachers seem to say, *Yes, I know before it was a suggestion, but now it is a firm command - sit down in that darn chair!*"

"You are totally describing Sylvie," grins Kate. "And you nailed the way she is with Phillip and Trevor. It's funny sometimes when they each watch the other with her, they wish for the deep conversation or the crazy antics that the other one shares with her. Her two fathers are so different, and while she thrives because they are different from each other, Phillip and Trevor seem to wilt and grumble as they privately wish to have it all."

"That is curious," Nicole says. "I would have thought they would love being unique and separate in Sylvie's mind."

"I think they each want to be everything to her," replies Kate. "Male testosterone maybe. I think it acts up without their brain calling on it. It just happens. But regardless, they are good with each other, although when they are out playing a game of tennis, I am not sure if winning the match has anything to do with tennis at all."

"And so, is Sylvie calling them both Dad?" asks Nicole.

"That remains messy," shrugs Kate. "Phillip is Dad. That was totally intentional and planned. Trevor's naming as Daddy apparently became initiated by Sylvie, although I highly suspect Trevor was whispering in the wings the whole time. Honestly, there is no chapter on this in any parenting book I have found, so I just let it all happen."

"How does Phillip react?" asks Dianne.

"Well, Phillip and Trevor don't overlap too much, and when they do, Phillip, as the grown up in this overall relationship, leads the way and just lets it be. I have seen a few raised eyebrows and grimaces, but nothing that needs bandaging up. And I make a point that if ever there is a need to step in for discipline reasons when they are both in the room, I do that. I would not want one of them judging the other in how they handle Sylvie when she needs some sorting out."

"Wise woman," says Nicole, raising her glass. "I toast you, Kate. This is all working because you are caring to protect their egos and you really care about how they are feeling."

"Thanks Nicole," Kate says, raising her glass. "I will toast too, not to me, but because I really want a sip!"

They laugh, sip together, comment on the sweet and tangy cocktail and catch up on their families, ageing parents, Dianne and Nicole's siblings, the summer, and recommended movies and books. Having nestled further into the cushioned wicker chairs, pulling warm sweaters and jackets around their arms and curled up legs, each has a pool of warmth that sustains them as they order a second cocktail and an obligatory large glass of water. As 6.30pm approaches, the sun has lowered in the sky and a sunset is approaching. The verandah hosts shadows of columns and rail posts, that become long tentacles stretching across their laps. Feeling the warmth from the fading sun as it peaks under the verandah roof and slides lower, they squint and smile and press their faces towards this last kiss from summer.

"Dinner, my dears?" asks Dianne. "Are we ready?"

Reluctantly, they uncrumple themselves, gather all up and head in.

## Dinner

Entering the small private dining room, that would have been a small lounge or office when the house was commandeered by one family, they are met with the dim lighting from low-lit wall sconces and their round, intimate candlelit table. They pull back the big heavy upholstered chairs, sit down and heave the chairs forward so that they are comfortably encircling the table. This wood paneled room with tapestry curtains and a large, wood burning fireplace, has been their annual town square, their place of confidence and where both simple truths have been shared and at times, protective and forgivable lies have been told. Its almost as if by taking their seat, there is an understanding that eggs will be cracked and dams will be broken. Words are the liquid that will flow. It has always been the case and so the question only remains, *What is on the menu for conversation tonight?*

"So how is Trevor's new job working out?" asks Nicole.

"Still to be determined, I would say," answers Kate. "I sort of wished he had stayed a bit longer at the last one. It had been barely a year before he moved. He seems to get impatient with what a job will bring him versus what he can bring to the job, or the company, or the product. I can see a little of that happening again right now and it has only been two months."

Both Dianne and Nicole are thinking, but choose not to share.

They see younger people wanting more sooner and expecting more before they have put in the work effort of their generation. But this will be an area of omission in their conversation, because it doesn't help and can only fan a flame if differences in age becomes a topic.

"Well, here is a first, ladies," Dianne breaks in, having reached into the centre of the table for the shared menu, freshly typed up and printed that afternoon. "We have a choice for our main course! While we will all be finishing every last drop of our *Seasonal Carrot & Squash Soup*, and eating every shred of our *Deconstructed Caesar Salad*, we are not assigned to a main course this year. You have the choice of *Arctic Char with Grilled Pears* or *Tuscan Chicken*."

"I am hearing white wine," says Kate, "If that sounds okay with you two?"

"Perfect," smiles Nicole, curiously noting that while Dianne's focus has always been the food, Kate's attention is generally fixated on the alcohol. Nicole is happy for them to lead in both areas. While she loves to cook, she is not a huge eater. And while she enjoys her afternoon beer during the week, and a glass of wine now and then with Dianne, she is not a big drinker. Her love is to be up early and out for a run, and too much food or alcohol the night before doesn't mix well with that.

Abigail arrives and introduces Becky who is assisting her tonight. She is a student at the local college and is studying hotel and restaurant management. They all smile, nod their heads and ask Becky about her program. True to form, Abigail cuts in and pulls them all back onto task, and asks Becky to describe the main courses in more detail and take the order. Next a bottle of chardonnay from Prince Edward County is selected, retrieved and poured. Shortly after, Becky returns with piping hot sourdough bread which is promptly smothered with butter and consumed.

"So, Dianne," says Kate, "Tell us more about this little boy in your class." During their bike ride Dianne had shared her concerns and the story of her visit last weekend to see Freddy's mother.

"Well," Dianne begins, "When I went to school last Monday, I was fully prepared to be hauled into Principal Wooley's office and reprimanded for dropping in on Freddy's Mom. But that didn't happen. It took until Wednesday, when he spotted me in the hall and called me over, for us to speak about it. But all he said was, *I heard you visited Margaret. She liked you. How is Freddy doing?* He kind of normalized the whole situation and if it wasn't for the fact that Freddy was missing Monday and Tuesday, and had only come back to class that day, I might have gone along with it. So, I said it was good that Freddy was back in school again, and I understood that Lulu had been away for a couple of days too, and then asked point blank, *Do you know why both of the children were away for two days?"*

"Dianne, are you trying to rile him up?" asks Nicole leaning in towards her. "You have a history of run ins with him. Do you really want to push him?"

"Nicole, this is about children. My filter fails terribly if I am concerned. And it was weird how he responded. It only confirmed that there was more to all of this."

"What did he say?" asks Kate.

"It's what he didn't say. He said he didn't know why they weren't at school. Which makes no sense. If the children were over with him on the weekend, and then not at school for two days right after that, you would think some level of dialogue would have occurred between he and Margaret. They are brother and sister and he is the children's uncle, who also heads up their school. One child being away, maybe it's a cold. Two children away at the same time for two days, it's likely something else."

"And how was Freddy when you did see him?" asks Nicole.

"I would like to say that there was some detectable difference that could have given me a clue about everything, but really he was pretty much the same, which isn't great anyways. Quiet, withdrawn, head down. At least he lets me talk to him and I get a few smiles. So for now, I am carrying him around with me. He has that same sweetness that is inside of our Sam. I just have a huge need to make sure he is safe."

Abigail and Becky arrive with the soup. It is a large bowl of bright orange. Likely a chicken stock with pureed carrots and squash, and it seems there is a hint of nutmeg and something else Nicole can't quite guess. It is delicious and they are all confident that butter and cream are responsible, but none of them will ask. They have learned to enjoy what they are given and that Abigail can sometimes take a question around a high fat or sugared ingredient as a criticism. So, they smile, say it is lovely and enjoy every spoonful.

"Do you think," ventures Kate, once they are alone again, "That it is the dad?"

"Well, that's the thing. I think it is him, but there is a part of me that suddenly caught myself mid-sentence when I was speaking with Margaret and I wondered if I was stereo-typing the scenario. She is tiny, but what if it is her?"

"Dianne, in my experience with you, you do have tremendous instincts around children and family dynamics," says Nicole. "Put aside being politically correct and not stereotyping. What are your instincts telling you?"

Dianne leans her elbows onto the table, interlocks her fingers and rests her chin on top of them. "Well, even though I haven't met him in person, from looking at that picture in their kitchen, Bill Preston is a big man. I think within his background something happened to him, and that is playing out with his children. I wish I knew more about his childhood, but he isn't from here. He grew up out east."

Nicole stares hard at Dianne. "Did you say Bill Preston? Is that who Freddy's father is?"

"Yes," replies Dianne, puzzled at Nicole's change in expression.

"You do remember who he is, right?" Nicole continues.

Dianne is still and slowly shakes her head. "I thought he looked vaguely familiar in the photo, but I don't think I have ever met him. I don't know him."

"You have! Don't you remember years ago when we were in the park with the kids and there was that big dad who got so physical with his little boy? He yanked his son's arm and you practically flew across the park to confront him."

Dianne sits back, her face noticeably pale. The warm blood circulating so happily from the day's ride looks like it is being sucked out of her body.

"That's Bill Preston?" Dianne says slowly. "I didn't know that was him. Poor Freddy. This has been going on for years!"

Kate, who has been watching their exchange, now asks for clarification about the long ago incident in the park with Freddy and his father. As all is confirmed, she joins the silence. They take in the enormity of this new understanding. If Dianne and Nicole had witnessed a moment of violence five years ago, how much trauma has this little boy been going through since then?

"You know it's puzzling," Nicole says contemplatively, "I know the Wooley family, but I didn't know that Margaret was married to Bill Preston. I haven't met her. But I know a couple of her brothers. She has five of them. Of course, you know Principal Woolley, Dianne. But there are four others. You would think that those men would have weighed in if they thought Margaret or her children were in trouble."

"I didn't know you knew Principal Wooley's family," Dianne says, "What are they like?"

"Nice family I would say. I know Principal Wooley can be tight with the rules and a bit sharp, but they seem like nice people. One of his brothers was interested in a cottage property I had listed, and while he didn't buy it, I met him a few times and he was lovely to speak with. They are a big boating family and he was interested in having a place on the water so that he, his siblings and all the cousins would have greater access to a spot for all their water sports."

"Maybe the brothers have tried to help," volunteers Kate.

"Maybe," says Dianne, pausing and clearly lost in thought.

"What is it Di?" asks Kate.

"I keep going back to something Margaret said," Dianne says slowly, a frown line appearing across her forehead. "It's the way that she said that Bill was away. But then she also assured me that the

THE GIRLFRIEND BOOK

children were now safe. At first blush that might mean they are safe because Bill is away. But where my radar is all screwed up is that her final words to me assuring me about the children's safety - well, it really felt like it was a permanent now."

"So?" Kate shrugs.

"I feel like something is banging on my head. It's the words that weren't said. She was telling me something. I think she knows with certainty that he isn't coming back."

"Well, that might be a good thing," Kate breaks in. "I mean if he stays away Freddy and his sister will be safe. That's good, right?"

"Yes, could be," nods Dianne. "But in my experience, a difficult parent might leave for a bit, but they always seem to come back. And its not pretty when they do. Margaret seemed to know that wouldn't happen."

"So," says Nicole, trying to follow the thread. "What are you really saying here?"

"I think something has happened to Bill," says Dianne.

"Wow," Kate exhales. "I did not see that coming."

"Have you discussed this with anyone?" asks Nicole.

"Just Tom. He has diplomatically told me to give this time. And I will. I find it all rather disturbing."

Nicole has leaned back, crossed her arms and is thinking quietly. Both Dianne and Kate look over at her and wait.

"One of Margaret's brothers works down the hall from Michael's dental practice," Nicole adds slowly. "I remember that there was a huge argument a few months ago, that we could hear coming from their suite. And then shortly after I saw Bill Preston storm by our glass doors towards the elevators. I remember thinking that it made sense because Bill seemed like an angry person and I just assumed it had been a blowup that was business related. They deal with a lot of suppliers and I had heard sometimes they were slow with payments. I didn't realize that Bill was married to their sister. Maybe it was a personal matter and not business."

They all look at each other. Dianne screws up her mouth and shrugs.

"Enough said," Dianne concludes, disturbed by all she is learning and wanting to close the subject off for now, so that she doesn't wreck their evening. "Clearly we are not Columbo," referring to a well loved detective show from their childhood. "But I will keep my eye out for Freddy. How can I not?"

As their bowls are cleared and their salads arrive, they revert to *remember when* stories, and reminisce about the blackout five years ago and their singing and dancing at Ricky's Road House. While its bar and dance floor are just a fifteen minute walk from them, they all agree that tonight they relish cocooning inside this quiet room and being able to talk without yelling over music. And then Kate mentions the discovery of the condom in Nicole's purse that night and the story Nicole told the next morning. Kate, not holding back, asks if that story had been true. Now that they all know about Nicole's past relationship with Nelson, Kate wonders about the truth of the story told about the condom being a party favour from a book club meeting.

Nicole grimaces and says, "I was just protecting you both from a much larger conversation."

This moves them into a wider discussion about sharing their lives, both the truths and sometimes the little lies.

"When would we lie to each other?" asks Kate.

"When we don't want to hurt each other," Dianne answers quickly, and then wonders if maybe that was too fast a response.

"Okay then," picks up Kate, "What is it Di that you are keeping from me, so you won't hurt me?"

"Nothing," says Dianne focusing on her salad.

"I am not sure this is a productive conversation," Nicole says, looking back and forth between Kate and Dianne. "I don't think any one of us outright lies, but at times it would be normal to omit thoughts that are still forming, and that you choose to hold back. Omission isn't outright lying, is it? Saying you don't know or aren't sure, when you do have a sense for the answer, might be a white lie, but we are built to mitigate damage around those we care about. And when it comes to opinions we have, who is to say that what we are thinking is correct? We could be very wrong."

"Wise words as always Nicole," Kate says as she picks up her glass of wine, sips from it and then lowers it slowly back into place. "Its interesting. One of Sylvie's books is on truth and fibs. Amazing how a fib sounds so much kinder than a lie. I think that is the point of the book. It gives the parent and child a way to formulate a conversation around lying that isn't so confrontational."

"I haven't heard of that book," says Dianne. "I am liking the sound of it though. I agree that the word *fib* is a more accessible one."

"This book," Kate continues, "Focuses on how when you begin with one fib, it puts up a little wall between you and others, and as you keep adding more fibs the wall grows higher and you gradually disappear. Very true, I would say."

"I agree," adds Nicole, nodding. "This whole escapade with Nelson, became a wall of lies. It completely separated me from Michael, and from you two. While that wall has come down with you, it still exists with Michael. But that is one wall that I won't take down by telling the truth to him. I am hoping that it will gradually crumble on its own over time."

"Did your therapist ever suggest you tell Michael?" Dianne asks.

"Therapists just ask you questions so you will find answers you can live with. She might have tried to lead me down that path, but what ever my responses were, it looks like we didn't end up there. I just don't see the sense in creating a huge shattering event right now. I should know what my intentions are for this marriage before doing that."

"So," asks Kate, "you are still not sure if you will stay with Michael? I thought maybe all was okay now."

"All is fine. It is okay, and maybe that is part of it. It is just okay. I am loving my work, being good at something and having this new economic freedom that the work brings. And maybe those were pieces I needed and I was missing them. Maybe now that I have that, I can recommit to my life here. Or, it might end up that the work and the independence it gives me will be the pair of binoculars that show me the way out. I don't know yet. So, keeping that episode with Nelson and me buried seems like the right thing to do."

Becky returns, tops up their wine, clears their salad plates and asks if they would like more sourdough bread. They show a measure of discipline and reluctantly shake their heads.

"While I am betting *your* fibs are not the size of my rather large one with Michael," ventures Nicole, "I am curious if you two have any fibs that exist between you and your husbands?"

Both Dianne and Kate contemplate the question, and Nicole finds it puzzling that neither of them jumped in with a quick *no*. She has just always assumed their lives with their husbands were pretty much open book.

"Back when Tom and I were dating in high school," begins Dianne, "I for sure told a few fibs when I was late getting together with him, or when I actually forgot we had a date. After being honest about forgetting the first couple of times, I reverted to fabricating other reasons. That did start to build a wall up between us. But since we got back together and have been married, besides his surprise party, I don't think I have lied to him. Wait, no, I am wrong. I lie to him all the time about how many cookies I have eaten when I make a batch. But I don't feel a wall going up on that one. Probably because we both know to take what ever I say and double it!"

Kate laughs out loud, knowing the cookie monster that resides in her friend. "You lied to me in university about how many cookies you ate all the time! But you're right. When both people know it's a lie, or a fib, which sounds so much better than a lie, then it doesn't build a wall."

Kate knows it is her turn, and she smiles. "I suppose, this is not the time to lie, when the question is about lying, right? So, with Trevor, yes, I do fib. I haven't told him about my Botox and filler treatments. Occasionally he has looked at me outright and asked if there is something wrong with my face. Its funny really. He basically *knocks the baseball out of the park* with respect to accuracy each time. It's always the day of the procedure or the next day that he notices something. And yes, that does put a bit of a wall up, that I am not sure how to address and take down. At some point I guess I will tell him. But does he really need to know?"

"I was wondering if you were doing something," chimes in Dianne, leaning over to examine Kate's face more closely. "You don't have wrinkles on your forehead. And I could have sworn you used to have more of a frown line between your eye brows. Does it hurt when they put those needles in? Are there any side effects?"

"Sometimes you can feel a bit fluish that night or the next day," Kate answers. "But it is very mild. How about you Nicole? I have often wondered about you. You have a smooth, youthful face. Any help?"

"No," says Nicole. "Just good genes so far." She finds this an uncomfortable topic, since in fact she has just begun visiting someone out of town for a little Botox. Since this is all still new, she dismisses it as a non-event, and decides to keep it under wraps.

"And how about fibs with Phillip?" asks Dianne.

"Okay, well when it comes to Phillip and Trevor, and their relationship with Sylvie, I would say omission is the fib that is frequently an undercurrent in conversations. If I was talking to Phillip about a visit to a private school for Sylvie, I wouldn't mention that Trevor was with me. If Phillip told me that one private school was notably better because how it could lead into a US university, I would not relay to Trevor that I heard that from Phillip. So, walls going up? Maybe. But frankly a few walls around those two is just fine."

In time their Arctic Char and Tuscan Chicken arrive, both with fresh steamed vegetables and double roasted potatoes. A second bottle of wine is opened, with Nicole letting Kate and Dianne drink the lion's share of the bottle. As the evening closes, chocolate torte and decaffeinated coffees arrive.

"So," begins Nicole. "This time next year, what would you like to see happen in your life?"

"That's a great question Nicole," jumps in Dianne.

"Hmm," muses Kate, "Very good question."

"I would like to have finished my first draft of my novel," says Dianne. "I have the outline, and I have begun work on writing it, but I do need to be more disciplined with protecting my writing time."

"That is so great that you are working on that Di," says Kate. "Do you want any help with proofing?"

"Maybe, but not yet."

"What is it about?" asks Nicole. "Why haven't you told me about this?"

"The storyline is one I have fumbled with for decades, so Kate knows about it from the early days when I was so excited about it. But it has been dormant for years. It hasn't come up, because I have done a good job ignoring it."

"What is it about?"

"A magical kingdom accessed through a child's attic," says Dianne, lighting up as she speaks.

"Sort of like a *Lion, a Witch and a Wardrobe*, but the wardrobe is substituted by an attic?" asks Nicole.

"You see Kate," Dianne says in exasperation, "I told you it was too close to that!"

Kate pushes back, "Every book with imagination that operates from our world to another world has some sort of portal within it. It has to!"

Dianne grimaces and scrapes her fork along her plate, capturing the final traces of chocolate from her torte. "Anyways, it is a fantasy for children, but you will be most welcome to read it as it develops. I will be wanting candid comments. No fibs! I am going to need some guidance to keep it fresh, original and not contrived. How about you Nicole, what would you like to see happen for you over the next year?"

"I have my eye on expanding my realty practice. I would like to bring on another realtor so we can share the work and collaborate in our marketing. I have seen others do it well, and think it would be great to have a partner. What do you think? If you were me, would you move that way?"

"Definitely," says Kate.

"It depends on who you are thinking of partnering with," says Dianne. "Do you know? I think Kate would agree that whoever you choose could help or hurt your brand."

"I agree," says Nicole. "And no, I don't have someone in mind yet. I just know a few folks I don't want to partner with so far."

"Interesting," thinks Kate out loud, "It would be great if you had a partner that could help cover you now and then. Weekends are precious, and sometimes you are going to want them back."

"We were lucky to kidnap you for these twenty-four hours," smiles Dianne, "Although I have seen you checking that pager, so it hasn't been a totally free day for you. And now Kate, your turn. How about you? What would you like to see happen by next year?"

"I would like to see Trevor thriving in his job, doing well, and en route to the prestige and income that seems so important to him. I think that will help us as a couple. He compares too much. He needs to be able to point to success that is his. He doesn't buy into *our success*. He says that so far it has been my success that has fueled everything. I am tired of trying to make it a joint achievement. He says it's a pitch and he won't be pitched to."

Dianne and Nicole listen, aware that there is anguish and a mounting history of issues within this subject. The easy answer is to reassure. They wonder if that would be a fib.

"I'm sure everything will work out," says Dianne, and Nicole nods her head in approval that these words have been said, but not because she believes them.

"Time helps all to work out," adds Nicole. Dianne nods her head too. Similarly, she is agreeing that these are good words to say at this moment, although she doesn't have complete faith in the actual outcome of this expressed sentiment.

"Thanks, you two," says Kate reaching out and holding each of their hands. "It's so good to have friends that care."

Later they head back to their two rooms and change into their warm, flannel pyjamas. Dianne crosses the hallway. Out of habit she politely knocks on the closed door but then shakes her head and barges into the big comfortable corner room. It is *their* room after all, or at least until it is time for sleeping and she withdraws to ensure they get some! They pull the long velveteen curtains, bounce onto the big double bed and pull out magazines that none of them read all year, but love to dive into together. It seems to be the one time of the year when they will care about *who is with who*, what dresses did they wear to an award show, and are those real body parts or enhancements. Inevitably, the evening stretches out past midnight, and their laughter and bond grows. They each still carry their own private insecurities, flaws and secrets. But the continued sharing of the progression of their lives provides common ground, and this contributes to a wide range of collective memories and inevitably adds layers upon layers to their friendship.

2010

# NICOLE

I love this room. The big, wide, double-paned windows, that pull the sunshine into the kitchen, but keep the rain, storms and cold out. This is where I have been happiest. Lively conversations with our children, gradually bursting out of their clothes each year as they grew bigger, bolder and brighter. Grazing through colourful cookbooks and experimenting with different flavours and dishes; all en route to a memorable meal. Delving into the newspaper with my morning coffee. Contemplating life with my afternoon beer. Staring out across the wide lawn and soaking in the colourful flowerbeds. And it is the room I find you sitting in, waiting for me when I get home, ready to ask me about my day.

But it is not really you Michael. It is my mind's image of you. A rather ethereal figure. I don't think of you as a sad ghost. You are more like a curious spirit. I speak to you and what I hear back is of course my own interpretation of what I think you would have said. In time you will join your bones in the ground. In time there will be silence when I can no longer pull up your face, presence and voice.

"So how were the Kavanagh's? Did they like any of the properties you showed them today?" Michael asks. Today you are seated comfortably, legs crossed, dressed casually in jeans and sporting that blue and white striped oxford shirt, that makes you look so handsome.

"It went well, thanks. They very much liked the Sampson place, but the price tag is scaring them a bit."

"Did you tell them that if they bought it, you might be their new neighbour?"

"No, best that I keep my move out of the conversation. I don't want them eying my new place and asking too many questions. It really is an exceptional spot. Both the location and the house. And I was very fortunate around the price point. That is a hard one to share with clients when they are facing a frothier market."

"Are you going to miss this house?" Michael asks, staring intently at me. You and I both know the answer to that question. I can't quite figure out why I keep having you ask me that. Maybe I am doubting my decision to move? By having you ask me this again and again, is it a way of testing myself to see if I really want to leave?

"Yes," I answer, "I will miss it. But it is time to move on."

Michael grimaces, and continues to look at me steadily. I have always liked his cool, blue eyes, but right now they seem softer. In fact, his whole body looks softer. But maybe that is because all the edges that define his body in my mind are disappearing. The more I think about him, it seems the more his physicality fades away.

It has been a very full and intense few years. Lots of growth, change and heartache. It all started in a good place.

Just four years ago, I was introduced to Amy. She was the same age as Jimmy, just twenty-one years old. She had grown up in a family of realtors in Peterborough and had met and married a young man from Port Colebrook. She landed here with some experience, few contacts, but carrying an incredible drive. She was also a wonderful human being. We clicked immediately. Within a few months we were informally helping each other with clients and within a year we created a formal partnership. In hindsight, it was perfect timing. It gave us a year and a half to solidify our working relationship before 2008, when the financial crisis threw a wrench into everyone's business plan.

With Amy being so capable and personable, I could totally trust her with a new referral from the city or an existing, demanding client. Knowing she was there I could plan a life beyond work and our town. Michael and I had a chance to break away and take some trips. We visited London, Paris, Rome and then pushed our boundaries the next year and flew to Bangkok and traveled through Thailand, Laos, Cambodia and Vietnam.

We finally found something we both enjoyed doing together. I learned to love museums and Michael learned to love new foods and become curious about why they tasted that way. And then that travel led us to watching documentaries together when we came home. Initially they were about countries we had traveled to or hoped to visit, but in time we enjoyed biographies and investigations into political and environmental issues. I learned to embrace Michael's cerebral interests through film, and he became more open to understanding points of view from a human connection perspective. And Michael seemed to finally taste what I was cooking and became curious about what I was doing in the kitchen.

We both grew.

The kids were appreciative of our new found relationship that was not based solely on tolerance. They noticed that we laughed occasionally. Tessa pulled me aside and told me, as if she were the adult and I was the child, that "I like how you two are making an effort to get along."

But there still was a divide between us. When Michael was working, his dental practice kept his mind busy and distracted. I sometimes wondered if Penelope, who took over my administrative work in the back office, and was always extraordinarily helpful, was perhaps involved with Michael beyond work.

"So, tell me about Penelope?" I ask candidly, as I reach into the fridge and begin to take items out to make a small, easy dinner. I don't really like to turn my back when Michael is visiting. What if he is gone when I turn around?

"What do you want to know?" he says, and I smile, glad to feel him still there.

Turning towards him, I ask, "Were you two ever intimate?"

His face seems to gradually become a little rosier, and he crosses his arms and stares at me. "What do you think?" Of course, he can't tell me anything new. I can only learn from him what I already know. After all he is just in my head and being projected onto that chair. But it helps to ask and to think things through out loud.

"She is a nice girl. Half your age. Pretty girl," I say. Who wouldn't admire Michael, a successful professional, with slightly greying hair, but still quite handsome? And if the boss's wife has been distant for years, and is now busy and thriving with her own work and newly found independence, maybe there is a visible crack there? I think I know the answer.

I pause for a minute and study my feet. Maybe now would be a good time to clear out what I have been holding onto for years. Even if it is only admitting it to a shadow of a soul.

"What about me?" I ask, raising my head and looking at him directly. "Have you ever thought I might have met someone?"

Michael unfolds his arms, leans back and stares at me. "It had crossed my mind."

"Really, what prompted you to think that?"

"We used to be closer. And then we weren't. You began to not comment on anything I said. Your mind was somewhere else."

"Why didn't you say anything?"

"Because I just assumed it would pass. And then in time I assumed that this was what marriage was. You know my parents. I think you would agree that what we had, began to look a lot like what went on in their home."

"Aren't you curious who it was?"

"Not really."

That was not what I had expected as an answer. But of course, this narrative is simply following a slow path that my mind can handle. I straighten up, breathe in deeply and say the name I have withheld for years "Nelson, Nelson Muir."

"The chiropractor?"

I say yes, and then explain how it started. It feels good to speak about this out loud. I speak about how in time I realized maybe I hadn't been a part of its instigation, but I was still very much a part of what it became. I ask you if you remembered Kate's wedding and the beach incident. You roll your eyes. You even laugh. I don't know where my mind found that reaction for you, but I like it. I share with you about how that was the turning point. I began to figure out what I had gotten into. And I explain that those therapy sessions I had been going to for a couple of years after that, were more to help me think straight than because of the deficiencies in our relationship.

"Well, that explains why Nelson always seemed to walk the other way when you and I were at school functions," Michael says.

"Yes, he did avoid you. I noticed that."

We are quiet and look at each other. I feel the urge to move over to you, and give you a conciliatory hug. But I can't. You aren't really there in a form to hug anymore.

"I am surprised at your response to this," I say, even though I know I have created the narrative.

"Me too," says Michael, "but then I am not in charge anymore." I smile at these words. After all, I have given them to you.

I turn back to the cold chicken, a leftover from last night and peel back the cellophane and begin to slice it with a knife. "Another unimaginative dinner I'm afraid," I say.

"That's okay," pipes up Michael's voice, "this type of body doesn't get hungry these days."

"So," I say, turning around again. I don't want Michael to leave. This has been a rather long visit. "I am going on my *Annual Bike and Pyjama Party* this weekend with Kate and Dianne. We are all turning fifty this year. After eighteen years we decided to make it a full weekend – two nights instead of one."

"How are they doing these days?"

"Kate is going gang busters. She was head hunted two years ago and moved to a startup that had some interesting software applications in development. Right up her alley. And now it seems one of them is looking very promising. Dianne thinks Kate is likely to hit it out of the park a second time when this company is bought out in a few years."

"That's great. She works hard that one."

"Yes, she sure does."

"And how about Dianne?"

"Dianne, hmm…"

I pull the lettuce, cucumber, tomatoes, and scallions out of the fridge and begin washing, dicing and tossing all together. Dianne has been amazing. The best friend a girl could have.

"Dianne is wonderful. I have been very lucky to have her looking out for me. She is busy, but never too busy for a friend. And she has had her hands full with work, the great interest in her first novel, and then that whole mess with the Prestons."

"Is that resolved now?" says Michael's voice from behind me.

"I don't know. I will get the full update this weekend. So, stay tuned."

"I am going to miss this kitchen the most I think," I say wistfully. "Truly the heart of our home, wouldn't you say?"

"Yes. Do you have to move?"

"Yes. It is time. It's time to move on."

I put down the food. Turn back towards Michael, but he is gone.

I feel myself crumpling up inside. An ache creeps up through my chest. It squeezes at my heart. I feel cold. My hands, my feet, all are numb. My eyes fill. My hands reach up to my chin. I feel a tear skitter down my cheek and it bleeds onto my knuckles.

I can hear your voice Michael, so clearly inside my head. I was here in this kitchen when I got your phone call. You called me from your cell phone just over a year ago. You were anxious and confused. Could I come and pick you up? You didn't think you should drive your car. The fact was that you couldn't figure out how to ask your body to drive it.

I raced out to find you. By the time I arrived, you had managed to get out of the car and you shuffled over to me. Your stance and your movement were both odd. You asked me to drive you to Toronto, to a hospital and to doctors, who talked with words that you understood and I needed translated.

Tests and more tests. Each giving answers we didn't want to hear. Jimmy and Tessa arrived and the fear in their eyes made you cry. We became a mess of four sets of arms reaching out, pulling in and holding on to each other, somehow thinking that we could keep you from falling over the edge.

Neurosurgery and recovery. And then they said it was okay for you to go home. But it was not okay. Nothing was really okay after that. You were not fixed up. They couldn't mend you. It was simply a matter of time.

Glioblastoma. A cancerous tumor that developed in your brain. Rare. The exact cause was not known. It did explain your recent headaches. I learned then that you had experienced dizzy spells too, and that the nausea over the past month was likely not from a flu bug. However, it was the muscle weakness that made you wake up and know that something was very wrong. You got in the car, but couldn't press down on the gas pedal. Then you couldn't get your brain to move your body out of the car. Your phone call to me came when you found yourself physically trapped, sitting silently in your car, in the parking lot at work. You told me you felt as if the world crashed down upon you at that moment. The price of your cerebral interest in medical science and health, is that you could assess yourself medically with more clarity than most.

And so, our home, this beautiful home, became our cocoon to escape to. Chemotherapy, radiation therapy and experimental drug therapies were discussed. An implementation plan was initiated. Your body took a beating and the kids and I, and family and friends hovered, cajoled, encouraged, and then wept. We lost you within three months. An embolism. We all felt robbed. Most would have had a year, and some more. But averages are made up of the near and the far. You left early.

I stare at your empty chair. This was one of our longer visits. But you are getting fainter. Maybe I should leave your spirit alone. I hope I am not bothering you. I wonder, "Will you follow me when I move?"

I did wait over a year before selling our home. That is what everyone seemed to recommend. I was even thinking maybe I would stay after all. But then I was visiting a new client who was hoping to put their small waterside home up for sale. I felt at peace as I walked through the front door. Each room wrapped its arms around me. None were too big and none were too small. Good bones. Beautiful flow. Each window I looked out of was a view I wanted to keep.

I turn back to the counter and add the slices of cold chicken on top of my tossed salad. I set the kitchen table for one, sit down with my meal and look out across the lawn. This is a beautiful setting, but I don't need to grow old with this one view. There are others to enjoy. It is time to move on.

# DIANNE

After a decade of living with characters in my head and three years of developing their story, finally those typed out words on the computer took their intended place. They became words on real paper and all bound together in a book. While I always believed I would finish the story, and would at least privately publish a few copies, as there are so many online self-publishing book choices out there, I did not envision that a wider interest for the book would ever develop. But Kate and Nicole, having followed the story that I was building over time, dove in with a plot of their own.

I had not fully appreciated the marketing power of my two best friends. While one marketed computer applications and the other real estate, they were both successful because of how keenly in tune they were with the consumers' mind. And when they read and loved my book and understood that it was written for the trusting, imaginative mind of the seven to twelve year old, they hatched a plan to publish a hundred copies in a rough, inexpensive format and send this out to a hundred grade three teachers across Ontario. The letter attached would be from me. Sincere and enquiring, it would explain my purpose and journey in writing the book and ask for their comments.

I still remember the morning that the first email response arrived. It was 6am on a Thursday and I had a hot coffee in hand. Having developed a habit of writing for an hour before leaving for school, I had just turned on the computer. As I searched for the piece that I had been editing the day before, an email notification slipped across the page and vanished. The name seemed familiar but I couldn't quite place it. I opened up my outlook and tracked it down. It was from one of the recipients of my book, and she absolutely loved the story. I floated to school and all through that day. Somebody out there, who I didn't even know liked my book!

Over the next few days, seven more emails came in. I referred to this initial group of responders as the *speed readers*. They must have received the book and read it within a couple of days. That was a good sign. But I did wonder about the others. Had they begun the book and then become disinterested and set it aside? Was the book still sitting in its package unopened? Or had the book found a home on a pile labeled *one day, way out in the future I might read this*?

Since my letter had asked for their comments, two of them did dive in with criticism. I would like to say it was constructive, but it didn't feel that way. I suddenly had new found empathy for anyone who had to face the written word of a disappointed reader. You sit quietly on the other end of a one-way tirade, unable to respond or defend yourself. The carefully chosen words of a critic, have a weight that sits on your chest and it is tough to push it off.

However, the other five responders had been very positive. They loved the characters, the plot, the subtle teaching of honorable values and the empowerment of the underdog. They had vulnerable children in their class who would benefit from the uplifting tale. They also mentioned that they had strong children in their class. They believed those children, when reading this book, might better grasp the power of empathy and learn to consciously make it a part of who they were.

But what made me gasp was when one teacher revealed that she was already halfway through the book with her grade three class, and they were mesmerized. Suddenly I felt I had truly gone full circle. I thought back to my racing mind in grade three as my teacher had read *The Lion, The Witch and the Wardrobe*. And while I had no fantasies of joining C.S Lewis in the history books, I simply loved the idea that I was helping young minds to travel into a special place.

Three weeks after Kate, Nicole and I had packaged up those one hundred books and sent them out, I felt at peace. Imagining one class of young children reading and enjoying my book was all it took to make me feel complete. I was curious as to what had happened with the rest of the books and what people had thought. But I was aware that human nature is such that we tend to reach out when we feel strongly, whether that is positively or negatively, and we tend to acquiesce when we are neutral. I just focused on the six beautifully worded and complimentary responses.

But then two days later there were five more replies, then eight more and the emails kept coming. While I had spoken with Kate and Nicole after the first batch, I waited another week and then reported back that we now had acknowledgements from thirty-two people – five didn't like it, but twenty-seven did! Kate quickly pointed out that having a thirty-two percent response rate was excellent. Three months later it had risen to forty-eight percent. The champagne cork flew across the backyard that weekend!

What happened next is something Kate and Nicole had predicted. Clearly one of those teachers either had a family member or a friend within a publishing house, and they had reached out to that person about the book. I got an email from Brooker House Publishing Co. and they asked if they could set up a telephone conversation with me. I froze. I called Kate and Nicole. While we had spoken about this potentially happening, I didn't have a script. Kate agreed to join the call with me and so we turned it into a conference call and had a wonderful conversation with a Janine Carter and Mr. D.J. Brooker. A few months later we had a book publishing deal. I say we because Kate, Nicole and I were in this together. They were my joint business partners, and I couldn't be happier to have one more reason pulling the three of us together. Although I was perturbed that they were both refusing a share in the profits, if we happened to have some one day.

"It's nearly eight," Tom calls out from the kitchen.

"Thanks hon," I call back as I close up the computer and resurface from the sequel I am writing. The mystery element is not co-operating this morning. I am a stickler about authenticity, even when it is fiction. Any tiny hint of being contrived sends me over the edge. I need a break to reconfigure this part of the plot.

"How did it go this morning Sherlock?" asks Tom, as he packs up his briefcase and slides my packed lunch across the table with a wink.

"Not great, but that just means something better is percolating that I don't know about yet."

"Positive attitude, that's why you're so good at this. By the way I heard from Sam this morning, he is planning to come home for the weekend."

"Is anything wrong?"

"No, school is great. He just wants a home-cooked meal and a quieter place to write an assigned essay."

"So, I guess you will be cracking open the cookbook then?" I smile. Tom is an exceptional cook and the one the kids turn to for their favourite meals. I bake pies, cakes and cookies, so he knows I will be joining him in the kitchen for a brief period to make a floury and sugary mess on the counter.

"I was thinking of checking in on Sara, to see if I can entice her home too," Tom continued.

"Good luck with that. She has only been back for three weeks. After pining for her friends all summer, I can't imagine her wanting to cart herself home before Thanksgiving."

"You're right," Tom concedes. "And it will be nice to focus on Sam. First year away, and he is coming home after three weeks? Not the Sam I know. I would have thought he would have lasted longer."

His observation seems unfortunately accurate. We grimace at each other, sensing a troubled wind may blow through the house this weekend.

We both throw on our fall jackets, wedge into our shoes that are lying by the front door, and give each other a quick kiss. As we head out to our two cars, a police car drives up and parks in front of our house. I feel my breath catch and fear floods through my arms and legs. Sam? Sara? Has something happened? Tom freezes too and we stand side by side like zombies as a police officer and another man dressed in a plain suit stride up the front path.

"Good morning. Mr. and Mrs. Fletcher, is it?" says the police officer.

"Yes," I respond, "Are the kids okay?"

"Yes, yes, no bad news here. Sorry, everything is fine. That's right, you have two children. They are fine I am sure. This is not about them."

Tom and I practically collapse with relief. I feel Tom's arm wrapping around me and pulling me in towards him, and while I am grateful for the support, I wonder if I too am holding him up. We have loved that our children are away at university and experiencing a new found independence, but every now and then we do have moments of worry. This one tops all of them so far.

"I was wondering if I might speak with you Mrs. Fletcher, Dianne is it?" says the man dressed in the dark, stiff suit. "My name is Detective Purdy."

"Yes, yes of course. But I was just heading into work. I'm at the elementary school in town and we start at 8.45am."

"Yes, I see. If now is not a good time, I am happy to speak with you after school. Would you be able to swing by the precinct on your way home?"

"Can I ask what this is about," enquires Tom protectively.

"Just a few questions about Freddy Preston, his mother Margaret, and the family."

I nod my head and take the detective's card. I promise to visit around 4pm and wave goodbye as they retrace their steps down our path and then drive away. Raising my eyebrows at Tom, and mouthing "This will be interesting," I climb into the car and back out of the driveway. "And so," I say aloud to myself, "The drama continues."

Driving along the sleepy little streets of our town, I am reminded how everything is never as it seems. One never knows what is going on behind any particular freshly painted door, or beautifully curtained window. And then when one suspects, and tries to step out and help, things can get very complicated.

It was some five years ago when I first visited Margaret Preston, in my quest to speak with her and her husband. I was searching for a way to help mitigate the harm that Freddy seemed to be experiencing. I didn't realize at the time, that I was the only one who had visited their home that weekend and that the time on either side of my visit was of great interest to the police.

A couple of weeks after my visit and conversation with Margaret, the word in town was that Bill Preston's brother had arrived. At first everyone thought it was Bill, because his brother looked so similar to him, but as he began asking questions about his brother, the news started to run through the community that Bill was missing. When I heard this, I called Tom. My imagination was on fire and I was scared to open my mouth to anyone but him.

"Margaret said that Bill had gone home to visit with his family," I said to Tom. "It seems like he didn't do that."

"There may be a legitimate reason he didn't go. Maybe there is a woman living somewhere else that he is involved with? Maybe he just needed a break from here, from his family, from work?"

"Maybe," I replied. That did seem plausible. If there was abuse in the relationship, he may have felt a need to flee – maybe even realizing he needed to protect his family from himself.

But then Max Petrella, a Private Investigator, showed up a few months later at the end of the school day, and asked to speak with me. He was a small, burly man, with a disheveled attire that reminded me of Columbo, the ruffled but shrewd TV character who played an ingenious detective. I thought at first, "Really, is he for real or part of an act?" But he was friendly, engaging and seemed quite smart. He also seemed genuinely concerned about Bill's disappearance.

"Thanks for speaking with me. Can I call you Dianne?" he asked.

"Yes, absolutely."

He took off his fall coat and joined me at my desk, sitting beside me in the guest chair. He pulled out a pad and pen from his inside jacket pocket, and then raised his head up to meet my gaze, and smiled warmly.

"So, I understand Freddy is in your class this year, is that right?"

"Yes."

"And I understand from speaking to Ms. Tapley who has Lulu in her kindergarten class, that you were concerned about Freddy's safety, and possibly Lulu's safety too. Is that right?"

"Yes." And so, I shared my concerns and the signs that I had seen.

"And I believe you brought this to Principal Wooley's attention, is that right?"

"Did you speak with Mr. Wooley?" I asked.

"Yes, I have."

"Well yes, I did speak with him."

"And what did he say?"

I looked directly at Max and wondered how much Principal Wooley would have said. It certainly wasn't in his interest to have it on record that he prevented a potentially valid complaint from coming forward.

"He asked me to leave it with him. Margaret is his sister, so he said he would handle it."

"And did he?"

"I don't know. I don't know what happened after that."

"But you decided to go ahead and check in with the family?"

"Yes."

"Did Principal Wooley know you were going to do that?"

"No"

"Would it be considered following the rules to go against what the Principal asked?"

I sat back slowly, crossed my arms and chewed on my lip. "Are you from the school board?"

"No," Max smiled and sat back in his chair. "As far as I know they aren't curious about any of this. I am not here to file a report on you. I've been hired by Bill's family in Halifax. They are trying to find out where he is. So, I was just curious why you decided to go against what Principal Wooley had asked you?"

"Well, I think he may have been too close to the situation. I justified it that perhaps his reaction was more personal than professional. I guess if it was my sister's family, I might want to jump in before a stranger did. So, I understand his reaction. But ultimately Freddy was my concern."

"What made you drive out that Saturday morning?"

I explained about sitting out on the porch with Tom that morning and then reading the news article about the man who had been abused as a child and no-one had helped him.

"So, tell me about your visit?"

I described driving over, remarked on how tidy and well kept their property was and then outlined the conversation I had had with Margaret.

"So, she said that Bill had gone east to see his family?"

"Yes."

"Did she say when he had left?"

"Not exactly, although I felt like I might have just missed him. But its hard to know if it was that day or a day or two earlier."

"And how did she seem?"

"Calm. Maybe tired. She is a tiny woman, and I couldn't get it out of my head how easy it would be for someone to hurt her."

"How did she react to your questions?"

"Well initially we spoke about children in general, and that was a lovely conversation. You see, I had said that I was there as part of a standard practice of dropping in to meet parents that I hadn't met before. But, that wasn't quite true."

"But that certainly sounds legitimate."

"Yes, it seemed to work. But when I finally raised up the courage to speak truthfully about why I was there, she shut me down. She was polite enough though and actually ..." I paused and tried to find the right words.

"What?"

"She was reassuring. It almost felt like she was empathizing with me for a moment. She told me everything was going to be okay and that the kids were safe now."

Max frowned, repeated what I had said, and then scribbled that down on his pad.

"Well, I think that is what she said to me. But please make a note there on your pad," I said, pointing my finger towards it, "That that is paraphrased by me. On a good day I don't remember the exact words any one person has said to me!"

Although, in reality in this case, I was one hundred percent sure that those words were correct. I had gone over and over them that day, that night and many times since. But somehow those words felt very private and I felt badly for sharing them.

"How did the inside of the house seem?"

"Fine, very tidy."

"Was there anything broken or that seemed out of place?"

"No."

"Did you see any suitcases or bags sitting out anywhere?"

"No."

"How about the children. Did you see them?"

"No, they weren't there."

"How about cars in the driveway. Did you see any?"

"Yes, there were two there."

"Two?" Max paused, nodded his head and wrote that down on his pad. "Could you please describe the cars?"

"One was a white truck, a bit dirty, but I'm pretty sure it was white under all that mud. The other was a basic dark grey sedan. I don't know my car models, sorry."

"Had you ever seen Margaret or Bill driving either of those vehicles before?"

"No, I really didn't know them."

"Did it seem strange that both vehicles were there, if Bill had left and flown out east? Wouldn't he have had to take one of them to the airport in Toronto?"

"Now that you mention it, that does seem logical. But maybe he took the bus, or rode there with someone else. There is a lot of ride sharing that happens here. Saves on gas money."

"Makes sense."

"Do you have any ideas where Bill is?" I asked. I did not expect Max to answer me, but I had to ask.

"No."

"Maybe there is someone else in his life that the family doesn't know about?"

Max smiled and winked at me. "Promise me you won't start sleuthing here, okay? We aren't sure what happened, but I can tell you from experience that when it's been over three months and no-one has heard or seen the person, a missing person's case is less likely to be one that ends up with an easy answer."

I nodded my head slowly, taking this in.

"I'm curious," Max continued. "What was Principal Wooley's reaction when he found out that you had visited his sister?"

I smiled, although maybe it was more of a grimace. I am such an open book. I wished I could say the Principal had been cross, because that would have made more sense. But I couldn't.

"He was fine," was my oversimplified answer, which was immediately pounced on.

"Fine, how do you mean?"

"Well, he called me over when he saw me at school, and just said he heard I had been over to meet Margaret, and that she had liked me. I was glad to hear that because I wasn't sure what she thought of me. But since then, I have seen her a number of times and she smiles and is very pleasant. So, all is good there."

And just when I thought we might be wrapping up, he perked up and began another line of questioning.

"How many times have you seen Margaret since that first Saturday?"

I then had to go through in great detail the eight to ten times I had spoken with Margaret over the past few months. Most of those encounters were when she was picking up the children and I just happened to be leaving right after class. But once we had run into each other in the grocery store and it had been a more relaxed and longer conversation.

"So, when she told you a month ago when you were speaking in the grocery store, that she hadn't heard from Bill, and that his family said he had never arrived out east to visit, how did she seem?"

"Calm."

"Not worried?"

"No."

"Did you find that strange at all?"

"No," I lied. She had displayed that very same cool demeanor that she had when she was saying goodbye to me at her front door. Totally in control. Assuring me all was going to be fine. I did find it unsettling, how a wife could be so neutral about a spouse. Good or bad, I would have expected some sort of expression.

"No?" Max queried.

"No. You have to remember that I don't know her well. Now, is that all?" I asked, "I should be getting home soon."

"Just one more question, if I could?"

"Sure."

"Freddy. What can you tell me about what he has been like since that weekend three months ago?"

"I would say, he has steadily come into his own. He has begun to volunteer answers in class and I can tell that he is making friends."

"Has he said anything to you about his dad being gone?"

"Not directly."

"What do you mean?"

"Well, he hasn't said anything to me, but I did hear him try to explain it to one of his friends a couple of months ago."

"What did he say?"

"Its odd really. He said *I think my Dad went for a long boat ride again.*"

"What do you think he meant?"

"I think he is trying to understand why his dad is gone and hasn't come back, and maybe in the past he went sailing or fishing for a while."

"Well, thank you. Listen, I very much appreciate you speaking with me. Here is my card, if anything else comes to mind. Is it alright if I follow up with you if I have anymore questions?"

"Yes. No problem at all."

As Max picked up his coat and headed for the door, and I began packing up my bag, he paused and looked back. I almost laughed, thinking that this is exactly what Columbo would do, and this final question would be the lynch pin, the most important question of all. I prepared myself for the big one.

"Could you direct me towards the men's room?" he asked.

I burst out laughing and he looked at me with great confusion. Being the open book that I am, I explained my love of Columbo and why I had laughed. He thankfully saw the humour in it too.

Later, as I drove home, my mind began picking up the corners of random items, and looking underneath them for any new ideas. This was the first time I had spent a concentrated period of time discussing Bill's disappearance with someone who was really interested in what had happened. Tom, the other teachers and even all the mothers, seemed to have limited capacity for the topic. Most just suspected he had left and didn't want to be found.

After that conversation I began to collect odd fragments of information. I learned from our drycleaner that Bill had left behind a new suit that he had coveted. I overheard one of Bill's friends at the hardware counter explain that the family had discovered that Bill had been booked on an Air Canada flight to Halifax on that Saturday back in September. But he never showed up for his flight. And when I was standing at the butcher's counter in the local IGA, I heard the butcher quietly confide to a customer, "Well, if I thought someone was laying a hand on one of my nephews or nieces, I would make that person disappear too!"

But then everything went quiet for years. Bill never reappeared. Max Petrella called me a couple of times over the first two years, but nothing after that. Now Freddy was in grade seven and seemed to be thriving. Lulu, in grade four, had been a joy to teach last year. She practically sparkled when she spoke. If something had happened to

Bill, to me it didn't matter. The children were safe, like Margaret had promised and their lives seemed to be unfolding happily.

Until last week. A body had been recovered from the bay. Or rather it was more like partial skeletal remains. It had been found when divers were trying to recover valuables from a sailboat that had sunk in an unanticipated storm. No one had drowned, thankfully. But the boat had been a show piece in the area. Its owner had outfitted it with expensive art and silverware, and his girlfriend had managed to have her full jewelry case inside her overnight bag. The insurance company, a little suspect of the loss, became involved in what would become a very thorough recovery of the sailboat. While the divers were scouring that area of Georgian Bay, they came across more than they were looking for.

No one had heard if the remains were in fact Bill's. But being asked to come in to speak with the police about the Preston family, seemed too much of a coincidence.

"This is going to be a long day," I thought, pulling into the parking lot and heading to class.

Seven hours later I walked into the local precinct and asked for Detective Purdy. I was shown into a small windowless room, with bright lights, two chairs and a table.

Detective Purdy was tall, broad shouldered and could have been intimidating. However, he was personable and seemed like a kind man. Later, Tom suggested that his gentle manner might have been an interviewing façade to make me feel comfortable and open up. He was not from our area. He had come in from Barrie. The advantage of not being from here was that he had no friends to protect in our town. The disadvantage however, was that he didn't know all the layers of relationships that were in place here.

"Thanks for coming in to see me," he began. "I am sure you have had a full day."

"Yes, it is always a full day, but I love the kids, so every day is a good one."

He smiled at that and I wondered if he had kids. In an effort to keep our meeting short I decided not to ask.

"I can appreciate it has been five years since Bill Preston went missing, however I would like to ask you a few questions if I may?"

He then proceeded to ask me a series of questions, very similar to the ones that Max Petrella had asked me in my classroom many years ago. As he asked me questions about the truck and the car in the driveway and about Margaret's assurance to me that the kids were safe, I realized he must have Max's notes and that this line of questioning was seeking to validate them. I wasn't sure how comfortable I was with all of this. That was all so long ago, and the children were doing so well. I hated to think of the trauma that might be brought back if too much was said.

However, it was when he asked about what I had overheard Freddy say to one of his friends about his father going for a long boat ride, that I felt myself drawing a line through the sand. Because in fact, Freddy and I had spoken again a few weeks after I had been interviewed by Max Petrella. I knew more about the boat ride comment. I had never told Max about it in the follow up calls. I had only told Tom. There may have been more to say, but I felt that to do so I would be breaking an unspoken promise with Freddy. I would be making a joke of trust.

Knowing that Detective Purdy had Max's notes and that he knew what Freddy had said to his friend, I was open to reiterate what I had said. "He thought maybe his Dad had gone for a long boat ride again."

"Do you know what he might have meant by that?"

"No," I lied. "I really don't know." I kept very still, willing him to move on, and not ask me anything more about speaking with Freddy.

Thankfully the questioning moved from Freddy to Lulu.

"I understand Lulu was in your class last year. Did she ever express any thoughts about what had happened to her father?"

While I had never asked her, Lulu had once tried to explain to me why only her mother would be coming to a parent teacher interview, and not her father. She had said, "Daddy won't be coming because he

got angry and everyone thought that he should go away for a while."
Staring at her small, serious face, I felt an ominous wave surge up and
my protective wall around her and Freddy became higher and thicker.

"No," I answered.

Detective Purdy then moved on to Margaret and nudged around
for any comments she may have made over the years. I was thankful
in that moment for Margaret's discreteness. I had absolutely nothing
to report.

He then asked detailed questions about each of Margaret's five
brothers. Since I only knew Principal Wooley, that is where he stopped
and focused. It occurred to me as he was prodding for information,
that Principal Wooley had also been tight lipped over the years. There
were never any casual conversations surrounding Bill's disappearance.
If the subject ever came up, he simply did not join in. I was thankful
that legitimately I had nothing to share.

As we wrapped up, I asked about the body that had been found in
the bay. I asked if it was Bill's.

"I can't discuss that with you," he said, looking down at his notes
and clearly not wishing to make eye contact. We sat in silence, but I
could sense the answer to my question. It was as if a voice was talking
out loud in the room. *Of course, it is Bill's body.*

Now that they had found Bill's body, the location of its discovery
would become part of the new narrative about what had happened
to Bill. The small dots I had compiled over the years were connecting
with ease. Driving home, I realized I had come up against an
imaginary property line that encircled Freddy's family. In my mind,
I had been sitting on this fence, pondering what I knew and how
best to protect the children. If Margaret and her family were aware of
Freddy's tearful conversation with me in the coat room five years ago
and that I knew about Bill's boat ride, they might understand that I
was in this with them. My silence about all of this, had me slipping
off that fence and walking up Margaret's driveway, hoping to join her
on the front porch. Except no-one was home. They didn't know I was
there.

# KATE

Life feels like it is constantly speeding up. Each morning when I step into work, it is as if I carefully walk up beside a fast-moving treadmill and begin to pace to anticipate the momentum on the running belt. Then I step one foot on and barely catch my breath as my other foot is dragged into action, and the full out marathon begins. It is sometime around 9pm that I can feel the treadmill beginning to slow. It never comes to a halt, and so I simply jump off, leave the room and try to re-enter home life, often unsuccessfully.

It has been like this for many years. Since my evenings are late, my time with Sylvie is captured in the early morning. At eleven years old, she is happy to get up early with me at 5.30am and natter away as I shower and prepare for my day. Sitting beside me on her custom-made, pink, cushioned bar stool, Sylvie is captivated by how I pamper my skin and draw on my face. Memories of sitting with my mother, and watching and learning from her, are clearly present. I can almost feel Mom standing behind us and smiling.

I miss Mom. I miss our conversations. The animated ones about her lively interactions with department store co-workers, shopkeepers and practically everyone she met. The serious ones about politics and social issues. The conversations full of observant anecdotes that made me realize how much my Mother watched, analyzed and judged. She would see and unearth the simple truths and the hidden lies. And now, while her body is wrapped in clothes that others now choose for her, sadly her mind finds it hard to pick a point of view, to debate or to discuss.

It took me a while to pick up on her unusual forgetfulness. Lost keys, a missed hair appointment, a confused phone call about why I wasn't home to help her with dinner. I hadn't noticed the increased use of lists and the yellow post-it notes that littered her fridge, her phone and a number of doors in her house. However, when she completely missed Sylvie's seventh birthday party and then forgot to pick up Sylvie at school when asked just a day before, I woke up and pulled my head out of the sand. Something was wrong.

Later on, when she got lost in her own neighbourhood and then left the stove on for the second time, burning a pan beyond repair, she agreed that her solo living days needed to come to an end. Fortunately, she had a good friend living in a senior's community. There was a floor in the building dedicated to those with developing dementia. I was thankful that the logical part of her mind was still intact and she accepted the need to be safe. She never fought me on the move.

It is strange what the mind decides to keep and what it will discard. For Mom, she gradually became indifferent about what she wore. For a woman who was impeccably dressed, I found that bizarre. However, when it came to her skin care and makeup, that was something she continued to be most particular about. Unfortunately she began to forget about the more current brands that she had coveted and the caregivers told me that she was always asking for moisturizers and lipstick brands that no longer existed. After these requests became extreme, one very industrious nurse had her nephew research the requested products and reproduce similar labels on his computer. Then they printed them out and pasted them onto my mother's current products. Apparently, Mom was ecstatic, stopped asking about the products (because she believed she had them) and constantly declared that her skin had never felt better!

God love her. I love her. Now four years later, she still knows me, most days. But our conversations are shorter. Phone calls are bizarre. When I see her in person I stand a much better chance of finding the woman I knew.

The sandwich years. Sylvie and Mom are the two slices of white Wonder Bread in my world. Trevor kids me, that, of course, that makes me the baloney in the middle. He helps to keep moments light when they could be dark. He too is pressed from two sides, although it is the traditional battle of home life and work that fight for him.

My hours don't seem to mesh well with Trevor. He tends to work late into the night and sleep longer than me in the morning. When I arrive home, he is either still at the office or engrossed with work in his study. If I try to coerce him to join me for a glass of wine or a sauna, I fail nine times out of ten. And in the morning, he is just beginning to open his eyes around 7am when I am heading out the door. A groggy "Good morning, have a nice day," is pretty much the one line of repeated communication between us through the work week.

Weekends used to be better when we made a point of sharing long lazy mornings, with fresh, hot coffee, and passing newspaper articles back and forth. Then, with Sylvie, the three of us would cook a full breakfast together and make a point of finding an activity for the afternoon. Bike riding, ice skating, museum and art gallery visits – the city always had something interesting to dive into. But with Sylvie's growing level of involvement in school and community sports, there are now swimming and volleyball practices, championship games, and as the fall arrives the skating lessons are starting up again.

On top of Sylvie's programs, Trevor and I are pressed to include the gym in our weekends, so as to contend with our ageing bodies. My fifty year-old arms, legs, abs and mind need lots of disciplined attention. Trevor at forty has been muttering that he needs to spend more time *buffing* himself up, which Sylvie and I find funny. He certainly has found a new relationship with the treadmill and the weight rack. I can appreciate how this all will help with managing the stress of his work, and so I am encouraging him. However, all of this leads us into a new pattern of waking to alarm clocks on Saturday, dashing out to deliver Sylvie to her practice or game, and then going our separate ways to our respective gyms. The plurality we once had in our lives has been invaded and we have become more isolated individuals. Our bridge is Sylvie and she is frequently absent.

But we know these are our busy years. We have demanding work, a young child, and on my side, a more dependent parent. We need to have family time, couple time and somewhere in all of that some personal time to breathe on our own. I don't think the breathing has been going that well. And I am not so sure how couple time is coming along either. It seems to have fallen to the very bottom of the list. But there is an optimism that we live with, that we will eventually figure this out.

"Good morning!" rings out a happy, hyper voice. Sylvie bounces into our room a full five minutes ahead of our alarm clock's scheduled blare. "Rise and shine you two!"

She plunges onto our bed, collapses on top of the duvet and nestles in between the two of us. "If we get up now, we can cook a breakfast instead of eating one from a box. Up you guys!"

Trevor pretends to groan, and then pounces on Sylvie and announces the manifestation of a tickle fest. Having been wide awake for an hour with thoughts ping ponging about in my mind, I am thankful it is time to get up. I laugh as their antics continue and feel truly warm and happy. I love to see them bouncing about. They have always had a wildly, playful relationship.

Trevor ducks as Sylvie vaults a pillow at him, and as he peeks up, he looks across at me with a sunny smile and winks. A warmth rises up. If I could, I would ask Sylvie if she would kindly go dress for the day, and I would reach out and pull Trevor to me, helping us both remember why we committed to share our life together. But this is a more widely shared moment and the day ahead will be the same.

"So, what is going on today?" asks Trevor. As involved a father as he is, he has never figured out one weekend from the next. He finds the family calendar is a complexity of colour coding that he would prefer to avoid.

"Volley ball practice at 9am!" shouts Sylvie.

"And then?" asks Trevor, clearly trying to figure out if there will be some free time for him during the day.

"Skating lesson at 2pm," I say, "And if we are lucky, we can all grab a lunch at noon together at some in-between location."

"Sounds perfect!" Trevor announces to Sylvie. "Our lives are yours to command!"

"Well, at least on a Saturday," I mutter.

Trevor glances across at me and grins. We are in total agreement. It has been a pact for the last few years that work can hold us hostage Monday to Friday, and even Sundays, if required. But Saturday is off limits and we are diligent at harassing each other if one of us pauses too long at a screen message on our phone.

Years ago, before I had children, I read a book by a doctor who said there were three ways to really show your child that you love them. First was physical affection; giving lots of hugs. Second was saying "I love you"; don't hold back. And third was making sure your child caught you watching them; a way for them to feel and know that they are the centre of your world. It was clear to me when I was a new Mom, that hand-held devices were completely destroying the possibility or frequency of the third one occurring. Looking around the playground I watched the delight of young children in a sandbox or on a slide, and then how they would turn to smile at their parent, only to find their mother or father buried in a piece of technology. The smile disappeared and the child carried on, but clearly a shared moment was lost. As much as I worked long and crazy hours, I made a pact with myself and then with Trevor, that when we are with Sylvie, we are truly *with* her. In addition to making sure she has felt loved and cherished, the upside for us has also been so many wonderful memories that might have been missed.

"Toad in a hole sound good?" asks Trevor as he heads to the closet and pulls out his jeans. He will be dressed and ready within five minutes, and knows that breakfast is best made by him as I will be trailing by twenty minutes.

"Yes, yes," shouts Sylvie, "Can I make the circle in the toast?"

"Absolutely. That part needs your artistic eye and focused precision."

Then they are gone and I sit up, pull back the sheets, stand and stretch. I can feel my shoulders seizing up from a seriously intense week. With any luck, those wanting to purchase the company I work for, will leave us alone for the weekend and be back to us on Monday with their revised offer. Life won't change as much this time as it did last time when the firm I worked for was bought. The share value I receive this time won't be used to buy a bigger home or change how we live. I will simply have a much larger investment portfolio. But, if this offer comes through it will create an uncomfortable reckoning again for Trevor and me. He is likely to stare in the mirror and ask, "But when will it be my turn to have a financial event like this?"

"Here Mommy, Daddy thinks you might like this," says Sylvie sweetly, as she carefully carries a mug with swaying swirls of frothed milk on top of the cappuccino.

"Thanks hon!" I reach out to carefully receive this offering and kiss the messy blond curls on top of her head. She raises up her head, just a foot below me now and smiles brightly, and then dashes out of the room. Our little sous chef is not one to leave her chef alone for long.

I continue to puzzle at how my work, which has been absolutely spectacular, is frequently the source of angst between Trevor and me. I love my job and the results are off the chart. I never expected the success that came from the multiple moves I have made in my career. I often feel my fairy godmother has worked overtime and sprinkled magic powder on everything I have ever touched. I had the good fortune of entering business when the norm was to stay with a big established company and climb the corporate ladder. When Trevor and I broke up and I fled a most respected job, I jumped into the fledgling tech startup market, that was craving some experience but didn't always have the money to pay for it. Since a *way-out* versus money was my priority, that market and me fit well together. How were any of us to know the opportunities there would be so lucrative? And once you were known to be a part of one success, you were interesting material for the next startup company with an excellent idea.

While my work has been good for me, it sometimes creates a division for us. Initially our ten-year gap in age provided Trevor with an understanding as to why I was tracking ahead of him. But in time it became apparent, that my early entrance into the tech startup market was becoming tough to catch up to. By the time he was leaping ship from the established large firms, the market was flooded with experienced Marketing Vice Presidents. It was hard for him to differentiate himself and find something that would give him an exponential pay back.

After showering and changing, I meet with myself in the mirror. I smooth on a light foundation. Touching up with concealer under my eyes and along the base of my nose, I gently dab some more over my three advancing age spots. I think about how to give Trevor the news about the potential acquisition of my firm with the least possible fanfare.

"It's ready!" shouts Sylvie from the downstairs foyer.

"Coming," I shout back, as I add a minimum eye, cheek and lip. I stop, push back from the counter and stare at my face. "It's Saturday. Be good. Focus on the moment."

Within an hour we have downed breakfast, charged to the car, dropped Sylvie on time at her school's athletic centre and Trevor has let me off at my club. He speeds off to his gym a few blocks away, and we know that over the next couple of hours we will both be working out and then covertly checking in with emails and work. But out of sight doesn't count, and as long as no-one reappears in a sour or distracted mood, it works.

"Let's try Buon Cibo," I say after our workouts, as I climb back into the car beside Trevor and we speed off to retrieve Sylvie. "I think the service is pretty fast there and it is just fifteen minutes from the ice rink."

Sylvie, Trevor and I wander through the mayhem of the high-end Italian supermarket and eatery. Everything looks delicious and our healthy metabolisms are in full gear after each of our respective workouts of running, biking, weight lifting and setting and spiking balls over a net. We settle on the pizza area, where I eyeball a huge, healthy salad being devoured by two women locked in a serious conversation. It reminds me that I am just a week away from time with Di and Nicole. I just pray this offer doesn't disrupt next weekend and our annual get together.

It is after the pizza has arrived, that so does an ill-timed visitor. Lost in the piping hot, thin crust pizza, with cheese and spicy sausage creating a taste sensation that we are all excitedly devouring, I didn't see Kevin until he was right on top of us.

"Well, well," he says, "That looks like a celebratory meal if I ever saw one!"

"Yes," I chime in quickly, seeking to deflect the meaning of his comment, "It's Saturday, we are together and life couldn't be better!"

"Oh yes. It could get better!" Kevin says with a wink. "You will be adding caviar to that pizza shortly Kate."

Trevor looks at me with a frown, not a bad one, just one that seems to say, "What the heck is he talking about?"

"Thanks Kevin," I say with a pasted smile and a tone I tend to save for telemarketers, "Can we take this up next week? Its Saturday and we are jammed between two sport practices for Sylvie."

"Sure," he responds, a bit stunned and maybe finally catching on that this piece of confidential news he is alluding to may not be common knowledge at this table. It seems everyone's interpretation of confidential is different these days. However, as I recall, we were all supposed to be zipped up about this until everything was firm.

Kevin nods, smiles and heads off, looking back once at me and silently mouthing, "Sorry".

"What was all that about?" Trevor asks, a line between his eyebrows growing unusually deep.

"Something that you and I can talk about at the rink," I say, understanding that between now and then I will have to find the messaging that has eluded me so far. I know there is no way I am going to be able to keep this quiet much longer. I need to get out in front of it before a public announcement is made. Dealing with what is coming now is probably better than having it surface during Trevor's chaotic work week.

"There's an offer?" he says.

Damn.

"Yes."

"A good one?"

I nod my head and then raise my eyes towards Sylvie, who is looking at us and about to ask a question.

"So, spicy sausage," Trevor jumps in, "I'd say that was a winner, eh?"

Sylvie nods her head as she dives in for another bite, and Trevor sits back, nods his head slowly and looks up at me. There is actually warmth in his eye. That surprises me. And his smile seems sincere and kind.

Later, as we are sitting at the ice rink, watching Sylvie and her small class practice their spirals, again and again and again, Trevor and I catch up on the offer. It first came three months ago, was turned down, was then refined and sent back and forth. And then a very good offer came in a week ago, and now is likely to return in an acceptable form this week. He knows I shouldn't be discussing it at all, and certainly not who it is from. While we are a private entity, the purchaser, as most would guess is large and therefore likely public.

"This will be the second time for you," Trevor marvels. "How will I ever keep up with you?" he jokes and squeezes my hand gently.

"It is pretty unbelievable. I thought this wouldn't happen for a few more years."

"Will you stay on?"

"I think so. I am pretty sure they want me involved, either working with them on our existing product or maybe for some other new developments."

"Wow, I won't ask how much until you can share the details. But I am guessing that after this one, you could call it quits and ride off into the sunset if you wanted to."

"Only if you were coming with me," I say and lean into him and wrap my arms around his waist. He responds and pulls me in close and kisses the top of my head.

We sit quietly, watching Sylvie. She glides forward gracefully and gently raises her back leg, holding it up for a good five seconds before carefully returning it to the ice, stopping and standing up straight as if finishing a long complex skate. And then, out of the blue, she looks up and over at us. We smile back and she beams.

# SEPTEMBER GIRLS' 50TH BIRTHDAY WEEKEND

## Friday

50. 365. 24. What's in a number? When one has 50 years to account for, each with 365 days and each filled with 24 hours, there is unquestionably, a *lot of living* in a number.

In a tribute to all of them turning fifty this year, Kate, Dianne and Nicole decided to make this year's annual get together two nights at Abigail's B&B instead of one. The plan was to arrive Friday morning instead of Saturday, and begin with a visit to the Scandinavian spa in town. While Dianne unpacked in her small, single room across the hall, Nicole settled into the larger corner room, which she shared with Kate. This room had become the designated sleeping quarters for the *quiet sleepers*. But Kate was no-where to be seen. Around 11am they receive a text to say she would meet them at the pools by 2pm.

Unperturbed, and realizing that Kate's job was in a busy period, Dianne and Nicole head over to the spa, change into their bathing suits and wrap themselves up in warm, white, terry towel robes. Picking out a hearty soup at the food counter, they choose a small table by the floor to ceiling windows and settle in for the first of their many wandering and well-loved conversations. They gaze out over the large busy warm pools, which are sending spirals of steam into the cool fall day. They remark that the small freezing-cold plunge pools are understandably empty. The pools are all neatly fitted around wooden sauna cabins, glass resting rooms and the spa's large steam room, which is housed in a round, wooden building with a copper roof.

Down below them and off to the left, a long, covered corridor connects the change rooms and showers to the massage rooms, where the weary wander and return as pampered pulp. They have massages scheduled for 4pm, so as long as the traffic behaves, Nicole and Dianne believe that Kate will arrive in time for at least one steam and a cold plunge before her massage.

"I love the feel of this place," says Dianne, looking around the room. Wooden rafters soar overhead and shiny, pine wood floors stretch out beneath their feet. "You can still smell the freshly cut wood as if this was all built yesterday."

"Looks like they will be firing up the fireplace soon," Nicole points out. The kindling sits wedged into the base of the stacked logs. An attendant seems to be searching for the matches. In a few minutes the crackling can be heard, and orange flames begin to curl and dance.

Dianne looks across at Nicole and smiles. "How are you doing my dear? Or rather, as Kate would remind me, I should be narrowing that question and just be asking *how is your morning going so far?*"

"Well, it has been with you. So that's a loaded question!" Nicole laughs.

They sit quietly and Dianne gives Nicole space to answer.

"Nothing moves," Nicole says.

"Where?" Dianne asks, looking out over the water pools, a little confused.

"At home," Nicole answers. "With Michael gone, everything is exactly where I left it. It is so strange to get up in the morning or come home at night and absolutely nothing has changed position."

Dianne refrains from commenting about how it drives her nuts when Tom doesn't put his coffee cups into the dishwasher.

"But Dianne, you asked about this morning. It is a very good one. I am feeling very much at peace."

"Good."

"It is healing to be with you, and to be here, and to have a weekend ahead with you and Kate. I am ready to mix in with people now, after wanting lots of time on my own. There was a lot to work out in my head. But I think I am there now."

"What were you working out?"

"Answers to questions, that in the end, I didn't really have answers for. But I had to figure that out."

"What were the questions?"

Nicole smiles, raises her eyebrows and sits back in her warm cushioned chair.

"Questions like – why did he die? How could I have changed things?"

"Big questions."

"Yes, but I understand no one knows for sure why some people develop glioblastoma. I could not have done anything to prevent his death. Even if I had picked up on an early symptom, the bomb was ticking. You can't stop it."

Dianne nods.

"But it's the other questions that have taken more time to examine and come to terms with," continues Nicole. "Were he and I really meant to be together? Was I just looking to move on to the next stage in life when I met him? Did I love him or was he just there at the right moment? Those are the questions that stump me."

Dianne sits back and tilts her head to the side as she looks across the table at her calm and reflective friend. So poised. So polished. At times open. At times closed.

"I am thinking if you can't answer those questions outright with complete conviction, then maybe that means there is no one answer. Maybe it was timing in your life that brought you together, but that doesn't mean you didn't have special feelings for him. You were fond of him and it was time to move along in life."

Nicole smiles and nods her head. For a busy place, it does seem to feel like a private circle of silence has engulfed them. They sit quietly and finish their soups.

"I think that is what a death brings," says Dianne, breaking the silence. "Large tracks of open quiet space to think and weigh. I remember feeling that way when my sister died. People who die seem to leave the rest of us behind to figure it all out. But then again, maybe we needed to figure it out to go forward. They just made us do it sooner than we might have."

"Hmm, true," Nicole agrees.

"But, even if you question your relationship with Michael," Dianne continues, "I am guessing you would never second guess having your family with him, right? I mean Jimmy and Tessa, without you and Michael, they wouldn't exist."

"I agree. That is where I have been ending up in my mind. If Michael and I happened, so that Jimmy and Tessa are here, then that is reason enough for us to have met, married and spent our lives together."

A helpful attendant asks if she can clear their soup bowls and they smile and thank her. Dianne looks out across the room to the food counter and describes to Nicole how appetizing the spelt chocolate chip cookies appear to be. A few minutes later Dianne returns with two hot lemon herbal teas and a large cookie to share.

By 12.30pm they have descended to the pools and have begun their spa rotation. They whisper to each other in the hot pool for twenty minutes and then submerge themselves for one full minute in the freezing cold plunge pool. Next, they rest for a half hour outside in the sunshine by the bonfire, wrapped in warm robes and seated in large Adirondack chairs. The cycle begins again with fifteen minutes in the sauna and then they tentatively dunk in the cold plunge pool for sixty long seconds. This is then followed by another half hour in silence inside the meditation house. Nestled into big, comfortable chairs, they look out through the large floor-to-ceiling windows and into a peaceful forest of tall, thin pine trees.

As 2pm comes and goes, Dianne and Nicole take turns popping outside to look for Kate, and around 2.30pm they wave at her as she heads out from the change room. They have saved the steam room for last. Unfortunately, it is also the one spot in the spa that requires complete silence. A few furtive hugs and welcomes are traded, and they head into the thick steam, climb up the oversized tile steps which act as row seating, and sit side by side at the very top. As the steam gradually clears, outlines of others appear; a few seated down to the left and one on the same level just four feet away. Then a huge gurgle and a hiss can be heard and a crush of new steam floods in through the roof and along the floor. Within a minute they are all back in a damp envelope of anonymity.

Later they remark that jumping into the cold plunge pool is never really a jump. It is more of a timid descent, step by step on the stairs. It requires a mind over body mentality. One has to force the brain to pretend that the spike of ice that the body is feeling is not really happening. They step in together, the water up to their waist. Then with a nod they drop down to their necks and start to count. Sixty seconds never felt so long. But the reward is worth it. As they ascend out of the pool it is as if their bodies have been given a magic forcefield that shields the cold and makes them feel that the cool September day is actually a warm, balmy tropical one. With only a towel wrapped around their waists, and carrying their robes, they spy three open chairs by the bonfire and head over to collapse into them.

"How was the traffic?" whispers Dianne to Kate.

"It was fine. I just got away late. Some big news to share ladies."

"Do tell," smiles Nicole, very much blissed out, and Dianne feels a wave of happiness to see Nicole seemingly at peace right now.

"Go-Cart has been purchased as of 9pm last night."

"You're kidding!" says Dianne jumping up and diving on top of Kate to give her a hug. "Congratulations!" she practically shouts, clearly too loud, and it feels like a hundred eyeballs are staring at them with disapproval.

"Sorry, sorry," Dianne says, crouching back into her seat and looking around at the unwanted audience she has created.

"But let's talk about it later" says Kate softly, "I am still processing a few things right now"

"We have our massages in ten minutes, how are you possibly

going to relax in there with all of that racing around in your mind?" asks Dianne.

Kate smiles and raises her eyes to the sky. "Not a bad problem to have in the scheme of things, but yes, my head will not be as settled as this freshly steamed body of mine."

An hour later they begin emerging from the massage rooms one at a time, padding over to the tea station in the massage reception area and picking up their receipts and tipping envelopes. Then their three blissed out bodies, wrapped in white robes, wander back down the long hushed corridor to the showers, hair dryers and makeup counters. By 6pm they climb up to the main floor reception, dump off wet towels and robes, deposit their tips at the front desk and head out into the sharp, early evening air.

## Friday Dinner

While tomorrow night will be their customary dinner in their private dining room at Abigail's, tonight they have a reservation at a small Italian restaurant in town. With appetites growing, they head over and arrive to a packed first seating, and are thankful for their booking.

Seated in the middle of the restaurant, they watch a wide variety of fabulous pasta dishes arriving all around them. They decide that the only way to do justice to the choice is to create a sharing menu between them. In time Gnocchi con Gorgonzola arrives, followed by Tagliatelle al Tartufo and Spaghetti alla Vongole. A large shallow bowl of arugula with thin slices of parmesan and a sharp lemon dressing is also ordered and leisurely consumed in the European custom, which is after the main course instead of before. Throughout a fabulous bottle of Amarone disappears and a second one is ordered. When their waitress asks cheerily if they would like desserts, they are unanimous that there is absolutely no room in their stomachs. Decaffeinated cappuccinos become the easy alternative, and the almond biscotti that arrive with them are dunked and happily eaten.

Kate has waved off conversation about her firm's sale until *later*, preferring to spend this noisy restaurant time catching up on everyone's children, family and life beyond work. However, as they finish up their meal and are sipping their cappuccinos, Dianne presses Kate to share details of the sale.

"Well, a few months ago this large public company, Sincofact approached us, and after a few rounds of offers and push backs, yesterday we accepted their offer."

"That happened sooner than you were expecting, right?" asks Dianne.

"Yes, we have our key product developed but we have a few others that are near the end of their development. We thought we might be more attractive after they were out and in use."

"I guess they gave you an offer anticipating success with those products that were in development?" asked Nicole.

"Yes, and a much larger offer than we had been forecasting. It was more than our financial models were indicating and more than we had been planning to begin soft pitching next year. I think they realized there was a great appetite for a more efficient process for online check out and payment systems and they wanted to lock us up. We might be too dangerous for them if another competitor with money came along and could take us over and grow. We knew we needed someone to take us out, but clearly they needed to ensure it was them and not someone else."

"So that is optimal then?" asks Nicole. "It's a best-case scenario, right?"

"Almost," says Kate, gnawing on her lip and flipping her cloth napkin about in front of her.

Dianne and Nicole watch and wait. They have known Kate long enough to understand that she will give them the next installment of the news, and that she is just figuring out how best to say it.

"They don't want me," she finally says.

Dianne's mouth drops and Nicole frowns. Those words don't make sense to them. Ever since they have known Kate, she has been

*Wonder Woman* in the marketing field. Her colleagues, who they have both met, have always had such high regard for her ideas and opinions.

"They are basically going to absorb us into their huge company. In the marketing area, they will pretty much keep our young team and a few of the admin staff, and let me and Gary go."

"You're kidding," says Dianne. "Aren't you and Gary part of the value of what they have just bought?"

"Maybe, but the true value is in the applications and the people who built them. We are the idea team that feeds into product development, and suggests subtle and sometimes not so subtle changes. So we are important, but I think that role gets lost when an observer looks at how we are set up. We look like we are just the marketing and promotion centre, and that piece would not be a unique asset. And they would have to pay us a fair bit to keep us, and I guess they didn't see the value in that. It was a shock. But it was also eye opening. There is ageism in the tech space and I didn't realize I had crossed that dotted line. My ego is a little bruised."

"So, when do you actually leave?" asks Nicole.

"One month today," grins Kate, with a somber and slightly frozen smile. "Looks like I will soon be available for school drop off and pick up on an ongoing basis!"

"Wow," says Dianne. "What does Trevor think of all of this?"

"Well, he was very supportive this week while we were waiting for the final offer, but I only told him about my not being a part of the go forward package when I was driving up here today. I only learned about that this morning."

Dianne reaches across to Kate and places one of her hands on top of Kate's. "Are you okay?" she asks searching her friend's eyes.

"I'm not sure yet. It was all a bit fast. I did like what I was doing. It's hard to think that it will all be gone in a month."

"Will you look for something else?" asks Nicole. "Or is it a bit too soon to know?"

"Well, we do have this budding author to hound. Dianne, I could show up once a week and whip you along through your second novel!"

"Yikes," laughs Dianne, "Not good for the creative process. We have got to find her another job, Nicole!"

"Seriously though," continues Kate, "It is unsettling. It's great to be able to realize my stake of the company, but it feels strange to think that their CEO and marketing team were sitting around discussing who to keep and who to let go. And then I became one of the people who they decided to punt. I am used to feeling part of the core, not the disposable part of a team."

Nicole and Dianne nod, but then Dianne lifts her cappuccino and says, "This still calls for a big congratulations, Kate. You helped make it all happen and you have now been a part of a second success story. Congratulations! And, Cheers!"

They all gently lift and tap their cappuccino cups together and promise to pop some *bubbly* tomorrow night to make it all more official and celebratory.

Later as they are strolling down the pretty main street, lit with tiny white lights, they peer into the windows of the closed shops. They slip fluidly between different topics. If ever anyone was to unwind the web of how one subject leads to the next, it would be a complicated mess of very thin fibers with loose association and curious jump off points.

Suddenly Dianne stops, raises her hand up and stands perfectly still.

"Listen," she says, as she cocks her head to one side for a moment and then points towards the steps descending from the street and into a basement bar. Dianne has picked up the sounds of the opening bars of *The Best*, one of their well-loved dance tunes.

The distant and muffled voice of Tina Turner is floating up the stairs, with a thudding base pounding between each line. They tear down the steps and pull open the glass door. The music swells, as if a hand had just turned up the volume dial from one to ten.

Plunging through the thick crowd, they strip off their coats and drop them in a pile of clothing that is building beside the dance floor.

They manoeuver their way onto the small dance area, full of hips swaying and raised arms flailing. They join in and bellow out the chorus with everyone. All are agreeing that the imaginary recipient of their adulation, is indeed *Simply the best*.

While the three of them sing out loudly, they are easily drowned out by the sound system. They feel the music pounding through their chests, and close their eyes and absorb the sound. Having watched Tina's video many times, they can visualize her striding across the stage in her sparkling sleeveless mini-dress. Reenacting her performance, Dianne lights up and takes four strides away from Kate and Nicole. She pauses and then presses her hands down over her hips and references an imaginary mini-dress. Paying tribute to Tina's fabulous long legs, she reaches down to her left ankle with her left hand, and suggestively drags her fingers up her left leg. With eyes watching and others cheering her on, Dianne repeats the move with her right hand, reaching down and then up and along her right leg. Then pausing in a dramatic pose for one beat, she swings her head back, sparks a huge smile and struts her way back to Kate and Nicole.

As often seems to happen when they find music they love, their singing and Dianne's performing attracts others and their circle of three grows larger. A group of four young women bounce into their midst and contribute a variety of animated moves. Then five young men, lumber on to the dance floor, precariously balancing their beer glasses as they stomp their feet in time to the rhythmic thud imbedded within the music. As the song nears its end everyone joins in, points fingers at each other, and hollers that *you're better than all the rest!*

While the goal had been to turn in early after their dinner, that plan has been thwarted. Over the next two hours they blend into the small club atmosphere of the underground pub, chattering with some local college students, a group of German tourists who are travelling across Canada and a young couple celebrating their second wedding anniversary. They notice that they are likely a decade or two older than the average patron but they love that no one seems to mind. Knowing there is a bike ride waiting for them in the morning, they stick to just one beer each. This is easy to do when Madonna, Lady Gaga, Cher and other voices are pulling them out onto the dance floor, where holding a drink would be an impediment to dancing freely with your soul sisters. Returning again and again to the bar for a glass of ice water works like a charm, and they are bright-eyed and alert when it is time to strike a path for home.

## Saturday Morning

"There you are," says Kate as she steps out onto the morning verandah on the east side of the old house. The light of the sun rising behind the maple trees sprinkles across the east lawn and up and along the deck's wooden slats. Kate is dressed in jeans, white runners and has layered a heavy, wool sweater over her soft, pink, cashmere pullover. Having slid out of bed, changed and not seated herself down for her morning ritual of preparing her face, Kate does not have her usual glow. Nicole also notices that Kate's eyes seem so small in comparison to the large bold blue eyes that usually peer out at the world. "Amazing what eye makeup can do", thinks Nicole. "Maybe I should pay more attention to mine."

Kate cradles a cup of coffee with steam wafting up into her face, warming her up in the cool September morning. "What a night," she continues. "That was fun! Have you been up long? I wondered where you had gotten to."

"I've been up for a little while. I love these early mornings," replies Nicole, wrapped up in two thick Hudson Bay blankets and nestled into one of the large cushioned wicker chairs. An empty coffee cup sits beside her on the table and Kate winks, picks it up and heads in to fetch Nicole a refill and to find herself a couple of blankets. A few minutes later they are side by side, sipping silently and listening to the sounds of the morning – birds chirping, the wheels of a bicycle moving along the street and then a series of light thuds as the Saturday morning newspaper is thrown and lands a few feet away from each of the many front doors along the street.

"And why are you up at 6am?" asks Nicole, eyeing Kate with maternal care. She senses that while Kate would be up early during the week, it would likely be her preference to sleep in if she has a free Saturday morning.

"Something just doesn't feel right," Kate says fidgeting with the fringe of the blanket.

"About the sale?"

"Yes, I got an email from Gary last night and I made the mistake of reading it before I went to bed. He is puzzled by the two of us being given packages. He thinks that when our younger team members were interviewed through the review period when Sincofact was looking at the company, somehow their value on past and current projects may have been overrepresented, and ours might have been underrepresented."

"Does he have any proof of that? Or is it just a thought?"

"Well, it was something that one of the younger team members said to him yesterday afternoon, that is bothersome. She was acting apologetic and then said, *I told the others we should have explained the full picture, not just focused on what we all did.* I would say that sort of speaks to possible misrepresentation of how our team worked together."

"So, what really is at stake here Kate? The current scenario is that you are given a package and you leave. You carry Sincofact's stock for a predetermined time frame and then keep it or cash it out. The alternative would have been you still get your equity, but you would have continued to work with them for a year or a few years? What would you have wanted?"

"That's a good question. I guess, I have always left when I wanted to and on my own terms. So, I would have wanted that. If I enjoyed their firm's culture, I would have stayed a while. If I found them too controlling, I would have left within a year."

"Are they known to be controlling?"

"Not really. Although I don't know for sure. I guess it just bugs me that I don't have the choice."

"How do you think the younger group could have misrepresented the value that you and Gary bring?"

"Well, Gary and I might have set the stage for that to happen. We wanted to protect the whole team and so we spent a great deal of time talking about how well the team worked together and how the ideas and talent was wide spread. The truth is that Gary and I are the two key people for ideation and follow through. We lead but we also do a lot of the work. The team is great, but results will be quite different without us. I guess I just wished the team had spoken as glowingly about us as we did about them."

"What is the average age of this new acquiring company?"

"I can hear your brain thinking out loud!"

"I'm just saying, your industry seems to have a lot of young faces in it."

"Well, Sincofact employees are closer to the age of our younger team members than to Gary and me. They are more in their thirties, and their founder is barely forty. Gary is fifty-four and I am *just* fifty. So, maybe we are not *cool* enough. I certainly don't have the same lingo as they do, although I always find it amusing to learn what their words mean and I was always open to learning them."

"Are you feeling like you are out in the play yard and there is a group pulling away from you? You are sort of standing on the edge as they look over their shoulder and move away?"

"Ugh, yes, that is exactly what I feel like. I hate it! Great analogy. Have you ever felt something like that?"

"Yes."

"Really," Kate says surprised, "When?"

"When I was in my last year of high school and when the kids I looked up to, were going away to university and I wasn't. They knew who was going away and who wasn't and they started this dance. You walked in the room and their circle closed in. You made a point of coming over to join them and they always seemed to have to be on their way. I hated it. Especially because I wanted to go too."

"Why didn't you go?"

"My marks were good, but my parents either couldn't afford to send my brothers and me, so they sent my brothers, or they were closet chauvinists, and didn't think I should go. While growing up they continuously signaled to me that the local colleges were excellent and they would love to have me stay close by."

"I never realized that, Nicole. I just assumed you hadn't wanted to go. Which I have to say I did find odd, because as I got to know you, in those early days through Dianne, I could feel your drive. I'm sorry to hear that the choice wasn't there for you."

"Yes, it was very much a missed opportunity. Maybe if I had rebelled, looked for a scholarship or financial aid, maybe I could have broken away and gone anyway. But I wasn't built that way. I listened to my Mom and Dad and followed their path for me. That is why it was so important to me that Jimmy and Tessa applied themselves at school and had the chance to go anywhere they wanted to go. I loved giving them that."

"Would you think about going to university now? There are continuing study programs for mature students that are supposed to be excellent?"

Nicole smiles broadly. "I have thought about it over the years. But, I hate to admit it, my wanting to go was really about going away with my peers, not the education. It was about wanting to meet interesting young people at a time of my life when I wanted to explore. So now, it is no longer on my wish list. I think it fell off in my thirties although it has always been a regret."

"And here I am grumbling about being kicked out of the game, when you weren't given a real chance to get into it."

Nicole looks directly at Kate and says, "Go right ahead and grumble. I don't resent you for doing so. If it wasn't for you charting the realtor path for me, I might never have had the chance at getting into a game at all. And real estate has been very good to me. So, thank you."

"Well, let me turn that around. Thank you. You have been good to me. You frequently help me to see things more clearly and not miss the point."

"And what is the point that you have now seen?" Nicole asks, tilting her head to one side and smiling.

"That I am old."

"Come on, you can do better than that."

"Ageism is setting in within the tech field. I had better get used to that. And I had better feel damn grateful for all the opportunity I have been given and I have seized along the way."

"Perfect!"

They sip the final remnants of their cooling coffee in silence. The sun has moved up through the scattered clouds and the day will be brisk but beautiful. They can hear the clatter inside as breakfast is being prepared.

"And what are you up thinking about this morning?" Kate asks Nicole.

"Just sensing Michael. Asking him what it is like where he is. He hasn't been answering that one. He seems to only answer questions that I have the content for and that I could figure out on my own."

"How close were you two when he got sick?"

"Hmm, we were friends for sure. And maybe we were as close as two friendly neighbours who speak frequently through the week. Over time that adds up. You know a lot of content about each other's lives. But he wasn't a feelings person and we had different interests, so it wasn't a soul mate scenario. We couldn't finish each other sentences for sure. Does that sound terrible?

"No."

"I think I feel a bit guilty for not being devastated that he is gone. I do feel sad. I know he wanted to live and at times I get really mad that he didn't get that chance. It is just not fair, is what I feel."

"Do you miss him?"

"Sometimes. Usually more when the kids are around and I want them to feel complete. I see the gap for them, that he isn't here, and that is when I miss him the most."

"Do you think if he had been well, you would have stayed together?"

"Our marriage was getting better. The travel together and the sharing of some new interests were all helping to bridge a big gap. I don't know. Maybe we would have stayed married. He didn't seem to be restless, and my restlessness was settling. I was settling I guess."

Abigail peeks her head out of the door and lets them know that breakfast is ready anytime. She comments on Dianne's absence and smiles and says, "There is always one sleepyhead". They definitely sense that Abigail has warmed up to them over the years. They learned last year from one of the housemaids that the fresh cut flowers that began appearing in their rooms a few years ago were the only fresh flowers in all of the guest rooms. Seeing two empty coffee cups she points at them, asks how they take their coffee, picks them up and returns with two fresh ones within minutes.

"The luxury of being served," calls out Kate, as Abigail leaves the verandah. "Thank you Abigail!"

Later when Dianne arrives, she is chided for sleeping in. "You know this does mean that you will be leading us in biking today Dianne," says Kate. "Your extra hours of sleep will be an additional battery pack strapped to your body!"

They all head into breakfast and to the sound of silverware clattering against plates and the chatter of other guests. They are met by the welcoming smell of bacon, fresh bread, and frying onions that will join vegetables and cheese inside Abigail's infamous large fluffy omelets. Eating well has always been a big part of their annual get together. With a day ahead to burn it all off, they dive in.

## Cocktails

After a full day of riding, having taken a more circuitous route than years gone past, their showers are lengthier than usual and afterwards they linger longer in their soft, terry towel bath robes. They joke that their bodies need some time to catch up to who those bodies belong to.

Dianne presses the start button on her CD player and the steady beat of drums fills the room. Phil Collins melodically reminisces about something seen long ago. *Can you feel it coming in the air tonight?* he asks. They sing along to the music, and question the mystery that surrounds the lyrics. Did the artist witness a drowning, see someone with his wife, or less believably, but what he reported when asked, were the words just what simply came into his head?

To mark their fiftieth birthday they had prepared in advance to have a chilled bottle of Bollinger champagne waiting for them. To toast the sale of Kate's company, Nicole had also asked Abigail that morning if she could pick up a small individual bottle of pink sparkling wine with a party hat and some streamers attached to it, as a small celebratory surprise for Kate. Spotting the little bottle, Kate laughs and pops on the hat. She unscrews the tiny bottle of Henkell Rosé and pours it into each of their champagne flutes. She thanks Dianne and Nicole and then raises her glass and toasts, "To the power of people and ideas creating a well received solution and then punting out those that helped!"

Dianne and Nicole immediately jump in saying that wasn't fair and that the moment needs something more positive. Nicole holds up her glass and says: "To Kate. Cheers to all your excellent work and congratulations on your success in business, at home and in life!"

"Hear, hear!" choruses Dianne, clinking Kate's and Nicole's glasses.

"Thanks," smiles Kate with a huge appreciative grin.

As they quickly sip through the light, pink, sparkling wine, Kate reaches for the main event. "And now, lets open this big, gorgeous Bollinger and toast us all!"

To ensure they don't damage Abigail's ceiling, Dianne suggests that they open up one of the windows as Kate removes the foil, untwists the wire and begins to gently turn the cork stopper back and forth. She then eases the cork further and as Kate feels the pressure building she leans and points the bottle outside the window. They yip and yell as the cork *pops* and flies up to the tree tops and across the back lawn.

Diane has slipped Kool & the Gang's CD into the player and *Celebrate* pounds out through the small boom-box. "There's a party going on right here," Dianne sings as they pour the bubbling pale gold *drink of the girls* into their flutes and begin to dance. This dry sparkling beverage is one of their favourites, and they swirl about to the music as they toast and taste.

"To turning 50, and cheers to 50 more!" says Dianne.

"To turning 50 with dear friends who have made many of those years easier to get through," joins in Kate.

"To turning 50. May we look back to today and be forever grateful for each other and the beautiful lives we have led and have yet to lead," adds Nicole.

"Killer toast Nicole," jumps in Dianne, and looking at Kate says, "I think she just buried ours."

Kate nods vehemently and they clink, sip, smile, laugh and dance. And then as alcohol will do to women who have not eaten for a few hours, the champagne proceeds to make the three of them exceedingly happy and the recipients of an overwhelming lightness of being.

As the song ends, Dianne changes the CD, finding one that has a selection of softer, easy listening tunes. They settle on top of the big double bed, scooping up their legs under their robes and balancing their champagne glass as they each find a comfortable spot to sit.

"I am thinking that both of you are about to step through portals to new lives," says Dianne reflectively, as they all lounge about on the beds, working their way towards the bottom of the bottle. "Those portals have happened in different ways, but they have created a parallel situation. You are both entering a new beginning."

"Spoken like an observant writer," kids Kate.

"Very true," agrees Nicole.

"So, describe what is ahead for you two as you move from here to there?"

"Well," says Nicole, "I have a move coming up into a beautiful home, which I am very excited about. Dianne, you have seen the house, and Kate I think the pictures I sent you do it justice. I bought it from the fellow who built it and then briefly lived in it. I am looking forward to the uncluttered contemporary feel of the place."

"It is a special place," echoes Dianne. "The clean lines, the soft wood, the huge windows, the light, the finishes. All so lovely. Nicole, it feels so right for you. "

"Is that builder building any more homes?" asks Kate.

Both Nicole and Dianne pause, sit up, stare at Kate and blink.

"Come on, this can't be new to both of you," continues Kate, "I have always said that one day when I had more time, I should look into a second property up this way. Looks like that *one day* is coming into play."

"Really!" beams Dianne, "I was never sure that you would."

"Well," says Nicole, "If you're serious, this builder is working on another place that I don't believe was pre-sold. I could check for you. It is on a nice piece of property on the water, and it is four seasons."

"Sounds good. Please do check Nicole. After all these years of referring city friends to you, it's my turn to find a great spot. And so Dianne, that will answer a part of your question. With more time I would love to be up here more, although with Sylvie in school, it will be on the weekends when she is not in activities, the holidays and the summer. But sorry Nicole, I interrupted you. What else do you have planned?"

"Well, I am also going to travel a bit too," says Nicole. "I know I don't want to give up work, and since Amy can handle the business while I am away, I booked a couple of weeks in October at a cooking school in Tuscany."

"That's fabulous," jumps in Dianne.

"And then maybe in the spring I'll go to Paris for a serious cooking course. I always thought that might be a great way to experience a new country or culture. Being there for a purpose. Learning something. And then I will keep an ear out for other interesting cooking schools in other parts of the world."

"What a great idea," Kate says, nodding her head slowly. "That is perfect for you. Maybe in the future, I could show up after one of those courses and we could sightsee and shop together!"

"Absolutely," smiles Nicole. "Maybe the three of us could travel together sometime soon!"

"By age fifty-five, if I take the early pension, I may have some freedom outside of the summer," Dianne says. "But the school system is pretty strict about no time off during the year if I am still working. Its strange really, how even though it is only five years away, I don't have a sense for what I will want. I may still very much want to be teaching my sweet little nine year old's. They fill me up everyday. Usually in a good way."

They all agree that Dianne has the best job ever, for her, and then suddenly realize they are ten minutes late for dinner and they had better get changed quickly before Abigail sends someone up to rap on their door. Within minutes Dianne has dodged across the hall to her room, changed and re-appeared. Nicole changes quickly too and she and Dianne head out the door. They tease Kate, who is doing a *quick* ten-minute face that they will see her by dessert. However, the bigger threat is the last line they throw out as they leave the room. "If you are not down in ten minutes, we will choose the wine!"

## Saturday Dinner

Descending to the dining room, Nicole feels the chill of the

September night and slides her hands into the warmth of the side pockets in her wool sweater. She feels the scratch of a paper's edge on her right hand and roots around and pulls out a small piece of paper. She opens it up, reads it and then smiles. Following Dianne into their private dining room she slips it back into her pocket, but the smile remains. Dianne turns to her and then frowns.

"What are you grinning about?"

"Nothing," Nicole says smiling, and with a noticeably light, happy air.

"Hmm, I beg to differ. That smile came from somewhere outside of this room," says Dianne. "You look like one of my kids when there is something afoot."

"Beautiful room," says Nicole, seeking to distract and looking about at the wood paneling, wood fireplace and their round dining table. The long, lit candles cast warm shadows onto the white linen table cloth.

Abigail enters the room as they sit down, and they begin to catch up on the day and the year gone by. She then reviews the menu and her suggestions for accompanying wines. A rather harried Kate arrives, slides into the third seat and Dianne happily hands her the wine list with a knowing smile.

As Abigail leaves the room, Nicole asks Kate, "How is your Mom doing?"

"She is in her own world these days," answers Kate. "But she seems happy in it. It is interesting to be around her, not depressing."

"Does she recognize you still?" asks Dianne. "I know you said that it was a bit of hit and miss these days."

"Yes, occasionally, but not every visit. She doesn't seem to have a clue who Sylvie is when we arrive, but Mom still gives Sylvie her full attention. Mom seems to be smitten by Sylvie as if for the first time, each time."

"That reminds me of the phrase I saw on a card", says Dianne, "*We will be friends until we are old and senile, and then we will be friends again!*" Will that be us, do you think?"

"Could be! And how are your parents these days?" asks Kate to both Dianne and Nicole.

"Well, Mom and Dad," jumps in Dianne, "They have been fixing up the house and they won't say if it's because they are going to sell it or because it needed it. Gemma and I think that they were thinking of selling it but now they have fallen in love with it all over again, so my bet is that they will stay."

"Funny thing is," adds Nicole, "That happened with my Mom and Dad last year. They headed down to Florida for their regular two months away, and thought they would list the house after they came back. They had it painted while they were away and came home and wouldn't budge."

"It's great they are all doing well," says Kate. "And it must be nice for them to stay where their memories were built. I have to believe that will be helpful as they age."

All through dinner, there is a constant babble flowing from their little room. An apple carrot pureed soup is served and consumed. An apple with gorgonzola salad appears and is devoured. The orchard out back has come indoors and they anticipate that the apple will be making a star appearance in each course to come.

While they have been talking now for over twenty-four hours, they never seem to run out of content. That in itself becomes the next topic of conversation. How can it be that it is so easy to bounce freely from one subject to the next, frequently having to come back round to a subject that was left hanging in the air when another one hijacked their thoughts and flung them in a different direction? They begin to ask each other about other friendships that may have had this same free-flowing pattern of conversation. Their talking comes to a halt. There is a moment of silence as they all think back in time.

"Before university I feel my friendships were a bit of a blur," says Dianne. "I was so busy spending time with everyone and I never really focused on developing strong, individual relationships. That was part of the problem for Tom and me during our doomed *round one* in our relationship. He was smart to leave me. I wouldn't have wanted to be a partner or friend to me in high school. I sort of missed the part about being there and giving time in the relationship. But I figured it out in university. I focused on a few good people. And really Kate, you were the acquaintance that grew to a friend, then close friend and then best friend. I hadn't really had a best friend until you."

"So, tell me about you and Nicole. You two knew each other in high school, right?" asks Kate.

"Yes, but not well," answers Dianne. "It was when I came home after university and after my teaching degree, that we got to know each other. I guess in that case we were already acquaintances, and then quickly became friends and then close friends, and now Nicole, we are best friends, right?"

"Yes," smiles Nicole. "I likely didn't make it easy for you to include me as a best friend for a while. I remember us getting closer, but I didn't know how to share my thoughts with you. I think you were happy that I listened to you, but I could tell you knew I was holding out on you. I gradually learned that to be a friend, there needs to be trust, empathy and vulnerability and it needs to go *both* ways."

"I wore you down!" says Dianne with a wink.

"You were for sure my first best friend," carries on Nicole. "And you taught me the *art* of friendship. So, while in high school I didn't have close friends, I do have a few more now. Amy from work, Juanita from the gym and Tessa, my daughter, I think of her now as a close friend too. And that friendship has grown from sharing and being open. All very different from what I was exposed to growing up in my family. And then of course, there is you Kate. I bet you also found me aloof for a while."

"Yes, but I could tell you were worth waiting for!" smiles Kate.

"How about you Kate?" asks Nicole.

"I used to have a friend in high school," says Kate, "Who I was very close to. Her name was Carlie. As you both know, I can be a pretty serious person, and so I didn't attract friends. I didn't know how to be a friend. I didn't know how to share my thoughts. I think I thought that the purpose of school was to do the work and do it well. I missed the part about the purpose of school was to learn to be a socialized person. Who knew?"

Dianne and Nicole listen, fascinated, as Kate hasn't talked about high school before. While they both attended school together, Kate was an unknown to them at that time, living far away in the city.

"So, I didn't talk freely with anyone really except for Carlie. I was in an all-girls school. Carlie had lots of other friends and you would think that that might have created a bridge for me, but it didn't. I just didn't seem to have the right things to say when I was around them. It didn't help that my Mom was very protective and I wasn't allowed to go on sleep overs with the girls in my class, which seemed to be the way everyone got together on the weekends. Mom was worried that there might be drinking and boys, which of course there were. So I stayed home and my relationship with classmates was pretty much during class. I understand it all now, but at the time I just thought I wasn't a likable person."

"It's hard to imagine you that way," says Nicole, with concern written all over her face. "That must have been very lonely."

"It was."

"But what about Carlie?" asks Dianne. "So, you two were at least able to really talk about things?"

"For a while. We were inseparable. We talked non-stop. But then one day, half way through grade thirteen, she just stopped talking to me. And not for a day or two, but for the rest of the school year."

"What?"

"I know. It was very strange. I couldn't figure it out. We hadn't had a fight or a difference of opinion. But basically, when I would come up to her to say hi, she would simply nod, say nothing and walk away. It was one of the worst things you can do to someone. Just freeze them out, without explaining?"

"So, why did she do that? Did you ever find out why?" asks Dianne.

"Well, I was pretty lonely that last year of high school and I never did figure out why during that year. But, in first year university, Carlie and I ran into each other on campus and she was friendly and animated and acted as if nothing had ever happened. I was totally confused, but thankfully more grounded. I had had a great summer and made friends at a sailing club where I had worked. And then Dianne, I had just met you and you were so open and inclusive. I felt I had this friendship thing a bit more figured out. So, Carlie and I agreed to meet up for a lunch one Saturday, and the best thing that happened was alcohol. We had a full bottle of wine, which was a lot for me in those days, and I finally got up the courage to ask her why she had stopped talking to me, and she got up the courage to explain."

Kate paused and Dianne and Nicole both lean forward.

"She had a crisis around her sexuality. I don't think she said it quite like that. But that was the reason. She had known she felt different about her attractions to women over men, but when she fully accepted that she was gay, she couldn't talk to me about it. While she and I were close, she realized that this was one subject she couldn't discuss with me. She didn't believe I would be able to understand her and she would feel devastated if I just disowned her. So basically, she disowned me instead, which when I said that to her, she went pretty silent and then said sorry. Maybe in fairness, she had more to deal with overall than me. But I think if she had been a true friend or maybe a more observant friend, she would have noticed how important she was to me, and how much that all hurt."

"What do you think you would have done if she had told you in high school," Nicole asks, curious as to how a young mind would deal with this.

"I think I would have been supportive. I might have wanted to know if she felt something for me, and we would have had to clear that up. But she told me at our liquored lunch that she hadn't felt that way about me, so we would have gotten through that. But the one thing that might have made life a bit odd, was that she did explain that there was a group of girls in our grade, that like her, were gay. And there were also some who were experimenting, who later determined they weren't. I had never picked up on any of that. Maybe she was right, I might have had a tough time understanding how to fit into that new reality around me, if suddenly I became aware of it."

"Did I ever meet Carlie?" Dianne asks.

"She waved at us a few times in the library, but she and I pretty much kept to a once-a-year lunch after that and then in our thirties we lost touch."

"So, in answer to the question we started with, Carlie is the person I had some of the most wonderful conversations with as a young person. Those conversations were free-flowing like ours. Until the last year of high school when it all dried up."

Abigail swirls into the room expertly carrying two plates in her left hand and one in her right. "Pork chops with apple and cinnamon, served with cooked kale and roasted potatoes," she announces as she places each one down. She then adjusts each plate so that the old family crest, from a long-ago unknown family, is sitting perfectly aligned with the top of the place setting.

They perform their *ooh's* and *aah's* and *it smells fabulous* and Abigail gives Dianne a small squeeze on the shoulder as she leaves the room.

"Do you remember how cold she was to us the first couple of years?" Kate says in a hushed whisper across the table. And that leads into the quietest of conversations about Abigail's journey from perfection-obsessed hostess to the warmest of women, and a much-admired business woman.

"We have all changed too over that time frame," remarks Nicole, to a lot of agreement. "We may attribute traits we have today as existing ten to twenty years ago, but the truth is, only some of them were really there then."

"Oh, God," says Dianne, "Can we just pretend we were who we think we were back then. I don't know if I have the concentration involved in the re-examination process."

"More wine," says Kate. "That will help."

They murmur appreciation for the tenderness of their pork chops and the delicious flavour and soft texture of the roasted potatoes.

Then Dianne stealthily passes Kate and Nicole her cooked kale. "You two can be extra healthy," she quips.

When their plates are being cleared away, they are informed that a chocolate brownie cake is on the way, in celebration of their fiftieth birthday. Within a few minutes Abigail returns singing "Happy Birthday to you" and is trailed by one of her cooks and two serving staff who are belting out the song. Placing the large iced chocolate cake with a blaze of candles onto the table Abigail remarks, "We just kept putting on as many candles as the cake would take. After all, you have 150 years between the three of you!"

The cake is absolutely amazing. Rich but light, and full of the purest of ingredients. It could never be confused for a Betty Crocker! They have generous first slices and after they are well along in their decaf coffees, tiny thin *seconds* are sliced and devoured. Kate, having gained full agreement from Nicole and Dianne, picks up the rest of the cake and marches into the kitchen to encourage the staff to finish it off before their little group of three feasts on it any further. "We need to be able to zip up our zippers and button up our buttons tomorrow, so please help us out!"

When she returns, Nicole suggests they head upstairs. She looks exhausted and suddenly they all feel it too. As they climb the steps, Dianne becomes quite serious and says that she needs to speak with them about something tonight, and that she just hasn't found the right moment to bring it up. Now with a mission, they head back to their two rooms, change into their pyjamas and gather in the big corner room. The drapes have been pulled across the large windows and the low lights on the bedside table cast a cozy glow across the room. Nicole sits comfortably against her two pillows on the double bed, Kate lounges on the single bed and Dianne settles into the room's sole armchair.

"It's about Freddy," Dianne says. "Do you remember the little boy that was in my class years ago?"

"Yes," says Kate, "The one whose dad went missing?"

"Yes, that's the one."

"There have been some pretty tough developments with that family," Nicole adds in. "I heard they just found the dad's body, right Dianne?"

"Yes, they officially announced that this morning. This is what I need to speak with you about."

Over the next few minutes, she reminds them about details surrounding her visit with Margaret Preston five years ago and her subsequent meeting with the private investigator. Nicole and Kate nod their heads as they recall past conversations about this. And then Dianne outlines what Detective Purdy asked her about this week.

"So," asks Kate, "From all you know, what do you think happened?"

"Well actually, I think I sort of know what happened."

Nicole and Kate look at her quizzically, and wait.

"What I am going to tell you has to stay with just us, okay?"

Kate and Nicole nod.

"Some five years ago, near the end of the school year, when Freddy was in my grade three class, I heard some muffled crying in the coat room. It was dark in there, and when I peered in, it took a moment for me to find him. He was sitting on the floor, alone in the back corner. He had his head buried in his sweater, trying to silence his crying. It made me wonder if this had been a strategy he had learned at home to keep himself safe. I knew it had been a tough time for him with his father missing and different rumours circling. There were rumours about abuse, rumours about his dad leaving the family and hooking up with someone else, and there were rumours about foul play. That's a lot for a little nine year old. I sat down with him on the floor and spent a good hour with him, just trying to talk with him and trying to get him to express how he was feeling. But he continued to be quite agitated and finally I clued in that there was something he wanted to say but thought he couldn't say it."

"I don't like where this is going," says Nicole, shaking her head.

Dianne looks at her directly, "Is it okay that I tell you about this, or should I keep this to myself?"

"I think this is something you need to share Dianne," says Kate sitting up on her bed, "Or you are going to turn into a Freddy hiding in a dark coat room."

Dianne looks at Nicole, and Nicole nods her head.

Dianne then relates the private conversation she had with Freddy.

*"I should have gone with my Dad."* Freddy said. *"He asked me to come with him but I didn't want to."*

*"Why didn't you want to go?" Dianne had asked.*

*"Because the waves were big and my tummy always feels sick when the waves are big. And then my Dad gets mad if I get sick."*

*"Well, that was a very good reason not to go."*

*"I don't know. My Dad kept asking me to come and my Uncle kept shouting, NO! FREDDY HAS TO STAY HERE! And my Dad kept calling me to join them on the boat, and my uncle kept telling me to stay in the house. Why did I do what my Uncle told me to do? I should have done what my Dad asked and gone with him."*

*"Do you know where they were going?"*

*"Fishing. They said they were going fishing on the boat. But then Mom said it was for a talk."*

*"Did you see them leave on the boat?"*

*"Yes."*

*"Did you see them come back?"*

*"No, Lulu and I went over to Uncle Henry and Aunt Irene's for a sleep over."*

*"Freddy, where your Dad went is not your fault."*

*"Yes, it is. I should have gone with my Dad. If I had gone on the boat with my Dad, he wouldn't have gone away."*

Dianne stops. Nicole sits shaking her head. Kate looks at them both, puzzled by Nicole's reaction.

"Kate," Nicole says slowly, "They found the body, or rather the remains of the body, in the bay a few days ago. The family said that he had gone to visit his mother out east. The family said he had driven to the airport. They even found his truck parked at the Toronto airport."

"Did the family say that he had driven his own truck to the airport?" Dianne asks.

"Yes, I remember Michael hearing about it from one of Margaret's brothers, who he golfs with. He said that Bill had driven the truck to Toronto and flown out east."

"I saw that truck in their driveway after he had supposedly left. No wonder the detectives kept asking about the cars," Dianne mutters.

"Dianne, did you tell Detective Purdy any of what Freddy told you in the coat room?" asks Kate.

"No."

"Dare I ask why?" asks Kate.

"Because I really do feel I was Freddy's trusted person at that moment, and I don't want to break that. And he told me that five years ago, and I don't want to see him being pulled through the mud on this."

"Did you lie to the police, Dianne?" asks Kate.

"They asked if Freddy said anything about what had happened to his Dad. Freddy didn't know ultimately what had happened to his Dad, so how could he tell me?"

"But Dianne," Nicole says slowly and carefully. "Clearly if you read between the lines of what that sweet little boy was was saying to you, you can piece together a conceivable answer to what might have happened. If the police are asking you what Freddy said about what happened, you did have a much fuller answer that you withheld."

They all sit silently. Dianne is visibly agitated, pressing her palms and fingers together, over and over again.

"Do you know which uncle it was that went out in the boat with Bill?" asks Kate.

"No," Dianne answers quietly, "And I am so thankful that I don't know. I never asked. I don't want to know."

"So, it could have been Principal Wooley?" asks Nicole.

"I don't think it was because that is where Freddy and Lulu went that afternoon. The movie I play in my head is that Freddy and Lulu go over to Principal Wooley's and enjoy a weekend with their uncle, aunt and cousins. They are all there. And I imagine one of the other brothers, who I don't know, as having a fight that gets out of control, or maybe being involved in a premeditated event. I don't know. I don't know what happened and who exactly was involved."

"So, you have known all this for five years?" asks Nicole, "And you never told anyone?"

"I told Tom. But since Bill was missing, Freddy's words about a boat ride didn't mean anything on its own. For sure, there was a thought in the back of my head about one of Margaret's older brothers stepping in. But until they pulled the body out from Georgian Bay, it was just a child's unfounded guilt that had been shared with me. Before they found the body, it was conceivable that Bill had just left and gone somewhere."

"So, what do you need from us?" asks Kate.

"Tell me I'm still a good person if I keep this quiet?" asks Dianne looking at them both, with doe eyes that seemed to plead for the hunter to put down the gun.

"Dianne," says Kate, shaking her head, getting up off of her bed and beginning to pace as she talks. "This is really serious. This is a very big secret for you to keep. I understand that you are looking at it from Freddy's side and wanting to protect him. But think about Bill's family wanting to know what happened and finding some sort of peace. There are many sides to this."

Kate stops and looks over to Nicole, hoping for some reinforcement. Nicole sits still, weighing her thoughts.

"Dianne," Nicole begins, "I understand your concern is for Freddy, so maybe look at it this way. His life was full of abuse, which we believe is now gone. But in its place there is now deception, and that is harmful too. You have often commented on how perceptive children are and their ability to know way more than they are told. Is it really a good thing for Freddy if the truth is buried?"

"Ugh, I should never have said anything to you two," grumbles Dianne, folding her arms and looking at the floor.

"It's not that you have said this to us that is the problem," says

Kate, "It's that you have this weighing on you. That is the problem. It's a moral dilemma."

"Yes," says Dianne with a laugh that is not a laugh. "It is a moral dilemma. Whichever action I choose will infringe upon a moral principle. Believe it or not, we talk about this in grade three, using slightly simpler language. I did not realize I was currently a walking poster girl for it."

Dianne can feel her shoulders cramping and she begins shrugging her shoulders and stretching out her neck from side to side. Kate, recognizing the rising stress in her friend's body, moves over to Dianne and pulls her up from her chair. She directs Dianne to sit down on the side of the bed and then Kate begins to knead her thumbs and palms into Dianne's shoulders. "Remember at university when we got so worked up about our workload?" Kate reminisces. "We became each other's personal massage therapists, and sometimes gently pushed and other times mercilessly pounded out the tension."

"Yes," smiles Dianne, "We thought we were carrying the weight of the world on our shoulders, when in fact it was a mere paper weight in comparison to what was ahead."

"Nicole," Kate instructs with a smile, "You need to get yourself over here too. Sit in front of Dianne, and put her to work on your shoulders. No bystanders allowed!"

Nicole complies and their conversation moves into comments around knots found, pressure points applied and the subsequent sharp pain incurred. This naturally moves into the sharing of thoughts about ageing bodies, keeping fit, drinking more water and getting sleep. At the mention of sleep, Nicole reminds them that that is what the night is for.

Kate reaches out to Dianne for a hug. "Just because we are moving on to sleep right now," she says, "Doesn't mean we are abandoning you and this topic."

"There is a lot to digest here," Nicole adds as she too joins in with a gentle hug. "It's a big deal, but we are here to help you think through this or help in any way we can."

"Thanks," Dianne says releasing them both, and padding towards the door. "I am pretty sure I am just going to stay silent and let it all play out on its own. Basically, I do have to pick a side. And I picked that side a long time ago when a troubled, little boy stared up at me in class."

Dianne heads to bed across the hallway and attempts to end the night with a light hearted note. "I hope these two sets of doors divided by a hallway will keep my snoring from reaching you!"

In the silent room that Dianne has left behind, Nicole and Kate sink into their pillows, pull up their warm covers, and express worry for Dianne and her preference to guard the family's decision to deceive. But soon sleep calls them and they sign off for the night. Their bodies are feeling the wear and tear of good wine, a day's ride, and muscles moving, ligaments lamenting and bones bearing the brunt of an active fifty-year journey.

2015

# NICOLE

It is a classic cliché. "When one door closes, another one opens up!" I used to preach these words to my children, in the same way my mother would say it to me. She would tilt her head lightly to one side as the phrase began, and then gently shift her head to the other side. It was if her head were tracing the path of a door opening up. The first time I caught myself tilting my head and saying those words to my children, I suddenly felt like a programmed robot. So, I took some time to examine those words, and in the end I found them valid and absorbed them as mine. Looking back over the years since Michael died, the closing of one door and the opening of another door is most evident. Michael remains a hugely important part of my life, but he is a part of a room in the past. His children carry parts of him forward. But for me, it has been best to not seek him out as I did in my first year. I let him rest and that has allowed me to have a new life beyond that second door.

It was four years ago, after moving houses that I began to truly transition into a new life. Tessa was visiting me for the month of August and she was fully enjoying her first extended period of time with me in our new home. I had just returned from my run and she caught me smiling and then carefully slipping a note back inside the pocket of my running shorts.

"Mom, what is that?" She reached out towards my pocket and I dodged her playfully.

"Just a little note of encouragement," I replied.

"From who Mom?" she asked, tilting her head and smiling broadly. "You know its okay if someone else comes into your life. Dad has been gone for almost two years now. Jimmy and I want you to move on. We hate the idea of you being here all alone."

I smiled but didn't feel ready yet to let her in. I was still processing what my life was and what I wanted it to be. I headed up to shower and carefully took the small crumpled slip of paper out and stared at the carefully scripted, hand printed letters. "Run to clear the mind, heal the soul and raise the spirit." I smiled and then slipped the piece of paper into the pocket of my running pants for the next day.

However, a week later when I arrived home from an open house, Tessa greeted me at the door, balancing a small wrapped package on her right hand as if it were a serving tray. Grinning she handed it to me saying, "Delivery for you. Hand-delivered by a tall, handsome gentleman, who was a little shocked to see me answer the door."

I smiled, and knowing that I would be hounded if I attempted to delay opening the package, I brought it inside to the kitchen table and carefully tore through the plain paper. A pair of bright, pink, arm warmers stared up at me. I laughed and then explained to Tessa that these sleeves were great to pull on at the beginning of a run when it was cold. Later on they were easy to slip off and put in your pocket when you were hot. As I removed the sleeves from their plastic wrapping, a small slip of paper with hand printed letters fell out onto the floor. Tessa pounced, picked it up and read it out loud. "We run not to get somewhere but to be present in the moment and to live that moment fully."

Playing detective, it took Tessa a few days to figure out who the man at the front door was, and then she cornered me to learn about what had been going on over the past year. It's amazing how much an attentive daughter can wring out of her mother, when she prepares her a tasty, home cooked meal with a fine bottle of wine.

Later, as I changed for bed and crawled under the sheets, I reached out and pulled my extra pillow closer and hugged it. The warmth I felt for Charlie grew so slowly, and I was amazed at the time it took to surface and then the intensity it reached. While over the years I had purchased my running shoes and training gear from a number of his different sporting goods stores in the area, I had only spoken with him a couple of times before Michael died. Those conversations were about the type of cross training I was working on and what shoes and running gear would work best. Michael's funeral was a blur, but I do remember Charlie coming to the visitation and thinking how kind he was to do that. Then a week later a warm, running jersey arrived for me, with a small hand printed slip of paper saying, "It's getting cooler, but your run is calling you out." I cried on the spot, and then tried to understand why. I couldn't.

When the fall came, a box arrived with a pair of Yaktrax inside it. These were contraptions to wrap around my running shoes so I could get great traction on ice or packed snow. I had been in the store a month earlier and Charlie and I had been talking about winter running gear. I had expressed a reservation about whether I would run outside this winter. The conversation had been light and friendly, and for the first time I noticed how lovely his brown eyes were and how his beautiful, black skin had such a healthy glow. His ready smile and hearty laugh were becoming intoxicating to be around. When the Yaktrax box arrived and I opened it up, a small hand printed note read, "Winter running clears the mind and warms up life". I took that note and slipped it inside my favourite sweater and carried it with me for months, pulling it out for a read whenever I needed a small boost.

In the spring I changed my running route and Charlie and I ended up bumping into each other one Sunday morning. He too was out for a run, and that chance encounter began many Sunday morning runs together, that concluded with coffee down by the docks, and time to really get to know each other. It was so easy to be with him. He wasn't in any hurry. He always seemed to have all the time in the world to talk about my children, his three boys, Michael's death, his divorce, my transition from housewife to the realtor business, and his not so smooth progression from playing professional football to building a small sporting goods chain, one precarious store at a time.

"Ever since I can remember, life was about football," Charlie shared in one of our first Sunday conversations. "My Dad and Uncle played all through school. My two brothers did too. And football gave me a scholarship to Notre Dame; a chance to go to a great university. I actually did go to class, and kept solid grades, although my teammates gave me a lot of grief when I didn't go out with them as much as they thought I should."

"Those must have been exciting times," I chimed in. "I never went to university, so I can't fully appreciate it, but I can imagine it."

"Yes, it was exciting. And when I got drafted to Cincinnati in my final year, I felt totally blessed. My parents were church people and I really felt that all their prayers had made it happen. But then just one month into my second season playing professionally, I was in a car accident. Among many injuries, I had a bad concussion and I wrecked my right shoulder. No amount of praying seemed to mend me enough to be able to return as a reliable receiver. It was strange that it wasn't football injuries that retired me. It was simply participating in the regular world that did me in."

"That must have been so difficult," I said, shaking my head. "To have such a big part of you stripped away." It was hard to imagine how one would adjust after years of honing a skill that is then no longer needed.

"Yes, it was difficult, in many ways," Charlie continued. "Like you, I married young. We even had our first son at that point. But Angela had married not just her university sweetheart but someone who she thought was a future football star. Sometimes I think she missed the football life even more than me. When my career got sidelined, she decided it was best that we all move back to Canada, where she had grown up and she had more family support. After years of being the one who led the way, I buried my pride and followed her to Toronto."

"You're a good man Charlie," I said, imagining the loss and change he would have had to absorb; the loss of a dream job and then a move to a new country.

"I wasn't the best man I could have been. I was a bit immature, even though soon I was a father of two, and a couple of years later we had our third boy. Angela became the key breadwinner in those early years. She was pretty dynamic, had a business degree and she put it to work. My English Literature major meant I could write well, but the job prospects for a new Canadian with that skill set were few. I ended up in a series of odd jobs, and started to drink a little too much in front of the TV."

"So how did the sporting goods store come about?" I asked, intrigued to understand how someone could move from odd jobs into an ownership position.

"I think my parents must have started their praying again," Charlie laughed out loud with his wide smile appearing. "Angela's older brother Terrance took me under his wing. He loved football and had always treated me as if I was still a star player. He worked in sales at a car dealership and he told me he did well because he was crazy about cars. He asked me point blank *What are you passionate about, Charlie?* And I didn't miss a beat. *Sports!* I said. *"Well then,"* Terrance said, *"That is what you need to be selling.* He was tenacious with me and helped me think through and research options, and together we found a sporting goods store, outside of the city, with an older owner who was open to me being a part of his exit plan in a few years."

"Very smart" I said clapping my hands together and sitting back. "That was brilliant!"

"Yes it was, and I give Terrance full credit for the plan. There were mishaps along the way, but over time I learned a lot, and then I began looking for other sports stores with elderly owners in small communities. It took time, and I made plenty of mistakes, but eventually the formula worked well." Charlie grinned and then became silent, as he picked up his coffee, took a sip, sat back and looked out at the boats lined up along the docks.

"And then?" I asked.

"Well, some people need to see their life moving faster than others. Some people want more things. Angela found my path a bit too slow for her. And then she found someone moving faster, who could give her more. I didn't see that coming. I thought that because we had our three little boys, the family was something she would protect. But she didn't."

"I'm so sorry to hear that. Were you able to find a way to share the children?" I asked. That had always been my biggest angst when I was tormented with the idea of my marriage with Michael breaking down.

"Yes, although as we tried to make it less disruptive for the children, I ended up letting her have the boys for longer periods. It seemed so unfair to me, that she was the one who initiated the break, and I had the kids less."

"I bet you were a great dad to those three little boys," I piped in. I truly did believe that he would have been.

"Yes, I was. Even with multiple stores to manage and goods to sell, I made being a *super-dad* my number one priority. I sometimes wonder if Angela and I had stayed together, would I have focused so intensely on being there for my boys? Maybe I would have been more relaxed about it and missed a lot of special moments." And then he smiled at me, winked and added. "One never knows if maybe what you have, is actually better than what you might have had!"

Those Sundays with Charlie were highly therapeutic. Running together and then sharing coffee with him, we both became very open about our lives, mistakes and successes. In time, I learned about some of the racial tensions that existed in Port Colebrook. That was something I knew very little about. Staring at this beautiful, kind man, it was hard to stomach the terrible things that whites could say to blacks, and then how those insensitive people could somehow carry on living in a vacuum of ignorance. I learned a lot from Charlie. I was thankful for his company. It was effortless to be with him.

But as the summer approached, life crept in. I had booked three weeks away at the rented cottage our family enjoyed each year. And Charlie and I each had children visiting periodically on weekends. Our string of Sunday runs vanished as fast as they had started. One Sunday I went running, twice as long as usual, hoping to bump into Charlie. I didn't find him. As I sat down by the docks having a coffee on my own,

I realized I missed him and maybe it was time for me to do something kind for him.

Remembering that in our conversations about food, he had expressed a love for Mexican cooking, I headed to the grocery store. I bought a host of ingredients and that night I set out to make a variety of empanadas. Carefully rolling out the pastry, filling some with spicy sausage and others with spinach and feta, I turned up the music and danced throughout. The next morning, I delivered a package wrapped in tin foil to his closest store. I was happy to be able to give it to one of his employees before he had arrived. The envelope attached had a small slip of paper within it. The hand printed words said: "Food is but one thing that sustains us. Sharing thoughts and dreams matter more."

Predictably, he called and our runs restarted, and shortly after our dating began.

Before Tessa headed back to Toronto and the new accounting job she had accepted after completing her CPA, I agreed to have Charlie over for dinner so she could meet him. However, the afternoon brought a difficult moment that pulled the evening down a dark path.

I was puttering around in the kitchen, fussing over a Mediterranean dish that involved multiple vegetables being roasted, when Tessa sailed in through the door declaring that her back finally felt unlocked. As I continued attending to the preparation of the dish, she marveled at the aroma in the kitchen and pulled her arms along the edge of the counter, turning her shoulders and breathing into a deep side stretch. She too was a runner and had been complaining about some creeping stiffness over the past week.

"Well, I think that chiro adjustment did the trick. Sometimes you need some help."

I paused, looked up at her and suddenly felt slightly light headed.

"What's up Mom?"

"Nothing. I just remembered I forgot to take something out of the fridge."

"What do you need?" she asked, moving to help.

I turned and blocked her path. Opening the fridge door, I stared aimlessly at its contents, finding the cool air helpful.

"Well, I am feeling much better," she continued as she squeezed by me and grabbed the orange juice, "and Nelson Muir said to say hello. Do you go to him too?"

"No, no I don't," I said, closing the fridge door and turning around to look at her carefully. My eyes tracked along her beautiful flowing dark hair, her long trim figure and curvaceous hips. Tight jeans and close-fitting t-shirts were normal for an attractive twenty-four-year-old woman to wear, but suddenly to me, she looked like she had practically nothing on. I hated to think of her in a room with *him*. Would the door be closed?

"What's the problem?" she asked, this time more annoyed than concerned. I guess my scanning of her body had been mistakenly taken as criticism.

"Nothing. Sorry. I just have some work things on my mind."

She stared back at me and then sighed as if exasperated by me. But then looking down at her phone, incoming texts became a compelling distraction.

I turned back to the fridge, pulled out a bottle of Pinot Gris, uncorked it, poured a large glass and nursed my way through the next hour of dinner preparation and the setting of our table out on the back deck. By the time Charlie arrived, I was on my third glass of wine, but instead of being a happy host, I was a puddle of mixed emotions. He caught wind of it within a few minutes and kept throwing me quizzical looks as Tessa carried most of the conversation during dinner.

The good news was that Charlie and Tessa got along wonderfully. The not so good news was that they each mistook my discomfort as signs that my relationship with the other was less than optimal. Charlie left thinking that I had issues with Tessa and Tessa told me I was clearly not comfortable with Charlie and that I acted so unnatural around him. Unfortunately, I then added a fifth glass of wine to my night and went to bed with absolutely nothing resolved.

Having woken during the night a few times, and having forced myself to drink copious amounts of water, I was able to rise early and run. Clearing my head, I decided on three courses of action, two of which involved no action. I would honour Michael and not tell Tessa about Nelson. I would not approach Nelson and seek any kind of complicated re-writing of history. And I would simply tell Charlie that I had had a migraine and found it difficult to concentrate and contribute to the conversation at dinner. I carried through on the first two, but thankfully re-scripted the last one. The next day Charlie and I had a *heart to heart* and his calm and understanding manner made the moment a gift. It allowed me for the first time, to fully share my life with someone and not keep secrets from them.

And now four years later our lives are more intertwined, with he and his world having moved in with me two years ago. He is a minimalist at heart, which meant that it was easy to open up closet space for him. But while he was happy to share his furniture with his adult children, he did bring along Lucy, a most *happy to see you* three-year-old golden retriever. The vacuum found it hard to keep up with the constant swirling tornedos of long hair, but I never felt more complete with all the additional long walks and warm hairy hugs. *Why had we never had a dog?* began to lurk in my mind. It is okay for life to be a bit messy. Some messes can bring their own kind of love.

Today I can feel our family is truly expanding. On top of building a life with Charlie and his children and grandchildren, my family is growing too. Jimmy is now married, and he and Shayna have had their first child. I am a grandmother – how odd to say that. Little Oliver is only three months old and looks like a cherub who has dropped off of a cloud. He is round, angelic, with white blond curls and crystal blue eyes – so much like the sweet little Jimmy I pushed around in a stroller so many years ago.

I head out to the grocery store to pick up supplies for our busy *end of summer* weekend coming up. Both Jimmy and his family and Tessa will be home, for a last hurrah before heading into September. Buzzing around the aisles with my list, checking off items as I dump them into the cart, my mind is jumping between visualizing the meals to be prepared and the anticipation of having everyone together.

As I fly up to the end of one aisle and prepare to turn the bend to the next, I nearly plough into a little blonde boy, whose eyes seem to line up with the top of my shopping cart. We are both shocked and immediately pull back, he with large blue eyes popping out and me with a growing frown as I puzzle over the child in front of me. I know that I have Jimmy on my mind, but if Oliver looks like Jimmy at three months, this little boy is the spitting image of Jimmy at five years old. I stare at him. He stares back at me.

"I'm sorry," I begin, "I was going way too fast…"

He looks up and grins and I catch my breath. I feel I have stepped back in time. Remarkable resemblance. How odd. But then suddenly not so odd. A woman appears behind him and scoops him up and turns to me with a huge smile, that suddenly retreats. It's Penelope.

"Nicole," she says, as she struggles to keep her smile frozen on her face. "How nice to see you."

We talk for just a few awkward moments, she introduces me to Theo, who shyly shakes my hand. She explains she is home visiting her parents for the summer.

"After Michael died and his practice was sold to Dr. Ambrose, I didn't feel comfortable working there. So, I moved out to Vancouver to be with my sister. She had a friend with a dental practice that had an opening. So that all worked out well."

I want to ask about Theo's father, but decide to let her offer up an explanation. Which she doesn't.

"How are Jimmy and Tessa?" Penelope asks. And I update her on their lives, and am surprised by her genuine interest.

"I had better be off," Penelope says, "Or I will be late for Mom and Dad's pre-dinner drinks. Always a ritual during Bar-B-Q season."

She hesitates and then sets Theo down and spins her cart around. Grasping Theo in one hand and pushing her cart with the other, she retreats down the aisle towards the cash register. Theo turns and stares at me over his shoulder. I know those eyes.

As she walks away, I am doing the math. Tilting my head as I size up the age of this child, I quickly conclude that there is a new dotted line stretching out from our family tree.

Driving home, I feel a bit lost in time and space. Michael has suddenly stepped through the door and out of the room where he has been resting. But I understand it is not him. It is just a piece of him. It does feel like the past has crashed into the present. I am now watching these two colliding waves begin to pull apart. There is this open ground of wet sand in front of me and I have a choice. I can let the waves crash into each other again or I can let it go and enjoy the walk on the beach.

# DIANNE

Should is a force. It empowers the speaker while pressing the listener up against the wall. Yet should is formed from an opinion on a matter. And any given matter can be picked up and looked at from multiple angles. Sara is home for a visit and with her comes her view on how the world should operate and how we all should be. There was a time when I would engage with my daughter to help her see the other side of the matter, but she is twenty-six now and so as a rule Tom and I no longer challenge her. Sometimes we listen and learn. Sometimes we stop listening.

Ever since Sara was little, she had an opinion. Never a doubtful child, she was always a strong rule follower. If the teacher asked the kindergarten class to pull out the blue cups for snack, she was quick to straighten out any fellow student who reached for the red or orange ones. If a school project was due on the Monday and she learned that a classmate handed it in two days late with no mark adjustment, she would fume for weeks. If she witnessed a stranger picking up an item in a store and attempting to leave without paying for it, her loud voice let the whole store know what was happening. It was simply her way of keeping the world in order.

As a teacher, I was fortunate to have had the training to spot early on that she was on the spectrum. As a mother, I loved her for all her idiosyncrasies as she strived to make the world perfect. As a compassionate human being, I often climbed the walls in agonizing silence. It was frustrating to live with someone who had an inability to be openminded. She could not accept that life was complicated and that people needed patience and time to solve problems. I was always amazed how she was so empathetic about issues, but seemed to lack empathy with individual people.

Today she is working with an impact investing firm, helping to research, profile and promote funds that invest in projects that make our community, our country and our world a healthier and more equitable place. She is above and beyond passionate about her work and has managers who help to keep her inside the lines with how she designs and markets their material. She basically has found the perfect job for her. Tom and I breathe in and out with great sighs of relief.

Sam too has come home this week for his summer holidays. I love it that Sara and Sam are both siblings and friends and have made a point of picking the same week to visit. I mentally place a big check mark beside *the kids will always have each other when we are gone*. My fixation on that topic likely comes from losing Caroline and witnessing how the twins, who were close to each other, have managed and thrived. The power and security of having a strong friendship with a close sibling is something I felt with Caroline as I grew up. It is comforting to see it in full force in both her children and mine.

Sam, now twenty-three, is thriving in the computer software industry. His childhood obsession with puzzles grew into a fascination around complex mathematical problems. Kate and Trevor spotted his unusual speed at comprehending computer games and software applications. They were keen to help him find challenging summer jobs while he was in high school and later on when he was in university. As a result, when he finished his engineering degree and entered the software field, his resume already teemed with experience. Through it all he has remained a sweet, caring soul, and his unsolicited hugs when he comes home, always fill me up.

Unfortunately, it is Sara and not Sam who is with me when I run into Margaret Preston. Sara's cold stare and gradual stiffening of her upper body inform me that she has developed a definite opinion about the participants in the Bill Preston drama that unfolded here ten years ago. I am grateful that she is unaware of my role, and that only Tom,

Kate and Nicole know what I know. While I am not a fan of secrets, there is nothing straight forward about this one and Sara's ability to look at the big picture is simply non-existent.

"Dianne, good to see you," calls out Margaret as she transfers her groceries from her cart and onto the checkout counter. We are parallel to her at the next checkout and have almost finished bagging up our groceries.

"Mom, let's go," says Sara in a controlled, low voice. "I don't want to talk to her."

"My goodness, is that Sara?" asks Margaret with a big warm smile, fortunately far enough away that she can't hear Sara's words. Margaret continues, "She is bigger than you Dianne!"

"Hi Margaret! Yes, Sara is towering over me these days."

"Mom, I want to go now," Sara whispers while fuming. "You shouldn't talk to her."

"Sara, why don't you take the groceries to the car, hon."

Sara glares at me, nods and pushes the cart out of the store and into the balmy August afternoon.

I finish paying for our groceries and then walk over to Margaret and help her bag up her items. "Sara, as you may or may not know, is not great with people sometimes. How are Lulu and Freddy?"

"Lulu had a good first year in high school. And Freddy, well he is happy to be heading away to university. Have you seen him lately?"

"I don't think I have."

"You would hardly recognize him. Not only has he shot up by a foot this past year, but his shoulders and chest have filled out, and even his cheek bones and jaw seem to have changed."

"It is amazing how boys can turn into young men overnight."

"He looks a lot like Bill actually," Margaret says quietly, "And that is a good thing right now. He likes the fact that he looks like the father he sees in photographs."

"Does he ask about his Dad?" I ask, as we begin to head out together to the parking lot.

"Yes. And for a long time now, I have been feeling that it is wrong to continue to lie to him."

I stop and stand very still, waiting for Margaret to catch up to what she has just said to me. We haven't had this conversation before. There has never been a mention of a lie. For years I have only ever heard the party line by the family that they didn't know what had happened to Bill and they didn't know how he had ended up in Georgian Bay.

But instead of catching herself, she stops and looks straight at me and says, "Could we get together and talk sometime? I know you could have told the police what Freddy said to you in the coat room about the boat, and I know you didn't. The police never asked us about Bill and his brother going out in the boat that day. They never learned about that. Thank you for keeping that to yourself."

To say *you're welcome* seems strange, and so I don't. We stand silently and then I nod my head.

"Yes of course, I'm happy to get together with you," I begin.

Over Margaret's shoulder I can see Sara is pacing. If she were a kettle, the steam would be peaking about now and the whistle would begin to blow. Sara's hands are now moving onto her hips and fury is a moment away. Time to deflect that pending volcano.

"Margaret, how about we go for a walk tomorrow? Would that work for you?"

We agree to meet up in the park down by the water at 2pm the next day, and we both go our separate ways. Margaret has a peacefulness I don't remember from years ago. Being calm and being peaceful are very different. I remember the former but not the latter. I head to the car, where I know peace will not be joining me on the drive home. To head off what is likely coming I stop, hold up my palm about two feet from Sara's face and say, "Stop, don't start. You and I see things differently and that is okay. Let me be me."

The next day a brisk August wind is blowing. The waves in the bay are choppy and it does feel strange to be meeting Margaret beside the water that was Bill's grave for many years. I shiver and I am not sure if that has been triggered by the breeze or by my brain, tracing Bill's name with a fingernail on a slate board in my head.

We stroll along the boardwalk, stepping aside from time to time to let those on bikes and rollerblades pass by. We catch up on the lives of our children. We talk about Sara, her lack of a filter and her ability to speak without being concerned about what others might think. "It must be so freeing for her to say what is on her mind and not have to shut it down," Margaret says. I glance towards her as she says this, wondering about how she has handled her own silence over the years.

Margaret then asks me about my next book. "I know they are supposed to be for children," she says as if there is an apology in the works, "But in your first two books, I just loved your characters and the words you used to express everything. I do think adults must be enjoying your books, too." I smile and thank her. It always feels good to know a reader is enjoying my work.

And then we find a bench, overlooking the water and sit, both staring out at the wide expanse of waves that are a chorus of peaking curls and crashes. We are silent. It is as if the play is about to begin and everyone needs to take their seats, put their program down, let the house lights dim, and then the show can start. Margaret begins to speak.

"I was the one who bought Bill his plane ticket to Halifax. I bought it a week ahead of time and I was so worried all week that he might find out about it. I knew we had to separate Bill from Freddy and Lulu and find a way for him to get help and to get better. So, the plan my brothers and I devised was that we would ask Bill to go back out east, to where he had grown up and stay with his mother for a year or so. His father had died two years earlier, so we knew he wouldn't have to contend with that terrible man. His father's anger had been so damaging to Bill and his entire family. We agreed that we would financially support Bill until he got a job out there. And then, if he received counselling and was able to keep a check on his anger, he could come back. We thought it might take a year or so, and then we would all be back as a family again. But, it all went terribly wrong..."

Her voice suddenly dips and seems to shake. I reach over and take her hand. She grimaces, looks down at my hand and then gives it a small squeeze.

"Bill's temper was his undoing. We had organized for my youngest brother Evan to take Bill out fishing. Over the years they had gotten along the best, so the thought was that Evan could have a *heart to heart* with Bill while they were fishing. I think Bill must have known that something was up that day. Evan was acting pretty intense when he arrived with his boat and I don't think Bill liked the way Evan was ordering Freddy to stay behind. Likely the tension continued to build even before Evan had stopped the boat, pulled out the fishing gear and then started to lay out the plan. As Evan tells it, Bill went absolutely mental when Evan began to explain what the family thought would be best. Bill had never hit anyone except me and the kids, so Evan was completely caught off guard when Bill's swearing and pacing back and forth turned into a full out attack on Evan. Bill lunged at Evan and took him down onto the boat's deck. What happened next remains confusing for Evan. Evan felt completely overpowered and at risk of being knocked out by Bill, and so when his hand found a gutting knife close by on the deck's surface he grabbed it. Suddenly they were fighting over the knife and rolling around on the boat's deck. Then Bill went limp and Evan realized he had stabbed Bill."

Margaret stops. She has pulled her hand away from mine and is clenching both hands together, opening and closing her fingers. Her shoulders are now hunched over her lap as she looks down at her feet. Her voice becomes weak and barely audible.

"Evan made two big mistakes. First he didn't drive the boat back right away - maybe Bill might have lived."

She clears her throat, looks out towards the water, and then speaks more firmly. "And second, he called my brother George, who of all of my brothers is the least capable of rational thought. Somehow when George arrived and Bill appeared to be dead, they worried that the police might not believe them. They thought the police might question Evan's story that Bill had lunged at Evan and that the police might not believe that the death was either accidental or in self-defense. You see, around that time both Evan and George had each spent a number of nights in jail for bar brawls and they had been the known instigators of some of those fights."

Margaret looks at me. Her face is small and drawn. For the first time I see all the many worry lines etched into her brow, temples and around her eyes. Her face has aged considerably since I first met her.

"So instead of bringing Bill back, so we could have the chance to explain everything, and the children and I could have the chance to mourn a father and a husband, they just made him disappear."

Her voice begins to rise as she appears to relive the moment.

"I didn't know where they had buried him! I guessed it was in the water, but they refused to say anything more to me. My own husband, was out there but I didn't know where! He was just gone."

She stares at me and seems to be checking to see that I am with her. I nod slowly. "Go on," I encourage, "It must have been a nightmare for you."

"Yes, it was. I was a mess. I had to stay out of public view for a long time because I was constantly tearing up. I did love Bill in a way that was hard to explain. His father had hurt him. He was broken. I don't think he ever meant to hurt us. I guess I loved who I thought he was when I met him and who I thought he might become again. But because of the story Evan and George began to tell, I couldn't mourn Bill publicly and I couldn't even mourn him within my own home. The family didn't want the children to know. They didn't want anyone to know. We all went along with the new plan, which was basically to pretend that the original plan had worked and Bill had left with the intention of flying out east to be with his mother. We went along with this new plan because we were all protecting Evan, who ironically had been trying to protect the children and me by asking Bill to leave."

She stops, purses her lips together and I can see that some tears have begun to track down her cheeks. She wipes them away with her finger tips and then shifts on the bench seat. She pulls herself up straight and a small smile appears along with an attempt at a short laugh, that ends up having very little sound.

"And then, suddenly there you were, at my house, just an hour after Evan and Bill had left on the boat and twenty minutes after Freddy and Lulu went to their cousins. I knew nothing about what was happening out on the boat at that time. I thought Evan and Bill were fishing and likely having a difficult conversation and then they would come back. I was worried that Bill would come back mad. But if that happened I had a bag packed in the trunk of my car and I would follow my children to my brother's. I thought I had everything under control. We had a good plan. I didn't want Bill's abuse to be reported to the police. That would set off a whole new level of anger, likely continued violence and we would have had the town's judgement to deal with too. Instead, Bill would leave, go out to Halifax and get better. The kids and I would be safe."

"That was a good plan," I say quietly. "A very good plan."

"And you know," Margaret says with an amused grin that came and went quickly, "I started making mistakes the moment you showed up. I messed up on the location of Freddy's supposed fall on the stairs. I was even the one who told him to say it was the basement stairs, because it is darker there and more believable that a child might fall in the basement then on the main stairs. And then as you were leaving and I caught site of Bill's truck in the driveway, I realized that was inconsistent with saying he had left. I just hoped you would stare at me as you drove off and not at the cars."

"You know, I didn't notice that inconsistency. But the private investigator did a few months later when he asked me how many cars were there."

Margaret nods her head and then continues in a more matter of fact voice. The calm and controlled Margaret is reappearing.

"So, I truly believe it was an accident, or maybe a court would say it was self-defense. Either way, Evan didn't mean to kill Bill. Of course it would have been better if he and George had laid out the truth with the police right away. But they didn't. Instead the truth was buried and it seems like everyone in the community has made up their own version of the story. And no-one has gotten it right."

"So, what does Freddy know?" I ask.

"He knows Evan and his Dad went out fishing. I think he told you he regrets not going, even though he really didn't have a choice. The story Freddy was told was that when his Dad came back from fishing, he packed up, drove to Toronto and flew to Halifax to be with his mother. We said that he was going to visit his family for a while and would come back when he wasn't so angry. It's amazing how kids will accept what they want to hear. Freddy liked the idea that his Dad would be back when the anger was gone."

"But when they found Bill's body in the bay five years ago," I ask gently, "How did he reconcile that with having seen his uncle and his father leave in a boat together?"

"That was tricky. He was thirteen. He was smart, perceptive and nobody's fool. We decided as a family to keep with our story. Bill had come back from fishing, had driven to Toronto and after that we didn't know what had happened to him. Some people suggested to Freddy that maybe his Dad had come back later on that year and had gone out fishing, but Freddy argued with them on that. More than anything, he was hurt by the idea that his Dad would come back and not try to see him."

"What do you think Freddy thinks now?" I ask.

"I think he knows I am lying. He knows we are all lying. He doesn't say anything, but if something about his father comes up, he just gives me a very long, hard stare and leaves the room. He has told Lulu that when he goes away to university, he won't be coming back. I don't have the courage to ask him if this is true and if he means that he won't ever come back, not even for a visit."

We both sit with these words hanging in the air. I think about Kate and Nicole and the tension that has rippled up between us over these past five years. While originally they would share their point of view when the topic of Freddy and his family would surface, now their mouths don't move and their eyes speak instead. To avoid the confrontation, I have become an expert at dodging the subject. They have continued to adhere to their early expressed beliefs that there is a cycle present and I am a part of it. While Freddy may have become free from his father's violence and abuse, the ongoing deception he is experiencing is itself a harmful force.

"How is Evan?" I ask. While I have lived with one small piece of this secret, I find it mind boggling to think that Evan has been carrying the weight of a hidden death for ten years.

"Not so good. That's why I wanted to speak with you Dianne. Evan is moving away from us, and has asked the family to let the truth come out. I don't think any of us will pro-act on that publicly, but finally I am able to tell Freddy and Lulu."

Margaret reads the surprise on my face and calmly continues.

"Initially Evan was traumatized by what he had done, but then he buried it and played along with everyone as if the fictional story we were all telling was true. But over the years, a deep-seeded depression set in. The guilt would seep up and he would wrestle with it - again and again and again. And then on top of struggling with the memory of what he did he became fixated on how wrong it was that he had made everyone an accomplice too. The irony in all of this is that in his attempt to speak with Bill and help me and my children, his own wife and children have lost him. We all have lost him. He isn't who he used to be."

We sit in silence. All at once, I feel completely incompetent at reading life. I had thought that silence would protect Freddy and yet it was pushing Freddy away from his family and it had clearly destroyed Evan. I had read things completely wrong. I believed we were all safely walking along a road way together that was in a traffic free zone. But now the blinders are off and I can see we were actually all in the middle of a highway with cars racing by that could hit us at any moment. I thought Freddy and his family were safe with the silence. But they were never safe. They were being hit in other ways.

"Don't see this as something you were a part of," Margaret says, somehow aware that I have felt involved. "You weren't. You didn't see the damage, because we all hid that too. And for a while, with their father gone, the children did do better. We brought in a child psychologist to help with therapy around the abuse Freddy and Lulu had experienced. I insisted that we not hide that any longer. So that helped. But family lies are insidious and over time Freddy knew we were not being truthful with him."

"How will you tell Freddy?" I ask.

Margaret breathes in slowly, bends her head back and looks up into the tree tops overhead.

"I am so tired of all the pretending," she says. "I don't have the words yet. I keep trying to find them, and I am so scared of using the wrong ones."

And then she lowers her head and looks at me with a new softness and continues. "And then yesterday, there you were in the grocery store; someone who is so good with stringing words together in such a lovely way. I suddenly felt like you had been sent to me. Do you think you could help me with my words, with what I will say to Freddy? I think the words will really matter."

I look into Margaret's eyes and smile. "The words always matter. And yes, we can look for them together. You will lead us to the right ones."

We stare out at the blustering bay and shine our faces up into the warm sun. I understand now that the peace I could feel coming from Margaret yesterday existed because she knew she would be telling Freddy the truth. She knew that she would soon be able to set down the sack of heavy lies that she had journeyed with for years. But she was still looking for the words. Words can be hard to find if you don't have a chance to string them together, articulate them out loud in a place of safety and then adjust them so they truly reflect what you mean to say. And in my life, I have found that girlfriends are particularly good in helping with that process. I look over at Margaret and smile, grateful to have a chance to make amends for my silence.

# KATE

I loved the majesty of this house from the very moment I saw it. Approaching from the street and climbing up the pathway, I gazed up at the pillars stretching up to hold the portico's roof. The classic symmetry of the columns and the long tall windows on the first and second floor cast a spell on me. I felt mesmerized standing in the presence of this grand structure.

I knew Mom would have loved it too. I could imagine her clasping her hands together, leaning towards me and saying, "Well my Kate, look at how far you have come. No doubt about it my dear, this is an exceptional house for an exceptional woman!" I missed her cheerleading. When she died from pneumonia last year, I realized that she had in truth been gone for a long time. Memory loss, fear and paranoia were followed by her brain becoming unable to tell her body what to do and how to fight illness. How she would have loved this fabulous house. I missed not being able to share it with her.

However, the inside of the house was another story. Multiple disjointed renovations over time had led to a confusing and confining interior. And so now that I am free from work and have the financial ability to reach out and take what I want, I buy the house and begin an eighteen month renovation. I will forever have respect for those who take on any type of building project. I had no idea as I began, what an immense journey it would become. The sheer number of continuously appearing decisions was daunting. The ability for something promised to disappear into ether was mind boggling. And the number of details that constantly crisscrossed the mind at all hours, without smashing into each other, reminded me of the crazy intersections that Trevor and I stared at in Hanoi. Mopeds continuously drove all four ways at once and mysteriously did not hit each other. My head hurt with all the house activity, but I loved it!

There were lots of wonderful moments through the renovation. The day the gutting had been completed and Trevor and I wandered through the beams and dust, hard hats on and tracing out the new rooms with our fingers. The day the new walls were up, mouldings and floor boards nailed in and all smelling of fresh paint. And as we approached the one-year mark, and the focus moved to fabrics, carpets and furniture, there was the pure joy of visiting design centres and absorbing the colours and feeling the textures. I truly felt like a kid in a candy shop with a rather large allowance and I could buy every jube-jube, chocolate bar and licorice stick I wanted.

During that time Trevor's work was going very well. He was busy, keen and optimistic. Combining this with my excitement of creating a new home for the three of us, we were all in a very happy place. We had a couple of fabulous, spontaneous holidays. In the grey of Canada's winter, we jetted off to St. Lucia and stayed in a coffee and cocoa plantation that looked out towards the two Pitons, the island's curiously shaped volcanic mountains. We scuba-dived off the coast, basked in the sun and drank liquid chocolate every day. The next month we traveled to Costa Rica during March Break and hiked and zip-lined in the interior and then snorkeled and swam along the coast.

As summer approached and we were still a couple of months away from the house being completed, I picked up the travel section of the newspaper one day and read a piece about villas in Tuscany. A week later we were booked for a month away, travelling first to Rome, then Florence and then out into the countryside to experience living under the Tuscan sun. A day before we were to leave, Trevor announced that as much as he wanted to go with us, it wasn't practical for him to go for a full month right now. I totally understood. I had been a part of that world once. I was just very happy that he would be joining us for our last two weeks of vacation, when we were in the villa.

Sylvie and I had a wonderful time with private guides in Rome and Florence, who brought the ancient world to life. And we had an even better time strolling Rome's Via del Corso and Via Condotti, and Florence's Via de' Tornabuoni. Sporting the top designer fashion houses, these streets presented colour, style and excitement. As much as I had tried not to spoil her, it was inevitable that Sylvie at age thirteen wanted to shop like her mother, and she was indignant if we strayed from designer brands when it was her turn to find something. She refused to buy into the fact that I might keep my Gucci dress or Hermes silk blouse for life, whereas her figure would soon outgrow anything that I bought for her now. Quickly I realized it was probably a very good thing that Trevor was not here for the first part of the trip to witness the parade of shopping bags and the *over the top* invoices.

However, it turned out that Trevor's work kept him longer than initially expected. Sylvie and I had to plot how to make his one week (instead of two) at the end of our trip absolutely sensational. When Trevor's car drove up the gentle bend of the driveway, through the gates and into the grounds of our hill top villa, Sylvie and I ran out to him in our soft, flowing, newly-purchased summer dresses. All was now complete. We hugged him and bubbled up all around him as we helped him with his bags and talked excitedly about the little towns in the area, the cooking school we had planned for the next day and our upcoming trip to Sienna. While jet lagged, he appeased us and changed into his swimming trunks and joined us in the swimming pool that overlooked the countryside. That night we had a cooking service prepare and serve a fabulous meal outside on the terrace. Later we sat with warm blankets as we watched the sun go down. It was perfect.

Flying home together, with sun kissed cheeks and bellies that cherished memories of the most delicate of raviolis, my taste buds continued to call out for a glass (or two) of an Amarone, a Piedmont's Barolo or a Tuscany's Brunello di Montalcino. I knew then and there that the large wine cellar in our new home would have a special section to pay homage to these wines and our fabulous trip.

In hindsight, if the wheels are going to come off the car, one could argue that the bliss of not knowing allows you to squeeze

more moments in ahead of time. But I guess in reality, they were
more lies. While my memory wants to embrace our time in Tuscany
as practically perfect, there is a corner of my brain that is not so
generous. It has a more accurate awareness about fact and fiction and
reminds me that truth was hidden at that time and it was about to
shift into view.

"I think that maybe you and Sylvie should move to the new
home," says Trevor, after he has sat me down in our kitchen, about
three weeks after we arrived home from Italy. "It is absolutely
fabulous, and every inch of that place reflects you."

I stare at him, taking in his words and nodding my head. "Of
course, we are going to move there. I think it will be ready within the
week. I'm so excited."

"And I think we shouldn't sell this place and I will stay here,"
Trevor says, his head bent down with his eyes focused on the porcelain
floor.

My mind stretches to make sense of the words, tunneling down
and around a corner that seems just too far away to reach. I can't
figure out the puzzle and so I simply ask, "I'm sorry, I don't
understand. Why would you stay here? We have an alarm system. It
will be safe until it sells."

"I think we need to separate," Trevor says.

My limbs become numb and then gradually very heavy. I can't
move. I become acutely aware of my chest rising and falling. My mind
feels as if a crow bar has reached in and jammed the wheel that turns
it. I can't think.

"What?"

"I am having a baby, or rather Tina is having a baby. I am going to
be a father."

"But you already are a father. You already have a family."

"Yes, and no. Sylvie is not my real daughter. She belongs to you
and Phillip."

"What?" Now I am angry. How could someone who for years has

made it his goal to have Sylvie treat him like her father, suddenly decide to hand that back?

"What are you talking about? Sylvie is a real daughter to you and you are a real father to her. Don't you dare hurt her by changing the life you have built with her!"

From then on everything seems a bit of a blur. I am not quite sure what he said and what I said. I don't recall if I am the only one that pushed and hit. We both cried, but our tears meant different things. Mine were for pain and hurt received and his were apologetic and came from guilt. But the further we talked and the more I learned about his new partner, this new child that was on the way and his narration about what his life now was and what he wanted it to be, the more I understood that he had another world he had been living in parallel to ours. It was not a new situation and it had been in existence for a year or two. The truth of his lies came forward. I soon realized that Humpty Dumpty had truly fallen off the wall, and that there were pieces scattered everywhere, and I couldn't possibly put them back together again.

Now a few years later, and with multiple therapy sessions under my belt, both professionally and with trusted girlfriends, I can see that I missed the subtle change that occurred in him when his father died two years earlier. In some of our short and infrequent conversations after our separation, I learned from Trevor that his father's death made him realize he did want his own children. It was important to him. It provided a connection to his past by helping to create a piece of him to go forward in the future. And of course, he couldn't talk to me about that because that wasn't an option for us, and he had begun to feel a widening of our worlds. We were in different stages of our life. I was moving beyond work and he was deep within it. And then when Tina, beautiful, young, peaches and cream Tina began working with him, and she seemed to understand him so well and dote on his every word, somehow late nights at work were easy to fabricate. In time she became pregnant, which was planned and they began dreaming of their future. Later after we had separated and his baby son was born, a piece of him arrived that would move out into the future as he had hoped. His son's name, not surprisingly, was little Trevor.

Shortly after that devastating tell all night in the kitchen, I made a deal with Trevor. If he kept Sylvie as a focused and important part of his life, I would be generous in the divorce. Thankfully Phillip had been very firm with me about having a cohabitation agreement when Trevor first moved in and then a marriage agreement when we got married. Phillip was seeking to protect Sylvie, and in the end he certainly did. I had a way to keep Trevor's attention and help him to be the good father to Sylvie I knew he could continue to be.

Children are resilient and Sylvie learned to adapt. Trevor made Sylvie continue to feel special and the bonus for her was that she now had a baby brother. Within a year Tina was pregnant again and Sylvie was hoping for a little sister. I worried that she would be replaced as her daddy's little girl. But she wasn't. When Carmela arrived Sylvie dove head first into sisterhood and Trevor became more attached to Sylvie as he saw a beautiful, generous side of her develop.

I knew it was only natural that I would experience waves of jealousy when Sylvie would scamper out the door and into Trevor's car and be whisked away for a weekend with her other family. While I had imagined losing Trevor in my earlier days, I had never contemplated that his leaving meant I would lose a bit of Sylvie too. There were parts of her life I could no longer share.

I was thankful to have the Georgian Bay property up north to retreat to. Nicole had searched and found the perfect escape for us five years ago. There was no debate with Trevor about who was going to be keeping this property. It was a part of a world I had looked forward to joining for years and now I had more time to do so. Sitting outside on the large wrap around verandah I could breathe in life and be thankful for the beauty around me and for those who made a point of not leaving me alone.

Nicole would drop by and lead me through a peaceful Yoga session on the lawn or would head into my kitchen and cook up a storm. Her calm demeanor and take-charge presence allowed me to let someone else look after me. It was beautiful to see her so happy with Charlie. He was such a good man and it was confirming to know there were still good men out there.

Dianne would ride over and demand I get on my bike and head out with her, or she would turn up with a few new draft chapters of her book and we would be lost in hours of collaborative editing. Between Nicole and Dianne, I was called up or dropped in on, at just the right pace. I had time to heal in the silence, and time to grow as they listened to me and sprinkled out thoughtful and valued words.

And then there was Phillip, who visited and was always a voice of reason and sound counsel. His warmth and humour made me laugh again, and his choice of fine wines seemed to uncork the bitter moments that I needed to express and work through with someone safe.

"Sweet Kate," Phillip says as he walks towards me on the verandah with a glass of red wine. "I need your opinion on this Margaux. It is a Chateau Malescot Saint Exupery. What do you think?"

I smile and happily accept the thin rimmed wine glass, which clearly he has brought with him, always a stickler to drink fine wine from equally fine stemware. I eye him with a pursed grin as I first swirl the glass lightly, then bring my nose to the edge of the rim.

"It smells warm and wonderful," I offer, and then take a small sip. "Full fruit, a little tobacco. I like the dryness."

Phillip's smile broadens, a small dimple just below the right side of his mouth puckers in. I love that little dimple. It only shows up with his big smiles, and I am so fortunate to be the recipient of many of those.

"You Phillip," I declare dramatically but playfully, and looking up at him, towering over me, "Are a fine wine. You are ageing well. You have good structure and temperament, and leave those who interact with you wanting more."

"If we hadn't already tried and failed at a love relationship," says Phillip taking a seat beside me, and adding his feet one by one to the shared ottoman, "I would be responding to that flirtatious nature of yours in an entirely different fashion."

"Do you ever think about what life would have been like if you had insisted on raising Sylvie with me?" I ask.

"Sometimes."

"And?"

"I would have slowed you down Kate," Phillip says, raising his glass of Margaux to the last rays of light as the sun is lowering in the sky. "And frankly, you would have worn me out!"

We both laugh, reach out and clink our glasses, nod our heads in agreement and soak in the early evening unfolding around us. The crickets are out and seem to have taken over from the chattering birds. There is a light, warm breeze coming up from the bay. It beckons the ear to listen, and the skin is thankful for its soft touch.

"So, who are you consorting with these days?" I ask, with a wink.

"No official consorts at the moment, although there is this woman Carol, I have begun to ask out. It does seem though that the odds of finding someone interesting are in my favour these days. There are more healthy women than men in their seventies."

"I admire the fact that you are mixing with those within a five-year radius of your age. I am sure there have been some thirty-something-year-olds who have tried to put the moves on you. You are attractive, both physically and financially."

"Yes," Phillip laughed, "But who is the bigger fool, them or me, to think that this wrinkled skin and arthritic boned body wants to be around its antithesis. Ironically, I feel younger by being with someone closer to my age. I don't have to live a life of constant comparisons."

"I can appreciate that," I say, nodding my head. For the first time I contemplate how much easier it might be to be with someone my own age instead of being with someone like Trevor, who was a good ten years my junior. Gone would be the comparing of my partner's tightly toned skin to my slackening outer casing each time we happen to pass by a mirror together.

"Are you happy Phillip?" I ask, for no apparent reason, except that I care.

"Yes, I am."

"Why?"

"Because life has been good. Professionally, I had many great adventures. Friendships, I have laughed and grown with the best. Health, I have been blessed. In life, I have been challenged and I have come through. I did love my wife, but when she changed directions and loved someone else, we got through that and I didn't shatter. I have loved many since. I met you. I created Sylvie with you. How special is that? And now I get to swoop in and help out when your misguided partner does a U turn. I have never professed to fully understand relationships, but I do believe Trevor is a wingnut."

"Is that a real word?" I laugh.

"If it's not, I am happy to find another one. I have a long list of words I could call him."

We both laugh, and the warmth I am feeling is more than the wine. How good it is to be with Phillip, just the two of us. He looks over at me and smiles and reaches out and gives my hand a squeeze.

"You know I love you Kate, always have and always will. Love doesn't have to be hot and heavy. It is an underlying truth. It just is."

I can feel the tears coming and raise my finger up at him and wag it like a school teacher. "Enough. Don't do that. You don't want to see ugly black mascara snow ploughing down my cheeks!"

We both laugh and ease back in our chairs.

Later, as I get up and head towards the kitchen to pull some kind of dinner together, I pass behind his chair and kiss the top of his head. Standing with one hand holding my empty wine glass I reach down with the other and enclose my hand over his his. "And Phillip, for the record, I have and will always love you too."

# SEPTEMBER GIRLS' BIKE RIDE
# AT 55

"I think our new bikes are throwing off our timing," observes Dianne checking her watch as they lock up their bikes from their morning ride and head down the stairs to the pub for lunch. "I hope they are open. It's only 11.30am."

"They might not serve us a beer until noon, but I'm sure the door will be open," chimes in Kate, reaching out to push the door and smiling as it gives way. They walk into the small, cozy restaurant with wood beams overhead and knotted wood floors below, and point toward their favourite table by the corner window.

"How do you like your new bike?" asks Nicole.

"I am loving it!" says Dianne enthusiastically. "I can't believe the difference. I am so glad you let me borrow your bike in the summer. It was night and day compared to the one I had been riding for twenty years."

"Charlie is the one to thank," says Nicole with a warm smile, remembering his astonishment when he had examined her bike for the first time and saw how few gears she had. "I had the same experience as you. I thought I had a great bike. It was old, but it worked well. But then pushing down the pedal on a lighter, efficient bike, it was almost magical! The ease, the speed, all noticeably different."

"It definitely shaved some time off on our way here," nods Kate. "Maybe we are going to have to look at extending our bike route this afternoon ladies."

"I just can't believe how you two put up with how slow I was last year," Dianne says.

"Well," Kate kids, "We had thought about ditching you a few times."

Over the next hour, the pub fills up with other cyclists, dressed in similar tight lycra shorts and colourful jerseys. Helmets, originally stored on extra seats, are gradually stashed under the table as every chair becomes occupied. Patrons at each table lean in. Elbows resting on tabletops. Cheeks pressed into curled knuckles. There is a hum of overlapping words and dotted laughter.

"How's Sylvie doing in her new school?" asks Nicole, after Joey has taken their order for three beers and three large Niçoise salads.

"She loves it," says Kate. "I found it so odd that she wanted to move schools last year. You would think that after all the change with Trevor leaving a few years ago, and her back and forth to Trevor, Phillip and me, that she might want to keep one thing constant. But its almost as if she craves continuous motion. She seems to thrive on it."

"Didn't she like her old school?" asks Dianne.

"She never loved it. It was highly academic and not built with the creative child in mind. And when she began making friends through skating that went to Tremont Academy and then learned about their arts and drama program, her ears perked up. When she visited the school for an end of year stage production she was blown away, and the push to change became a full-time obsession."

"How did Phillip feel about that?"

"Funny thing was that Phillip was very supportive, and it was Trevor who was out of touch. While Phillip was very keen for her to get into a school that was a great feeder for a US Ivy League school, I think he figured her out early on and realized that wasn't really where she was going in life. Trevor still clings to the hope that it might still happen. As long as I'm paying for it, of course."

"What about you?"

"It's still a dream. But I realize now it isn't real. Which seems to be the way with a lot of dreams I've had over the years."

The mood shifts, and Dianne and Nicole instinctively reach out. Dianne pressing one of Kate's hands and Nicole squeezing the other.

"The benefits and annoyance of just being three of us at a small round table," smiles Dianne, "We can grab you easily at anytime."

Kate purses her soft lips into a tight smile and nods her head.

Joey arrives with beers and a boisterous "And here they are! A little piece of local culture for each of you!" The little town of Eisenberg has flourished with the success of the local brewery and the brew pub staff always make a point of ensuring everyone feels welcome and a part of their happy place. While in the early years they refrained from having a beer at lunch, that all fell apart the year of Kate's separation. That year they transgressed into a three-hour lunch with multiple beers, a rather dreamlike bike ride home, and a short nap before dinner. Later, an agitated Abigail had to rap loudly at their door to wake them up for their evening meal. Since then, they have transitioned to each having just one beer at lunch, and they unanimously agree it has been a positive addition to their bike ride.

"And how is Sam coming along with his new girlfriend?" asks Kate with a wink. She knows that Dianne is very protective over her son. While Sara is a force and acts with unbridled confidence, Sam who is younger and now twenty-three, is more pliable, sweet and trusting, and has had instances where others have dominated him.

"He is sort of beaming these days," answers Dianne tentatively. "Rebecca adores him – who wouldn't?"

"And?" asks Nicole.

"And, I think its okay. But I overheard something at a Bar-B-Q we had this summer that was a bit disturbing. Tom and I were off to the side, our back to the group, helping with dinner preparation. It was as if we weren't there really. And Sam and Rebecca and four of their friends were sitting around in a circle with their drinks discussing growing up, the world ahead and how everything suddenly changes when children arrive. Out of the blue Rebecca just said *Well, even though my body can have children I'm not going to have kids, so I won't have to deal with that.* It was so odd. It sounded so final, not even light, questioning or challenging. Just matter of fact."

"What did Sam say?" asks Kate.

"That's the strange part. I turned around and looked over and he was just sitting there, silent. He didn't react or respond. It made me think he must have heard this before. They must have spoken about it."

"Did you ask him about it?" asks Nicole.

"No. But I do worry about it. I will have to say something sometime. But not yet. They have only been together for six months. I have made it a practice not to jump in too fast. I would prefer to give the kids space and save my words for when I really need them. A parent's words tend to have more weight if they aren't used constantly."

"Good tactic," says Kate, "I should look into developing that practice. For sure some issues are bigger than others and it would be good to have some dry powder around for the big ones."

Joey is back, and three large salads land with panache in front of each of them. "And" he says, "Our infamous fresh buttermilk buns are just out of the oven. I will be right back." In a flash, he has disappeared and reappeared with the promised basket of buns, soft and steaming, buttery and delicious.

"I have to say though," continues Dianne staring at the melting pad of butter she has placed on her piece of freshly torn bun. "It hurts to think that Sam is potentially absorbing Rebecca's point of view about children. I have always told Sam and Sara: *You are the best thing your Dad and I ever did.* I said it so much that if I ever said *you know what the best thing your Dad and I ever did?* they would holler back: *We are the best thing you ever did!* It was super cute when they were little, and as they got older it was endearing. And just last Christmas Sam topped it off by hugging me goodnight on Christmas Eve and saying *I'm glad you and Dad made us.* How can a sweet boy like that not want to be a dad too one day? He would be an amazing father!"

"He *will* be an amazing father," soothes Nicole. "Its good you are giving it space and time. They are young and there is still lots of change to come if they are only six months into their relationship."

"My only regret about children is only having one," says Kate solemnly. "I agree with your statement Dianne. Sylvie is the best thing I have ever done. Funny how I have Phillip, not Trevor to thank for that. But I do wonder about the two children I lost. It can be haunting at times. What might they have been like? And then there is the other question. Would Trevor have stayed? That part becomes confusing. The further I move away from him, the less I like him. He doesn't seem to be who I thought he was."

Dianne and Nicole can feel Kate sliding backwards again. While it has been a few years since her separation, it is only a year now since the divorce. Through the separation Kate had lots of time to learn about Trevor's deceptions, both with Tina and with bank accounts and investments, that Trevor had managed for them. While their pre-nup was very clear about their own individual earnings, and named accounts, when funds were built up in joint name, that protection disappeared. Somehow during the year leading up to Trevor's leaving, there was a flurry of activity that seemed to distort the historic nature of these accounts. With Phillip's insistence, his accountant intervened and brought in forensic accountants who helped to restore the truth and nail the coffin shut with respect to Kate ever trusting Trevor's word again.

"So, while I am not in love with Trevor anymore. I do think about those ultrasounds and the tiny little hearts pumping. Those tiny moving shadows were en route to becoming real little people."

"I understand," offers up Nicole. "They are always with you. Those babies may not have had the chance to appear in this world, but they each had a spirit."

"You feel it too?" asks Kate. Nicole nods solemnly.

Dianne looks from Nicole to Kate, and then back to Nicole again. "Am I missing something here?" she asks.

Kate looks at Dianne and tilts her head towards Nicole. "I know that two miscarriages was terrible. But Nicole having three. Very tough."

Dianne sits silent as stone. She knows nothing about this. She feels herself drifting back from the table, and it's as if a webbed casing is creeping up and around her two best friends. They are wrapped up together. She is on the outside.

"No," says Dianne quietly, "I don't know."

Now it is Kate who is taken off guard. While the three of them have become the best of friends over the years, for a long time she had felt like the outsider. Often she felt it was she that was often uninformed. Dianne and Nicole had known each other longer, lived closer to each other and so visited more often. It just seemed illogical to Kate that Dianne would have missed knowing about Nicole's miscarriages.

"Look Dianne," says Nicole, "They happened a long time ago. I never talked about them. But when Kate went through her miscarriages I felt I should speak with her about them. It hurt to talk about them, but she was hurting. So I shared with her what had happened."

"But when did you have these miscarriages?" asks Dianne. "Did I know you then? Or was it before you had Jimmy? Was it before I came back?"

Nicole leans back, crunches up her paper napkin and then begins to smooth it out, before giving up and crunching it up again. "It was after Tessa," she says looking straight at Dianne.

Dianne thinks back to their visits while the children were young. Nicole had Jimmy a year before they first started getting together, and then Nicole had her second child Tessa. Within a year of Tessa being born Dianne became pregnant and Sara came into the world. A year later Dianne was pregnant again and Sam arrived. And all through that time, they pretty much saw each other every couple of weeks and shared their lives, or so she thought.

"So, while I was pregnant with Sara and then with Sam. Is that when you miscarried?" Dianne asks.

"Yes, one for one, and then one in-between," Nicole says with a smile that is not really a smile and more of a painted line on a mask.

"Why didn't you say anything?" demands Dianne. Her voice sounds hurt, but Kate can hear some anger building, which is unusual for Dianne, but Kate understands. This is rather a big deal to have missed out on for so long. Nicole's history of holding back was playing out here in a major way.

"Look," says Nicole, taking charge, "Remember who I was back then. I wasn't an open person. I hid a lot of what I felt. If I could have told anyone at that time, it would have been you."

"But why didn't you?"

"Think about it, Dianne," Nicole continues. "When you suddenly lose a baby, and no-one can tell you why it happens, and you are getting together with someone you care about, and they are really excited because they are pregnant, is that the time to share the news? I didn't want to scare you. You were so happy. So excited. I wanted to protect you."

"Sorry," mumbles Dianne, feeling a shift and beginning to understand. With her involvement in protecting Freddy Preston, she knows that a secret can be kept so as to protect. She understands this.

"But the hurt you would have been going through?" says Dianne, "I wish I could have been there for you. It's true though, I would probably have become scared about my own child. You know me well. I do recall being a little anxious a number of times during my pregnancies."

"A little anxious?" Nicole says tilting her head with a grin.

"Okay, very anxious might be a better descriptor," continues Dianne. "So, I guess I should be saying thank you. And also, I am so very sorry to hear about your miscarriages. That must have been such a painful time in your life."

As the table is silent, Dianne soaks in the past and its meaning. She is struck by the action taken by her friend. To have been experiencing such grief three times and choosing each time to keep it silent so as to let her live through two happier, less anxious pregnancies, that was one of the most unselfish acts she could imagine.

"Thanks Nicole," Dianne says. "You are the kindest friend."

"Hey, hey," jumps in Kate, "She is *one* of your kindest friends!"

"Of course," smiles Dianne. "How did I get to be so lucky?"

They return to their neglected salads and comment on the freshness of the lettuce and the lightness of the dressing, fully aware they are seeking a new subject.

"Well," begins Nicole, "I wasn't quite sure how to introduce this topic. When we were riding I told you a bit about the kids, but it seems that Michael had one more child that I didn't know about."

Kate and Dianne pivot their heads in unison towards Nicole as if they were dolls and a button had just been pressed at the base of their necks.

"What?" says Dianne.

"In August I ran into a carbon copy of a five-year-old Jimmy at the grocery store," laughed Nicole. "This sweet little boy and I nearly collided, and then his mother came around the corner and it gradually all made sense."

"Penelope?" asks Kate.

"Yes," nods Nicole looking curiously at Kate, "How did you know?"

"Don't you remember how you used to talk about how Michael was spending more time after hours at work?" continues Kate. "You seemed to doubt that it would take that long for Penelope to learn the administrative role you had left behind."

"Yes," Nicole says, nodding her head, "I forgot I had verbalized that. It's true, I suspected something might be up. But I was busy getting on with building my career and I wasn't sure if I was leaving the marriage or staying. I sort of blocked him and her out of my mind. But I never imagined a child might be the output of his time with her. Clearly this child is his, but this little boy was born after he died because she was never visibly pregnant when she worked for Michael at the office."

"Do you think Michael knew Penelope was pregnant when he was dying?" asks Dianne gently.

"I don't think so. Michael, affair aside, was an honorable person. If he had known, I think he would have stepped forward and wanted to provide for an unborn baby. It would have eaten away at him if he didn't, and I never saw signs of him being worried about Penelope. There was nothing left for them in the Will. I've been thinking about it a lot this past month. I have moved from moments of hurt, to moments of anger and then I fade back into a quiet place, where I don't feel anything bad towards Penelope. I actually feel a bit haunted by her sweet little boy's eyes. I was the one who was inattentive to Michael. And Penelope was attentive. Maybe he cared for her, but I don't think there was a huge fire burning. He never asked to see her when he got sick and the one time she came to visit she was with the other office assistant and the visit was short."

"If she knew and didn't tell him," reflects Kate "That was rather honorable on her part. She didn't want to pile that on him when he was so sick."

"I agree," says Nicole. "She moved out west after the funeral and after the practice was sold. She now lives with her sister in Vancouver. I have been wrestling with the knowledge that there is another child of Michael's out there. But getting angry doesn't make sense when I examine my behaviour in our marriage over the years. As you both know, I didn't know if I was coming or going at times. But where I have landed is that it does make sense to try to help this little boy. He is Michael's son and I think Michael would want to help in some way. I just don't know for sure how to do that."

"That would be a kind thing to do," Dianne says softly, "What help would you like to give?"

"I was thinking that maybe I could help with a university fund?" Nicole looks back and forth between her two girlfriends for feedback. "But I think maybe I should do more. Maybe some sort of monthly financial assistance. It would be good to know Penelope could comfortably enroll her son in sports and other programs, and handle the hungry, growing boy body she has on her hands."

"That sounds like welfare," blurts out Kate, and then apologizes. "Sorry, that was a bit blunt. What I mean is that maybe instead of a monthly payment, maybe an annual gift might work better. Penelope has already displayed her independence by coping on her own and she might find an ongoing payment a constant reminder of support."

"That's a good thought Kate, and absolutely no offence taken," says Nicole. "I am finding it confusing to see clearly on this one. Even the idea of tracking Penelope down for a conversation, that she might avoid because she thinks that it might be a confrontation, sets my mind spinning."

"And what about Jimmy and Tessa," asks Dianne, "Are you going to tell them about this?"

"That is where my brain really starts to hurt," says Nicole. "I don't want to dishonour Michael in any way. I don't know if Michael would have wanted his children knowing that he was part of another relationship. And then maybe Penelope may have views of whether or not it might be a good thing for Theo to know about his half brother and sister."

"Theo?" asks Kate. "That's such a sweet name."

"Theodore was Michael's middle name," nods Nicole contemplatively. "It is a nice touch that she did that."

Joey arrives holding a tray with three shot glasses. "A shot of brandy for each of you from the gentleman cyclist across the room." He signals towards a table by the door, and they all look over with curiosity. Dianne and Nicole draw a blank as they survey the four men seated together, with one rather handsome, slightly greying and refined looking man raising his glass towards them. He is sporting raised bushy eyebrows, a rugged jawline and a huge charismatic smile.

"I can't believe it!" exclaims Kate. She is clearly pleased and jumps up and heads over. While they are in their mid fifties, Kate's disciplined diet and orderly regimen at the gym has allowed her to keep a striking silhouette. Combined with her ongoing maintenance of porcelain skin, and regular visits to the dermatologist's chair, it is no wonder that it seems like the room parts like the Red Sea as she walks across it. While every table has their own conversation in play, a number of patrons appear to have taken a short recess, so as to watch this image cross the floor.

Dianne and Nicole look at each other, shrug their shoulders and grin. It is what they want for Kate. They would love her to meet someone. They just aren't trusting of her ability to navigate men. They remember her string of mishaps before Trevor, and they were alarmed and surprised to see the pattern reappear over the past year. For a smart woman who was so tuned in to details in her business life, they both found it rather curious how many signposts she seemed to miss along the man path. At fifty-five, it was a toss up as to which was the biggest dating time bomb – was it the married man who forgot he was married or the serial charmer, with no intentions of remaining in one relationship? Kate had met a couple of both. So, the question was, which of one of these was the gentleman who had sent the brandy shots?

Kate returns to the table, picks up the brandy shot, raises it up and smiles across the room and then turns towards Dianne and Nicole. "Okay ladies," she says as she sits down, "Drink up!" On command they clink their shots and throw them back, the heat and spice trickling through their chests. While a brandy shot at lunch is not part of their regime, they have become relaxed with age and are open to stretching their biking rules.

"So?" quizzes Dianne.

"He is a new money manager I met," says Kate. "His name is Kenneth. He is very smart, interesting and a lot of fun to be around."

"How did you meet him?" asks Nicole.

"Well, I was at a fundraiser for the Museum a few months ago. I was on my own. I had decided to get out and try to meet people, and so I bought a ticket. I was wandering through the exhibition of Egyptian Art and stopped at this one large, exquisite statue of a Pharaoh and his Queen. The stone was so smooth and I found the faces mesmerizing. I was just standing there staring at it and a voice behind me said *Art is beautiful, but it is not a good investment.* It was a bit jarring, but it all made sense when I learned that he had an investment firm."

"Interesting pick-up line," nods Dianne, "Do tell more."

"Well, during the night he did concede that some art can be a good investment, but in general he believes that there is a lot of art on people's walls that will likely re-sale at a fraction of what it was bought for. He explained that people tend to hold onto their art for life, so they don't often experience the re-sale process. To which I pointed out, that with divorce, one does experience the re-evaluation of assets during one's lifetime, but true to his point, that can be a time when one finds out that art hasn't kept up with its original purchase price."

"So, by this time he knows you are both a past buyer of art and a divorcée," says Nicole, "And how does this dance continue?"

Kate purses her lips and glares at Nicole, "What dance! I don't think he is really interested in me. He is more interested in my money."

"Have you invested with him?" asks Dianne.

"Just a little. And it has done well. So, I may invest some more."

"You say that he is not interested," says Nicole, tilting her head to the side and glaring at Kate, "But how about you? Are you interested?

Kate laughs, looks up, shakes her head and leans in towards her girlfriends. "Okay, you know me too well. I find him breathtaking. I enjoy being around him. He is divorced and currently single. Maybe with time, something might happen. I actually thought something was happening when he called me up and asked me if I would like to come as his guest to the Toronto Art Fair. Turns out that his company was one of the sponsors and he had invited a ton of people. It was rather funny actually. I arrive, thinking I was sort of his date, only to meet up with him and a large circle of people standing around, and then find out they are all his guests too."

"You're kidding," laughs Dianne.

"It was a classic record scratching moment. I had trolled Bloor

Street, found the perfect form fitting dress that was still modest enough, had my hair styled in that loose, messy fashion forward way, and then spent twice as long at my makeup mirror to ensure I looked as natural as a fifty-five-year-old woman can allow herself to look. And then, it wasn't actually a date. It was my investment manager asking me along with his other clients for a night out to look at paint thrown from all angles at paper."

Laughing and then quizzing Kate about the actual art seen, they wrap up the bill with Joey and head for the door.

As they pass by Kenneth's table, Kenneth reaches out and playfully grabs Kate's wrist.

"Hey gorgeous," he says, "Have you read the prospectus? Let me know. Happy to take you through it in person, one on one."

Kate smiles and leans in "It's the weekend, I am with my girlfriends, and so that won't be happening until next week. Have a good ride!" Kenneth and his friends echo the sentiment.

Walking up the steps to the bike, they all blink in the brightness of the early afternoon. Kate walks ahead and begins to unlock the bikes. Dianne looks over at Nicole, who has pulled back.

"What is it?" asks Dianne.

"I think a fox has entered the hen house," says Nicole.

"And that hen is totally oblivious?" asks Dianne.

They nod and head to the bikes, where an animated Kate is practically bouncing.

With the added alcohol, and their longer lunch, they agree not to extend their route this year, but promise to do so next year. In the past they have raced home for cocktails, but this year the mood is different. Whether it was the added brandy shot or meeting up with Kate's Kenneth (that has Kate a little hyper and Dianne and Nicole a little wary), they are less needy to get back to Abigail's for their first drink.

They pedal along in the sun, enjoy the mild breeze and take in the day. They catch up on Nicole's continued advancement with her real estate business. She and Amy have three associates now working with them, and business has continued to be a steady upward climb. They discuss whether Dianne should retire next year with her full pension, or keep teaching which only adds an insignificant incremental amount to her pension each year. Clearly the education system is seeking to retire the aged to make room for the young. They debate *But should the young be taught by the young or the experienced?* They ask Kate questions about her new consulting work that has her helping biotech start ups that are full of founders half her age, but curiously open to her advice. It seems that this industry, as opposed to the education system, values experience.

As they bike along the open stretches beside Georgian Bay, the wind blusters up and a chill sets in. They zip up their jerseys, and add another layer of clothing. Seeing white caps forming in the bay they look overhead. The sun is still blazing but there are some ominous clouds beginning to form. They quicken their pace, as they remind each other of past years where they were suddenly deluged by rain that poured from clouds that looked quite similar to those forming above them.

## Cocktails

Arriving at Abigail's they head in for warm showers. Wrapped up in cozy robes, they each cradle a glass of Kendall-Jackson Chardonnay. For the past couple of years, they have fondly referred to this wine as simply Kendall, imagining him as a friend who has so kindly produced such a delicious and reasonably priced wine for them. Dianne curates the music. Initially they bounce around to the Fine Young Cannibals, singing out that *She Drives Me Crazy* and then they settle down to the haunting melodies of Enya. Nicole pulls out the pretzels, and they crunch, munch and sip through their story telling.

Kate and Dianne nudge Nicole to elaborate more on her relationship with Charlie. Over the years Nicole has learned it is safe to speak about affection, but she always needs a little help to get started. She smiles warmly as she shares stories of her bike trip with Charlie from Amsterdam to Bruges, the cooking course they took together in Morocco, and their precious Sunday mornings. Sundays are reserved for them to read and pass articles and thoughts back and forth, which have had them learning together about national and global issues in great detail.

"Last year when Ebola struck West Africa," says Nicole, "We were reading one Sunday and there was a tiny article about an outbreak. Then as the weeks went by, we began to see the number of infections grow through Guinea, Liberia and Sierra Leone. I didn't know anything about these countries before. While Charlie can't fully trace where in Africa his ancestors came from, he likes to point out with a smile, that we all came from there if you look far enough back in time. Learning about their challenged health care systems and watching the death rate settle in around sixty-seven percent was so upsetting. It was terrifying to think that if you contracted Ebola, you were more likely to die than survive."

"That was very disturbing to watch," adds Dianne. "Some of my nine year old's must have been watching the news, because they came into class pretty upset. They were asking whether it would come here. How do you answer that truthfully? It did reach the US and Canada is a blink away. There are a few cases in the US now. So I said, *It could, but we are doing all we can to prevent that.* That is how I answered, but of course, I ended up with a call from a parent who wanted to know why I said that Ebola was coming to Canada."

"Lost in translation for sure," joins in Kate. "It is scary though to think it is transmitted from body fluids. Watching all those white and blue hazmat suits worn by both the medical care workers at the hospitals and the porters who would carry the bodies away, it looked like a science fiction movie."

They continue to contemplate the challenge of diseases around the globe. And Nicole debates that while medicines and vaccines can help, they take time and money to develop. And there is a constant push and pull between medicine for profit and medicine to help everyone. Who will pick up the reins and lead the charge to do the right thing? They all sit quietly contemplating this and they feel quite ill-equipped to answer.

Dianne breaks the spell with a small whisper, "Anyone like a little more Kendall?" Wine glasses reach out and they turn to an easier conversation about flavour and taste buds, acknowledging that they are seeking to escape the last subject.

In time Kate brings up Kenneth again. It's as if throughout she has been thinking about him, and wondering when to re-introduce him as a subject. Dianne and Nicole can sense Kate's interest, and are loathe to be unsupportive, but are confused about what their role is at this stage of life. She is not a naïve teenager or a *twenty something*. But they don't know of a guidebook for friends of the fifty-something divorcée. How do you keep them out of trouble?

"Don't you think Kenneth is rather handsome?" Kate begins.

"Well, yes," says Dianne, "He is rather beautiful to look at." She looks across at Nicole who is frowning at her, and she is reminded that encouraging Kate may not be the end goal here.

"And he is teaching me about investing in a way that is more engaging than others I have worked with," continues Kate. She recites learning about index investing, passive vs. active management, commodities and limited partnerships. Since Tom is the one who handles investments in Dianne's family, Dianne listens open mindedly, but finds it all a bit beyond her. Nicole listens with a more critical understanding. Out of necessity after Michael died six years ago, she has had to personally learn to handle their investments and learn how to invest the life insurance proceeds she received. With the continued healthy profits from her business, she has successfully managed her growing wealth with research, trusted advice, patience and avoiding anything that seems too good to be true.

"So how much have you invested with him so far?" asks Nicole. While she and Kate regularly discuss finances, Dianne is uncomfortable with Nicole's rather direct financial question to Kate.

"$250,000 so far. And it was in strategies that are shorter term and liquid – the analogy he uses for these are that from a time frame perspective, they are like a short hike, where after just six months to a year, a return has appeared."

"And what about this next one, with the prospectus that he mentioned?" continues Nicole. "What is that all about?"

"Well, that will be a couple of million dollars and it will be a longer-term commitment. That is more like hiking along *Hadrian's Wall*. I had to look up Hadrian's Wall after that meeting to understand what he was talking about. Turns out it is a very long wall that was erected when the Roman province of Britannia needed to protect themselves from the Scots. So, with that type of investment, which is invested in a combination of private resource-oriented businesses, I need to leave the money alone for a much longer period – for seven to ten years - so that it can grow without interference."

Nicole's curiosity is piqued. The term *Hadrian's Wall* is something she has heard in the recent past but she can't quite place where.

"Seven to ten years is a long time," Nicole comments. "I gather there is a premium paid to you because you are losing your liquidity?"

Kate smiles and nods, "Listen to you! Impressive. Yes, because I can't touch this investment for a while, the return is targeted in the mid to high teens, net of fees."

Nicole knows that with Kate's two equity events, a couple of million dollars is less than ten percent of Kate's overall net worth. So, it is not that this sum would be too much for Kate to invest in one well thought out investment. It is something else that seems to be scratching on Nicole's brain. *Who* you invest with, was one of the key principles she had learned and it had kept her out of trouble. Kate's chance meeting with Kenneth at the Museum, the short time they had known each other, and the charm that appeared to be a part of the mix, made Nicole feel uncomfortable about Kate's relationship with her new manager.

Checking the bedside table clock, they suddenly spring into action. Time has again sped up on them and they have a roaring fireplace and a candlelit table waiting for them downstairs. Having decided that tonight they will head downtown for some dancing after dinner, they pull on slim, dark pants and smart crisp cotton shirts that will breathe when the dance floor heats up. As Dianne appears from her room, her large silver loop earrings hang just below her short, blonde hair. They catch the light and Nicole reaches out to touch them. In turn, Dianne compliments Nicole on her fanciful dangling silver fan earrings, that are peeking through Nicole's shoulder length bob. Kate teases them about their attention to fashion details, commenting *what a bunch of girls we are*. And then Dianne and Nicole make a fuss about Kate's classic, large diamond studs that seem to wink as she settles her long, dark mane behind her ears.

## Dinner

As they walk into the private dining room, light and airy piano music is playing, accompanied by sounds of a soft drum brush and a woman's smoky, sultry voice. The room feels like a boudoir in Paris. They notice changes within the room since their visit last year. There are new purple paisley curtains drawn back with thick velvet sashes. The walls have been lightened to a soft cream and the fireplace mantle has been cleared of all the trinkets. They can hear the logs crackling as they begin to burn and one thuds as it shifts and settles into place.

Their three heavy, comfortable chairs sit waiting at their round table. The starched white linen cloth shimmers and the tall tapered candles, wedged into silver candle holders, are lit and beckon them to sit down and begin.

"This always has a slight feeling of being at a séance," Dianne blurts out, and then quickly checks behind her to ensure they are alone.

Abigail smiles at the doorway, "Well, I would say that you ladies practically have one of those, every year. With the depth you seem to dig into, if I was a spirit, I might come for a visit."

During this year's catch up with Abigail, she is relaxed and not in her usual rush to steer them to the menu. It has been some twenty-three years now that they have visited each fall. Kate asks Abigail if she has plans to retire. Abigail smiles and turns on the charm, "The day after you three stop coming here, well that might be when I might consider it."

As Abigail shares the theme for the evening, the Parisian music floating in the background begins to make sense. Tonight, is a toast to France. Having travelled to Paris, Dijon, Marseille, and Bordeaux last year, Abigail has been busy seeking to replicate what she tasted. *Soupe à l'oignon*, choice of *Ratatouille* or *Coq au Vin* and then a *Tarte Tatin* will be served tonight, and everyone is suitably impressed. A dry Chenin Blanc is ordered to begin the meal, with plans for a bottle of Chablis with the main course and a Sauterne with the dessert. Kate marvels at the wines Abigail has brought in to pair with her French cooking. Abigail smiles broadly and retrieves the first wine from the cellar. She uncorks it, allows Kate to taste it and then pours a generous glass for each of them.

"So Nicole, how is Jimmy and fatherhood coming along?" asks Kate. "I can't believe you are a grandmother!"

"It's a beautiful thing to watch your son with his own child. But it is not the grandchild alone that I am smitten with. It's watching my son light up!"

Nicole suddenly remembers their afternoon conversation with Dianne about Sam and his girlfriend's lack of enthusiasm for children. Understanding that this could limit the chance for Dianne to be a grandmother, Nicole shuts herself down.

Dianne shakes her head and says "No, no. Keep going Nicole. I want to hear about Jimmy, and not an edited version of it."

Nicole nods, assures Dianne it will all work out with Sam over time, and then describes how Jimmy, who can be so serious has become a clown around his new son. He is seeking a more balanced work and home life and is the happiest she has ever seen him.

"And Tessa," asks Kate, "Anyone in her life?"

"Maybe," answers Nicole, "But I don't think I am supposed to know. I do love how she and Charlie have become so close, but sometimes she shares things with him and Charlie is not sure if I am supposed to know. And then when he tells me and clearly I didn't know about it, he feels badly as he realizes that he must have been told not to say anything and he has forgotten."

"But that is not fair for her to do that with you and Charlie," chimes in Dianne. "Charlie is your partner, your confidante. Tessa shouldn't be wedging herself between you two."

"I'm glad you said that Dianne," says Nicole, "That is how I feel too, but I wasn't sure if I was being petty. I do want them to like each other and to be close. I just feel odd that she tells him things first and often in confidence."

"So," asks Kate, "There is someone?"

"I think it may be her roommate," Nicole answers, reaching for her glass and sipping this rather tasty piece of the Loire Valley.

Dianne and Kate pause, sit back and process this. Tessa is rooming with Anne Marie, who they have all met. She was the yoga instructor in town before deciding to move to Toronto around the same time that Tessa was attending school in the city. Fortuitously, a couple of years later they had met up around the time that Tessa was looking to upgrade her accommodations, having begun a new higher paying job in a marketing PR firm. They understood that they shared a beautiful apartment overlooking the lake.

"Well," says Dianne, breaking the silence. "How do you feel about that?"

"Spoken like a therapist Dianne," Nicole replies with a grin. "I am fine. It's a bit of a paradigm shift, for sure. But it doesn't change who she is or who I am. It's strange to think though that as her mother I didn't observe she preferred women. I did notice she never spoke about men. She always had boys that were friends. But she never seemed to swoon over any of them. That is the part I observed and found interesting. I thought she was very level headed with men, and in time would find one of them engaging."

"So, she hasn't actually had this conversation with you yet?" asks Kate.

Nicole shakes her head. "But I think she will soon. Charlie has been encouraging her to do so, and I think he is about ready to let her know that he has told me."

Abigail and one of her serving staff arrive with the *soupe à l'oignon*. As they carefully set down the earthenware bowls full of caramelized onions and beef broth, with bubbling cheese encrusted on top of crusty croutons, Abigail explains that this type of soup dated back to Roman times. Apparently, it was traditionally a peasant dish, although the current version dates from the eighteenth century. She elaborates that the unique flavour comes from the caramelization of the onions along with the adding of brandy during the slow cooking process.

"Brandy twice in one day," chirps up Kate. Abigail's eyebrows raise and Kate happily replays a rather long version of their encounter at lunch. Abigail takes all in, as a good hostess does, and then escapes back to the kitchen.

The soup is fantastic and the conversation turns to food, cooking, and Nicole's recent venture into holding themed cooking classes in her spectacular kitchen overlooking Georgian Bay. She has created a package that provides a cooking class for eight people and she has gifted this to three charitable groups in town as an auction item. So far two of them have been auctioned, raising money for the local hospital and the food bank. She has now hosted two fun filled evenings, one an Italian cooking class and the other centered around Turkish cooking.

"What a great idea Nicole," says Kate, "I need to sit back and figure out a way to help out and give back. For sure it won't be in the culinary field."

"You could help out in the medical research area," suggests Dianne. "Tom was talking about it just last week. There are lots of innovative medical devices that need help to move towards commercialization. But our health system, while full of brilliant scientists, doesn't have great marketers and business people. He is trying to get his boss to allow some of their engineers to do some pro-bono work, but he said they need other business experience in there too."

"Hmm, that does sound compelling. Maybe I could speak with Tom?"

"Absolutely."

After the soup bowls are cleared away, Nicole's *Ratatouille* arrives, followed by *Coq au Vin* for Kate and Dianne. The Chablis is opened and chills a little longer at the side of the table, as the Chenin Blanc is emptied. Kate teases that their drinking is not what it used to be and they are running behind.

"Dianne, did the publisher get back to you about the cover illustration for your third book?" asks Nicole.

"Yes. They are hoping that the illustrator will be able to carve out time to do it after Christmas. Three more months to wait on top of the two we have already waited. Its crazy to think that the cover of the book is holding up the printing and launch of this book."

"I think we all underestimated the time lag in the publishing business," says Kate. "Remember when your first book was picked up so quickly? Everyone was amazed. It can take authors three to ten years to get a publisher interested in their first book. Yours happened in five months."

"But then," chimes in Dianne, "There was the editing, re-editing, cover illustration, business and marketing plan details. Followed by the *tut tutting* that I can't travel to the number of book readings because I teach and am not allowed time off during the school year. Did I not mention that I was a school teacher when we started?"

"Well," says Kate raising her glass, "At least all the effort created a well received book, even if it was received a good two years after it went into the mammoth grinding machine."

"Well, it gave me lots of time to write the sequel," says Dianne cheerfully. "I did appreciate not having the pressure of critics looking over my shoulder. They didn't know about the first book yet, so I could write the second one in peace."

"Do you think this delay with the book cover is because you

decided to go another direction with your third book?" asks Nicole. "I mean, if you had agreed with them and done a trilogy, instead of insisting that the story ended after two books, do you think this third publication would have gone faster?"

"For sure," interrupts Kate. "For sure it would have gone faster. They had all of the inroads built because of the first two books, it would have been very easy to shoot the third one through. That illustrator would have been pulled off a job is my bet. The publishers are very fond of a proven story line."

"But," says Dianne, "I am writing for the joy of it and the message I want to share. So, I am good with the decision. I actually like this new book the best. I prefer the world my characters have entered and I am in love with the little heroine. This might be one that I could create a trilogy around. But I will have to wait to see where the characters and their world take me as I go along. Its always an adventure. I never quite know where it will all land."

"It is really quite remarkable to watch you create these worlds," says Kate, sitting back, nursing her glass of wine. Then she perks up and declares, "Anytime you want to jump into mine and rewrite it, feel free to do so!"

Abigail returns with the server to clear their plates away. Dianne and Kate make a big fuss over the *Coq au Vin*. Nicole peppers Abigail with questions and compliments about the *Ratatouille* and then announces, "I think I may have the menu right in front of me for a French themed cooking class, although it sounds like parts of it may be more work than some participants may want in their evening out. I am learning that within each group there are those in the cooking class that want to cook and there are those that simply want to watch and eat."

After, as they sit resting, a young man enters the room and stokes the fireplace and adds more wood. They engage him in playful conversation. He is a university student, working here on weekends and is clearly trying to determine how much conversation is appropriate to have with guests. He initially holds back, but as Kate and Dianne continue to pepper him with questions, common points begin to intersect. It turns out that he is in school with students who have come from Port Colebrook, and he asks if they would know Freddy Preston. Thankfully he doesn't notice the pause in the air at the mention of Freddy's name. Dianne quickly jumps in with some kind words about Freddy, and then as the young man leaves the room, Kate and Nicole turn to Dianne, their eyes asking for the inevitable update.

Dianne has known this moment would come and she has given it great thought. It is time to admit that the deception within Freddy's family has had a toll on the family, and so she concedes that what Kate and Nicole had suspected was true. Keeping a secret had been harmful. While she doesn't share the exact details, she explains that Margaret has now told Freddy the truth, and soon Margaret will share it with Lulu too.

"How did Freddy react?" asks Kate.

"He was angry," Dianne replies. "He said some terrible things to his mother, and then he methodically sought out each of his uncles. Let's just say, that didn't go smoothly. Some physical restraint was needed."

"So, are you going to tell us what happened to Bill?" Nicole asks.

"No," Dianne says. "I think it is best if you know what the town knows, which is basically a mish mash of the truth. I still believe that it is not my story to tell. And that way, you two are more removed from all of this. Is that okay?"

Kate and Nicole look at each other, nod slowly and then look back at Dianne.

"Just promise us that if this secret starts to hurt you, you will come to us?" says Nicole.

"And remember," Kate weighs in, "We don't want walls going up between us, okay?"

"Okay," Dianne says, "I promise."

They sit back, peer at each other with resolved grins and realize that they had best change the topic. It has been some time since they have been able to touch on the subject of Freddy and end the conversation without angst present.

"So Kate," jumps in Nicole, "how is Phillip?"

Over the next few minutes, they learn about Phillip's new relationship with Carol. Both Kate and Sylvie approve. Carol is just five years younger than Phillip, who is now seventy-five, and she keeps Phillip active with sports, long walks and dinners with friends. Kate talks about Phillip's ongoing love of golf, tennis, living in Florida, visiting Sylvie and Kate, and his insatiable appetite for anything with nuts.

"I swear," says Kate, "Phillip has died and gone to heaven if you show up with peanut brittle or make him a pecan pie! And he is so much more relaxed than the man I met years ago who lectured me about my finances, and followed every investment and career move I made."

Nicole leans forward. A frown has surfaced on her face. "Does Phillip know about your investing with Kenneth?"

"No, and I think its about time I did some investing on my own. Kenneth thinks so too. He spends a lot of time with his clients to help them understand the details, so they can be independent and make their own decisions. I can't imagine bringing Phillip in to watch over me on this. It would be embarrassing. I'm fifty-five. I'm not a child!"

"Are you sure that someone you have only just met is someone to trust with that much money?" Nicole continues. "The term *Hadrian's Wall* actually sounds ominous to me. I guess I don't like the idea of being separated from my own money for long periods of time. Investing is never a straight line and its safer if there is flexibility."

Kate seems to be oblivious to Nicole's growing anxiety on this subject. "Don't worry, I am doing my due diligence. It will be fine. Although, I doubt you and Kenneth would see eye to eye, Nicole. He is not a big believer in putting too much money into second and third properties. He calls them *Mirages*– they look like a great investment but..."

"They are *over extenders of capital?*" asks Nicole, finishing Kate's sentence and sitting up straight. The haziness around the *Hadrian's Wall* analogy, when mixed with the *Mirage* term, suddenly allowed her brain to rearrange some puzzle pieces and bring the answer into focus that had been eluding her all evening. She now clearly recalled a client who had been bidding on a property last year and was beside herself because she couldn't get her investment manager to release funds that were supposed to be available to her. She claimed that the *Hadrian Wall* period had concluded many months ago and all the funds were to be deposited to her account, but the date to receive them kept moving out in time. While Nicole did not understand the *Hadrian Wall* term that was being used, she clearly remembered this woman's investment person continuing to advise her to stay invested with him and to stay away from real estate. Having worked with properties for years, that both appreciated in value and provided a lot of enjoyment, Nicole found the term *Mirage* quite offensive.

"Yes," laughed Kate, "Exactly! Properties beyond your principal residence are *over extenders of capital*. That is what Kenneth believes. And you have to agree that properties do eat into cash flow more than people expect. They constantly need servicing. Lots of extra payments come up for taxes, maintenance and unexpected expense surprises."

Nicole nods. She thinks. How will she share tactfully with Kate all that she knows about Kenneth? How will she outline what came to light as she helped her client through a messy round of threats and appeals, in order to have the money released?

"*Tarte Tatin*, accompanied by your Sauterne" announces Abigail, who has been standing at the door listening and now walks through the door with the tarte, and is followed by a server carrying their sweet dessert wine. As she places the upside-down apple pie in the middle of the table, adjusting the candle sticks so as to make room, she explains that it is believed this tarte began life as a mistake. Back in 1898 the hotelier Stephanie Tatin was making a traditional apple pie, when she accidentally burnt the apples, sugar and butter. To hide her mistake, she placed the rolled-out pastry on top and put it into the oven. This upside-down dessert was a hit and became the hotels signature dish.

"So, mistakes can sometimes be good," Abigail says with a smile, and motions to the server to pour the Sauterne. "In cooking, and sometimes in life mistakes can lead us somewhere new. But, there have also been lots of mistakes in the kitchen that you can't fix. That also happens in life."

Kate, Dianne and Nicole nod in agreement.

"Well said. Abigail, any other wise words for us?" Kate chides.

Abigail pauses, stands back and folds her arms. "Don't push each other off if you don't like what you hear. I think you know each other better than you know yourself. Keep listening to each other."

The room is silent. Abigail nods, stares directly at Nicole, nods again and leaves the room.

"Did God just speak?" asks Kate with a laugh.

"Maybe," says Nicole softly, exhausted just thinking about the conversation she will have to navigate in the near future with Kate.

"Okay, enough. Who is going to cut into this wonderful *Tarte Tatin?*" asks Dianne.

As the decaf coffees arrive and they enjoy bites of their tarte and sips of their sweet golden wine, they revert to memory sharing and *remember when* becomes the beginning of every story. After so many years, there are lots of memory boxes to unpack, some that one or two of them have vivid images of and others that all three recall clearly. Ageing minds becomes a topic for a moment, and then they overturn that and delve into holiday and travel plans for the year ahead.

As they wrap up dinner and are about to head upstairs to grab their coats and purses, Nicole breaks away and checks in with Abigail. She finds her leafing through some cookbooks at the back of the kitchen, a steaming herbal tea keeping her company.

"Why did you look at me like that after you spoke to us?" Nicole asks.

Abigail pulls out the chair beside her and motions Nicole to sit down and join her.

"I'm glad you picked up on that. That man Kate is talking about. I don't like it. She is clearly enchanted by him. And when money and a single woman are courted, I'm sorry, I get wary. Plus, you are wary too. My bet is on you understanding this all better than Kate."

Nicole then shares the pieces with Abigail that she has only just put together. She expresses that she could be wrong. It might be a different person. But she will be checking in with her business partner and the client and will get all the facts straight before confronting Kate.

They sit quietly taking it all in, shaking their heads and thinking.

"Thank you for not being the perfect hostess Abigail," says Nicole with a grin.

"Pardon?" asks Abigail.

"Thanks for listening in and for not minding your own business. It helps that I am not going to be rattling around in my head on my own tonight. I will sleep a little better knowing that you too think I'm heading in the right direction."

"Be prepared that she may still shrug it off. If he is as charming as he sounds, he likely has a hold over her. She may need a really good hit over the head. Men are conned by beautiful women. And women are conned by beautiful men. Nothing new in that."

"If I have to, I will speak to Phillip. I do have his number. It feels awkward, but maybe that is why these things happen and don't get stopped. Friends don't like to get into each other's business, especially when its about money. And the shark that is hunting is counting on the bystander preferring to stay dry and leaving him alone with his catch."

After a few more shared words around people, life, food and cooking courses, Nicole heads up to join Kate and Dianne. With suspicion turned to conviction, hesitation has turned to a resolve for action. She doesn't know exactly how she will knock Kate over the head, but she is committed to figuring out *this Kenneth*.

## Dancing

The three of them stand side by side in the vanity mirror in the large corner room, slightly inebriated from the wine they have enjoyed throughout dinner. They pull out their lipsticks one by one and each of them draws a smooth creamy line across the soft skin of their lips. Nicole's is an orange rose colour. Dianne's is a soft pink. Kate's is a defiant red.

"Let's go," shouts Kate, reaching for her coat.

"Do you want to head back to that little pub bar we stopped into a few years back?" asks Nicole.

"No," jumps in Kate decisively. "We are heading to Ricky's Roadhouse."

"That was a long time ago," smiles Dianne. "It was a bit of a zoo."

"I'd be up for a smaller place," suggests Nicole.

"Come on," grins Kate. "If we are going out, we might as well go all out!"

And so, charting their course, they move swiftly in the cool autumn night along the sidewalks, jay walking and skipping lights so that they don't have to stop and risk the chill fully soaking into their bones. It dawns on all of them, and they comment, on how the warmth from alcohol helps to dull the sharp icy pinch of the night. The reward awaits as they open Ricky's front doors and the pumping hot air blasts against their cool faces. The smell of spice, grilled foods and garlic jumps forward and the DJ's music pumps out with full force.

The opening lines from Madonna's *Express Yourself* is beginning to express itself throughout the room, and Dianne is practically bouncing as she lights up and looks back and forth between Kate and Nicole. They wave Dianne forward, motioning that they are happy for her to go dance, and they will figure out a table for them. Dianne pauses, and then takes off to the dance floor, sure to meet up with fellow dancing soul mates.

Kate and Nicole follow the hostess to a table in the middle of the room. Nicole checks out Dianne who is bopping about on the dance floor, nodding her head in agreement that one shouldn't settle for second best and agreeing with Madonna that you have to *Put your love to the test*. While Nicole smiles and sits down, Kate remains standing and peers carefully around the room, doubling back and retracing parts of the room she has already scanned. Nicole sits back and eyes Kate, and grins knowingly.

"So Kate, are we expecting someone?" Nicole asks, having to shout over the noise in the room.

"What?" Kate asks, sitting down and picking up the menu and then cocking her head towards Nicole, blinking in an exaggerated manner that begs a stage.

"When exactly did Kenneth and his friends mention they might show up here?" Nicole shouts.

"Any time now," Kate answers with a wink. "You can't blame a single girl for trying to spice up things, right?"

It was true, thought Nicole. Kate was single. There was nothing inappropriate for her to orchestrate an encounter with Kenneth, who was also, apparently single. Nicole decides that tonight she will pull back from her current instinct to find the jugular vein in this new investment advisor.

As Madonna's voice fades away and the music winds up and into a new song, Dianne pops off the dance floor and finds them.

"Nice table," she says, "But for the next great song, you must come out and dance, okay?"

Nicole smiles, but doesn't nod. She is thinking maybe she has drunk less than Kate and Dianne and she may end up being too serious for a fun night out. This is when a tray of shots would be helpful, but she will be the last one to suggest that. As it turns out, it's as if her nemesis has read her mind, and suddenly Kenneth, his three friends and a tray of tequilas shots have landed at the table.

And now all starts to move in slow motion. Chairs are added to the table and their group of three is suddenly seven. The noise of the dance floor is dwarfed by the low, strong voices of men with big chests, rugged jaws, wide shoulders, and confident, handsome faces. The focus is you *must* join in and down the shot. *No* is not an acceptable answer, and *yes* becomes the easy, but inevitable way to another yes. And then a second tray of tequila shots arrive.

Next, Kenneth has ordered B52's, which he describes as the perfect after dinner drink.

"A layer of Kahlua, with a layer of Baileys Irish Cream and topped off with Grand Marnier," he announces, "What better way to end a meal!" Everyone drinks one, some impacted more than others.

Kate and Dianne join in without abandon, whereas Nicole pauses before succumbing. Kenneth is fascinated by Nicole's hesitation. He stands, circles behind her chair and crouches down, reaching his arms along side each of her arms which are resting on the table. His head is an inch from the right side of her face.

"I see you," Kenneth says to Nicole. His voice is just loud enough for her alone to hear. "You are watching. You are not sure about all of this."

Nicole turns abruptly to face Kenneth head on, and is met with a soft smile and eyes that practically sparkle.

"I'm not as bad as you think," Kenneth says, with a seriousness that makes him seem less inebriated than his friends.

"But I don't think you are all good," says Nicole.

"Who is all good?" Kenneth winks. And then he adds, "So Nicole, you are a runner?"

"Why do you ask?" asks Nicole.

"I can see how your flesh lies lightly and evenly along your bones. It is beautiful."

Nicole freezes. She suddenly feels undressed. She can see Kate on the other side of the table looking at her with a pensive frown and she can tell that Kate is trying to make out what is being said.

"Thank you," Nicole answers, feeling the alcohol forming a layer of protective insulation around her, but still aware that things are not as they should be.

The music begins to seep through Nicole's consciousness. Maybe she can now hear it because Dianne is madly waving at her and pointing her thumbs towards the dance floor. This gives Nicole's brain the chance to change lanes from Kenneth's attention to the dance floor. She hears the iconic voice of Cher filling the room and she jumps up, steadies herself and then leaves the table and heads with Dianne to the dance floor.

Nicole welcomes the anonymity of a mass of people enjoying the music. It is a safe haven. She floats with the sound and energy around her. She watches as Dianne begins to do *her thing* and step into the role of Cher. While Dianne does not have Cher's long lean body and fish net stockings, she certainly knows all the words of the song and inevitably finds a few others on the dance floor who do too. Soon Dianne and her new found dancing friends are off into an elaborate shared enactment of Cher's concert performance.

Nicole smiles at the words within Cher's song, asking if you *believe in life after love*. "Yes," she says out loud to no-one, "I do." Her new life is now with Charlie, after a quieter, disappearing love with Michael. Knowing she is in a mild but pleasing alcoholic trance, she tunes out the world and reminisces with a peaceful smile as she dances on her own.

While the music pounds, and many flail about her, Nicole floats pleasantly into a mindless state. And then a smiling face looms in front of her. Kenneth is reaching for her hands and playfully begins to jive with her, slowly pulling her towards him and then pressing her away. Nicole finds this mildly irritating and pulls back wondering where Kate is. Looking about she spots Kate dancing beside Dianne. Kate is casting a pained look towards her and Kenneth, and Nicole attempts to move away. But with the dance floor filling, it is tough to find open space to move to. Everyone is being pressed together and now two intoxicated young women have pulled Kenneth and Nicole into some sort of team rugby huddle. Nicole finds this all very confusing. Too many hands are moving from shoulders to waists and hips. As the dance floor begins to form a human wave, with an undulating movement floating around the room, Nicole can feel an old but familiar panic rising. She shakes off the touch of others and pushes out through the crowd.

Cher holds her final note. The dance floor breathes in and out, and then launches into another frenetic song. Nicole, feeling a little nauseous, heads towards a nearby door that has been letting patrons out into the cool evening air. Dianne follows her and immediately pounces.

"What are you doing?" Dianne asks.

"What... are you ... talking about?" Nicole answers, her words spaced more than her head intends.

"Kenneth, that's what I am talking about. I know you wanted to keep him away from Kate, but you seem to be getting a bit cozy with him yourself"

"I'm not doing anything! He just popped up."

"Well cut it out. Its pretty confusing for Kate. I can tell she is about to lose it."

"Maybe, I should just head out," says Nicole. "I am not feeling that great and if I drink anything more, I am liable to pass out."

"No, no, no. Sorry, please stay," pleads Dianne. "Let's just stay away from Kenneth and you and me can stick together."

As they head back inside, they weave through the restaurant and bar and can see that Kate is holding court at the table. Her animated story has caught Kenneth's full attention and his three friends have moved in close. Hands brushing arms. Another hand reaches out and squeezes her leg. A hip engages her hip. From afar, an octopus comes to mind, and Dianne and Nicole stop and watch.

For a brief moment, Kate looks up and sees Dianne and Nicole, but then she turns away, clearly signaling she would prefer that her two friends keep their distance.

"I think Kate is fully aware that Kenneth is a bit of a player," says Dianne. She pauses and then shakes her head as she continues, "I know I am not a financial person, but it seems to me if she is not sure she can trust him with us, how can she trust him with her money?"

Nicole turns and looks at Dianne. She couldn't agree more, but isn't sure if she is capable of stringing together a constructive sentence as a response. She simply blinks and nods.

Over the next hour, Kate enjoys Kenneth's full attention and Nicole makes a point of visiting more obscure corners of the room or dancing on her own with Dianne and some new found friends on the dance floor.

As the evening wraps up, Adele's voice comes out over the sound system. Powerful and melodic, it is a perfect song for an intimate dance. Kenneth and Kate are in a slow, close embrace on the dance floor, and Dianne and Nicole sway and grimace as they watch their friend.

As Adele laments that *sometimes it lasts in love, but sometimes it hurts instead*, the room comes alive with voice. It is as if every woman in the room croons along with Adele, and relives a past love that pushed them away. Nicole smiles watching the puzzled faces of the men around the room. If they watched closely, they would see and learn about women and their frazzled emotions, and maybe some do.

Thankfully when the music stops and the lights are turned up full, Kenneth's friends have additional unfolding plans to attend to. All of these plans include more alcohol, and so Dianne and Nicole are able to pry Kate off of Kenneth and drag her home. As they wander back to their B&B, Kate is predictably effervescent and starts to plot out her call on Monday to Kenneth and her plans for getting together with Kenneth next week to look at her portfolio.

Nicole shakes her head and stops in the middle of the sidewalk. She pauses, and then speaks bluntly and with force. "Kate, you have got to separate your personal relationship with him and the money side of things."

"I will, but it would be best if you stay out of it," Kate says coolly, staring at Nicole straight on.

"Kate," adds Dianne, "We are just trying to help."

"I don't need this kind of help," Kate continues, with anger forming. "And I don't need either of you speaking to Phillip about

Kenneth either. I need your word that you won't call him or try to interfere. Okay?"

"Okay," Dianne says, feeling like child, and not liking it.

Nicole remains silent.

"Nicole?" asks Kate. "Do I have your promise that you will leave this alone and keep Phillip out of this?"

"Yes," says Nicole.

Nicole's *yes* seems to be the only answer that would allow them to move past this moment so they can head home to bed. But her *yes* is a reluctant one. The pressure to answer screams of coercion. Later, Nicole calculates that it was not Kate forcing Nicole to answer, but rather Kenneth's force over Kate that was creating the situation. Inside Nicole's head she can sense her brain busily redacting her promise. But she decides to keep that to herself for now.

2020

# NICOLE

To think that what wrapped our minds up in knots a few years back was about how to pull Kate out of pending trouble. It seems like such a small thing now, in comparison to the complexities that 2020 brought.

But back in 2016, we were on a mission. After searching out a number of frustrated investors who had difficulty in liquidating and leaving Kenneth's investment fund, Dianne and I were consumed with debating Kate about her decision to invest more with Kenneth. In the end I did call Phillip and explain all to him. He stepped in, but with a different set of tactics. Working behind the scenes with a private investigator, he was able to piece together a string of relationships that Kenneth was having with a number of his female clients, ranging in age from twenty-one to seventy. While Kate seemed able to excuse Kenneth for inconsistent reporting details and potential but unproven fraud, learning that he was in fact bedding a number of his clients, while stealing casual hugs and kisses from her, woke up the dragoness within her. His smile and charismatic way were no longer something she found charming. Instead, she stormed in and confronted him, and in time dislodged her investments, or at least most of them, as some losses did occur.

But my part in this ended up severely damaging my friendship with Kate. She was furious that I had pulled Phillip into the picture after she had expressly told me not to tell him about Kenneth. I thought that after she was distanced from the situation she would understand and be happy that I had helped. But she seemed to have little time for me. She said I wasn't who she thought I was and she would never trust me again. Dianne has worked hard to smooth over this rather big bump, but Kate remains noticeably distant and politely tolerant when she is around me. It is as if I have regained my very early position as an acquaintance, and that the built-up friendship over the years has evaporated. Kate will carry on with lively stories and laughter, but she almost acts as if it is just her and Dianne alone in the room. I don't seem to exist when she is there. Besides running into her a couple of times shopping in Port Colebrook, I have only seen her at our annual bike rides and dinners. Kate arrives just in time for the bike ride, puts on an act through dinner and leaves the next morning before breakfast. I have been relegated to the single room and Kate has been wearing industrial ear plugs as she shares the larger room with Dianne. I know if Dianne wasn't pleading with her, she wouldn't be showing up at all. I think it may be time for me to just step away from this, because I don't really know what *this* is anymore.

Dianne has explained to me that Kate was incredibly embarrassed by what happened. She has had a hard time accepting that if Phillip hadn't stepped in, she would have lost a lot more money along with her self-respect. Dianne says that Kate feels a permanent change in how Phillip views her now and blames me for that. She thinks Phillip has started to treat her more like a child than an adult, and she finds it infuriating. Dianne believes that Kate is blocking the truth and she simply won't revisit what really happened and deal with it. Somehow Kate has re-written the story and believes that she would have come to a realization on her own and extracted herself without help. Dianne and I grin and raise our eyes to the sky, not believing that would ever have happened but feeling powerless to change her mind.

But breaking away from that toxic relationship, did allow Kate time to figure herself out and make some better choices. She met Ellery. Through Dianne, I learned that Ellery was a quiet, smart, unassuming scientist turned Professor, who was in the process of retiring and joining a couple of advisory boards. Apparently, Kate had told Dianne that there weren't electric sparks flying, but that was nice for a change. I was really happy for Kate. But when I saw her last and said so, she glared at me and said, "And so I suppose you would like to take credit for this, because you got me out of Kenneth's clutches?"

Thankfully, I have lots of other distractions in my life. Charlie and I continue to thrive together. We have wonderful visits with both his children and mine, and the grandchildren are growing in number. Jimmy has three and Charlie's boys now have six between them. And then there is the new addition of Theo and Penelope in our lives.

Four Christmases ago, suspecting that Penelope would come home to visit with her parents, I tracked her down and asked her out for a cocktail. As we sat on the bar stools at Bellamy's, she fidgeted with her purse as we waited for our *Naughty but Nice* Cocktails to arrive. I had rehearsed my lines with Dianne, and was thankful for Dianne's blunt and open style that allowed me to comfortably begin by just blurting it all out.

"Penelope, I shouldn't assume anything, but I want you to know that I am totally okay if something happened with you and Michael."

Penelope went completely still and raised her eyes to me with some alarm, but with a touch of curiosity.

"I may be wrong," I continued, "But Theo reminds me a lot of Michael, and that is a good thing, I promise."

"How long have you known?" Penelope asked slowly, her face flushing as she looked down at the bar's counter top.

"From the first day I met you and Theo in the grocery store. Theo looked just like Jimmy."

Penelope nodded slowly, and a strained closed mouth smile stretched across her face.

"Did Michael know?" I asked.

"No. He didn't. He was so sick. I didn't want to give him one more thing to worry about."

The bartender, having been busy mixing and shaking up bourbon, orange, ginger and cranberry, appeared with a big smile and a boisterous *Merry Christmas!* as he placed a colourful concoction down in front of each of us. We picked up the martini glasses, eyed each other, raised our drinks in a small, silent toast, and then sipped. It was delicious, and I think we both found the alcohol helpful. Over the next hour, we relived the year leading up to Michael's death and then how each of us had dealt with it afterwards.

"What you need to know, Nicole," Penelope said at one point, "Is that Michael would never have left you and your children. He made that very clear. I think he believed that you were in a bad patch, and that you two would eventually figure out how to get out of it."

"So, what were you hoping for in your relationship with him?" I asked carefully.

"I was pretty young and naïve. I see that now. I was smitten by him. I loved his serious intensity. His occasional smiles made my day. And he really praised me for the work I was doing and I know now that I didn't get enough praise growing up, so I was enamored with being told I was good at something. I just thought somehow things would work themselves out."

I asked about what Theo knew about his father, and Penelope said that she had told him that his Dad's name was Theo and that he had died before he was born. She decided it was best not to call him Michael and so chose Michael's middle name instead. She had told Theo that his father would have loved him very much. She admitted that she wasn't sure if that was true, and she didn't know what would have happened if Michael hadn't gotten sick and had to deal with a child outside of his marriage. But for the sake of Theo's sense of self worth, that was the version of history she had decided upon. She wasn't sure what she would do over time as Theo was beginning to ask more about his father. What did he look like? What did he like to do? Where did he grow up? Did he have brothers and sisters? She was finding it was getting tougher and tougher with a six year old to tactfully change the subject.

In time we got around to the topic of how she was doing financially. It turned out that she was managing fairly well on her salary, since she lived with her sister's family where rent was low and there was built in baby sitting. Theo had pseudo siblings in his cousins, and her brother-in-law's family had accepted him as another grandchild to keep an eye on and help out with. She knew she had been very lucky about all of this. And she had been dating someone over the past six months, who was kind to her and Theo, and she was beginning to see a healthy future there too.

Remembering Kate's advice from the year before when we had all been close and had pondered through ways to offer help, I asked if I could help with an annual gift where maybe some of it could go towards sports and extracurricular programs for Theo today, and some of it could be invested for his future university or college education. I have to say I was pleased to watch the surprise in Penelope's eyes and then her adamant pushing away of the gift. While it confirmed what I had hoped about her character, it did mean that it was going to take a little longer to get her to accept the gift. But nothing that a second round of *Naughty but Nice* cocktails couldn't fix!

Later on, as we wrapped up our conversation, gave each other a tentative but warm hug and left the bar, I slipped Penelope an envelope, saying, "This is not money. It is worth more." She opened it and pulled out a four by six inch photo. A smiling Michael looked up at her.

"Please take this for Theo," I said, staring at her intently. "You will know when you might want to give it to him. It makes sense that he will want to know where he came from. It's okay to tell him."

I watched as her eyes filled up. She blinked and the tears came loose and rolled down her cheeks. Her pretty face contorted with emotion and her shoulders trembled. I wondered about the pain, loss, sadness and worry that this young woman had carried for the past six years. I marveled at her sweetness and resilience. I concluded that Theo had a really good Mom.

Now four years later, I couldn't be happier when Penelope and Theo visit each summer and Christmas. And after Penelope and Mark were married last year, Mark visits with them too. I love to see the way Mark engages with Theo and ruffles his hair affectionately as he passes. He seems like a kind man and that he will be a caring dad. A few months after her marriage, Penelope approached me and suggested that now, since Theo did have a family, maybe the annual gift should stop. I asked to discuss that in person when she was home in the summer, and then I pulled her out again for cocktails at Bellamy's.

"Penelope, if Michael were here, he would be helping," I said as we sipped our Smokey Paloma's, the tequila, grapefruit and smoked salt packing a solid punch in our mouths.

"I don't know if that is true. I sometimes think that maybe he would have been angry and have pushed Theo and me away. I am thinking that maybe it is time to just move on."

"You had a private relationship with Michael, and I won't pretend to know how you each felt about each other. But what I do know is what Michael stood for and believed in. I know you weren't sure if Michael would have helped, but I can tell you for sure that he would have. And if Michael were here and if he was watching Theo grow up, he would be so impressed with you as a mother. He valued family and children. He was always a devoted father. While I am sending the gift to you each year, you and Theo have to understand it is absolutely a gift from Michael."

Thank goodness for Penelope's openness to reason and her ultimate wish to love and be loved. She was able to accept the logic that each gift she accepted helped me as much as it helped her and Theo. I needed to know that I was doing what Michael would have wanted. It made me happy.

This was also a good time to speak face to face about how she and Theo had found meeting Jimmy and Tessa, my two children and his half brother and sister. From watching them all meet the summer before, I had thought it had gone well, but what I didn't know was how they had all kept in touch since then. Jimmy had sent a birthday gift to Theo this year and Tessa had visited when she passed through Vancouver on business. I found it interesting that my children hadn't told me about this, but realized that they, like me, were finding their own way forward on how to adapt to the results of their father's affair.

In time we would likely talk about it more freely, but for now I would wait for them to find the words.

And then 2020 arrived, and the world turned upside down.

2020 was to have been Charlie and my year of travel and discovery. With Amy and our team able to handle our growing real estate agency, I was beginning to step back from work. With Charlie in the midst of selling his sporting goods chain to Craig and Angie, a young couple who were keen to have their own business, he too had time opening up. We made plans in January to ski for ten days in Vail with friends. February would be a month in a rented home on the Atlantic Ocean in Florida, with Jimmy's family visiting us. March would be our time to be home and then on April 3rd we would head to South Korea and Japan for six weeks of travel. The plan then was for our spring and summer to be home, enjoying Canada, and in the fall we had a cooking course in Lisbon, followed by travel through Portugal and Spain with Dianne and Tom.

The first part unfolded beautifully.

Vail. The crunch of snow boots, the rattle of the gondolas and the swoosh through feathery white powder. I can still feel the warmth of the sun and the cool of the cold. Skiing with Charlie was a movie all of its own. His athleticism was in full display. He said that moving through the freshly fallen snow was like *carving cream*. We visited the powdery back bowls up top, glided through open glades and pounded short radius turns through evergreens and naked blonde aspen trees. Bluebird skies on one day gave us time to gaze out at the stunning mountain range. A blizzard the next day provided an adventurous and nail-biting time to bundle up, stay close to each other and watch carefully for out of bound markers.

Après ski was always the time to gather with friends and make a few new ones. Inside cozy bars our cool skin would hit the sudden heat of wood burning fireplaces. Climbing the stairs, in our full ski gear with worn out quads and glutes, we enjoyed Almresi, a little piece of Austria with old, stressed wood floors, beams over top, carved chairs and alpine table cloths. Pulling up our stools at the long wooden bar, we joined friends for a crisp, cold beer, a cider type gluhwein and large hot pretzels with a choice of mustard or spiced pork lard. Prost!

The next day our Après ski brought us to a packed Pepi's for cold, light Pilsners served in crockery beer mugs. Rod Powel, an icon in the après ski life of Vail, entertained with guitar, songs and stories. We stayed for a couple of lively sets and then headed off for dinner. Somewhere across the ocean the COVID-19 virus was traveling from China to an Italian ski resort and then on to Vail. Six weeks later, Rod would become Eagle County's first coronavirus victim.

In February we settled into a beautiful home by the ocean in Del Ray Beach, with a covered verandah where we could soak up the warm blustering breeze coming off the Atlantic. Walking the long sandy beach, with a wide brimmed sun hat, I loved the feel of the sun kissing my skin and my toes dancing in the water. Charlie preferred to jog up and down the beach, but I loved to walk in the sand. That gave us each time to think and soak in this sunny place, and then we spent the rest of the time together golfing, biking or flipping through pages of books we had saved up to read while we were away.

When Jimmy and his family arrived to join us for our last week, the world was beginning to move down a surreal ramp, that felt very slow at first, but had no back up button, and in time would speed up. While we moved freely and felt safe during our first three weeks in Florida, during our fourth and last week it was clear that the coronavirus had boarded planes from Asia and Europe and it was beginning to quietly spread in North America.

While no cases had been reported loudly around us yet, I remember random actions I took, that now tell me that my brain had registered what was coming. Instead of using the mats provided to us in our morning yoga classes at the Colonial Hotel, during our last week I went out to Marshalls and bought new, safe yoga mats for each of us. While visiting grocery stores, drug stores, and big box stores I began to look for hand sanitizers, and found it curious and alarming that I couldn't find any. And whenever a stranger began a bout of coughing or sneezing nearby, instinctively I would pull the family together and bolt out the door.

Our last evening in Del Ray was a Saturday and we had reservations in *The Office*, a family friendly restaurant on Atlantic Avenue. Looking back the whole evening seemed perfectly cast as a super spreader event, if by chance someone social, loud and gregarious with the infection had shown up. Packed together with Jimmy, Shayna and our three little grandchildren, we were just one of forty tables jammed side by side. Everyone was involved in animated conversation, laughter and diving into their ribs and barbeque chicken. Later we walked along Atlantic Avenue, Charlie and I holding hands, rubbing shoulders with strangers on the packed side walk. Jimmy's family dodged and darted past happy and intoxicated tourists and peeled through the open retail stores and candy shops. We were not oblivious to what was coming, but as yet we weren't taking the full safety measures that we would soon learn to live by. We felt life was about to change, but for that moment we hung on to the night and enjoyed being anonymous in the large, friendly crowds. I remember feeling extremely awake and aware and pulling in the energy around me. Soon we, like Asia and Europe would be running for cover. That stroll along the Avenue felt like our last hurrah.

Ironically there were hot spots developing in Florida, but thankfully we didn't fully understand this until we were all back safely in Canada. Arriving home during the first week of March, we were fortunate and avoided the mass line ups in the airports when Canada called its citizens home a week later. With stay-at-home orders and non-essential travel cancelled, our year of travel slipped away. We became stationary and an empty calendar stretched in front of us.

While for some life became simpler, ours was initially mixed with creative chaos. Amy and I worked with our realty office to reinvent how to help sellers sell and buyers buy. During shut downs it was quieter and then when restrictions were lifted, the market became frenetic and a record number of transactions happened. 2020 became a very profitable year. Similarly, Charlie dove in to help Craig and

Angie re-configure how to sell sporting goods online, arrange smooth curbside pick up procedures and then how to reopen with safe protocols when restrictions eased. While real estate was spurred by the wish for a bigger or better living space or a more cost-effective living arrangement if one was overextended, sporting goods soared as the masses began to look at how they wished to reconfigure their free time. Bikes, skateboards, running shoes, cross country skis, snowshoes and more flew off the racks and shelves, and the sporting goods industry experienced a boom in business. Inventory for Charlie's stores eventually became the problem, as supplies from out of country or overseas thinned, some becoming paralyzed in the Port of Montreal strike.

In time, when Charlie and I could see our respective businesses were surviving, and in fact thriving, we were able to pull back and be thankful for having such capable people in place. We joined the quietly cocooning part of the population, who were slowing down and enjoying the simple pleasures in life. Our runs and bike rides became more precious. Our occasional safe visits with family or a few friends out on the back deck in the summer, were golden moments relived for weeks. Lucy, our golden retriever, loved this new world, where we were around, which meant more walks, cuddling and treats. We both pulled out old hobbies and interests that had never been put aside on purpose; there simply hadn't been enough time to fully explore them. Charlie built up a wood working shop in the garage and in time family members began to receive personalized sitting benches. I pulled out an old guitar and with the help of online tutorials and my teenage camp song books, I toughened up calluses on the finger tips of my left-hand and became lost in music of years gone by.

As a parent, there is always a fear present about the welfare of one's children. I lived hoping the kids could beat COVID if they were infected, and then suddenly that challenge surfaced. Shayna called in May to let us know that Jimmy and the whole family had tested positive and they were all in quarantine in their little home in

Toronto. They had been visiting with another family, seeking to form a bubble with them. Unfortunately, the mother of that other family had been exposed to the virus through a parent in a long term care home.

I had such a difficult time with staying put, not visiting and not swooping in to help. Two years earlier during the flu season I had arrived with fanfare to help Shayna when she and two of her three children were bed ridden with the flu, and Jimmy was in the US at a conference. Making homemade soup, doing the laundry, and reading stories to little Jamie, Carrie and Campbell, was as much therapy for me, as it was help for them.

How can you not be *doing* something when those you love are hurting? With COVID, I was instructed to stay in my home and let that sweet, sick family of five, battle it out on their own. Jimmy never fully shared all the details, but for two weeks he said, they went down a black hole. The combination of dealing with splitting headaches that medication couldn't fully relieve, the debilitating aches and pains in joints, and the odd sensation of lungs in jeopardy was terrifying. The children's symptoms were milder, but the fear Jimmy and Shayna carried 24/7 about the wellbeing of their three little ones, added a layer of constant worry and a heart stopping terror whenever a child called out. By June they were fully recovered, and thankfully there were no lingering lung concerns. They hadn't dodged the bullet, but they had survived it.

Tessa, pregnant and in her last trimester with her first child, was always on our minds. While we all avoided medical facilities where a sick person might be seeking help, Tessa was entering them on a regular basis, as she was considered a high-risk pregnancy due to elevated blood pressure readings. In late April she gave birth to Michael, cherishing her father's memory by giving her son his name. She and Anne Marie then went into hiding with their new baby. With remote work the norm, they could run life behind closed doors and keep out the danger lurking outside.

Charlie and I had to satisfy ourselves with drive by visits to see little baby Michael. We would drive an hour and a half to Toronto and park outside their recently purchased small semi-detached home. They in turn would stand in their front bay window, curtains pulled back, waving and smiling and communicating through a cell phone. Initially we could see a little tiny bundle in their arms. In time that grew into moving arms and legs, and a little bald head turning towards us and then away. By the summertime, we were able to join them on the back porch and once we all could easily access COVID tests, we coordinated testing and a real visit. While I was delighted to be able to hold and cuddle this beautiful new grandson, the wave of joy and love that overwhelmed me was when I could finally hug my daughter, this brand-new mother, and hold her close and breathe her in.

Now it is mid October. Gone is the heat of summer with long walks on safe open fairways, biking everywhere, and visiting comfortably on back porches. Back in late September, Dianne called and said that since it wasn't safe or possible to gather at Abigail's for our annual retreat, she and Kate thought that we could set up a date for an end of season bike ride. I asked Dianne if Kate really wanted all three of us on the bike ride, and she insisted Kate did. I am finding that hard to believe, and I did suggest to Dianne that maybe it was time for me to move on. But Dianne was pretty tenacious. She called back yesterday and instructed me to be ready. With time more flexible these days we are following weather apps, poking our heads outside each morning and waiting for the perfect warm, sunny day. The call will come any time now, as there seems to be a temporary warm front moving in.

# DIANNE

It seems like each day I am encountering a curious scenario that could be scripted within one of *The Twilight Zone* episodes. These moments certainly fit the definition of *lying within the mental state between reality and fantasy.* I wonder what Rod Serling, the creator of this 1960's TV series, would think of our world in 2020. Having included fantasy, science fiction, absurdism, dystopian fiction, suspense, horror, and psychological thriller into his themes, often concluding with an unexpected twist, I suspect he would find inspirational material all around us today.

Through door #1 - *the grocery store.* The meat, fish, frozen vegetables and eggs are sold out. Toilet paper, paper towels and every form of disinfectant has evaporated. The household cleaning aisle stretches before me like a bowling alley, the shelving on both sides pretty much looking like vacant gutters. The flour is gone. Where did all those yellow bags go? However, the image that is still etched in my mind is an elderly gentleman, with a scrunched up brow, pushing an empty shopping cart up and down the grocery store aisles. I must have passed him four times, and still nothing had moved into his cart.

Through door #2 - *the hardware store.* Clearly all the shoppers were scared silly to be there. We all avoided each other, turning down an aisle whenever another shopper was approaching. This was before masks had been mandated although a two metre distancing was recommended. But the staff seemed to have missed that memo and stood close together in groups of four to five people, talking and laughing. If there was an airborne particle to share, they would all have been a party to it. However, the surreal moment was when I received a "Can I help you?" from behind me. I turned around to find a smiling twenty year old a foot from my face, who seemed absolutely confused when I pulled back in alarm.

Through door #3 - *the reading of "The Globe and Mail" online.* What is astonishing is that the only news is COVID news. The subject of one hundred percent of the articles on the home page and inside each of the sections of the paper is COVID. Generally, it is reporting on the spread of the virus, the cancellations of events and the devastation to multiple industries. At one point I made a concerted effort to find a non-COVID article so as to avoid the subject. I couldn't, and so turned off the iPad and picked up the book I had bought just before heading into lock down. However, Erik Larson's *The Splendid and the Vile*, a recounting of Churchill's experiences during the Blitz, was hardly the escape I was looking for. As I turned the pages and the bombs rained down on London for a year, killing forty-five thousand Britons, I found an uncomfortable parallel forming. While the Londoners lived with uncertainty every night, not knowing if it would be their last, the world I was living in was on pins and needles, waiting for an invisible enemy that might appear and strike at any moment.

Tom and I were so fortunate that with my retirement from teaching last year, Tom took a two month leave from work so we could travel. We explored parts of Canada, the US and the UK, basing our path on book readings that my publisher had arranged. At the time I snapped so many pictures and didn't know what I would do with them all. But in the end, they became a great escape when the pandemic hit.

During the first few months of COVID, I simply did not have the hope and optimism needed to visit my imaginary worlds and write. I couldn't find characters and messages to develop. I decided to put the writing on hold and instead focus my attention on creating a photo book of our big trip. Not only did it allow me to side step my writers block, but it also provided a way to document and relive, in great detail, a very special time in our lives. Tom would lean over me as I progressed and his stories were added to mine as the pages developed. After a full month of compiling and editing, we proofed the final copy, paid the charge, pushed the send button and in three weeks our much-anticipated photo album arrived in the post.

Do I miss teaching? Yes. Do I miss teaching through COVID? No. Am I worrying about my past students and all the children seeking to learn and grow through this difficult time? Absolutely. Can I do something to help? Let me try.

During the summer, I reached out to the web of grade three teachers through a blog that had been created during the time of my first book, and that continued to be a source of connection with a community I knew. I asked if I could help in any way, and many began to book me for Zoom appearances with the classes they believed they would be teaching either in person or online in the fall. My task would be to read in the most animated way for five to ten minutes from one of my books, talk for five to ten minutes about being their age and loving books and wanting to write my own one day and then open the floor for questions. If we could incite a wish to read or write stories, then maybe that would help to reinforce that, even at age nine, you can take control of your newly closed up world and find a creative force to help power you through it.

Tom too, found a way to help through the company he worked for. Carmichael & Sons Tool & Die Inc. was considered an essential service company as it produced parts for both the auto industry and for a number of manufacturing companies. With the early shortages of personal protective equipment, Tom identified that his company had a large supply of the N-95 masks that were desperately needed by front line workers. He knew their plant workers would be fine with lower calibre masks and brought this forward to Henry Carmichael. Henry was delighted to help and made a point of personally driving the boxes of masks to the local hospital. Next, Tom approached Henry about retrofitting one of their unused machines so that it could produce protective face shields for front line workers. Henry was ecstatic with the idea. Tom had always enjoyed working with Henry, and had been loyal and stayed for over twenty years even when others tried to hire him away. His reason for staying was in full display when he went in one night to pick up some files that he had forgotten to take home and found Henry tinkering on the machine they were in the final stages of retrofitting. The plant was empty, but there was a light on in the back of the shop floor. There was Henry bent over with a flashlight fiddling with one of the sprockets. Seeing Tom, he looked up and smiled. "Should be good to go tomorrow Tom. Thanks so much for initiating this. We can't kill the virus, but we can do our part to help to keep people safe." The next day boxes of face shields were rolling out the door and heading to hospitals throughout our region.

Both Sara, now 31 years old, and her boyfriend Connor, became our biggest fans. They loved to hear about the initiatives we had both built. It was strange to see our daughter, who had always been highly critical of how the world worked, veer away from negative comments and make a point to become part of the solution. Identifying that there were so many isolated elderly men and women living on their own in their community, Sara and Connor developed a network of friends to take on the charge. Through phone calls, Facetime and Zoom conversation, they created a friendly outreach program, and then tacked on a free pick up and delivery service for groceries and medical prescriptions. I saw their relationship strengthen in a most beautiful way during this time. And for the first time, I saw the softer, kinder side of Sara come out. I wondered if perhaps she had hardened as she grew up so she could battle the world. But then when the real battle came, she found that by taking down that armour she could in fact do more and handle life better.

And sweet Sam? Well, two years ago, after three years in a relationship with Rebecca, he realized that he loved her but not enough. He loved children more. He wanted to be with someone who wanted to share a future family with him. I found this difficult to share with Kate, since Trevor had left her so he could have children of his own. But Kate caught me side stepping the news and in her typical, direct style, informed me that Sam was no Trevor and she was so happy that Sam had made the decision. Of course, it helped that Sam had always been the lovable child that Kate had been smitten by. He could do no wrong in Kate's eyes.

The shut downs and isolation during this time were particularly hard for Sam, who was on his own. At twenty-eight years old, he was doing well financially and so a year before COVID hit he had moved out from years of rooming with friends and now had his own place in Toronto. He worked remotely from his small rented condominium, and felt like a hamster in a cage, especially when he hopped on his bike, that was set up on a stationary trainer and looked out over the city and the masses of tall condominium buildings. He imagined himself running madly on the hamster wheel. "Just call me Harry the Hamster" he would say, each time we talked to him. We courted him to come home and take over his room for sleeping and Sara's old room as his office, but he wasn't ready to leave the city just yet, even if he no longer participated in it. I think his optimism that life would return to normal sometime soon was higher than most.

But in early June, after three months of isolation, he hit a wall. We could tell from our weekly Zoom video calls that he wasn't sleeping well and suspected that on top of not shaving he wasn't showering much either. Then one day we saw a gaunt and disoriented face staring at us through the computer screen, and his voice and wandering conversation was most disturbing. Tom and I got off the call, jumped in the car, drove to Toronto and landed outside Sam's door. It took ten minutes before Sam let us in. It was a disaster and he was definitely out of sorts. Over the next twenty-four hours, as we helped to clean up both him and his living space, we reached out on-line and through friends, trying to find a counsellor or therapist. The system was completely tapped out. Sitting Sam down and talking through his mental state became circuitous. In the end we just asked him to trust us and let us bring him home for a short stay. Somewhere deep inside Sam, there has always been a core that trusts. Thankfully it was still there, and he slouched into the back of our car and slept the whole way home.

After a few weeks at home, where a local therapist opened up evening hours so as to accommodate the demand of so many young people in need, Sam surfaced. Gradually the cheery, optimistic young man returned. As the summer progressed, he began to split his time between the city and coming up for short stays with us. And as he experienced that staying with us, meant that he could easily grab a game of golf through the week and ride his bike on trails that weren't packed with people, his childhood home began to become a preferred location for living through the pandemic. And later on, we learned that a friendly encounter with a young woman on the bike trail was definitely an additional reason for the amount of time he spent with us during the summer and fall.

As the leaves are changing, but life and plans stand still, a long winter stretches before us. There are whispers that vaccine results will soon be shared and we are all holding our breath, hoping for the miracle shot that will stop us all treading water and let us swim to the shore and climb out. I am tired of having to remember each step in a self established regime. Drive car to the store of targeted purchase. Park car. Place mask over mouth and nose and ensure it is properly attached. Pick up mini purse and ensure wallet, keys and hand sanitizer are in it. Lock car. Enter store. Sanitize hands and cart handle. Move quickly and efficiently up and down the aisle following the arrows on the floor. Don't get within two metres of another shopper or be prepared for a steely glare or the odd fit of rage.

And through this difficult year, the heartache of missing time with Nicole and Kate persists. While I keep in touch with each of them separately, it is completely depressing to have lost what the three of us had when we were all together. I can appreciate Kate's point of view that Nicole made a promise and she broke it. But equally I understand why Nicole broke that promise and I am very glad she did. I certainly didn't have the courage to do what she did. I think Nicole understood better than me the extent of the financial damage that Kenneth could do. And I believe that for Nicole, her actions were visceral. Having had a past where Nelson had some sort of control over her for years, she could not stand by while Kate was manipulated. I don't think Nicole even stopped to think, "Should I do something about this?" She just did whatever it took to protect Kate.

I have tried to explain this to Kate. She listens with a flat face and then changes the subject. I feel for Nicole. I know she misses our band of three, and is beginning to push back, resigning herself to the fact that the friendship won't be restored.

Fortunately, I do have another outlet for girlfriend companionship. In March, when we all went into lockdown, my three writing buddies and I began a 5pm Friday night Zoom. Two years ago, I attended a writer's retreat in Prince Edward County. Held at a small, local hotel, the program provided intriguing lectures, quiet time to write, and social evenings to share new writing and fabulous food. But best of all, I met Kim, Mary and Carol. While our writing styles and the genres we wrote in were different, we all agreed that when one has a book on the go, which was pretty much always, it was like having a monkey on your back. It was always on your mind. By the end of the program, we had formed *The Monkey Club* and we kept in touch as each of us went on to finish our next book.

When COVID hit, Kim reached out with a Zoom link to all of us and we began what has become a cherished weekly event. At 5pm each Friday we close out the week together with a cocktail hour. We cover all kinds of subjects, although the US elections, racial riots, the *orange* man leading our southern neighbours and his non-response to the pandemic, have been dominating our discussions of late. Each of us have our drink of choice, with champagne being a favourite and a good cabernet beginning to make a showing as the weather has turned cooler. Some weeks we sign off as we hit the one-hour mark, and some weeks we are on a roll and the clock disappears. We have watched each other rotate between busy and tired, optimistic and happy, and worried and sad. We aren't always having the same type of week as each other, which means we do seem to take turns steadying the boat and turning up the light at the end of the tunnel. It has become a very much valued anchor each week, in a world that is constantly shifting and drifting.

# KATE

"Ellery? What kind of a name is that?" quizzed Sylvie, screwing up her face into a ball as we strolled along the Halifax Harbour walk. I had come to visit her during her third year at Dalhousie University where she was studying creative non-fiction, journalism and plenty of unfiltered self-expression.

Knowing Sylvie's fascination with language, I too have become curious about words and was prepared for her question. "Well, the name is related to Hilary, and is a derivative of hilaris, which means cheerful, which Ellery certainly is, however I would never stretch it out and call him hilarious. He is definitely not that." I smile, thinking about Ellery and the blanket of calm that surrounds him. It is peaceful to be with him, but lately I have been wondering if his relaxed nature is possibly bordering on boring. My smile fades somewhat and Sylvie watches, tilts her head and knits her brow.

Over the next hour walking the seawall and enjoying an unseasonably warm January day, I share with Sylvie how my new relationship is progressing. I knew that she would be doubtful, as she has witnessed a number of my rash choices since my divorce six years ago. However, with the encouragement from Dianne, I had come out to speak with her about Ellery, since this relationship, now six months along, was different in a good way. There was absolutely no worries or angst. He was smart, reliable and gentle. Life was smooth. The reason for my discussion with Sylvie was to begin to prepare her. I knew that soon Ellery and I would broach a decision about living arrangements and I wanted to be sure Sylvie had time to meet him and hopefully approve.

A month later, during her winter break, Sylvie came home and met Ellery. She was a little distant at the beginning, but warmed up over the week. While he was all science and she was entrenched in the arts, they were both well read and shared an intense curiosity about politics and current affairs. They were also skilled debaters. I generally felt ill-prepared when I sat down with them and a contentious topic came up. But staying quiet and letting them both have the floor turned into a good thing. In a short period of time, they grew to fully appreciate each other. Mission accomplished!

During the summer, with Sylvie's *thumbs up*, Ellery spent a lot of time under our roof – well, actually two roofs, as we rotated our time between the city and up north in our Georgian Bay property. While initially I had thought Ellery would give up his condominium, he didn't seem in a hurry to do so. At first I was perplexed. He had initiated the idea of living together early on. I had just assumed that would mean becoming full time partners, and sharing the same home.

When Phillip heard from Sylvie that Ellery was spending a lot of time with us, and might move in, the phone rang.

"My dear Kate, promise me you will be diligent?" Phillip asked. "Do work out a proper cohabitation agreement, won't you?"

I had to reassure him that we weren't quite there yet, and frankly, it exhausted me to think about having to go down that path of discussion. As I got off the phone, I sat back and tried to figure out the reluctance and ambivalence I was feeling. Ellery was a nice man. But maybe Ellery too was sensing that spending time together didn't have to mean spending our entire lives together. Dianne had teased me that maybe I was involved in a *friends with benefits* situation, which startled me. I had never been casual with relationships before. Being a black and white thinker, I seemed to be confused by the grey I was in.

2019 brought Sylvie's graduation and her launch into a year of global travel. And then 2020 screeched that travel, and all travel, to a halt, and life changed for everyone.

Looking back, March 2020 was insane. While just seven months have passed since then, it feels like a very long time ago. I know that if Phillip, who is now eighty, had been well, he would have carried the weight through March and shielded me as much as possible from the commotion and uncertainty surrounding Sylvie's precarious situation. But with him being so frail after his recent fall, and convalescing temporarily in a care home, our roles with Sylvie were suddenly reversed. In the past I would indulge her and he would bring her down to earth. I would encourage her towards adventure and he would clean up the mess. I always knew he had her back, and my back. He would keep us safe. And then he fell, and became both disoriented and less mobile. We now needed to care for him and ensure he did not become distressed. And so, I hid the truth from him.

I didn't let him know that while the world was grappling with the beginnings of a global pandemic, his precious daughter was trapped in Peru. Martial Law had been imposed when President Martin Vizcarra issued a nationwide state of emergency declaration and overnight ordered the borders closed. No-one was allowed in or out. Sylvie called from Cusco on March 16, completely void of her annoyingly high level of autonomy and strong self-confidence.

"Mom, the borders are closed. All the flights are cancelled. And they won't let us leave our hostel! Can you get me out of here?"

Good question. Let me check my rolodex. Nope. Don't seem to know one single person who lives and works in Peru, let alone that would have any sway with the Peruvian government. At first, I defaulted to thinking of the world as basically full of rational people. That helped to keep me calm. If there were Canadians in Peru who wanted to come home, surely, they would be allowed to do so. But what I started to realize as the days went by and Sylvie and I continued to talk anxiously through our cell phones, was that the world, each country, the politicians and the population were all in a brand-new pressure cooker. Irrational and random behaviour was highly likely.

On March 17, Sylvie reported that when two of her friends had tried to go out to the grocery store to get food for everyone because the hostel was only serving one meal a day, they were accosted on the street by locals. Xenophobia seemed to have set in and the citizens believed that North Americans had brought the virus to their country. Then on March 19, a half dozen Peruvian soldiers barged into their hostel with assault weapons and shouted at them all in Spanish. Basically, the message was that they were to stay in their rooms and not leave the hostel. Later they could hear a strong high pitched buzzing noise. It was like a very loud and annoying mosquito that would not leave. Soon after, they spotted a drone moving in and around their building, and realized with remorse that the outside back garden, hidden from the street, was now totally out of bounds.

When Prime Minister Justin Trudeau and the Canadian government posted a statement that it had no plans to repatriate Canadians from other countries, and then stayed quiet about those who were trapped within countries with closed borders, I flipped. While Ellery was supportive, how I missed Phillip's reassuring touch on my shoulder, gentle smile and then how he would turn around and fix everything at warp speed. If Phillip were here, he would soothe me for a moment and the next second he would be on the phone, pulling out all the stops and setting our world straight. Thinking of him, I got on the phone, and searched for how to pull out the stops so that I could somehow bring Sylvie home and restore an equilibrium to our lives.

Through social media, I learned that while there were millions who had been traveling and were now changing their plans, lining up for planes and coming home to Canada, there were thousands of people trapped behind multiple closed borders. Online, I met some of the parents and friends of the five thousand or so trapped in Peru, and we all began a constant push through every politician, public figure and celebrity that we knew to bring our children, parents and friends home. I have never spoken to so many different people, every day, for so many days. I learned it was important to corral everyone you knew. It always seemed that the person you reached out to with lower expectations would surprise you and know someone with influence. And then there were those that you thought could help for sure, and they sometimes were slow to take action, and that would always be remembered.

While cell phones are a blessing for the immediacy they bring, they are also a curse when the voice is scared, the news is unsettling, or the battery dies and the silence that follows ignites the imagination, running it wild with worry. Those ten days were some of the most intense I have ever experienced. What is the role of a parent, but to protect, help and bring their child home? I fell asleep each night to nightmares of men in fatigues hunting down Sylvie and her friends, blaming them for deaths in their country. I woke each morning in a panic, because she was still not safe and so very far away.

And then we heard that the Peruvian government had agreed to let three Air Canada flights land in Lima on March 24, 25 and 26. The first would bring Peruvians home, and all three would be allowed to evacuate Canadians. The flight was posted as $1,400 a seat and the booking system would open up two days ahead of each flight. The March 24 flight sold out in minutes and anyone on a slower internet connection missed out. Sylvie and her friends watched in horror as the hostel's computer screen began to spiral after just the first few data entry attempts. None of them would be on that first plane.

Hearing Sylvie's distressed encounter with the booking system, Ellery and I pulled together a group of friends and we were all ready to dive onto the system for the next flight and secure a ticket for her. The theory of this plan was good, but it turned out that practically every family trying to get their family member home on that flight was doing the same thing. The system crashed. We waited patiently for a sign that it was up and running again, but when we pounced, we were too late.

Third time lucky? As the first plane of evacuees was leaving Lima on March 24, we stood by for the release of the March 26 tickets. We had enlisted over forty friends at this point, including a rather anxious Trevor, who had also pulled together some of his friends. I broadcasted to the group, so as to inject a friendly, competitive spirit, that whoever was successful in booking Sylvie a ticket was invited to pick a case of their favourite wine from my cellar. I have to say I had some very serious contenders standing by. In the end it was sweet Sam, Dianne's son who nailed it. When I got the call from him that Sylvie's seat on the flight was fully booked and he didn't want the wine, he just wanted to be called when Sylvie touched down in Toronto, I broke down and wept uncontrollably. And when two days later, when she walked out through the sliding doors at the airport and into my arms, I wept again. I cried with relief and with remorse. Relief that she was home and remorse that Phillip was unable to share any of this. It was the first time I had ever been a knight in shining armour. I missed the glow of Phillip in that role. But it was good to know I would be able to figure things out. He had taught me well.

It was also through this ordeal that I learned a truth about myself, and it didn't make me feel good. I learned that I was happy to have Phillip go above and beyond for me and I realized that I did not do that for others. My experience in bringing Sylvie home was the first time I could point to some sort of heroics. And as I puzzled through this, a nagging feeling began to develop. Someone else in my life had bothered to go all out for me and I had shut her down. Nicole had fought for me. She had understood the trap I had been in. Looking in the mirror, I didn't like what peered back at me. But then I packed that thought back into a box and put it up on a high shelf in the back of my mind. There was too much going on to think it all through.

With Ontario in a state of emergency, it meant that by the time Sylvie arrived home on the 26th, the city had become a shell of itself. Cars were parked in driveways, outside homes or under apartment buildings. The traffic lights had nothing to direct. No cars. No people. After a large, frantic shop, many of us had enough food to last a few weeks. Everyone simply hunkered down. Everyone that is, except essential workers, which was an eyeopener to all of us about who really made our world go round. We totally understood the importance of our medical care workers, but we quickly learned that those working in grocery, drug and hardware stores, auto repair, garbage collecting, plumbing, electrical, and driving buses and trains, were all front line and allowed life to function for the rest of us who could work and manage from the safety of home offices.

With Ellery's history of asthma, we knew that his respiratory system was compromised and he would not do well if he became infected with this virus. By the weekend, the three of us made the decision that it would be better if Ellery and I headed up north to our Georgian Bay property, and Sylvie would stay in Toronto. Ironically, Ellery had been the one to cling to Toronto during March, having been so engaged in playing hockey twice a week and climbing up a tennis ladder at his club. But then the emails poured in about the closing of ice rinks, sports clubs, business and social clubs. Our appointment books simply tipped over and pretty much every business and social engagement came sliding off the calendar. Suddenly there was nothing keeping us in the city.

Sylvie, on the other hand, felt that her people were still in Toronto and she wanted to stay. While she promised social distancing, I don't think I really believed that she would follow through with that. She did form a small group of five friends, who ebbed and flowed between their homes and worked on keeping out new entrants. Generally, they were successful, but every now and then a new name would be mentioned and I just tried to keep my mouth shut. It was all too complicated to navigate one's own life, let alone pretend to have advice for someone else's.

Driving out of the city was simply very odd. We left on a Friday morning around 8am, when generally all arteries in and out of the city would have been plugged, and all inner-city roads would have been stop and go. The route we took was the same one we had always used in the past, but no-one was on it. Listening to the traffic report was rather humorous. It felt like a skit from Saturday Night Live.

"And now over to Jim, for the traffic report" said the radio commentator.

"Thanks Carrie. The traffic. Well, there is none. So Carrie, it's back to you again!"

However, after an hour when we turned off the highway and

drove along the back country roads, a sense of normalcy began to creep in. The winter trees stretched naked to the sky. The vast fields covered by thick snow, sat silent.. The sun beamed down and reflected off the metal tops of farm equipment, storage barns and slick, icy patches on the road. For the first time in two weeks, my mind calmed and registered that while the world was upside down, there were parts of it that were carrying on as before. It would be possible to take long walks and be safe. When the snow cleared, we could bike. And when the summer came, we could swim. All was not gone. Some of it would still be there.

Pulling into the driveway and unpacking the car did feel a little bit different, knowing we would be here for an indeterminant amount of time. But once we were settled in, there was an unusual peace. It was so strange not to have a set date for our return to the city.

Firing up my computer and staring at my calendar, I gazed at the wide-open spaces that kept appearing as I clicked forward, week by week into the future. In time, the calendar refilled as board and committee work resumed. In addition to my work with two small Bio-tech firms, I had taken Dianne and Tom's advice a few years ago, and was helping with a commercialization project with researchers at an inner-city hospital in Toronto. With the world's new appreciation of the value of research, it was interesting to witness a more motivated investment community beginning to appear.

I now enjoy rising up each morning when my body wakes up. I no longer use an alarm clock. I don't go to bed very late and I am never overtired. I open my eyes, slip out of bed, wrap myself in a soft robe, wiggle my toes into plush slippers and push the espresso machine button. I watch the sun rise. And when it is overcast, I watch the sky lighten, bringing in another day. And blissfully, I don't have to make my face up every morning. Ellery seems to be oblivious to when I do or don't wear makeup. I sometimes wonder if he really looks at me or if his sense of me is simply a floating aura versus a figurative being. When he wakes up and wanders out to the large picture windows in our living room, he smiles, leans down to me on my swivel chair, says "Good morning, you," and gives me a faint kiss. He looks right at me, but I wonder constantly, "Is he really seeing me?" My lack of foundation, mascara and blush, never seems to register with him. I get the same smile and kiss as I did in the city when I had spent an hour putting on my face.

Enjoying a couple of weeks where I had pushed off early morning commitments, I decided to make that pattern a permanent practice. I simply didn't book anything willingly before 10am. That allowed a few mornings for reading and a few for workouts. One of my friends from the gym reached out to our personal trainer, with whom we had enjoyed years of spinning and training. Along with another friend, we formed a small virtual exercise group of four, grinning at each other through Zoom. Now our Monday and Friday get togethers have become the bookends for our work week. We start with a 7.30am coffee and conversation, and by 8am we are moving into mobility exercises, always finding new muscles to wake up and work. As the months have passed by through lock downs and the loosening of rules, our coffee time has grown longer as we share highs and lows, help each other think through personal worries, and gradually nurse along our ageing bodies, curious minds and sometimes troubled souls.

Thinking back to those early days, there definitely was a *shock and awe* period we all experienced. The news coverage pulled us into a vortex where we could spin for days. It was perplexing to watch the different ways people interpreted the virus. There seemed to be two extreme camps of thought – paranoia and denial. I was very much in the paranoia zone and it was always jarring to run into friends or colleagues who seemed to think the social distancing rules were too extreme, the virus was a bad flu, and who were overly optimistic about how this would all blow over soon. But when Sylvie reported that Trevor was going down that thought path, I picked up the phone. He was a bit too close to Sylvie to leave this thinking unchecked.

"Hi Trevor," I said calmly, "How are you all?"

"Great," he answered tentatively, "It's unusual to hear from you. Is everything okay?"

"Yes, as okay as things can be. I just wanted to check in with you to make sure we were on the same page with being careful and encouraging Sylvie to be careful."

"Okay," Trevor replied. "I see why you are calling. Being careful. Hmm. But you do know this is all getting a little blown out of proportion, right?"

"Why do you say that?" I asked, as this was the reason for my call. What was he thinking?

"This is just a very bad flu. Most people come through this just fine. Its crazy that they are closing businesses and shutting down the economy. The politicians are overreacting. They are too scared to think through this logically. They want to make sure they appear totally concerned and understanding about the individual, so they will get re-elected. They aren't thinking about the damage to the collective. They don't know what they are doing."

"But people do die from this Trevor. It's real."

"Yes, but it is mostly older people who are already sick."

"Many of the older people are just old, they aren't sick until they get this." While Trevor and I had grown apart over the past decade, we had shared a lot of similar views when we were together. I had always found him to be reasonably rational and I felt disoriented by his comments on this.

"Look, I have a friend who got it," Trevor continued, "And he said it was like a truck had hit him for a week or so, and then he was fine."

"Do you really believe that is how its going to progress for most people?" I asked.

"Yes, I do. And shutting down people's livelihoods and making us take our kids out of school, when the kids don't even get the virus, that is nuts. We are going mental here trying to work from home and cope with the kids at home too."

"I can understand that is a lot to manage," I said, wondering that maybe his views came from a high need for them to be true so that his life personally could get back on track.

"Look, we just have to let this virus take it's course," he continued. "We can't stop it. It will move its way through the population. It needs to. People will get sick and yes, some will die. But it will be just a small percent or two. And then our population will gradually build up an immunity towards it, and then we are back to normal."

"What if Sylvie is part of that percent or two?" I ask, trying to flatten the anger in my voice.

"She is young and healthy. She will be fine Kate."

"But what if she wasn't fine Trevor? Wouldn't you have wished she had been careful, taken precautions, been safe?"

"What are you really calling me for, Kate?"

"I just want to make sure that we both are encouraging Sylvie to be careful, limit who she is with, work remotely – which she can do as a writer. Can I ask you to do that?"

"So, can I be just like you?" asks Trevor bluntly. "Is that what you are asking? You want me to tell her to be paranoid? Careful, the virus is around every corner and it is coming to get you. Is that what you want me to be saying to her?"

I sighed, and he heard it. We sat on opposite ends of the phone in silence. His version of me did sound extreme, and realistically, it was accurate. That is what I was like and what I wanted. But I knew that I needed to concede somehow here, or I wouldn't have made an inroad with him at all.

"I'm sorry Trevor," I began slowly, "I agree, I am weighted on the paranoid end of this. Could you and I meet half way on this?"

"And what would that look like?" he asked.

"I don't know," I murmured. "Maybe, if we see her being careful, we don't interfere with that. If she wears a mask, we don't make fun of that. And if she chooses to go out and be with friends, I wont jump all over her. Maybe, we are just agreeing to support what ever view she takes on this."

"Okay, I can do that," Trevor said. "I suspect she will follow your way of thinking more than mine, although with her investigative writing, I wouldn't be surprised if over time she is influenced by others who think like me. I am not alone in believing there is some type of conspiracy going on. There are those that gain when others lose out. And there are a lot of people losing out. Someone out there is happy about that and is perpetuating the fear, because it is helping them."

My head was almost cramping as I talked to Trevor. I was trying to twist my mind around his words to make sense of them. It's true there were winners and losers and it was infuriating to watch the inequity widen. But there were so many conspiracy theories that were circulating and most felt like science fiction. I found it hard to even contemplate tackling a rebuttal.

"Thank you," I said. "I mean it Trevor. Thank you."

"Okay, but Kate, try not to dive down a dark hole."

"Okay Trevor, I'll try not to. Bye, take care of yourself."

"You, too. Bye. Make sure you don't stop living your life, Kate."

I left the call mildly exhausted and curiously pondering. We both saw each other at extreme ends of the issue. Was I too far to one end, and not open to a real middle ground? As I thought about my low tolerance for extremism and my historical preference towards compromise, I could see that I was fine to apply that to most issues. But when something was about life and death and personal safety, my compromise gene evaded me. It seemed to have completely disappeared.

While fear was present, it was curious to watch at this time, as humans turned to humour. Humour seemed to cushion fear, and was a release valve for even the most serious of us contemplating the present and the future. I had always credited humour for bringing laughter and fun in life's wonderfully happy moments, but I had not fully appreciated its consistent appearance in our more dour and anxious times.

Sometime at the end of March, when we all had the chance to experience keeping our distance, long shopping queues, toilet paper shortages, and alcohol as a nightly sedative, the email jokes, skits and musical performances began to arrive. While we may have had work emails to read and return, they were mixed in with friends and family sharing daily messages that ranged from vaguely funny to absolutely hilarious. Passing the ones along that we liked, we all added into the whirlpool of material in play across the globe. In some small way, each funny video or joke posted, passed on the message that even in this darkness I see the sunny side of life, and there is a tomorrow for us all.

Whether it was because life slowed down or because I was learning to relax, I found that I started examining life and relationships more closely. I felt more strongly about those who were important to me. I knew I lived and breathed for Sylvie, but I hadn't fully appreciated how attached I was to Phillip until I was blocked from seeing him. Because of the caregiver rules in the care homes during the COVID shut down, Phillip could only have one named visitor, and that became Carol. Sylvie and I were delegated to virtual visits through an iPad that we had bought and given to Carol. As long as Carol was there, Phillip seemed to be able to figure out how to use the device. But gradually over the months, we began to notice his cognitive decline.

Sylvie and I talked about Phillip and how much he meant to each of us. While he had lived outside of our physical home, he had been that constant, formidably strong protector. We noted that sometimes, when you have someone like that in your life, it can make you bolder, step forward sooner, and allow you to take more chances. This can be good, when these risks are constructive and building opportunities. But maybe sometimes, the choices are more poorly thought through, or purposefully sloppy, when you know there is someone who will pick up the pieces.

"Mom," said Sylvie, "It does feel strange, knowing he isn't able to swoop in and help anymore."

"I understand," I echoed. "I miss asking him for advice now too, although I still always wonder – what would Phillip have said, or done?"

"You did a great job getting me out of Peru," Sylvie added, reaching out and squeezing my arm.

"I learnt from the best!" I said, which was something I said to myself often.

"Well," Sylvie continued, "You and I had best be more careful about the messes we get into, right?"

"Yes, good point. That is very true. Although you are your father's daughter," I smiled and winked. "And I suspect you will likely not get into so many messes going forward."

In time when a second caregiver was allowed in, Sylvie took on that role. She reported back that Phillip's mind was failing and he became particularly perplexed when the dining room was closed and he was told to stay in his room. For a man with such a bright mind, his frustration with what seemed irrational, was hard to live with. Absorbing the severity of the virus and the need for isolation was something he had never had to understand when he was well, and somehow his weakening mind would not accept it as a new truth.

As the spring approached, the opening of golf courses was a bright, ray of spectacular sunshine. All across Ontario, golf courses that had appeared to be a part of a declining industry, were receiving lots of enquiries about membership. Who would have thought to describe golf as the perfect social distancing sport? While the after-game drinks, lunch or dinner were on hold (at least during the early days), it was so easy to lug your own clubs to the course, pull them around and play safely.

It was around this time that Ellery began to pull back from our time together. We had headed out for our very much anticipated first round of golf. Following COVID protocol at that time, it was just the two of us. While we talked sporadically on the front nine, the back nine comments were solely golf specific, and the air between us felt empty. It was as if, after two full months in isolation together, we had run out of things to talk about. Later that night he mentioned he had to meet a contractor at his condo the next morning and would be staying in the city for a few days. I was surprised to learn he was renovating one of his bathrooms. And then I was surprised how much I was looking forward to a few days on my own. While he did return, the visits became shorter, with longer gaps in between and by mid summer I was single again.

I found it curious that I had no tears. I realized that a *nice* relationship didn't really carry great emotion within it or when it ended. And as I began to engage again with friends and colleagues, sitting safely outside on sunny decks, I realized how much I had missed doubling over with laughter and being challenged by a new line of reasoning. I became aware that a sense of humour and intellectual intrigue were very important to me and somehow they had slipped out of my life over the past year. I made a mental note that time was finite and that if I added someone into my life again, they could not be a solo venture, but instead would need to be a part of my collection of friends.

Dianne, always open with her thoughts, was good at reading situations. She summed my time with Ellery up simply, and upon reflection, perfectly. "You and Ellery appreciated each other for the good people you each are. But I don't think either one of you moved on to falling in love with that lovely person."

And so that is when Dianne became my regular golfing partner. We met up twice a week. We loved our afternoons of walking and talking. Initially, our post game conversations were held in the parking lot, but as the summer progressed and the first wave of COVID eased, we enjoyed cocktails on the outside verandah that overlooked the green of the 18th hole. There was something so sensationally civilized about sitting in the sun, and being served in a social setting. We both relished that time and clung on to the moment, so aware that the fall was predicted to bring a second wave, renewed shut downs and we would all climb back into our hobbit holes.

It was in late September, during one of our post golf conversations on the club's verandah, that Dianne went quiet and then launched into one of her blunt, unfiltered attacks, where I became the target.

"Kate, I have been doing a lot of thinking about friendships and what makes someone a friend and what makes someone a best friend. I think friends share, care and warm you up when they are around you. I think best friends do that, but ultimately there is more that is going on. Over time the shared values and experiences create anchors and there is a quiet understanding that you are there for them no matter what."

"Dianne, I know where this is going."

"You are wrong about Nicole."

"No, I'm not," I shot back instinctively. But over the past few months, as I had been thinking through my relationship with Phillip, I had also been re-examining my reaction to Phillip's and Nicole's interference many years ago. My conviction about the accuracy of how I perceived everything had been dropping. It didn't help either that Sylvie was starting to voice her disapproval of how I had cut off Nicole. I am not sure where she got all her facts from, but likely she had been a curious fly on the wall way back, and she had overheard Phillip and me as we fought and debated.

"Kate, you do realize that the way you cut off Nicole is worse than how that friend of yours in high school cut you off?"

"No, it's not. Nicole broke a promise and interfered in my life. My friend in high school was in a personal crisis and shut me off."

"I beg to differ. You were in a personal crisis. Nicole came in to help you and you shut her off."

"Look, we have been through this many times, can we just drop it?" I asked, knowing that Dianne was on a mission, and might not.

"No, because we actually haven't been through it even once. You just keep stomping on it and then dropping it. And I am sorry but you and Nicole are both my best friends and I owe her as much as I owe you, and I just won't *not* talk about it any longer."

"Well, this is a rotten way to end a great afternoon, Dianne," I said and then stood up and picked up my golf hat and purse. "If you don't mind, I think I will get going."

"I do mind Kate. And if you get going, and don't stay and talk this out with me, I'm not golfing with you again." Dianne's face has noticeably reddened and she is uncharacteristically serious. She adds, "I'm not riding my bike with you either."

"Good God, Dianne," I murmured as I sat back down and slumped back into my chair.

"Kate, I want you to talk through your version of what happened five years ago and for the first time I am going to be totally honest with you about what I think really happened and you are going to listen to all of it."

I could feel an instinctive wish to bolt, but because I couldn't, the next best thing seemed to be to waive the young waitress over and ask for two glasses of chilled Chablis. Dianne glared at me. I thought she would be happy to see me ordering wine. It did signal I was staying to talk. Surely, she would soften up a bit now. But she just continued to remain silent and stare at me. I wondered if maybe this was a negotiating technique. While she was known to blurt things out, over the last few years I was aware that she had become more skilled in building an overall strategy before she jumped into a contentious issue.

"Okay then," I began. "So, I am to recount what happened, and then you will give your version. Is that right?"

"Yes."

"Well, as you will recall, I met Kenneth, and he was very charming and we sort of got involved. And unfortunately, he was not as good at investing as he made out to be. However, if everyone had stayed out of it, like I asked them to, and they promised they would, I would have figured out Kenneth on my own and would have left."

I paused as our wine arrived, and the young waitress, fully masked, carefully placed a napkin down for each of us and set the large glasses of chilled wine on top. I reached out and took a sip, thinking about what else to add to the series of events that had happened years ago. Dianne is strangely silent. She is definitely using some kind of *draw the other person out* technique.

"So, Nicole," I continue, "Even though she had promised not to tell Phillip, calls Phillip. She tells him about Kenneth, and Phillip gets involved. Phillip digs up some very unflattering details about Kenneth. When Phillip confronts me with his findings it is beyond embarrassing. And this definitely destroyed for some time the very special relationship Phillip and I had. Dianne, you say a best friend is there for you *no matter what*, well I would say that doesn't include breaking a promise and going behind your back."

I then sat back with my wine, signaling I am done.

"Why do you think Nicole called Phillip?" Dianne asked. She still hasn't touched her wine and she is staring at me with such concentration, I have to look away.

"She didn't like Kenneth," I answered. "She didn't think I could look after myself. She likes to get into people's business. She steps too far and likes to take control."

"Let's examine those statements," Dianne said, now picking up her glass of wine, raising her glass at me and then taking a sip.

"First – she didn't like Kenneth, you say. In hindsight, maybe you don't like him much either, now that you see what she saw, what I saw and many others came forward and confirmed. So, I wouldn't take not liking Kenneth against her. She understood him before you did.

Second – she didn't think you could look after yourself. That's true. She didn't. That might be the toughest one for you to come to terms with Kate, but the truth is you weren't looking after yourself and you made no signs of trying to. You were oblivious to what was going on. Or if you knew, it was self-destructive behaviour. You were giving more money to someone who any rational-minded person would have avoided."

"I was beginning..." I started, and Dianne held up her hand.

"Stop, it is my turn to be speaking," Dianne said. "Your role is to listen. So, third - you said that Nicole likes to get into people's business. Well, that's a bit unfair. I haven't seen that behaviour from her at all. In fact, she tends to stay out of people's business. She is one of the most private individuals I know and she totally respects the privacy of others. What I saw her do with you is not treat you like other people and stay quiet, in fact she treated you in a special way. She treated you like a best friend and she got involved."

"You respected your promise," I jumped in, knowing I could squeeze in a short retort.

"In that moment, Nicole was a better friend to you than me," Dianne pounced back. "If I had the guts, I would have called Phillip, but I was thinking too much of the consequence of dealing with you. Nicole was clearer minded. Protecting you was more important than dealing with your backlash."

I stayed quiet and sipped my wine, and thought. Why did I fight all of this, still?

"Fourth," Dianne leaned forward as she sought to drive her final point home. "Nicole steps too far and likes to take control? Is that really what you think? Please, where is that coming from? Sometimes what one says about others tells us more about the person speaking than who they are speaking about. Kate, you are the one who likes control, and frankly you lost it here. Nicole stepped in to help you get it back, so don't go saying she stepped too far and it was her taking control because she likes to. Ridiculous."

Dianne paused, then nodded her head and sat back. "I'm done," she said.

"But she really wrecked my relationship with Phillip for a while," I said quietly.

"No Kate," Dianne answered. "You did that all by yourself."

I pursed my lips, folded my arms tightly across my front, and exhaled slowly. I thought back to the multiple fights Phillip and I had when he confronted me about Kenneth again and again. I had been obstinate and wouldn't accept his findings and he was livid that I could be so thoughtless with how I was running my financial affairs.

"You know Dianne, I think what really hurt, was when Phillip told me I was being a terrible role model for Sylvie. He pointed out that my success in business didn't mean much if I was willing to blow it away carelessly. And then he questioned me about what does it mean if you show your child that you can be conned easily by a man, even when your friends try to help you.I hated that he called out my role as a mother and questioned it. And I fumed that it was one of my friends who had told on me. I felt humiliated and betrayed."

"I understand Kate," Dianne said leaning towards me. "I really do. But I think you misplaced that anger. The anger would have been best directed at yourself, and at Kenneth, not at Phillip, Nicole or me."

I nodded and then asked something that had been on my mind for a very long time. "Tell me Dianne, I know its petty, but was there ever something that went on between Nicole and Kenneth?"

"What?" Dianne said with a laugh. "Are you kidding me?"

"I know. It might seem farfetched and not make sense to you, but that night when we were out dancing together, Kenneth was so attentive to Nicole. And then for weeks after, he always asked about her. I found that confusing. And then when she told Phillip, I had this strange sensation that she was clearing the floor for herself."

"Oh Kate, you have to know that is not true."

"But why was Kenneth like that with her?"

Dianne smiled and then offered her thoughts on this. "I think Kenneth knew that Nicole was on to him. He was paying a lot of attention to her because yes, she is attractive, but maybe he knew to keep you tied to him he needed to pull her in too. You know what they say - how do you keep your enemies close? Make them your friends. That sort of thing. And I bet he kept asking about Nicole to see if you would offer up what Nicole might be saying against him, so he could combat it."

I nodded. I could see everything more clearly now. It helped to better understand that final piece. The idea of Nicole with Kenneth had been troublesome even though it was so unlikely. Dianne's explanation helped the puzzle fit together. Being in charge of my own messes now, I certainly had a big one to fix.

"Thanks Dianne. Sorry for pushing back on this for so long. Thanks for dragging me back through it."

"I'm sorry I didn't force you through it sooner. If I start to challenge you a bit more in the future, please know it will just be me trying to straighten out any lines that get crossed. I've learned they don't always unwind by themselves."

As we finished our glasses of wine, Dianne mentioned our *Girls Annual Bike Ride*. It was already late September, and while we understood that we couldn't stay at Abigail's, we could still find a spectacular day for a good long ride down by the bay.

"How about we find a time in October?" Dianne proposed. "There is always a warm weather patch that seems to raise its head during October and brings a few gorgeous days."

"Perfect," I said, looking forward to the ride, but dreading my conversation with Nicole. "Are you sure Nicole will come?"

"Well, you haven't been easy to be around Kate, but deep down I think she has always been hopeful that you would come around."

"Will you tell her everything is okay?" I asked sheepishly.

"Are you kidding me?" Dianne balked. "After all this time, that can only come from you. And you know that."

"Yes," I said, "I know."

# OCTOBER GIRLS' BIKE RIDE
# AT 60

When Kate saw that the weather channel was forecasting 23C for Wednesday, just two days away, she called up Dianne. "I think we found our day. Shall I conference in Nicole?"

"Yes," Dianne said, adding cautiously, "Have you spoken with her one-on-one yet?"

"No. I was going to suggest that maybe she and I could meet up a half hour before we ride."

"Sounds like a good plan. So yes, do pull Nicole in on the line." Dianne held on and in a moment the three of them were all on the line.

"Well ladies," began Kate, "I think tomorrow is the day. Are you ready?"

"Absolutely," said Dianne, "The bike is in great shape, even if I'm not, so I think I will be able to keep up with you two!"

"It will be great to see you both," pipes up Nicole, in a slightly forced cheery voice.

"You girls are in luck," says Dianne, "I am planning to bake a fresh batch of my special cranberry, walnut and chocolate chip cookies. They will be our pseudo sixtieth Birthday Cake, as cake and frosting do not pack well in a knapsack."

"I can bring a curried chicken salad," offers Nicole.

"Tempting" says Kate, "But I'm just not comfortable with sharing food yet. I've been reading too much about transmission of this virus, and while we are safe biking and meeting outdoors, for now I think I will keep with the two meter social distancing guideline and munch along with you from my own picnic bag."

Dianne asks about Kate's reading and she and Nicole listen somberly as Kate shares a confusing array of data. Some of it contradictory and all of it a bit mind-numbing. Hearing the silence on the other end of the phone, Kate eventually stops, shelves the rest of the findings, and they all agree to meet at 10.30am at the docks to begin their ride. Their mission will be to not have a scripted destination, but rather to ride along the water's edge and pick pretty stops for lunch and an afternoon tea.

"Nicole," Kate adds in, "Would you be up for meeting me around ten? I have some apologizing to do, and I think I should let Dianne off the hook of having to hear me babble on."

The phone line is silent. Kate becomes anxious, Dianne is slightly pensive, and Nicole moves from surprise to a wide, growing smile.

"Yes," Nicole answers. "Ten works. See you then."

Sure enough, Wednesday is stunning. Bright blue sky. Warm sun. The water is calm and the usual crisp fall breeze seems to be sleeping as Kate and Nicole meet up at the docks. They each give a stilted wave from a distance, fasten on their face masks, lock their car doors and walk towards each other. Kate points out some stairs leading down to the lower docks and they head over, sit down on either end of the top step, ensure they are safely distanced, take off their masks and look out at the marina below.

After a short polite conversation around the gorgeous weather, the difficult past year and hoping both of their families are safe and well, Kate clears her throat and begins.

"I'm sorry Nicole, for blaming you for everything. I was wrong to do that."

Silence follows. They both look out at the boats. Kate was expecting Nicole to say something back. Nicole doesn't want to interrupt Kate in any way.

"I mean, I wasn't thinking clearly back then," Kate continues. "Being so wrong about Kenneth. Being confronted by Phillip. Feeling embarrassed. Foolish. Stupid. I struck out at you. Your broken promise and involving Phillip, it was the only thing I could think of to blame. I latched onto that. Clearly, I didn't want to blame myself. I was wrong to do that. I'm sorry."

Nicole feels her mind is tied up in a knot. A warning light flashes. Don't say anything. After four years of being set aside by Kate, Nicole doesn't trust her brain to feed her the right words.

"Look, I read it all wrong," Kate adds. "Over the past eight months, I have been coming to terms with losing Phillip."

"Is he okay?" Nicole blurts out in alarm.

"Physically, yes. But he fell last year and he has been in a care home. And then he fell again and hit his head, and his mind is just simply fading. We have lost who he was."

"I'm sorry to hear that," says Nicole. "I know he has been a very special person in your life."

"Yes, he has been. I didn't always realize it at the time, but he taught me about how being there to back someone makes them stronger and safer. He did that for me. He did that for Sylvie. And what I have realized Nicole," and Kate turns and looks directly at Nicole, meeting her hesitant gaze, "Is that you did that for me too. I just didn't understand it at the time."

Nicole holds Kate's eyes, and nods her head. "I see," are the only words that surface.

"Also, the whole thing became such a personal affront when Phillip challenged my role modeling, or lack of it, as a mother. That hurt the most. While maybe I could handle being stupid, I could not absorb being a bad mother. I deflected that one by making you the target of my anger, instead of taking the blame full on."

Nicole nods again.

"And," Kate continues, "An added irritant that didn't help, was that Kenneth seemed to find you rather fascinating."

"What?" bursts out Nicole, her eyes reading complete confusion.

"I know," Kate laughs, "I vetted this with Dianne a couple of weeks ago, because I had been burying it. But it is true. Don't you remember that night when we were all out together?"

"Yes, I do," Nicole says, "More than I care to, actually."

"Well, he kept asking about you after that night. Dianne says that he probably could sense you were on to him, and it was better to make an enemy into a friend. Maybe that was true. But I think he found you attractive, and that sort of set me off a bit too."

"I had no idea," Nicole says. "I think he simply romanced a lot of people to get what he wanted, whether he was after their money, or maybe some short-term affection or advantage."

"It was always a bit of an emotional zig zag with him," Kate admits. "He had a way of pouring out attention and affection that was so completely overwhelming. I would feel I was the most important person in his life. And then he would blow that up by gazing at a good-looking woman walking by in a way that was more than just observational."

"Do you know what has happened to him?" Nicole asks.

"I heard that he was spotted with a badly bruised face and he was hobbling around the city a few months ago," Kate grins. "Apparently he was investing money that turned out to belong to the mob. I heard he didn't realize that, and that the client didn't take very kindly to the delay and then the discount he suggested when they asked for their money back."

"Yikes," Nicole laughs. "Are we allowed to be a little happy about that?"

"Yes," beams Kate. "We are. Anyways, all to say Nicole, I really and truly am sorry. I value what you did for me. I understand it all better now. I am sorry for being obstinate and proud and not reaching out sooner."

"Forgiven," chirps up Nicole, sporting a quivering smile and a set of wet eyes. "I've missed you."

"I've missed you too," says Kate, blinking back tears.

Gazing out again at the boats and the vastness of Georgian Bay, they sit in the morning sun and enjoy soaking in the sound of each other's voice and the warm presence of a far away friend who has returned. They catch up on Charlie's comforting presence in Nicole's life, Kate's break up with Ellery, and her worry about facing an isolating pandemic winter on her own.

"Hey" shouts Dianne from the parking lot. "You two lovebirds made up yet?"

They laugh and walk up to the parking lot. While they can't physically hug each other, they stand a good two meters apart and send air hugs to each other. Then bikes are removed from racks, thoughtfully packed knapsacks are pulled out and onto their backs, helmets are fastened and they are off.

With thanks to the Grand Trunk Railway that began laying down tracks in the mid 1800's, these old rail beds are now smooth, paved, traffic-free biking and walking paths. Wide enough to comfortably fit two riders side by side, the paths allow the three of them to take turns riding as a pair with the third person trailing. Then when an area widens, and no pedestrians or cyclists are in sight they squeeze in the three of them in one tight row. They laugh when this happens, and then become aware that they are hardly the COVID recommended two meters apart. Kate falls back, apologizing for her paranoia.

While they have taken water breaks along the way, it is as they reach the two-hour mark, and their stomachs are grumbling, that they seek out some large flat rocks down by the water's shore. They find a series of smooth granite slabs and each of them selects one that is comfortable and gives them a safe distance from each other, while forming a friendly circle for the three of them.

"Has anyone heard about how Abigail has been doing through all of this?" asks Kate, pulling up her knapsack onto her lap and unzipping the top.

"Yes, I have," says Nicole, opening up one of her kitchen hand towels and laying it on a small flat section of her rock, "I was in Ellington in late August and swung by. I didn't intend to go in to see her, I just wanted to check if the B&B sign was still there. I wanted to be able to go on looking forward to the future and knowing there was a chance for all of us to go back there again one day."

"Did you see her?" asks Dianne, pulling out a couple of Tupperware containers.

"I did. As I was driving by, I noticed a large sign on the lawn promoting prepared meals and baked goods. So, I parked, put my mask on, walked up the front path and knocked on the door. There was a loud *Come on in*, and there she was, along with a couple of other masked warriors, working away in the kitchen."

"How did she seem?" asks Kate, unwrapping her sandwich, and poking the overflowing avocados and tomatoes back inside the two thin pieces of grain bread.

"She was refreshingly the same. Totally upbeat and positive about life. They had managed to pivot early, and have built a significant size clientele that would prefer to not cook every night. She said some of her clients are ordering twice and even three times a week."

"Good for her," says Dianne. "She is a force to contend with. That's great that the pandemic didn't shut her completely down."

"I suspect too," ponders Kate, "That she likely doesn't have much debt. She has had the property for a long time now. While she continually made small improvements each year, it always seemed that she did so without worry. I think she probably came into this financially sound."

"I agree," adds Nicole. "She also told me that about twenty percent of what she is cooking and preparing is being given to the local community shelter. So I think she is in good shape. She has even devised a way that a customer, if they want to, can join in and help with a *2 for 1* scenario. The customer pays for two meals, but only takes one home. The other one is added in to the twenty percent that she is taking to the shelter."

"Always liked that woman," says Kate, munching on her carrots, celery and lemon hummus. "This feels so strange to be eating away here and not offering you two anything!"

"I know," adds Dianne, "Food is such a big part of what we have all grown up sharing. As kids if you opened up a pack of gum, you instinctively shared. As adults we are no different. I miss the giving.

Truth is, it makes us feel good to share. So, I guess I miss that feeling good part. And speaking of what makes me feel good, I also really miss dancing. While I turn up the volume and dance on my own at home, its not the same. Do you remember that first time when there was the power outage and we went to Ricky's Road House?"

"That was so much fun," jumps in Nicole.

"Funny thing is," Dianne continues, "We had no idea back then when we were singing along with Aretha Franklin's *Who's Zoomin Who*, that Zoom would have a whole new identity twenty years later. It would be fun to put that music on quietly in the background during a Zoom meeting and see if anyone picks up on that."

"That music would be perfect for Zoom if they ever had to advertise themselves online," jumps in Kate, "But I somehow think they don't need to spend a cent on marketing these days. You'd have to be living in a rabbit hole not to know who they are."

"Dianne, I miss the dancing too. But, I really miss the hugs," says Nicole thoughtfully. "I am so lucky to have Charlie, and he gives great hugs, but I miss being able to spontaneously hug the kids, the grandkids, my parents, you two, and others who were just part of that circle of hugs before all of this."

"We are all missing out on a lot of oxytocin that used to be in our lives," agrees Kate.

"What?" says Dianne, "I thought that was bad for you?"

"You are thinking OxyContin, the opioid medication," jumps in Nicole. "Kate means oxytocin, known as the *love drug*. It is inside you. It calms your nervous system and it boosts positive emotions."

"And it lowers your blood pressure," says Kate, "And your cortisol, which is the stress hormone, so you feel less anxious. And it also enables a higher quality of sleep. So, if you think about it. The world is in a pandemic, a very stressful predicament, and we aren't allowed to hug, which would have been a very helpful way to activate oxytocin and help us all to reduce some of the stress."

They continue to talk about the strain and anxiety they each feel, remarking that just the act alone of talking about it is therapeutic.

They talk too about how over the years the power of being able to voice and share, always seemed to help with clarifying the muddle that could develop if you kept thoughts locked inside your own head. Being able to articulate thoughts in a safe place, allowed clarity to form. Ideas to help with fears, problems and worries could be launched. Solutions for issues surrounding family, work and life, could be batted about and resolved.

Kate is concerned about her growing isolation. She feels cut off from Phillip both physically and mentally. Even when they have a phone or video call, she finds it hard to reach the man she knew. And she feels the pandemic has forced her to limit her visits with Sylvie, who has developed a much wider group of city friends that Kate is worried about being exposed to. She doesn't know who Sylvie's friends are interacting with and can only imagine the intricate web of people connected to Sylvie, if they were to actually map it all out. She finds it mind-boggling how this invisible virus has so profoundly changed free-flowing interactions. She loves being up north, being closer to the outdoors and feeling safe, but the "walls don't talk" she says sadly, referring to the silence of living alone.

Dianne worries about her mother, who is now on her own after her father died three years ago from a sudden heart attack. While she and her sister drop in each week, that still leaves long days all week where she is on her own. Occasionally, she learns that her mother has been spotted out getting her own groceries, instead of ordering in. One day she heard that her mother attempted to drop in at one of the retirement homes to see a friend, and was promptly turned away as they were in lockdown and were dealing with COVID spreading among their residents. While 83, and diabetic, two strikes against you if you contract the virus, her Mom vacillates between following the guidelines they have set out together and throwing them out the window.

Nicole has fears about her father, who is in the later stages of a lung disease. He is gradually losing his breath, and is now on oxygen. To her it looks like an extremely slow version of COVID; fluids gradually filling up the lungs and the eventual inability to breathe. He is eighty-five, never smoked, and was always fit. And then two years ago her parents came back from Florida, where they had rented a bungalow for a few months, and he found that he was getting out of breath climbing the stairs at home. It seemed to happen all of a sudden, but apparently the disease is gradual, and unnoticed at the front end. So, he is on her mind a lot. She was scared at first to visit, in case she brought COVID into the house, but her father has made it perfectly clear now that he would prefer to see her and her brothers as often as possible, and die sooner, then not see them and die anyway within the next year or so.

By this point they have all finished their lunches, the mood is somber and they have repositioned themselves on their respective rocks, so that they are facing into the sun and looking quietly out over Georgian Bay. The calm waters of the morning are beginning to chop. White crests rise, foam appears and then arched waves pound down and into the next rising surge.

"I like Amazon," perks up Kate, breaking the spell. "I know that there is a swath of the population that is condemning them, and I do scratch my head when an item the size of my wallet, comes packed in a box as big as a large piece of luggage, but I like them. I never really ordered much on line before COVID, always preferring to be able to pick up what I was buying and examine it first, but I am an ardent convert."

Dianne smiles and shakes her head, loving Kate's ability to knock them back into a happier moment. "Well, of course you love it," Dianne kids, "You are shopping! And you can shop when ever you like and for what ever you fancy. How could you not love it!"

"Sylvie made a great point last week about why our psyche loves it so much," Kate continues. "When we go to a store we search and find our purchase and we get a small high as we buy it, right?" Dianne and Nicole nod. "But when you buy online, you get that high as you search it out and buy it and then you get that feel good feeling again when it arrives and you open it up. Two distinct periods of time, separated by a couple of days, but definitely promoting a buzz twice!"

Nicole laughs and nods her head in agreement, "That's profound. I agree. Sylvie has nailed it. That is so true."

"So," says Kate, narrowing her eyes and dramatically looking from Nicole to Dianne, "Tell me. I know there have to be some positive things going on in your lives, even though we and the world are in this big mess. I shared Amazon. What have you found to be a plus in all of this?"

"Masterclass," says Nicole, without missing a beat. "With lots of empty time to fill during that first lockdown, I had heard about it and so checked it out online and then signed up. I think it was $225 for a year and it allows unlimited classes on a wide range of topics that are curated by industry experts."

"So, what classes did you take?" asks Kate.

"Well, I signed up because I thought I would try the guitar lessons, but that was a mistake. When Carlos Santana started to talk about *just feel the music* and *go where the music takes you* I realized I was way over my head, and I might be better off with finding guitar basics in a traditional online course. But, as life tends to do, while heading somewhere for something specific, you find lots of other interesting things along the way. I signed up for guitar but found a host of other subjects that I had a lot of fun with."

"Like what?" asks Dianne.

"Make-up with Bobbi Brown," grins Nicole, raising her eyebrows as she looks over towards Kate. "I am not wearing any evidence of that course right now, but Kate, I do now understand some basics around applying effective eye makeup, so watch out. I am learning the secrets!"

"I had better look into this," pipes up Dianne, "Or it will be me on the slow bike all over again, and I will be trailing behind two wide-eyed diva's as you cross the room!"

"Just so I don't appear as shallow as I am," adds Nicole, "Let me also say that I spent some very good sessions with Jane Goodall learning about conservation and Annie Leibowitz understanding why my photographs have always considerably lagged hers."

"Annie Leibowitz!" exclaims Dianne, "I would pay $225 in a second just to listen to her. I love her work. So, I would just have to google Masterclass, and go from there?"

"Yup, simple to join and it is great just popping around the site and sampling all the introductory videos by different people. There are some great writers there too, Dianne. You might find them interesting to check out. I did the Margaret Attwood course, and found her mesmerizing. I don't have any plans to write, but found it fascinating to learn about the various components of writing. I have a much greater appreciation, Dianne, about your work and all who write."

"And what about you, Dianne?" asks Kate. "Something positive that you are doing, that is actually a direct result of the disruption this year?"

"Photobooks," says Dianne decisively. "I looked into making one for the big trip that Tom and I did last year, and it turned out really well. It was a pretty substantial book, and I loved the process of laying it all out and then adding commentary from both of us. So, I went back to some family holidays and started to edit and compile digital files and then went on to do three smaller photobooks. Each one is quite different from the next. While I am a words person, I am also highly visual, and I love being able to combine both parts in one medium."

"I would love to see them, Dianne," pipes in Nicole, "It could be the inspiration I need to create some semblance of order for all the pictures I've taken over the years."

"I've learned that you just have to break it down into something that has meaning to you. It makes it easier to edit and decide what you really want to portray in the book. You simply can't let it be everything. So, decide what is it that you are really trying to say and then show that."

Dianne thinks about the two, small carefully wrapped packages she has inside her knapsack, and ponders whether to bring them out now. But Kate has clapped her hands together and is raring to go for their next leg of the journey, which will only be an hour or so ride in search of a perfect spot for *tea*. They have all been carrying thermoses of tea, along with something sweet to eat at their final stop.

Back on their bikes, their riding has become less hurried and their conversation more contemplative. Kate shares her worries about Phillip, whose spirit is failing and who feels trapped in a care home that was supposed to be a temporary place to heal and not his full time residence. Kate hopes that the vaccines being developed and ending their trials soon will be the ticket they are all hoping for. Word is that the government will seek to inoculate front line workers and the staff and residents in retirement and care homes first. So that may be the one redeeming factor for having Phillip living there.

"Your Mom's experience in a home was so different," reflects Dianne, riding beside Kate, while Nicole takes a turn behind them.

"Yes," answers Kate, "I often think about her, and I am so glad that during the progression of her disease, she wasn't in today's environment. She was fortunate to be in a safe, relaxed and social setting. As she manouevred through losing her short-term memory, and then confusion over words, or the purpose of an object in front of her, there was a warmth around her. She didn't have to deal with having to understand masks and social distancing. That would have intensified the paranoia that she was already beginning to battle."

"I was reading about the seven worst foods for your brain this week," perks up Nicole, pulling up a little closer. "Of course, the punch line should be that I don't remember any of them. But I actually made a huge point in memorizing them, just to be sure I didn't embarrass myself."

"I hate to think what is on that list," calls out Dianne, dropping back a bit so Nicole can ride side by side with Kate.

Nicole continues on and recites each of them out loud so Dianne and Kate can weigh in.

"One - Sugary drinks." They agree that none of them are keen on those anyways.

"Two - Refined Carbs." This is annoying for all of them as they do love a good Montreal Bagel and the occasional fabulous crusty baguette.

"Three - Foods high in Trans Fats." Dianne laments that her homemade cookies fall into this category, and Nicole offers to share an almond butter recipe that is safer.

"Four - Highly processed foods." Kate and Dianne grin, both agreeing that these make dinner prep so much faster. But they have been trying to follow Nicole's lead in banning these from the house when possible.

"Five - Aspartame." A cheer goes up from them all because this substance has been avoided for years.

"Six - Alcohol." A hushed silence is followed by Kate shouting out "Next!"

"Seven - Fish high in Mercury." Stories then follow about friends impacted by this and how without testing you don't really know how much you have in your system. They all make a mental note to look into asking to be tested for this.

"It's strange now," says Dianne contemplatively, "We are all sixty years old now, and the idea of memory loss is not something far off and distant. We have seen it happen around us, and we are all having moments grasping at words that eludes us."

"I find too," adds Nicole, "That while I remember the concept or theme in newspaper articles and magazines, I don't remember the pieces of data that made the argument being expressed so impressive. This means that if I want to retell what I read, my version is much less compelling, because I can't quote the statistic or remember the name of the person or the place involved."

Kate adds in, "I have started making a point of finishing an article, sitting back and deciding what three points I am going to try to remember. I focus on this, find those points, and then sometime in the next day or a few days later, when I remember, I will test myself. Of course, what is curious about this is that the article I read is usually online and so I can't just pick it up to check my accuracy. So, it's an interesting habit, but frankly, I don't really know how I'm doing."

"Well," says Dianne, "When my Mom was concerned about her memory and had some tests, I went with her. What I remember, and that was reassuring, is that the doctor said it was very normal to forget names, dates and data points. What is more of a concern is if you forget going places. So, if you go shopping in Toronto and you can't remember the name of the stores you went into or how much your lunch bill was, that is okay, but if you can't remember that you went to Toronto, that is a problem. That is my current barometer for this subject, and so far, I seem to be aware of where I have been."

"Well," laughs Kate, "This year that has been a low bar to jump since we are all basically staying home most of the time!"

They carry on through a particularly winding part of the trail that is thinner and the pavement has turned to softer sand that snags the bike wheel more easily. They ride for a while in single file. While voices aren't filling the air, conversation seems to carry on in each of their heads, as they pull up memories, images, and *notes to self* of a to-do item that has popped into their head. Quiet time, and being together and being apart – this has always been a part of their rides in the past, although usually they know they have a wide expanse of together time ahead with cocktails, dinner and pyjama time. Not this year. But they still have a tea stop, and a final loop back to the cars.

Coming out of the forested path, they circle down off the trail to the water's edge. There is a small park with a few scattered picnic tables, all empty on a Wednesday afternoon. They select the picnic table out by the point and space themselves out, Dianne and Nicole on one side but sitting at the very end of their bench, and Kate on the other side and in the middle. After they are settled, their eyes measure and realize that they are pretty much just one meter apart from each other vs two, but none of them say anything. It is a simple lapse during the exhaustion of having to constantly make each moment of life fit the rules.

Hand sanitizers appear and they each go through the motions of cleaning off their hands. Then individual thermoses are pulled out and steam wafts up from the small cups they each pour. Dianne plunks down three individually wrapped Ziploc bags in the middle of the table. Each bag holds two large golden cookies bursting with huge chocolate chips, cranberries and walnuts.

"These were made by me yesterday morning with all the handwashing protocols and I wore a mask while I made them and then bagged them. So, they are as safe as what you buy in a store, plus they have been in total secure lockdown within their individual bags for coming up to thirty hours now. What's a Happy Birthday without something sweet to help celebrate?"

Kate and Nicole smile and then laugh, looking first at each other and then back to Dianne. Fingers scoot out towards the Ziploc bags and they happily retrieve them.

"These are a piece of heaven," says Kate savouring her first bite. "I have to say I did forget how good they were. Thank you Dianne, and cheers to you and Nicole. Happy Birthday!"

"Yes, thank you and Happy Birthday to you both too," joins in Nicole. "I actually brought a package of store-bought cookies hoping to get you two to share them with me, so I am happy to keep those out of sight. Completely unappetizing compared to these."

"I brought a few tangerines along with some Lysol wipes," adds Kate. "So, I think if we each wipe off our own tangerine before we peel it, we are safe, right? Do you think one day we will look back at all of this and think we were nuts? Will we wonder if all our protective measures were too much? Once the fear is gone we may question our protective actions. We will need to remind each other that our fear was very real."

With their protocol established for sharing, they relax and wind into some quiet reflections on the past year. They recount the tiny sixtieth birthday parties they each had with their spouse/partner and one or two kids. They promise to throw a joint birthday party next summer, if it's safe to do so. It is something to look forward to and to plan for. They remark how so much of their pre-COVID lives involved planning for something in the future. A child's university graduation ceremony, meant bookings of a hotel, a special restaurant and transportation for the weekend. A grandchild's birth involved the offering of time to visit and help, and taking a trip to the city to assist with the shopping for a crib, highchair and accessories. And then there was the travel they all enjoyed. Wading through travel magazines, researching destinations online and gradually piecing together a special trip.

They kid about the type of planning they are involved in today. It is all about being super diligent. Drawing up of the grocery list, to ensure that the number of trips in a month are minimized. Making sure the hand sanitizer and the masks are fully stocked in the car, in your coat pocket or in your purse. A different kind of planning. Today it was about efficiency and safety, versus steps towards something exciting.

They catch up on their children and their comings and goings. Kate's Sylvie is freelance writing and beginning to write screenplays. She has a couple of friends who are in film and she is finding writing dialogue a refreshing change from prose. Nicole's Jimmy has his hands full with both he and Shayna working remotely from home, and trying to manage their three young children underfoot. Tessa and Mary Anne are enjoying parenthood, and are beginning to worry about how they will socialize little Michael over the next year. They are considering forming a bubble with another family who also have a baby boy. Dianne's Sara has become the diamond in the rough. Once a pretty self-centred person, Sara is thriving in both her day-time work and her community volunteer work. She and Connor seem to be eyeing a bigger place with an extra bedroom, and Dianne thinks they might be contemplating starting a family. And Dianne's lovely Sam is spending more time in Port Colebrook these days as there is a very sweet young woman in his life.

"You will never guess who it is," says Dianne with a big smile.

"I met Sam biking this summer with a young woman, would that be her?" asks Kate.

"Probably, what did she look like?"

"As I recall she had long, dark hair, and a big smile. She sort of sparkled – a happy girl. But then of course, if she is with Sam, who wouldn't be!"

"Yes, that's her. And that my dears, is Lulu Preston."

"Freddy's little sister?" asks Nicole.

"The very same. She is about six years younger than Sam, full of energy and they are very sweet together."

"Very small world up here," smiles Kate. "How are Margaret and Freddy doing these days?"

"Well, after COVID cut so many of us off from each other, it was so refreshing to run into Margaret at the grocery store one day and catch up as we pushed our carts around, two meters apart in the aisles. But everyone was so serious and it seemed like we were committing a misdemeanor to laugh in the store, so we decided we had best take our talking outside before we got kicked out. Then we started walking together once a week, every Tuesday morning, through the rain, heat, wind and soon I guess, we will be ploughing through the winter snow. So, *how is Margaret?* Well, the answer is that she is doing better now. There were a couple of years after Freddy left, where she was quite depressed. Freddy didn't call. He didn't visit her or respond to any of her calls, emails or letters. Freddy kept in touch with Lulu so Margaret always knew where he was, but Margaret said she had an ache for years that wouldn't go away. But then her brother Evan tracked Freddy down and visited him repeatedly. Margaret suspects that Evan had been in therapy and was seeking redemption. Part of that *making amends* was to ensure that Freddy wouldn't continue to blame his mother for something that Evan had done. Something worked. Freddy came back for a visit two years ago, and while he won't be coming back to live, he is no longer estranged from his mother. They are mending and getting closer again."

"So, Evan was the brother responsible for Bill's death?" asks Nicole.

"Yes," Dianne says looking first at Nicole, and then at Kate. "It was either self-defense or an accident. It wasn't premeditated. But clearly, it was a nightmare and all poorly handled. No-one knows where Evan is right now. The authorities don't seem to be asking about him, so the family is hopeful that in time, he may choose to return. However his marriage had broken up before he left, and everyone is worried about the children. Margaret finds the irony haunting that Evan has now become the missing father. "

"And how about Lulu?" asks Kate, "How does she seem?"

"She doesn't carry the weight of what happened in the same way as Freddy did. Margaret was able to tell her about her father's death in a way that Lulu could accept. Sam asked me about what happened to Lulu's father, and I said it was best if he speak with Lulu about it. I didn't want to lie to him and say I didn't know. I told him that it was not my story to tell."

A cool wind brushes up from the bay, and they sit quietly. No-one feels the need to ask more questions. It is time to let this subject go.

They can all feel their time together coming to a close. The sun that was bright, hot and high in the sky when they started this morning, is beginning to arch downwards in the late afternoon. The wind is kicking up on Georgian Bay and they each stand and begin pulling out and putting on another layer of warmth for the ride home.

"Before we go," says Dianne, "I have something for each of you."

Kate and Nicole stop, Kate tilting her head to the side and Nicole raising her eyebrows with a question mark.

Dianne pulls out two small wrapped packages. She explains the procedure she went through to make them safe. She hands one to each of them. "It is just something small, but I wanted something that the three of us would all have. I have a copy at home too."

"Thank you," says Kate, "That is so kind of you."

"I wish I had something for you," says Nicole.

"Stop it," interjects Dianne, "You don't even know what it is. Just open it up."

Together, Kate and Nicole pull the gift out of its bag, untie the pink satin ribbon and carefully pull up the taped edges of the soft green wrapping paper. A thin book appears. The front and back of the book has a mix of bicycle wheels in all different sizes, spiraling across the cover. Behind the wheels, the long raised dock at the end of one of their favourite riding paths is visible. The title on the front of the book is simple and direct. *The Girlfriend Book* are the words that stare up at them.

Over the next ten minutes, they are all smiles as they begin to leaf through the pages and Dianne points out anecdotal parts. Inevitably this brings laughter and then some tears as the message and the meaning of the words sink in. Dianne then encourages them to wrap them back up and have a read through it later tonight. "I will be reading it again too and thinking of you both," she adds.

"This is so unfair," yells out Kate. "I need to hug you, Dianne!"

Nicole rises to the occasion and takes over, ordering them to put on their masks, form a circle facing inwards and keeping two meters from each other. "Now, reach your hands forward, but don't touch. Be calm, stare at me and each other. Now imagine our arms around each other. Can you feel them? I am hugging you. Can you feel that?"

Anyone looking out towards the point that day would have wondered "What type of strange meditation are those three women practicing?" While looking rather odd, there was an energy that they could all feel. A realist might stack it up to one's imagination. A mystic might cite something more spiritual. However, for them, it was simply a group hug. They could sense it all around them and they didn't want it to end.

The bike ride back to their cars was the shortest part of the day's loop, and soon they were taking off helmets and knapsacks and strapping their bikes back onto their bike racks. They all agreed that the day had been as special as they had hoped for, and would be a memory to hang on to over the winter ahead. Kate begins to reiterate her apology to Nicole, and Nicole shuts it down quickly saying Kate was forgiven and they were onto the future. They promise to figure out dates for snowshoeing and cross-country skiing once the snow begins to fall. And, in the meantime, the biggest goal is to continue to stay safe and well.

Later that night, when they are home, after Nicole and Dianne have shared their day with Charlie and Tom, and Kate has reached out to Sylvie to update her on the joy of mending a friendship, they each find some quiet time on their own. They pull out Dianne's book and nestle into a comfortable chair. First touching the cover, the front and the back, and staring at the many wheels, they recall Dianne pointing out that there were twenty-seven wheels in total, each one marking a year they had ridden together. Then they open up the book and read through the story of their friendship.

Over the next two hours they follow the recounting of their many years together. Special moments – some are funny, some are sad, and many are heartwarming. All tracking how their listening, trusting and sharing had allowed each of them to grow stronger and take new and unknown paths. Twenty-seven years sewn together beautifully over just seventy pages. Dianne had made a point of explaining that there were only three copies, and there would only ever be three copies. They were to think of it as a personalized card, not a book. But Kate and Nicole, after finishing the book, connect with each other and then together reach out and call Dianne to insist. This is not a card, this is a book, and simply the best one they would ever own.

# AUTHOR'S NOTES

Although I have been fortunate to have shared my life with a multitude of girlfriends, the characters and plot within **The Girlfriend Book** are purely fictional. This story was written not as a memoir, but rather as a means to capture the overall spirit and warmth of the special relationships that develop from sharing and articulating life's journey with friends.

# ACKNOWLEDGEMENTS
# & THANKS

This book was written between the fall of 2020 and the spring of 2021, while the world moved through wave two and three of the COVID-19 pandemic. Writing a short story that morphed into a larger one, allowed me to escape from the news and to ensure that I put my day job into a more defined box. During this time, there are many who encouraged me and who helped in ways they may or may not know.

First, thanks to my husband Richard, who always asked about how the "book" was coming along, even when it was only ten pages long. You helped me to imagine what this piece of work might grow into.

Thank you to my three adult children, Patrick, Jacqueline and Scott, who over the Christmas holidays were mildly curious as I headed into my study to write, and refrained from teasing a fragile, new writer.

Thank you to Margaret Attwood and Joyce Carol Oates. Working through your Masterclass Programs on line in the early days of October 2020, gave me insightful writing tips, the confidence to experiment and a burning wish to express.

Thanks to Kim Shannon and Mary Throop for being open to read through my first full draft, and for encouraging me to further develop some of the characters. Kim, your comment that "The reader wants to be part of this group, and enjoys spending time with them" was valuable reassurance that it wasn't just me who enjoyed escaping into the pages. It was fuel I needed to keep going.

Thank you to Jen Sievenpiper, Kelly Meighen, Gisèle Robitaille and Donna Tranquada for your attentive feedback while reading through the first published version of this book. Your solicited editorial comments were very much appreciated.

Thanks to Nicole Hambleton, for your candid thoughts on life in our weekly morning walks, and for helping me think through how to handle one of the sensitive areas in this book. I always grow during our conversations.

Thank you to Gisèle Robitaille and Libby Wildman for so many wonderful years of friendship. While my friendship with each of you is separate from the other, and while neither of you is characterized in this book, you will likely recognize within this story, the love of bike riding and dancing, the joy of humour and laughter and the cherished sharing of deep confidences. I look forward to continuing these with each of you.

Thank you to my son Patrick for your creative talent and insightful counsel during the design of the cover. It was precious to have a piece of you involved in this endeavor.

And thank you to my mother, Barbara. You were the first person to read my fledgling first few chapters, when my characters were in development and their futures were still unknown. Thank you for your curiosity about the characters and your subsequent questions around women and friendships, which signaled to me that there was a compelling story to imagine and write.

# ABOUT THE AUTHOR

Gwen Harvey, founder of a wealth advisory firm in Toronto, is an experienced writer of business briefs, newsletters and commentary. This is her first work of fiction.

Gwen is married and has three adult children. She, her husband Richard, and their Bernese Mountain dog Bear, split their time between Toronto and the rolling hills of Mulmur, Ontario.

CPSIA information can be obtained
at www.ICGtesting.com
Printed in the USA
BVHW071339100222
627930BV00001B/1